IRIS AND RUBY

Rosie Thomas is the author of a number of celebrated novels, including the bestsellers *White*, *The Potter's House*, *If My Father Loved Me* and *Sun at Midnight*. Once she was established as a writer and her children were grown, she discovered a love of travelling and mountaineering. She has climbed in the Alps and the Himalayas, competed in the Peking to Paris car rally, and spent time on a tiny Bulgarian research station in Antarctica. She took inspiration for this book from a trip to Egypt and a dramatic excursion into the desert. She lives in London.

Praise for *Iris and Ruby*

'Thomas can write with ravishing sensuality.'

KATE SAUNDERS, *The Times*

'Her evocation of wartime [Cairo] has all the raffish, glittering brittleness of life on the edge . . . touches on the varieties and nuances of love between men and women, and the power of family relationships to enhance and destroy lives.'

ELIZABETH BUCHAN, *Daily Mail*

'Whether brilliantly conjuring the past – the colour and life of wartime Cairo, the loves and the losses, the friend-ships made and severed – portraying Lesley's stifled life or capturing Ruby's tangled emotions, Rosie Thomas creates unforgettable characters and settings. She's a superb writer.'

Choice Magazine

Praise for Rosie Thomas

'Rosie Thomas writes with beautiful, effortless prose, and shows a rare compassion and a real understanding of the nature of love.'   *The Times*

'Honest and absorbing.'   *Mail on Sunday*

'A master storyteller.'   *Cosmopolitan*

'Thomas' novels are beautifully written.'
                                        Marie Claire

'Terrific . . . a real weepy.'   *Sunday Times*

'A story full of passion . . . will keep you reading long after bedtime.'   *New Woman*

By the same author

Celebration
Follies
Sunrise
The White Dove
Strangers
Bad Girls, Good Women
A Woman of Our Times
All My Sins Remembered
Other People's Marriages
A Simple Life
Every Woman Knows a Secret
Moon Island
White
The Potter's House
If My Father Loved Me
Sun at Midnight
Constance
Lovers and Newcomers
The Kashmir Shawl

ROSIE THOMAS

Iris and Ruby

HARPER

Harper
An imprint of HarperCollins*Publishers*
77–85 Fulham Palace Road
Hammersmith, London W6 8JB

This paperback edition published 2006
15

First published in Great Britain by
HarperCollins*Publisher* 2006

Copyright © Rosie Thomas 2006

Rosie Thomas asserts the moral right to
be identified as the author of this work

A catalogue record for this book is
available from the British Library

ISBN: 978 0 00 793710 3

Typeset in Sabon by Palimpsest Book Production Limited,
Grangemouth, Stirlingshire

Printed and bound in Great Britain by
Clays Ltd, St Ives plc

MIX
Paper from
responsible sources
FSC www.fsc.org **FSC˘ C007454**

For Louis, Solomon and Misty.
The new generation

CHAPTER ONE

I remember.

And even as I say the words aloud in the silent room and hear the whisper dying away in the shadows of the house, I realise that it's not true.

Because I don't, I can't remember.

I am old, and I am beginning to forget things.

Sometimes I'm aware that great tracts of memory have gone, slipping and melting away out of my reach. When I try to recall a particular day, or an entire year, even a damned decade, if I'm lucky there are the bare facts unadorned with colour. More often than otherwise there's nothing at all. A blank.

And when I can remember where I have lived, and who I was living with and why, if I try to conjure up what it was like to be there, the texture of my life and what impelled me to wake up every morning and pace out the journey of the day, I cannot do it. Familiar and even beloved faces have silently melted away, their names and the dates of precious initiations and fond anniversaries and events that once seemed momentous, all collapsed and buried beyond reach.

The disappearing is like the desert itself. Sand blows from

1

the four corners of the earth and it builds up in slow drifts and dun ripples, and it blurs the sharpest, proudest structures, and in the end obliterates them.

This is what's happening to me. The sands of time. (It is a no less accurate image for being a cliché.)

I am eighty-two. I am not afraid of death, which after all can't be far away.

Nor do I fear complete oblivion, because to be oblivious means what it says.

What does frighten me is the halfway stage. I am afraid of reduction. After a lifetime's independence – yes, selfish independence as my daughter would rightly claim – I am terrified of being reduced to childhood once more, to helplessness, to seas of confusion from which the cruel lucid intervals poke up like rock shoals.

I don't want to sit in my chair and be fed spoonfuls of pap by Mamdooh or by Auntie; much less do I want to be handed over to medical professionals who will subject me to well-intentioned geriatric care.

I know what that will be like. I am a doctor myself and as well as remembering too little, I have seen too much.

Now Mamdooh is coming. His leather slippers make a soft swish on the boards of the women's stairway. There is nothing wrong with my hearing. The door creaks open, heavy on its hinges, so that I can see a corner of the pierced screen that hides the gallery from the celebration hall. A light shining through the screen stipples the floor and walls with crescents and stars.

'Good evening, Ma'am Iris,' Mamdooh softly says. The deferential form of address has become so elided, so rubbed with usage that it is a pet name now, Mum-reese. 'Have you been sleeping perhaps?'

'No,' I tell him.

I have been thinking. Turning matters over in my mind.

2

Mamdooh puts down a tray. A glass of mint tea, sweet and fragrant. A linen napkin, some triangles of sweet pastry that I do not want. I eat very little now.

The shiny coffee-brown dome of Mamdooh's bald head is blotched with darker patches and big brown irregular moles. Out of doors in the harsh white sun I know he always wears his tarboosh. To see him lifting it in two hands and firmly settling it on his head before going out to the market is to be taken back to the time when the red flowerpot fez was essential wear for every effendi in the city.

Mamdooh is holding out my glass of tea. I take it from him, hooking my fingers through the worn silver hoops of the holder and poking my head forward to breathe in the scent.

'Auntie has made baklava,' he says, encouraging me by turning back the napkin on the plate.

'Later. Go on now, Mamdooh. You must have some food yourself.'

Mamdooh will not have eaten a mouthful or taken even a sip of water since before sunrise. It is Ramadan.

When I am alone again, I drink my tea and listen to the sounds of the city. The cobbled street outside my screened windows is narrow, barely wide enough for a single car to pass, and beyond the angle of wall that shelters my doorway there are only the steps of the great mosque. The traffic that pours off concrete ribbon roads and submerges the modern city like a tidal wave is no more than a dull rumble here. Much closer at hand are shouts and laughter as families prepare their evening meal and gather to eat in the cool dusk. There's a rattle of wheels on the stones and a hoarse cry of warning as a donkey cart passes by, and then a few liquid notes of music as somewhere a door opens and shuts. Hearing this, it might be the same Cairo of sixty years ago.

3

Some things I can never forget. I must not. Otherwise, what do I have left?

I close my eyes. The glass tips in my fingers, spilling the last drops of liquid on the worn cushions.

Sixty years ago there were soldiers in these streets. Swarms of British officers and men, New Zealanders and Australians, French, Canadians, Indians and Greeks and South Africans and Poles, all in their dusty khaki. The city was a sun-baked magnet for the troops who flooded into it, whenever the war in the desert briefly released them, in search of bars and brothels. Turning their backs on the prospect of death in the sand, they drank and fucked with all the energy of youth, and Cairo absorbed them with its own ancient indifference.

After all, this war was just another layer of history in the making, contributing its dust and debris to lie on top of thousands of years of ruins. There is more history buried along this fertile strip of Nile valley than there is anywhere else in the world.

One of those soldiers from sixty years ago was my lover. The only man I have ever loved.

His name was Captain Alexander Napier Molyneux. Xan.

He wore the same khaki bush shirt and baggy shorts as all the others, distinguished only by badges of rank and regiment, but there was a further anonymity about Xan. He was neither flamboyant nor mysterious. You wouldn't have singled him out in a crowd of officers at the bar in Shepheard's Hotel, or at any of the raucous parties we all went to in Garden City or Zamalek, simply because he seemed so ordinary.

The absence of peculiar characteristics was intentional. Xan worked deep in the desert and it was one of his talents to blend into the scenery wherever he happened to be. He

4

rode a horse like the cavalry officer he really was, but if you saw him on a camel with a white *kuffiyeh* swathed over his head and face, you would take him for an Arab. At the Gezira Club he played tennis and fooled around beside the pool like any other ornament of the Cairo cocktail circuit, but then he would disappear for days or a week at a time, and even in the hothouse of Anglo-Egyptian smart society there would be no whisper of news or even gossip about where he might have gone. He vanished into the desert like a lizard darting under a rock.

I loved him from the moment I first set eyes on him.

I remember.

New roads and concrete tower blocks and shopping streets have obliterated much of the Cairo we knew then, but in this evening's reverie every detail of it – and of that first evening – comes back to me. I have revisited it so many thousands of times, it seems more real than my eighty-two-year-old reality.

At least I haven't lost this, thank God, not yet.

This is how I recall it:

It was an airless night thick with the scent of tuberoses.

There were two dozen little round tables set out in a lush garden, candle lanterns hanging in the branches of the mango and mimosa trees, and beyond tall windows a band playing in a panelled ballroom.

I was twenty-two years old, fresh from the wartime austerity of London, drunk on the glamour of Cairo as well as on champagne cocktails.

Giggling, my friend Faria led me over to a table and introduced me to a group of men in evening clothes. There was a bottle of whisky and a phalanx of glasses, cigar smoke competing with the tuberoses.

'This is Iris Black. Stay right where you are, Jessie, please.'

But the young man with pale yellow hair was already on

his feet, his head bent low as he lifted my hand to his mouth. His moustache tickled my fingers.

'I can't possibly sit still,' he murmured. 'She is too beautiful.'

Inside my head I was still the London typist, making do on a tiny wage in a basement flat in South Ken, but I had learned enough in my weeks in Cairo not to glance over my shoulder in search of whoever the beauty might be. Here, in this exotic garden with the band playing and the orchid presented by my evening's date pinned to the bodice of my evening dress, I knew that she was *me*.

'Frederick James. Captain, Eleventh Hussars,' he murmured. And then he released my hand and stood up straight. He was slim, not very tall. 'For some reason, everyone calls me Jessie James.'

His arm crooked and his fist, lightly clenched, rested just for a second on the smooth flank of his dinner jacket.

There were plenty of rather fey young men in Cairo. I had several times heard the RAF boys collectively described as 'the flying fairies', but Jessie James didn't seem to belong in quite the same category. In spite of the hair and the well-tailored evening clothes, he looked tough. His face was sunburned and there was a shadow in his eyes that went against his playful manner.

'How do you do?' I said.

'Ah, she is so nice, our Iris,' Faria gurgled. 'A good girl, from a diplomatic family. When she was twelve, you know, her daddy was Head of Chancery right here in Cairo. She is practically a native citizen.'

Faria was one of my two flatmates. Two years older than me, the elegant daughter of a prosperous Anglo-Egyptian family, she had taken me under her wing almost as soon as I arrived. Faria was engaged to the son of one of her father's business associates and liked to tell everyone that as she was

6

practically married, she was ideally placed to chaperone Sarah and me. Behind the backs of whoever we were talking to she would then deliver a huge wink. In fact, Ali was often away, on business in Alexandria or Beirut or Jerusalem, and Faria would have benefited from the attentions of a chaperone rather more than we did.

We were drawn into the group. Chairs were brought over and placed at the table as the officers eagerly made room. I accepted a glass of whisky, at the same time looking around the glimmering garden for my escort. Sandy Allardyce was one of the young men from the British embassy. He insisted to anyone who would listen that he was desperate to get into uniform, but so far he was still chained to his office desk. I guessed that he felt uncomfortable in the company of so many men who were actually fighting, and that he dealt with this by drinking too much. His pink face had turned red within an hour of our arrival at the party.

'So you lived here as a young girl?' one of the officers asked. The man next to him clicked his lighter to a cigarette and I glimpsed his face, briefly lit by the umber flare.

'Just in the holidays. I was at school in England most of the time.'

Faria was laughing extravagantly at a joke made by one of the others, her head thrown back to reveal her satiny throat and the diamond and pearl drops swinging in her ears.

Jessie leaned forward to command my attention again. 'Are you looking for Sandy? I saw you dancing with him.' He had noticed my anxiety.

Gratefully I said, 'Yes. He brought me to the party. I ought to go and find him. He . . .' I was going to add something about the orchid, I was already fingering the waxy tip of one of the petals.

Then the man with the cigarette moved his chair so the light from one of the candle lanterns threw his face into relief. There was a blare of music from the band and a burst of applause as a dance finished. I looked at him and forgot whatever remark I had been on the point of uttering, not that it mattered. Cairo party conversation was profoundly superficial.

The man's eyes were bright with amusement. He was dark-haired, dark-skinned. He might have appeared saturnine if there hadn't been so much fun in his face.

He leaned across the table. I saw the way his mouth formed a smile. 'Don't dance with Allardyce. And if it's a choice between Jessie and me – well, that's not really a choice at all, is it?'

'Ale*xan*der.' Jessie pouted.

'Not now, dear,' the man said. He drew back my chair and I stood up, he put his hand under my arm.

'Xan Molyneux,' he said calmly. We walked across the lawn together, under the branches of the trees. The heat-withered grass smelled acrid, nothing like an English garden. I had never felt so far from home, yet so happily and entirely not homesick.

'I'm Iris.'

'I know. Faria did introduce you. Is she a friend of yours?'

'Yes. We share the same flat. Sarah Walker-Wilson lives there too. I suppose you know her?'

I can't bear it, I thought. Every man in Cairo adores Sarah. In the six weeks since I had moved in, Sarah had not spent a single evening at home.

Xan inclined his head until his cheek almost touched mine.

'The three flowers of Garden City,' he murmured. Garden City was the quarter of Cairo where we lived. I wasn't sure if he was making a joke or not.

We reached the dance floor. Xan's expression was serene and he was humming the tune as he took me in his arms. He didn't enquire whether or not I thought it was a jolly

8

band, or if I was going to Mrs Diaz's shindig in Heliopolis tomorrow night. We just danced. He was a good dancer, but I had had other partners who were better. It was more that Xan gave the steps and the music and me all his attention, which made spinning round a crowded floor to the tootling of an Egyptian band seem singular, invested with a kind of magic. Laughter shone in his face and the pleasure that he was obviously taking in this precise, isolated moment radiated out of him. I felt energy beating like a pulse under the black weft of his coat, transmitting itself through my hands and arms and singing between us, and an answering rhythm began to beat in me. We both felt it and we were swept along, becoming more absorbed in the dance and each other. We looked straight into one another's eyes, not talking but communicating in a language I had never used before.

That first dance seamlessly ran into the next, and the one after that.

I stopped being drunk on champagne and whisky, and grew intoxicated with excitement and the music and Xan Molyneux's closeness instead. I saw the bandleader glancing over his shoulder at us, and some other couples were eyeing us too, but I didn't care and Xan was looking only at me. We had exchanged hardly more than a dozen words but I felt that I knew him already, better than anyone I had met in Cairo.

I also felt a clear, absolute certainty that from now on all things were and would be possible. Happiness became wound up with anticipation to a point of tension that was almost unbearable, and it made me suddenly giddy. As Xan swung us in an exuberant circle I tripped and overbalanced on my high heel. A hot skewer of pain stabbed from my ankle up my calf and I would have fallen if he hadn't wrapped his arm more tightly round my waist.

'Are you all right?'

I drew in a breath and blew it out hard to stop myself howling.

'Just . . . twisted it.' The dancers formed a circle round us.

'Here, I'll carry you.' He slid his other arm beneath my thighs, ready to lift me off my feet. At that moment I saw Sandy. He came steaming through the dancers towards us, crimson in the face, the studs popping out of his shirt front. His eyes seemed to swivel in opposite directions.

'What's going on?' he shouted. 'Molyneux. You . . . what d'you think you're doing?'

'Helping Miss Black to a chair,' Xan drily replied, straightening up. 'She has twisted her ankle.'

I took a step away from his side and nearly fell over, Xan immediately lunged to my rescue, and we almost toppled in a heap. As we struggled to right ourselves in a tangle of arms and legs I laughed up at him, in spite of the pain in my ankle, and I heard a wounded bellow from Sandy. He came flailing at Xan and caught the collar of his evening coat. Xan let go of me and twisted round to face Sandy who planted a wild punch on his jaw.

'Leave my girl alone,' Sandy shouted, but having landed his awkward blow the belligerence was visibly draining out of him. He gazed around at the circle of onlookers but he couldn't see any ready support. His big, shiny red face seemed to crumple inwards, oozing whisky from every pore. I watched miserably, balancing on one foot, wanting to tell the sticky air – but for Xan to hear – that I wasn't Sandy's girl at all, and feeling ashamed of the impulse.

'You know, I really don't want to hit you back, Allardyce,' Xan drawled. One hand slipped into the pocket of his coat. He sounded amused, not at all perturbed. 'It would make such a mess.'

'He's right, it would,' another voice chipped in. Jessie

James had appeared, with Faria beside him. Her sharp eyes took in everything. She held out her arm and I leaned on it as Sandy caught hold of me on the other side. His hand was hot and damp, and there were little glittering rivulets of sweat running from his hairline to his stiff collar. He jerked his head at Xan and Jessie, but he was already in retreat.

'It's not funny.'

'Are we laughing?' Jessie innocently asked.

Sandy turned away from them and muttered to me, 'C'mon, s'get another drink. Be all right.'

Faria clicked her tongue. 'No it won't. I'm taking Iris home. Can't you see she's hurt?'

The band started playing again and the other dancers turned away, losing interest.

The next minute I was hobbling into the hallway, supported on one side by Faria and with Sandy weaving on the other. A huge crystal chandelier dripped diamonds of light over our heads. I felt rather than saw Xan and Jessie at the back of our ungainly procession as Lady Gibson Pasha came surging towards us, both hands outstretched as if to catch me. Our hostess wore a gold turban and a collar of egg-sized emeralds.

'My dear, my dear girl, you poor thing. You must put your foot up, we need an ice pack.'

She was clapping her hands, calling at a passing servant to bring ice. I wanted to stay near Xan and to get as far away from Sandy as possible. I was also longing to get home and lie in a dark room to disentangle the chaos and amazement of the evening.

'It's nothing, really. I'm so sorry, Lady Gibson. Just a silly sprain.'

'Daddy's car and driver are here,' Faria said. 'We'll go home. I'll make sure Iris is looked after.'

Sandy vehemently nodded his head. He had gone pale

11

now. Another servant was at hand with Faria's little swansdown bolero and my mother's Indian shawl, which was my evening wrap. With Lady Gibson's instructions floating after us we hobbled out of the front door. Amman Pasha's chauffeur was waiting at the steps with the big black car. He opened the door and I was handed into the expanse of cream-coloured leather. Sandy collapsed beside me, gasping and tugging at the ends of his tie to undo the bow. Faria slipped in on the other side.

The car began to roll over the gravel. I twisted round to see through the rear window and caught a last glimpse of Xan and Jessie standing side by side at the foot of the steps, black head and blond, watching us go. I couldn't really see Xan's face, but I thought he was still smiling.

'God,' Sandy groaned. 'Bloody hell.' He screwed his black tie into a ball and stuffed it in his pocket before letting his head fall back against the seat cushions.

'We'll drop you at the embassy,' Faria said coolly and leaned forward to give the driver instructions in Arabic. We swept over the Bulaq Bridge and I saw the broken mosaic of yellow and white lights reflected in black water as we turned south past the cathedral.

Faria yawned. 'Oh dear. I completely forgot to tell the poet we were leaving. Whatever will he think?'

It wasn't a question that required an answer. Jeremy – known as the poet – was the most fervent of Faria's admirers, a thin and mournful young man who worked for the British Council. Ali was away and Jeremy had been her escort for the evening. He would think what he presumably always thought: that the exquisite and careless Faria had given him the slip again.

Sandy had passed out. I could hear the breath catching thickly in the back of his throat. Whisky fumes and Faria's perfume mingled with the smell of leather and the uniquely

Cairene stink of kerosene and incense and animal dung. Faria took a Turkish cigarette out of her bag, clicked her gold lighter and inhaled deeply. I shook my head when she held it out to me. The pain in my ankle was intense and the faint nausea it engendered made my senses keener. I let every turn of the route print itself in my mind, the black silhouette of each dome against the fractionally paler sky, the hooked profile of an old beggar patiently sitting on a step. Every detail was significant and precious. I wanted to absorb each tiny impression and hold it and keep it, because tonight was so important. I never doubted that.

We stopped near the embassy gates and shook Sandy awake. He groaned again and muttered incoherently as he flopped out into the road. The car swept on. Over the top of the embassy building, behind the flagpole with the limp folds of the Union flag, I could see the tops of huge trees shading lawns where I had been paraded for tea parties as a child. I liked to slip away and gaze at the Nile beyond, slow olive-green, flagged with the sails of feluccas.

Later I lay in bed with the wooden shutters latched open and watched the sky. My bandaged ankle throbbed but I didn't mind that it kept me awake. All I could think of was Xan, whom Faria had hardly noticed and who had left me stricken with desire from the moment I saw him. Shivers of laughter and longing and anticipation ran through me as I lay there, slick with sweat, under my thin cotton sheet. On that first sleepless night I never doubted that Xan and I would meet again. I would tell him I wasn't and never had been Sandy Allardyce's girl, and we would claim each other. That was exactly how it was meant to be.

. How simple, how innocent it seems. And how joyful.

Garden City was set beside the Nile, an enclave of curving streets with tall cocoa-brown and dirty cream houses and apartment blocks deep in gardens of thick, dusty greenery. Our apartment belonged to Faria's parents who lived in a grand house nearby. There were wood-block floors and heavy furniture, and every room had a ceiling fan that lazily circulated the scalding air. There were big metal-finned radiators too, that occasionally emitted hollow clanking noises and dribbled rusty water. Faria never noticed the heat and her black hair stayed like a glossy wing instead of frizzing in the humid blast as mine did, but she was afraid of feeling cold. When she was going out at night she always slipped a little bolero of white feathers or a silk velvet cape over her bare shoulders.

My room was a narrow, high-ceilinged box at the end of a corridor away from the main part of the flat. The furniture was on a humbler scale and there was a view from the window of a jacaranda tree in the next-door garden. I didn't know Faria and Sarah very well but they were lively company, and I was pleased to have such a comfortable place to live. It was even conveniently close to where I worked, at British Army GHQ, just off Sharia Qasr el Aini. I was clerical and administrative assistant to a lieutenant-colonel in Intelligence called Roderick Boyce, known to everyone as Roddy Boy. Colonel Boyce and my father belonged to the same London club and had hunted together before the war. A letter from my father, and an interview during which my prospective boss reminisced about my father taking a fence on his big bay mare, were enough to gain me the job.

The morning after Xan and I met I got up early to go to work, as I had done on every ordinary day since I had come back to Cairo.

In the stifling mid afternoons the streets cowered under the hammer blow of the sun out of a white sky, but at 8 a.m. it was cool enough to walk the few streets between the flat and the office. That day, with my heavily bandaged

14

ankle, I had to take a taxi. Roddy Boy looked at me as I half hopped to my desk, supported by a walking stick belonging to Faria's father.

'Oh dear. Tennis? Camel racing? Or something more strenuous?'

'Dancing,' I replied.

'Ah. Of course.' Roddy Boy chose to believe that my social life was much more hectic and glamorous than it really was. 'But I hope your injury will not impede your typing?'

'Not at all,' I said. I rolled a sandwich of requisition forms and carbon paper into my machine and forced myself to concentrate.

When at last I came home again Mamdooh, the *suffragi* who looked after us and the apartment, greeted me in his stately way: 'Good afternoon, Miss Iris. These were delivered for you an hour ago.'

'Oh, beautiful.'

There was a big bunch of white lilies, gardenias and tuberoses. I buried my face in the cool blooms. The intense perfume brought back last night even more vividly, candlelight and music and cigars and Xan's face. Mamdooh beamed. He was pleased for me; usually the bouquets were for Sarah.

I sat down awkwardly and opened the envelope that came with them. There was a plain white card with the words *I hope your ankle will mend soon*. It was signed simply *X*. That was all.

Mamdooh was still standing there in his white *galabiyeh*, waiting for more. Faria complained that he was too familiar and that what time she came in at night was none of his business, but I liked the big man and his broad smiles that were always accompanied by a shrewd glance. Mamdooh missed nothing. Faria's mother was probably aware of that too.

'Just from a friend,' I said.

15

'Of course, Miss. I will put in water for you.'

The flat often looked like a florist's shop. Sarah and Faria didn't even ask who my bouquet was from.

I admired my flowers and waited, but a week and then another went by. The whole month of June 1941 crawled past and I heard nothing more from Xan.

In my outer office at GHQ I typed reports and delivered signals for Roddy Boy, and chatted to the staff officers who hurried in and out to see him. As a civilian I was on the lowest level of clearance, but because of my family I was judged to be safe and many of the secret plans that flew in and out of Roddy Boy's office crossed my desk first.

The Allied troops, except for those besieged in Tobruk, had withdrawn into Egypt and the Germans were at the Libyan border. In an attempt to dislodge them, in a brief flurry of GHQ activity during which Roddy Boy didn't withdraw for his usual long afternoon at the Turf Club, Operation Battleaxe was launched.

'We can't match their bloody firepower,' Roddy groaned from behind his desk.

Almost one hundred of our armoured tanks were lost to German anti-tank guns, their smouldering wrecks lying abandoned in a thick pall of dust and smoke. Many of their crews were dead or wounded.

As July approached I began accepting every invitation that came my way. I went to cocktail parties and tennis tournaments, fancy dress balls, and poetry readings at the British Council, scanning the crowds for a glimpse of Xan. I sat beside the pool at the Gezira Club every lunchtime, always in the hope of hearing news of him.

Just once, I met one of the other officers who had been at his table at Lady Gibson Pasha's party.

'Xan?' he said vaguely. 'I don't know. Doesn't seem to be around, does he?'

16

He had simply vanished, and Jessie James with him. My certainty about us ebbed away. Maybe he had been posted elsewhere. Maybe he was married. Maybe – could that be possible? – he really did prefer other diversions.

Maybe he was dead.

I kept my fears to myself. What I felt seemed too significant and also too equivocal, too fragile, to share with Faria and Sarah.

'You're very sociable these days,' Faria said with a raised eyebrow.

'It's as easy to go out as to stay in.' I shrugged.

Then, at the end of the first week of July, on an evening when the heat made it an effort to dress to go out, even to move, the telephone rang in the hallway and I heard Mamdooh answer it. His big round head appeared in the doorway.

'For you, Miss.'

'Hello?' I said into the receiver.

'This is Xan,' he said. 'May I come and see you?'

I laid my head against the door frame, electric shocks of relief and delight chasing up my spine. I managed to answer, 'Yes. Now?'

'Right now.'

'Yes,' I said again. 'Yes, please come.'

That was how it was.

I open my eyes on the dim, silent room. There is spilt tea on the cushions, some sticky drops dark on my front. I am overwhelmed with sleep now, too tired to sit up and tidy myself. It doesn't matter. Who will see, except Mamdooh and Auntie?

Sleep. Dream. Always the dreams.

Shit. Double shit and fuck, Ruby said to herself as she caught a glimpse of what lay beyond the doors. Is *this* what it's like?

It was dark outside. Beyond a barrier there was a heaving

17

wall of heads and waving arms and shouting faces, harshly lit and shadowed by sickly overhead neon lights. The airport was clammily air-conditioned, but she could already feel the heat rolling towards her through the doors as they slid open and hissed shut again. The crowd of arriving passengers pushed her forward, catching her rucksack with the protruberances of their own baggage, jerking her from side to side. The doors opened once more and this time she was part of the gout of humanity they disgorged.

Hot, humid air rushed into her lungs. Sweat immediately prickled under her arms and in her hairline.

A chorus of yelling rose around her. Hands grabbed at her arms, tried to hoist the pack off her back.

'Lady! Taxi, very good, cheap.'

'Hotel, lady. Nice hotel.'

'Stop it,' Ruby shouted. 'Leave me alone.' She hadn't bargained for this onslaught. Alarmed, she wrenched herself free of the clutching hands but another dozen pairs replaced them, tried to propel her in different directions.

'Taxi here! Lady, I show you.'

She became aware of a stream of honking cars beyond the immediate crowd, a fringe of palm trees with ragged leaves outlined against a sky dimly peppered with stars, a snake of headlights along an elevated road. The noise and the heat were overwhelming. Ruby glared into the boiling sea of dark faces, moustaches, open mouths. At the back of the throng was a younger face, imploringly watching her.

She dragged an arm free, pointed at him.

'You. Taxi?'

Instantly he dived through the scrum of bodies, grabbed her wrist with one hand and snatched her rucksack with the other. Ruby kept her smaller nylon sack tightly pressed to her side. They scuttled through the mass together and emerged into a clearer space beyond.

'Come,' the man shouted, pointing over the roofs of a hundred hooting black-and-white taxis. A packed bus roared in front of them, missing them by inches.

The driver's taxi was parked under one of the palm trees. Two ragged children were sitting propped against it. The driver gave them a coin, threw her rucksack into the boot and opened the passenger door. With relief Ruby sank into the back seat. The springs had collapsed and stained foam padding bulged through a split in the brown plastic seat cover. The interior of the car smelled strongly of cigarettes and cheap air freshener.

The driver thrust the car into gear and they roared forward, then jerked to an almost immediate halt in a queue for the exit road. Even though it was dark, the heat was intense. Ruby had never encountered this phenomenon before. She closed her eyes, noticing that even her eyelids were sticky with sweat, then forced them open again. She mustn't switch off, not yet. The driver flashed her a smile over his shoulder. His teeth were cartoon-white in his brown face. He did look young, not much older than herself.

'Where you go?'

She unfolded the sheet of paper that she had kept in her jeans pocket all through the flight and read out the address.

'Why you go there? I know nice hotel, very clean, cheap. I take you there instead.'

'We're going where I told you,' Ruby insisted. 'No arguing. Got that?'

This amused him. He laughed and slapped his hands on the steering wheel.

The traffic began to move. There were roads everywhere, the sodium-lit elevated sections crazily perched over complex intersections, all hemmed in by drab concrete tower blocks and hung about with giant advertisement hoardings. The faces of huge women with black eyebrows and cows' eyelashes mooned at each other over the street lamps. Every foot of road was clogged with hooting cars and trucks and big blue buses. The road signs were written in a code of squiggles and dots.

Ruby lounged in the sagging seat and stared at it all. Her face was expressionless but inwardly she was fighting to maintain the defiance that had buoyed her up since leaving home. Now that she was actually here, she realised that she had hardly considered her destination. To get away and to stay away, that was what she had fixed on. But now all kinds of other problems reared up, competing with each other for her attention. She didn't know how to handle this place, not at all. And nobody knew where she was; no one was looking out for her arrival. It was far from the first time in her life that she had been in the same situation, but never in quite such an alien setting.

She felt a long way from home, but she bundled up that thought and pushed it aside.

'How much?' she demanded. She had changed the rest of her money into Egyptian pounds at the airport exchange. It made a reassuringly thick wad, which was why she had decided to splash out on a taxi. The thought of trying to find a bus had been too much to contemplate.

The driver swung the wheel to overtake a donkey cart laden with saucepans and tin bowls that was plodding along the inner lane of the motorway. He shot the smile at her again.

'Ah, money, no broblem. Where you from?'

'London.'

'Very nice place. David Beckham.'

'Yeah. Or no. Whatever.' At least they were moving now, presumably towards the city centre, wherever that might be. Airports were always miles away in the outer bloody suburbs, weren't they?

'My name Nafouz.'

'Right.'

There was a pause. Nafouz reached under the dash and produced a pack of Marlboro, half turned to offer it to her. Ruby hesitated. She had run out and she was longing for one.

'Thanks.' She lit it with her own Bic, ignoring his.

'You have boyfriend in Cairo?'

Ruby gave a snort of derisive laughter. 'I've never been here in my life.'

'I be your boyfriend.'

She had hardly looked at him, except to notice his teeth, but now she saw the creases in the collar of his white shirt, and the way the inside of his black leather jacket dirtied the fabric in crooked ribs. His black hair was long, combed back from his face. Quite nice, really.

She lifted her head. This, at least, was familiar territory. 'In. Your. Dreams,' she said clearly.

Nafouz's delighted laughter filled the car. He drummed his hands on the wheel as if this was the funniest joke he had ever heard.

'I dream always. Dreaming cheap. Cost nothing at all.'

'Just watch the road, all right?'

She huddled in her corner, smoking and looking out at the wilderness. She had been abroad before, of course, with Lesley and Andrew to places like Tuscany and Kos and the Loire valley (how dull *that* one had been), but she had never seen anything like this steaming mess of concrete and metal. As they got nearer to what must be the middle of the city the traffic jam got even worse. There were long stationary intervals during which she peered down the side streets. There were tiny open-fronted shops with men sitting smoking at tin tables. Shafts of light came out of open doorways, shining on women with black shawls over their heads who sat on stone steps with children squirming around them. There were crates of globular shiny vegetables and crooked towers of coke cans, a thick litter of rubbish in the gutters, scrawny dogs nosing at it all. Men selling things from trays yelled on the street corners, other bent old men pushed hand barrows through the traffic. Neon lights blinked everywhere and there was the endless honking of horns.

'Busy place,' she said at last, wanting to make it smaller and less threatening with a casual phrase.

Nafouz shrugged. 'Who your friends here?'

He was either being nosy, or he was concerned for her. Neither was welcome.

'Family,' she said discouragingly.

They were winding down smaller streets now, leaving the main thoroughfares behind. Ruby glanced upwards and saw onion domes and tall thin towers pasted against dark-blue sky. The street was so narrow that there was only room for one car to pass. The women sitting on their steps lifted their heads and stared as the taxi slid by. There was one great dome just ahead, cutting an arc of sky, and a trio of thin spires that rose beside it.

Nafouz stopped when he could go no further. The street had become a cobbled alley and it took a sharp-angled turn just in front of them. A stone pillar blocked the way. In the angle of a pale blank wall was a door with a small flight of stone steps leading up to it.

'Here is place,' Nafouz announced.

Ruby stared at the door. She could just see that it was painted blue, old paint that had bubbled to expose wood split by the sun. She hadn't at all worked out what to expect, but it wasn't this. There was nothing here to give any clue to what or who might be inside.

She summoned up her resolve.

'Yeah. How much money d'you want?' She opened up her

22

nylon sack and her Discman and headphones and an apple and tubes of make-up rolled over the seat.

'Fifty bounds.'

'*Fifty*? D'you think I'm stupid or something? I'll give you twenty.' She opened her wallet and fumbled with torn filthy notes.

'From airport, fifty.' Nafouz wasn't smiling any longer.

'Get lost, right?' Ruby gathered up her belongings and hopped out of the car but the driver was quicker. He ran round and held down the boot so she couldn't retrieve her rucksack. They squared up to each other, faces inches apart.

'Twenty-five,' Ruby said.

'Fifty.'

'Give me my fucking *bag*.' She kicked his shin as hard as she could. Unfortunately she was only wearing flipflops.

Nafouz yelped. 'Lady, lady. You are not behaving nicely.'

'Really? Now hand over my bag.'

'You pay first.' But Nafouz was relenting. This tourist's resistance earned a glimmer of his respect. Usually they just gave in and handed over the money. 'Thirty,' he conceded.

'Fuck's sake.' But she sighed and took another note out of her purse, crumpling it and flinging it against the sleeve of his leather jacket. Nafouz's smile was restored. Thirty Egyptian pounds was the going rate for a ride in from the airport.

Ruby took her rucksack and hoisted it over her shoulder. With the wires of her headphones trailing and the contents of her other bag spilling in her arms she marched up the stone steps without a backward glance. She heard Nafouz reversing the car the way they had come, then a squeal of tyres as he raced away.

As soon as he was gone she regretted the loss of even this brief relationship. Maybe she should have asked him to wait. What if there was nobody here? What if the address was

23

wrong? Where would she go, in this city where she couldn't even read the street signs?

Then she lifted her head and straightened her shouders again.

There was no door knocker, nothing. She knocked on the blistered paint. There was a smell of dried piss in this alleyway, competing with all the other stinks.

There was no sound from within.

Ruby clenched her fist and hammered even harder. Some poem that they had all been made to learn at school floated into her head and, without thinking, she yelled the words in time to the banging: '"Is there anybody there," said the Traveller?'

The door suddenly creaked open, revealing a six-inch slice of dim light. Ruby was so startled that her voice trailed away in a squeak. She could just see a big fat man in a white dress.

She said, 'I am Ruby Sawyer.'

Having taken one look at her, the man was already trying to close the door again. Ruby's foot flew out and wedged itself in the crack. She wished for the second time that she was wearing proper shoes. She repeated her name, louder this time, but it clearly wasn't enough.

She added loudly, 'I am here to see my grandmother. Let me in, please.'

The resistance diminished a little. Immediately she put her shoulder to the door and pushed hard. It swung open and she fell inwards with a clatter of spilled belongings. The man's face was a dark purplish moon of disapproval. He frowned, but he did help her to her feet.

Ruby looked around. Her first impression was of the inside of a church. There was a stone floor, musty wood panelling, a pale, weak light suspended on chains inside a glass vessel. A smell of incense, too, and some kind of spicy cooking.

'Madam is resting,' the man said frigidly.

The best course was obviously to be conciliatory.

'I don't want to disturb her. Or disturb anyone. I'm sorry if I made a noise. But, you know . . .' The man didn't help her out. He went on impassively staring at her. 'I . . . I have come all the way from London. My mother, you see . . . Um, my mother is Madam's daughter. You know?'

There was another silence. Whether he knew or not, the connection didn't seem to impress him. But at last he sighed heavily and said, 'Follow me, please. Leave this here.' He pointed to her bags. She relinquished them with pleasure.

He led the way beneath an arch and through a bare room. Behind a heavy door there was a flight of enclosed wooden stairs. The lights were very dim, just single bulbs in the angles of walls, shaded with metal grilles. They went up the stairs and along a panelled corridor. It was a big house, Ruby thought, but it was dusty and bare, and all the stairs and corners and screens made it secretive. A place of shadow and whispers. It was much cooler in here than it was outside. A faint shiver twitched her skin.

The man stopped at a closed door. He bent his head and listened. She noticed that his face had turned soft and concerned. There was no sound, so he lifted a latch and eased the door open. There was a light burning in a teardrop of crimson glass, a carved divan seat piled with cushions under a shuttered window. In a low cushioned chair with a padded footstool a very old woman was propped up with her eyes closed. A spilled glass lay on the kelim rug.

Ruby took a step forward and she opened her eyes.

Dream? Someone I used to know who was buried beneath the sand while I was looking elsewhere?

I am afraid of these spectres who loom up out of the past. I fear them because I can't place them . . .

Fear makes me angry.

'Mamdooh, who is this? What do you think you are doing? Don't let people walk in here as if it's a public library. Go away.'

The woman, apparition, whoever she is, doesn't move.

Mamdooh kneels down, picks up the glass, puts it back on the tray. I can see the blotches on his old, bald skull. At once I feel sorry, and confused. I put my hand out to him and it's shaking. 'Forgive me. Who is she?'

The woman – very young, strange-looking – comes closer.

'I'm Ruby.'

'*Who?*'

'Your granddaughter. Lesley's daughter.'

'You are *not*.'

Lesley's daughter? A memory disinters itself. A pale, rather podgy child, dressed in a wool kilt and hairslides. Silent, yet somehow mutinous. Have I got that right?

'Yes, I am. You are Granny Iris, my mother's mother, Cairo Granny. Last time I saw you I was ten. You came for a holiday.'

I am *tired*. The effort of recall is too much. Poor Lesley, I think.

'Does she know you are here?'

The child blinks. Now I look at her, I can see that she *is* hardly more than a child. She has made the effort to appear otherwise, with startling face paint and extraordinary metal rings and bolts driven into nose and ears, and with a six-inch slice of pale abdomen revealed between the two halves of her costume, but I would put her age at eighteen or nineteen.

'Your *mother*. Does she know?'

'No, actually.'

Her answer is deadpan but, to my surprise, the way she delivers it makes me want to smile. Mamdooh has picked up the tea glass, tidied the tray. Now he stands over me, a protective mountain.

26

'Ma'am Iris, it is late,' he protests.

'I know that.' To the child I say, 'I don't know why you are here, Miss. You will go straight back where you came from. I'm tired now, but I will speak to you in the morning.'

'Shall I send Auntie to you?' Mamdooh asks me.

'No.' I don't want to be undressed and put to bed. I don't want to reveal to the child that sometimes this happens. 'Just get her to make up a bed for, for . . . what did you say your name is?'

'Ruby.'

It's a prostitute's name, which goes well enough with her appearance. What was Lesley thinking?

'A bed and some food, if she wants it. Thank you, Mamdooh. Good night, Ruby.'

The girl gives a sudden smile. Without the glower she looks even younger.

I make my way to my own room. When at last I am lying down with the white curtains drawn around the bed, the longing for sleep of course deserts me. I lie staring at the luminous folds of muslin, seeing faces and hearing voices.

Majestically disapproving, Mamdooh led Ruby downstairs again. A little old woman, about five feet tall, with a white shawl wrapped round her head and neck, appeared in the hallway. They spoke rapidly to each other.

'You would like to eat some food?' Mamdooh asked stiffly.

'No, thanks very much. Had some on the plane.'

'Go with Auntie, then.'

Ruby hoisted her luggage once more and followed the old woman up the enclosed stairs and through the shadowy galleries to a small room with a divan under an arched window. Auntie, if that was the name she went by, showed her a bathroom across the way. There was an overhead cistern with a chain, and the bowl was patterned with swirling blue and white foliage. There was an old-fashioned shower head as big as a dinner plate and a slatted wooden board over the drain, and a blue-painted chair with some folded towels.

'Thank you,' Ruby said.

'*Ahlan wa sahlan*,' Auntie murmured.

When she had gone, Ruby peeled off her clothes and dropped them on the floor. She got under the thin starched sheet just as she was, and fell instantly into a dreamless sleep.

CHAPTER TWO

'No, no, don't worry at all. I just wondered if she and Chloe might be together . . . Yes, of course. Is she? In Chile? How marvellous. Give her my best wishes, won't you? Yes, that would be lovely. I'll give you a call. 'Bye.'

Lesley replaced the receiver. 'She's not there either.'

Her neat leather address book lay open on the side table, but there were no more numbers left to try. She had been through them all and none of Ruby's friends or their parents had seen her recently. None of Ruby's friends who were also known to her mother, at least. There weren't all that many of them.

Andrew was sitting in an armchair in a circle of lamp-light, a pile of papers on his lap. A vee of wrinkles formed in the centre of his forehead as he stared at her over his reading glasses.

'She's nineteen. It's really time she started taking responsibility for herself. You can't stand in the firing line for her for ever.'

'I don't think I do,' Lesley answered mildly. 'Do I?'

Andrew exhaled sharply through his nose, pulling down the corners of his mouth to indicate disagreement without bothering to disagree, and resumed his reading.

Looking away from him, at the pleasant room that was arranged just how she wanted it, with the duck-egg blue shade of the walls that was restful without being cold and the cushion and curtain borders exactly matching it, Lesley felt anxiety fogging the atmosphere. Concern about Ruby distorted the room's generous proportions and made it loom around her, sharp with threatening edges. The air itself tasted thin, as if she couldn't draw enough of it into her lungs to make her heart beat steadily. Lesley knew this feeling of old, but familiarity never lessened the impact.

Where was Ruby? What was she doing this time, and who was she with?

One day, Lesley's inner voice insisted, the unthinkable will happen. She shook her head to drive away the thought.

She never experienced the same anxiety about Edward, Ruby's half-brother. Edward was always in the right place, doing the right thing. It was only for Ruby that she feared.

Justifiably, Andrew would snap.

Lesley closed her address book and secured it with a woven band. They had eaten dinner and she had cleared it away. The dishwasher was purring in her granite-and-maplewood kitchen, the central heating had come on, the telephone obstinately withheld its chirrup. Ruby had been gone since yesterday afternoon. She had slipped out of the house without a word to anyone.

Just to break the silence she asked, 'Would you like a drink, darling? A whisky, or anything?'

'No thanks.' Andrew didn't even look up.

'I'll go and . . . see if Ed's all right with his homework.'

Lesley went slowly up the stairs. At the top she hesitated, then tapped on her son's door: 'Hello?'

Ed was sitting at his table. The television was on at the foot of his bed, but he had his back to it and she saw an exercise book and coloured pencils and an encyclopaedia open in front of him.

'How's it going?'

'OK.' His thick fair hair, the same colour as his father's, stuck up in a tuft at the front and made him look like a placid bird. He was the opposite of Ruby in every single respect. He rolled a pencil between his thumb and forefinger now and Lesley was aware that he was politely waiting for her to go away and leave him in peace.

'No word from Ruby,' she said. 'I really thought she'd ring this evening.'

Ed nodded, looking thoughtful. 'You know, I don't think we should worry. She's probably staying in town with one of her mates. It's not like it's the first time she's just forgotten to come home, is it?'

For an eleven-year-old, Edward was remarkably well thought-out.

'No,' Lesley agreed.

'Have you tried her mobile again?'

Only a dozen times. 'Still turned off.'

'Well, I think we should just tell ourselves that no news is good news. She'll probably ring you tomorrow.'

'Yes. All right, darling. I'll pop in later and say goodnight.'

'OK.' He had his nose in his book again before the door closed.

Lesley went along the landing to another door at the far end. The thick sisal matting, expensively rubber-backed, absorbed the sound of her footsteps. She leaned against the handle for a moment, then walked into the room.

It was dark and stuffy, and the room's close smell had a distinctly brackish quality to it.

Lesley had already looked in here two or three times during the day but the otherness of Ruby's bedroom, the way it seemed to rebuff her, never failed to take her by surprise.

31

She felt cautiously along the wall for the light switch, then clicked it on.

The smell was from Ruby's collection of shells. She had lost interest in adding to it at least eight years ago but the cowries and spindles never quite gave up the traces of fish and salt locked in their pearly whorls. The wall cabinets that Lesley had had put up to display them contained a jumbled, teetering mass of sandy jars and broken conches. The collection had never been properly organised or catalogued. Ruby had just wanted to get specimens and keep them, piling up her acquisitions greedily but carelessly, as if she were building a dam.

She moved on to shells after her enthusiasm for collecting autographs had waned, and after shells lost their fascination she became obsessed with beetles. There were boxes and cases of preserved specimens on every flat surface.

Lesley crouched down beside a row of mahogany display cases and peered through the dusty glass fronts. These had cost Ruby all her pocket money and every Christmas and birthday present for years, and the contents still made Lesley smile and suppress a faint shudder at the same time. Some of the beetles were two-inch monsters with stiff jointed legs, minutely articulated antennae and folded wings with an iridescent polish. Lesley had always recognised that they were exquisite as well as interesting, these skewered trophies of Victorian entomologists that had so fascinated her twelve-year-old daughter.

Other items in the collection were just matchboxes containing tiny shrivelled items that Ruby had pounced on in the garden, trapped and kept. Lesley smiled again at the memory of absorbed Ruby crouching beside a bush of artemisia, her latest discovery caught in her cupped hands.

'What are they all? Do you know?' Andrew used to ask.

'Yes,' Ruby would answer flatly, offering nothing more.

'Why do you like them?'

'They're beautiful. Don't you think?' She would turn away then, not looking for an answer, as if she had already said too much.

'At least it's not spiders,' Lesley had said appeasingly to her husband once she was out of earshot.

The beetle passion eventually faded like its precursors, but Ruby would never consider selling any of her acquisitions or even allowing them to be stored up in the loft. Almost everything, including the shoeboxes full of autographs, was in this room.

Lesley kept her eyes averted now from the case containing a single enormous conker-brown insect that looked like a giant cockroach. There was hardly room to place her feet among the boxes and cartons, the scribbled drawings and pages torn from magazines, discarded clothes and spilt tubes of make-up. It was impossible to tell what, if anything, Ruby had taken with her. She stepped gingerly across the floor and sat down on the rucked-up bed. She placed her hand in the hollow of the pillow, but no warmth lingered there.

Every corner of the room, every shelf and cupboard and drawer, spilled hoarded belongings. Nothing was in any order. The collecting seemed to have little to do with quality, only quantity. To having and holding, Lesley guessed, maybe as a way of shoring up a world that might otherwise crumble. But for all the random, chaotic and overwhelming material clutter, the impression that it now held was of emptiness.

Ruby had gone.

Lesley placed her feet together and rested her hands in her lap as if to offer up her own composure in response to the room's disorder.

Ruby hadn't gone like her contemporaries were going, on well-planned gap year travels to Asia and South America or amid clouds of A-level glory to good universities. Not mutinous, truanting, dyslexic and serially expelled Ruby. She hadn't passed any exams, or spent a summer raising money to fund a year's work with children in Nepal or wildlife in Namibia. Ruby had left the family house in Kent to lodge with Andrew's brother and his family in central London, supposedly while she was attending sixth-form college. But college hadn't lasted long and in Camden Town, Ruby had spent her days hanging out with new friends that none of the Ellises approved of. Then, just recently, she had abruptly moved back home again. She passed long hours closeted in her room and when she emerged she spoke only when spoken to. Andrew chivvied her for decisions about a career. Making a contribution to the world, as he called it.

Ruby had lifted her black-painted eyes and stared at him as if he belonged to a species she didn't recognise.

Nothing could have enraged him more.

And now, she had simply removed herself altogether. The absence of Ruby swelled to fill her bedroom and bled outwards, hollowing the comfortable house.

'I love you,' her mother said to the motionless, smelly air.

Tenderness and longing sprang from the marrow in her bones. The feeling was turbulent, baffled, nothing like the calm, sturdy love she had for Edward, or her regularly thwarted affection for Andrew.

Her love for Ruby was the deepest passion in Lesley's life.

The silence deepened. There was no ready explanation to be found, in this room or anywhere else, for what had gone wrong with her daughter. Or with me, Lesley added meticulously. It wasn't that she blamed Ruby for being difficult. She took all the responsibility for that on herself, which further irritated Andrew. In their late-night conversations or in the car on the way to deal with another of Ruby's situations she had asked the same questions over and over: *what have I done wrong? Have I been a bad mother?*

34

'You have lacked a role model,' Andrew tended to say.

One thing did strike her with peculiar certainty now: this time the departure was final. Wherever she had gone, by her own choice or – *please, let it not be that* – under compulsion, Ruby wouldn't be coming back.

Lesley bent her head. She examined her knees in their second skin of smooth nylon mesh. She picked at a loose thread in the grosgrain hem of her skirt and, to her shame even though there was no one to see, tears suddenly ran out of her eyes and dripped on the fabric.

Ruby opened her eyes.

White light poured in through the arched window, filling the bare room until the air seemed almost solid with floating particles of dust. It wasn't the sunshine that had woken her, however, but a burst of chanting. The words were incomprehensible, delivered in a rich sing-song voice distorted by heavy amplification. She pushed back the sheet and scrambled to look outside. Her eyes widened in amazement.

In the street below, rows of men were kneeling on mats laid over the cobbles, with their foreheads pressed to the ground. They made a patient sea of white- and grey-clad fish backs, the soles of their feet turned innocently upwards like so many pairs of fins.

The city was stilled. Ruby rested her own forehead against the thick greenish glass and tried to hear the prayers.

A few minutes later a wave broke across the sea as the men kneeled upright and then stood up. The mats were casually whisked away and movement flowed back into the street again. Two little boys chased each other up some steps and scuttled through a doorway. A handcart loaded with fruit trundled past, pushed by two men. Realising that she was hungry, Ruby reluctantly turned from the inviting view.

The house was so quiet. The stone walls must be very

thick, she thought, as she wandered along the outside corridor. She couldn't remember which way Auntie had brought her last night and the layout of interconnecting rooms was confusing. Here was a broader corridor with seats facing a carved screen with little hinged trapdoors in it. She peered casually through one of the propped-up hatches and was surprised by the grand double-height space it overlooked. This big hall was almost unfurnished except for a long table and some high-backed chairs pushed against the walls. At the far end was a low dais backed by a wall painting of entwined flowers and fruit and exotic foliage. Huge lamps of iron and glass were suspended on chains from the arched roof. It would be a pretty good space for a party, she reflected. If you half closed your eyes as you peered through the screen you could see the whirling dancers and hear the beat of the drums.

After another full circuit of the gallery Ruby opened a low door and found a staircase. She ran down the steps and peered into the big room from this lower level. From down here the gallery was completely concealed.

She suddenly sensed that there was someone behind her. Whirling round, she came face to top of head with Auntie.

'Hello,' Ruby said brightly.

Auntie peered up at her. '*Sabah il-kheer*,' she murmured. Her face was like a walnut. She didn't smile, but there were quite kindly-looking creases at the corners of her eyes and mouth.

'I'm looking for my grandmother.'

'Mum-reese,' Auntie agreed, nodding. She indicated with a small hand movement that Ruby should follow her.

The house wasn't really as big as it appeared. Just a few steps round a corner brought another surprise.

Ruby said, 'Oh. It's lovely.'

At the heart of the old house was a little open courtyard. It was enclosed by terracotta walls pierced by simple rounded arches faced with grass-green and turquoise glazed tiles. In the four corners were big square tubs of trailing greenery and to one side a waterspout splashed into a green glazed bowl. The trickle of water was loud in the small space. A lemon-sharp slice of sunlight obliquely bisected the court-yard and in the shady portion was a padded chair. Iris was sitting there watching her. Her thin grey hair was held up with a pair of combs and she was wearing an elegant silk robe with a faint pearly stripe. She appeared less tired than she had done the night before. But she also looked displeased.

Ruby considered. She wanted to find a way to stay, not just because to come here at all had been a last resort and she had no intention of being sent back home, but because it was so intriguing. Therefore she must say something appropriate, find a way to ingratiate herself. A shadow of a thought passed through her head – an acknowledgement that she was quite out of practice at making herself agreeable. She didn't even know what to call this disconcerting old lady. She was way too unfamiliar and beady for 'Granny', which was how Lesley referred to her at home. Not that Ruby's mother talked about her own mother very often.

'Hi,' she said in the end, shuffling her feet.

Mamdooh had to remind me when he brought my morning tea that we have a visitor. The night was a long one, and it was after dawn when I finally slept. And then, dreams.

Now here is the girl. She wears peculiar, ugly clothes. Are they the same ones as last night? A pair of dusty black trousers, safety-pinned in the front across her plump belly. The legs billow out from the knee like sails, and they are so long that they drag on the ground. The hems are all dusty and torn. When she takes a step I see that her huge shoes have soles four inches thick, so she isn't quite as tall as she seems. On the top half, or third because the garment is so shrunken that it exposes six inches of white midriff, is a little grey thing with some black motif on the front. She has so many silvery rings on her fingers that they reach up to her knuckles, more rings in her ears, one in her nose, and a silver stud pierces her top lip. She hasn't washed this morning, there is black stuff smudged round her eyes. Her face is round, pale as the moon, and innocent.

She slouches forward and utters some monosyllable I can't hear.

Why is she here?

I search the layers, broken layers, of memory. Piecing together.

Lesley's daughter.

'Don't you have any proper clothes?'

She sticks her chin out at me.

'These are proper.'

'They are not decent.'

Her eyes meet mine. She scowls, then thinks better of it. Her metal-cased fingers pluck at the bottom of the vest garment.

'Too short?'

I am already tired of this exchange. There is a white shawl across the arm of my chair and I hold it out to her. She shakes out the folds and twirls it like a matador's cape, and I am struck by the grace of the sudden movement and, yes, the happy exuberance of it. It's pretty to see. Then she seems to remember herself. She knots my shawl awkwardly over her breasts so it veils her stomach.

'Sit down.'

Obediently, she perches on a wooden stool and leans forward.

'Y'know, I don't know what to call you. You're my grand-mother and everything, but it doesn't seem right to say Granny. D'you know what I mean?'

It hardly matters what she calls me. It's a long time since

38

I have been anything except Mum-reese or Doctor Black. 'My name is Iris.'

'Is that what you want me to say?'

I rest my head on the cushions and close my eyes.

After a minute, maybe more, she murmurs, 'Iris?'

The line of sunlight is creeping towards us. I rouse myself again.

'Have you told your mother where you are? You'll have to go back home right away. You do realise that, don't you? It's very inconvenient, this . . . this appearance in my house. You must telephone her at once, tell her where you are, and say I told you, to . . .'

A shadow crosses the child's face.

'Yeah. I know, I know. Thing is . . .' she half stands and rummages under the shawl in the tight pocket of her trousers. She produces a small silvery object. 'My mobile doesn't work out here.'

'Is that a telephone? You can use the one here, I suppose. It's through there. Mamdooh will show you.'

'Right. OK. Um . . . I'm really hungry, though. Is there something to eat, maybe, before I call home and tell them everything's cool?'

'Auntie is bringing it.'

Auntie and Mamdooh arrive together. Auntie's quite lively with curiosity now but Mamdooh is offended, I can see from the way he puts down the tray with exaggerated care and doesn't look at the girl. It doesn't matter. She'll be going back where she came from, maybe not today but certainly tomorrow. What was her name?

It comes back to me surprisingly easily. Ruby.

Ruby's eyes lit up at the sight of breakfast. She was very hungry indeed, and here was a bowl of fat purple figs and – lifting a little beaded cloth that covered a bowl – thick creamy yoghurt.

39

There was a basket of coarse bread, a glass dish of honey and a plate of crumbly, sticky little cakes. There was also a battered silver pot, a tiny wisp of steam rising from the spout.

'Thank you, Mamdooh. Thank you, Auntie,' Iris said. 'We'll look after ourselves now.'

Ruby drew her stool closer.

'Pour me some tea, please,' Iris ordered. Ruby did as she was told and put the glass on the table beside her. The tea smelled of summertime.

'Mm,' Ruby said, after a long swallow. 'That's so good. What is it?'

'Don't you know? Mint tea.'

'I like it. We don't have it at home. Well, maybe Mum does. She drinks those herb tea things, but I shouldn't think they're like yours. Can I try some of this?'

Iris nodded. She watched as the girl spooned honey onto bread and ate, biting off thick chunks and chewing with strong white teeth. Honey dribbled down her chin and she wiped it off with her fingers before greedily licking them too. After the bread and honey she turned her attention to the figs.

'How do you eat these?'

Iris showed her, slicing open the skin to reveal the velvet and seed-pearl interior. Ruby ate, her smudged eyes screwed up in a comical spasm of pleasure. She followed the figs with most of the bowl of yoghurt and then drank more tea.

'Aren't you going to eat anything?' she asked.

'I'll have one of those.' Iris pointed to the triangles of baklava. Ruby put the pastry on a plate, handling it as if it were burning hot so as to be seen to limit the contact from her own fingers, and set it next to Iris's glass of tea. Then she stretched out her legs, sighing with satisfaction as she looked around the little courtyard.

40

'It's like another world. Well, it *is* another world, of course. Glorious Araby.'

'What did you say?'

'When? Oh, that. I dunno, it's from a poem or something, isn't it? Don't ask me who wrote it or anything. I suppose I read it or heard it. Probably bloody Radio 4, it's always on in our house. You know how some things you don't try to remember, quite weird things like bits of poems or whatever, they just stay in your mind? And other things you're supposed to remember, however hard you try it's just like, *phhhhht*, and they're gone? Stuff you're supposed to learn for exams, mainly?'

'If it matters, you will remember it. You have to hope for that.'

'Depends on what you reckon matters.' Ruby laughed, then caught sight of her grandmother's face. It had fallen suddenly into lines of anguish and the powdery skin under her eyes looked damp with tears.

She bit her lip. 'Did I say something wrong?'

Iris reached a hand inside the sleeve of her robe and brought out a handkerchief. She dried her eyes carefully and tucked the hanky away again.

'I am becoming forgetful myself,' she said. She made a little gesture with her hands, swimming them through the air and then closing them on nothing. It made Ruby think that memories were slippery, like fish.

'That must be frightening, sometimes,' she ventured.

'It is.'

'What can you do?'

Iris turned her head to look full at her. 'Try to . . . try to capture what you can't bear to be without.'

Ruby didn't understand this but she nodded anyway. The sound of water splashing from the little spout filled the courtyard. The sun had crept closer and now the thin stream sparkled like a diamond necklace.

'Well,' Iris said in a different voice. 'Have you had quite enough to eat?'

'Maybe one more of these.'

She bit into another pastry. Sugary flakes stuck to her lips and she darted her tongue to retrieve them.

Mamdooh came through one of the arches and stooped beside Iris's chair. It was time to move it further into the shade. As she watched him helping her grandmother and settling her again Ruby noticed he wore the same tender expression as last night, as if Iris were a little child.

While they were talking quietly together, Ruby stared up into the parallelogram of sapphire-blue sky. She could just see the tips of towers, topped with slim bulbs of stone and spikes bearing crescent moons. There was a whole city on the other side of these walls, the teeming place she had seen out of the taxi windows last night. Now that she had found her feet she was longing to explore it.

'Mamdooh is going to the market now,' Iris said.

Ruby leapt up so eagerly that her stool tipped over. 'Can I go with him?'

Iris lifted her hand. 'You will have to ask Mamdooh.'

'Please may I come with you?'

He had round cheeks, rounded eyelids, full lips the colour of the breakfast figs, but his bald head was all speckled and his eyes were milky. His stomach made a sizeable mound under his long white robe. He didn't look as old as Iris or Auntie, but he wasn't young by any means. He looked Ruby up and down as she stood there with Iris's shawl knotted round her midriff.

'To the market, Miss?' He sounded doubtful.

'I'll, um, put a cover-up shirt thing on? I've got one in my bag. I could help carry the shopping, couldn't I?'

'I do this for many years, thank you.'

'I'd really like to come.'

Iris closed her eyes. 'Show her the market, Mamdooh, please. She will be going home to England tomorrow.'

He bowed. 'Of course.'

When she came downstairs again with a man's shirt buttoned up over her vest, Mamdooh was waiting for her. He had a woven rush basket over his arm, and a faded red flowerpot hat set squarely on his head. A black tassel hung down towards his left eye. Ruby felt a giggle rising in her throat, but Mamdooh's expression quelled it.

'Is this OK?' she meekly asked, indicating her cover-up.

His nod was barely perceptible.

'If you are ready, Miss?'

They went out through the blue-painted door and the sun's heat struck the top of Ruby's head. She took the few steps to the corner and looked up at an ancient crenellated wall, a cluster of smaller domes surrounding the large one and the three slender towers.

'What is this place?' she called to Mamdooh who was making stately progress in the other direction.

'It is the mosque of al-Azhar. We are going this way, please.'

'It's very old.'

'Cairo is a place of history.' The way he said it told Ruby that he was proud of his native city and his reverence made her want to know more of it. She quickened her pace to catch him up again, and they swung down a narrow street and out into a much broader, almost Western-looking one. Out here there was a roar of traffic and hooting and tinny amplified music, and they were caught in a slow tide of people before Mamdooh ducked down into a tiled modern subway not much different from the one beneath Oxford Circus. When they surfaced again Ruby blinked.

Mamdooh beckoned her. 'Khan al-Khalili bazaar. Follow close to me, it is easy to be lost here.'

He was right. It would be the easiest thing in the world to lose yourself in this maze of tiny alleys leading away from the almost-familiarity of the main street. There were canvas awnings looped overhead, and in their welcome shade the brightness of the crammed-together shops and stalls was dazzling. The merchandise was piled up and hung in tiers so it seemed to drip stalactites of hectic colour. One shop was crammed with interesting-looking brass and ceramic hookahs, another niche was festooned with belly dancers' costumes gaudy with nylon fringing and glass beads. Another little recess was shelved from top to bottom with hundreds of glass jars containing oils in all the shades of precious stones. Next door open-mouthed hessian sacks spilled ochre- and saffron- and pearl-coloured grains.

The footpaths between the stalls were choked with people and wooden carts and porters with boxes piled on their heads. There were men in Western clothes, and others in *galabiyeh* and tarboosh like Mamdooh. There were women robed in black from head to toe, others in trousers and sturdy blouses with just a scarf wound over their hair. Ruby was startled and slightly affronted to see that there were numbers of Western tourists, pink-faced and too tall, uncertain in response to the urgent demands of the stallholders. In Iris's secluded house she had felt as if they were the only two of their kind in the whole of Cairo.

The shopkeepers competed for Ruby's attention as she went by.

'Lady, look-see. Just looking, no charge. Very good prices.'

Urchins plucked at her shirt, holding up novelty lighters and boxes of tissues and bottles of water. Even in the shade it was hot, and the air felt saturated with moisture. Her shirt was soon sticking to her back and thick hanks of hair plastered themselves to her forehead and the nape of her neck. There was a continuous *ssss-ssss* of warning at her back as porters and carters hauled and pushed their loads into the depths of the bazaar.

She followed Mamdooh's bobbing tarboosh, realising that if she lost sight of him she had no idea which way to turn. A memory came back to her of being a small child, shopping with Lesley in a department store. She had lost herself in a forest of legs and bulging bags, and she fought her way between them, stumbling forward and then back again, a wail of panic and outrage forming in her throat. Big faces had bloomed over her head, and hands reached out to catch her as she screamed and screamed. It could only have been a minute or two before Lesley found her, but it had seemed like hours. She resisted the impulse now to catch and hold tight onto Mamdooh's white skirts.

An even smaller capillary led away from the alley of shops, this one enclosed by rickety houses with overhanging upper storeys that reduced the visible sky to a thin strip. There were wooden benches lining the house walls, all heaped high with vegetables and fruit. One stall was a mound of figs with skin as smooth and matte as the softest kid leather, another was a tangle of bitter-looking green leaves. Mamdooh stopped, planting his legs apart and surveying the merchandise.

Stallholders surrounded him at once, thrusting up polished aubergines and bunches of white onions for his attention. Some of the offerings he waved away, others he condescended to pinch or to sniff at. Once an item had received his approval, there was a convoluted exchange obviously relating to the price. Finally, at length and with ceremony, a purchase was wrapped in a twist of paper in exchange for some coins and Mamdooh stowed it in his straw basket before moving a couple of paces onwards.

Ruby had never seen shopping taken as seriously as this. She found a space against a dusty wall and watched in fascination.

Mamdooh glanced back once or twice to check on her. When he realised that she wasn't going to interrupt him, or wander off and cause trouble, he gave her a small nod of approval. And then, when his shopping was complete he tilted his head to indicate that she was to follow him. At the corner he spoke to an old man sitting on a stool beside a couple of rough sacks. Another coin changed hands and now Mamdooh passed the twist of paper straight to Ruby. She bit into a sweet, creamy white nut kernel.

Mamdooh treated her just as if she were a kid, she thought. It was quite annoying, but at the same time – well, it was restful, in a way.

They threaded their way back through the porters and tourists and stallholders and customers, a slow mass of hot humanity that made urgency impossible. Ruby tucked herself behind Mamdooh and watched the faces as they bobbed towards her and were borne past.

Slanting sunlight just ahead revealed an open square. There were walls of sepia-coloured stone, the dust-coated leaves of rubber trees casting patches of shade on broken pavements, and a pair of faded sun umbrellas rooted in pillars of concrete. At two tin tables, bare except for ashtrays and a folded newspaper, sat a handful of old men.

They raised their hands or mumbled greetings to Mamdooh, who responded with two or three brief words. Several pairs of eyes, red-rimmed or milky, turned towards Ruby.

She understood the situation at once. Mamdooh came out to do the household's shopping, then retired to this café or whatever it was for an hour's talk with his friends, and her presence was an impediment to this pleasant interval in his day. She lifted her hands and raised her shoulders in apology as Mamdooh prepared to move on.

She said hastily, 'I can find my way back, you know, if

you want to stay with your friends for a bit. I found my way last night, didn't I?' She remembered Nafouz and his taxi.

Mamdooh looked genuinely shocked at this suggestion.

'That would not be at all right, Miss. We will be going home at once. Mum-reese will look for you, perhaps.'

The *perhaps*, and the pinch of the lips that went with it, betrayed more hope than conviction, but Ruby knew there was nothing more to be said about going back by herself. Farewells were exchanged with the old men and Mamdooh sailed across the square. But now, Ruby sensed, she was walking with him rather than in his wake. The impression was confirmed when he remarked in a conversational voice, 'Market, very old also.'

'How old?'

'Seven hundred year.'

'Ha. Just think of all the buying of things.' Centuries, Ruby thought, of leather and herbs and perfume and figs. The notion made her shiver a little.

'Selling,' Mamdooh corrected her. He rubbed his thumb and forefinger together. 'Selling, very important.'

They both laughed at that. Mamdooh's shoulders shook and his head tipped back, but his tarboosh didn't fall off.

They came to the wide street from a completely un-expected direction and ducked through the stream of buses and cars. They were walking companionably towards Iris's house when an extra-loud volley of hooting caught their attention. There was a black-and-white taxi parked where the alley finally became impassable to cars. The faded blue of the door was just behind it.

'Lady, lady! We look for you!' a voice shouted.

Nafouz was leaning out of the driver's window and banging with his fist on the car door.

Mamdooh moved fast for a man of his bulk. He streaked across to the taxi and shouted at Nafouz, flapping his big hand towards the open end of the alley. From the passenger side of the car another young man climbed out and hung on the lintel. He looked like Nafouz, but a little younger. He was grinning and shouting back at Mamdooh, thumping on the car roof, clearly enjoying the scene. Two or three small children gathered to stare.

. Nafouz slid out of the car. He appealed direct to Ruby. 'We are friends, yes? I bring you, last night.'

'No.'

'Lady?' Nafouz's eyes were wide, hurt pools.

'Yes, I mean, you drove me from the airport. That doesn't make us friends, does it?' She had kicked him, for one thing.

Nafouz turned away to burrow inside the car. Ruby looked at the other young man. He had the same slicked-back hair as Nafouz and a similar white shirt, but cleaner. He smiled at her.

'I come all the way, bring this for you.' Nafouz had re-emerged. He was holding out a CD case with a hand-coloured insert, a pattern of swirls and tendrils in red paint and black ink. Ruby looked at it. Her name was spelled out among the tendrils. Jas had painted the insert, and he had burned the CD inside it for her. It was one of his own mixes, just about the last thing he had made for her before . . . Before he . . .

She held out her hand. The CD must have fallen out of her bag as she scrambled into or out of the taxi. She would have been sad to lose it.

'It's only a thing, baby,' Jas would have said. 'Things don't matter, people do.'

But she had so little of him.

'Right. Well, thanks,' she muttered.

She was about to take the case but Nafouz drew his hand back, teasing her. Her fingers closed on thin air, but Mamdooh was quicker. The case was tweaked out of

48

Nafouz's grasp and slipped into the deep pocket in the seam of Mamdooh's *galabiyeh*.

There was a sharp exchange of words before Mamdooh turned back to Ruby. 'If you like, Miss, you give him a little money. But it is not if you do not want.'

Ruby looked at the two young men and they stared back at her. An awkward flush of colour crept up her face as she felt the space of cobbled alleyway widen between them. She wished she hadn't denied being Nafouz's friend; she would have much preferred to be that now rather than the possessor or otherwise of a few Egyptian pounds.

'How much?' she muttered, in shame.

Nafouz was equal to the moment. 'Twenty bounds,' he said brightly.

Mamdooh clicked his tongue but Ruby rummaged under her shirt for her purse as the two young men watched with interest. She took out a note and Nafouz whisked it away. He winked at her.

'You take a tour? I show you Cairo. Special Cairo, my brother and me. Not tourist places. Real city.'

Ruby hesitated. She would have loved to pile into the taxi and go cruising through the streets with them. She could smell cigarettes and the plastic seats of the car, and feel the hot diesel-scented air blowing in through the windows.

Mamdooh had already mounted the steps and produced a key for the blue door.

'Another time, maybe,' she said lamely. There were priorities, other matters she had to deal with first.

The younger brother came round to Nafouz's side of the car.

'I am Ashraf.'

'Hi.'

The door was open, Mamdooh was waiting with the basket of vegetables at his side. The brothers were waiting too.

'My name's Ruby.'

Their faces split into identical white smiles. 'Nice name.'

'I've got to go now. But I'd like to take a tour, yeah. Have you got a . . .' She made a scribble movement in the air for a pen, but Nafouz dismissed it.

'We find you.'

'Miss?' Mamdooh said, holding the door open wide. His forehead was serrated with disapproval once more.

'See you, then.'

Ruby marched up the steps. The taxi noisily reversed down the street in a cloud of acrid fumes.

In the cool hallway Mamdooh blocked her way. 'It is important to have some care, Miss. You are young, in this city there are not always good people. Not all people are bad, you must understand, it is just important that you make no risks. Do you understand what it is I am saying to you?'

He *was* treating her like a child. In London, Ruby did what she wanted. Lesley and Andrew didn't know what that involved, nor did Will and Fiona who were Andrew's brother and his wife. She was supposed to be their lodger, but – well, after a while they had given up on telling her what to do and what not to do. That was because of Will. Even though Fiona didn't know about him, the three of them had ended up in this kind of silent contract, where nobody saw anything or said anything in case it led to somebody seeing and saying everything. That was how Ruby summed it up for herself, at least.

And there had been some bad interludes. Ruby had seen and once or twice done things that she didn't like to remember. The memories came back anyway, in the night, and they made her sweat and feel sick. The memories had a way of changing and speeding up so that they were like horror films of what might have happened to her. Her skin crawled, and she would twist and turn under the covers to try to make them stop and go away. She even wished for Lesley to come and tell her it was all right and she was safe.

But usually in the end she fell asleep somehow, or the daylight would come and she'd wonder what she had been so afraid of. The important thing to remember was that she had survived. Going back to people's places when she shouldn't have done. Doing too much stuff, or just drinking. Not knowing where she was or where she had been. Feeling like nothing, less than nothing. But that happened to plenty of people, didn't it? Not just her.

Luck or cunning, Jas had said. That's what you need to survive, in this day and age. It was important to have both. She could just hear his words, see him breathing out a snaky ring of blue smoke as he spoke.

So Ruby was sure she understood exactly what Mamdooh was saying and was certain that she could deal with whatever might happen to her here. She was impressed by her own cunning and her luck wouldn't desert her.

'Yes,' she said stonily. She stood and faced him, giving no ground.

Mamdooh tucked the handles of the basket over his arm.

'Mum-reese resting now. Later, she will speak to you.'

And order her home. Ruby knew what he meant her to hear, but she gave no sign of it.

Left to herself, she wandered through the house.

It was less opulent than it had looked in last night's incense-scented darkness, and even more neglected. The great lamps that hung from the vaulted roofs were thickly furred with dust, and more dust lay on the stairs and on the broad sills of the windows. Cobwebs spanned the dim corners. The rooms were barely furnished with odd, unmatching chairs and tables that looked as if they had been brought in by an incoming tide and just left where they landed. There were no books, ornaments, or photographs – none of the cosy

51

decorator's clutter that Lesley arranged in her own house and those of her clients. There was nothing, Ruby realised, that told any stories of Iris's past. Nothing accumulated, even after such a long life. She was quite curious to know why.

This morning, Iris had told her that she was becoming forgetful. She had made a swimming movement with her old hands, as if she were trying to catch fish. And there had been tears in her eyes.

Didn't framed photographs and bits of china and books help you to recollect?

Ruby frowned, trailing her finger through the grey film on a wooden chest and recalling her grandmother's words. She had said something about capturing what you can't bear to be without. It was the word capture that resonated.

When she was small, Ruby distanced herself, she had felt all wrong. She couldn't read and write as well as girls in her class, and she was endlessly in trouble. A way of making sense out of her confusion had been to collect and keep things. By piling them up in her room she could make herself bigger than they were, so even if what she collected represented only a strand, a tiny filament of the world's appalling abundance, it had still seemed to offer a measure of control. But shells and beetles were inanimate. In that, in the end, collecting had disappointed her because the world was so swarming, inchoate and threateningly living, and it had bulged and gibbered and danced outside her bedroom window, making her boxes of beetles seem nothing more than childish detritus.

'Growing up is so very hard to do.' Jas had yawned when they talked about this.

But if you wanted to capture memories that threatened to swim away like fish? How would you do that?

An idea came to Ruby. It was a very neat, simple and pleasing idea that would solve her problem and at the same time be valuable to her grandmother. It was the perfect solution and she was so taken with its economy that she ran up the nearest of the house's two flights of stairs towards the door that she had worked out must be Iris's. She hovered outside for a moment, with her ear against one of the dark panels.

Then she tapped, very gently. When there was no answer she rapped more loudly.

'Auntie? Mamdooh?' Iris's voice answered.

'It's me. Ruby.'

There was a long silence. Then the voice, sounding much smaller, said, 'You had better come in.'

She was sitting in the same low chair as last night. There were pillows behind her head, a rug over her knees. Ruby read bewilderment in her face.

She stooped down beside the chair and put her hand over Iris's thin, dry one.

'Am I disturbing you?'

'No.'

'I went shopping with Mamdooh. I think I got in the way of his routine, but it was really interesting. He told me there's been a market there for seven hundred years.'

'Yes.'

The monosyllable came out on a long breath. Iris was obviously almost too tired to speak and her fragility gave Ruby a hot, unwieldy feeling that she could only just identify as protectiveness. She wanted to scoop up her grandmother and hold her in her arms. But even as she chased this thought to its logical conclusion – Iris would not appreciate being handled like a rag doll – the old woman seemed to summon up some surprising inner strength. She hoisted herself upright against the cushions and fixed Ruby with a glare.

'Have you spoken on the telephone to my daughter?'

Ruby quailed at this sudden direct challenge. 'Um, no.'

'You are disobedient.'

'I didn't say I was definitely . . .'

'Why have you not done so?'

There was now the opportunity to make up some excuse, or to try a version of the truth. Ruby understood already that it would be advisable to aim for the truth, at least where her grandmother was concerned. She withdrew her hand and took a breath. 'It's really because I don't want to go home. I was hoping you wouldn't make me.'

Iris studied her. Her gaze was very sharp now, all the weariness and confusion seemed to have evaporated. 'Why is that?'

'It's quite a long story. If I could stay here with you for a while, I could maybe tell you . . .'

'That is not possible.'

Ruby bent her head. The sonorous, amplified chanting that had woken her this morning suddenly filled the room again. 'What is that?'

'The call to prayer.'

'Oh. All right, I'll ring Mum and tell her where I am and there'll be a mega fuss and outcry, and I'll go home. But if I could stay here, just for a few *days* or so, not a lifetime or a year or anything, then maybe I could help you.'

There was again the steady gaze. 'This morning, with my shawl. You did a little . . . almost a dance. I liked that.' Iris smiled at the remembered image.

'Did I?'

'How do you think you can help me?'

Now it was Ruby who made a small unconscious gesture with her hands, as if trying to catch darting fish. 'You told me you are sometimes forgetful.'

'Yes. So?' Sharply.

'I walked round the house this afternoon, and you don't

seem to have any belongings, the kind that help you to remember the past.'

'I have lived a long life, in different places. Most of them primitive. I have learned that so many material possessions are just that, material.'

She was saying almost the same as Jas; *it's just stuff, baby.* There were connections here, twining around herself and Iris and the old house and even Mamdooh, and Nafouz and his brother, and the old men in the café. Ruby wanted to stay, more than she had wanted anything in a long time.

'Go on.'

'I thought, I wondered, if you told me what you want to . . . to capture, maybe I could be the keeper of it for you. I could be the collector of your memories. I could write them down, even. I could be your am . . . what's the word?'

'Amanuensis.'

Ruby's pale face had been animated, but now a heavy mask descended. She turned her head and looked out of the corner of her eyes. Iris hadn't seen her look sullen before.

'Not that, maybe. I'm dyslexic, you know. Bit of a draw-back.'

'Are you?'

'It's not the same as being thick. But sometimes it might as well be. To all intents and purposes.'

'Thank you for making that clear. You don't seem thick to me.'

'But maybe we could tape-record you? Like an oral history project. We did one at school, with the old ladies from the drop-in centre, about the Blitz.'

Iris laughed at that. Her hands loosened in her lap, her face lost its taut lines and her eyes shone. Ruby suddenly saw a young girl in her, and she beamed back, pleased with the effect her company was having.

'How useful to have previous experience.'

'I didn't mean to compare you.'

'Why not? I remember the Blitz. The beginning of it, anyway. Then I came out here, to Cairo, to work.'

'*Did* you? How come?'

'That's the beginning of another long story.'

They looked at each other then, as the last notes of the muezzin crackled and died away.

It was Iris who finally broke the silence: 'Go and talk to your mother. You may use my telephone, in the room through there. And when you have finished I will speak to her myself.'

Ruby stood up and went through the interconnecting door to Iris's bedroom. It was very bare, containing nothing more than a bed swathed in white curtains and a couple of wooden chests. A telephone stood on the table on one side of the bed, and on the other there actually was a framed photograph of a man and a woman. Managing not to stare at it, she walked deliberately round to the opposite side and picked up the receiver. After two or three attempts, she was listening to her mother's mobile ringing.

Lesley answered immediately, of course.

'*Ruby*? Ruby, are you all right? Thank God you've called. Tell me, what's happened? Where are you?'

Ruby spoke, briefly.

Her mother's voice rose. 'You are *where*?'

She closed her eyes.

CHAPTER THREE

When I replace the receiver I see that my hands are shaking.

I return to the other room where the child is waiting for me.

'What did she say?' she asks.

The anxiety in her round face tells me how much she does not want to be packed off back to England. I sit down to collect my thoughts and she fidgets with impatience, twisting her legs and picking at the stud in her nose.

I can give her the gist of my conversation with Lesley, but there is so much else that I would find harder to put into words.

'Leave your nose alone or you will set up an infection. Your mother has been worried about you. I told her that I thought you would be safe enough here.'

At once, the anxious expression breaks up into a smile that contains glee and satisfaction and a measure of triumph.

I am beginning to understand that Ruby's innocence is shot through with calculation. Maybe the innocence itself is calculated. And I realise that the notion interests me more than anything has done for quite a long time.

'So I *can* stay for a bit?'

Our separate conversations with Lesley have had a further curious effect, of course. That she is in opposition to both of us makes partial allies out of Ruby and me.

'I would like a drink. A proper drink, I mean. Will you call Mamdooh?' I say.

I am stalling for time because with part of myself I fear the loss of privacy that having her here will inevitably mean. I want to be alone to concentrate on the past, in order to hold on to it for as long as I can. Yet maybe the offer of help that Ruby made is less naïve than it sounded; maybe there is something in her idea.

Wearing his disapproval like an extra robe, Mamdooh brings in a tray with two glasses, a jug of water and a decanter with a couple of fingers of whisky in the bottom. I have no idea when I last drank Scotch.

'Mum-reese, you will have plenty water with this?'

'No, thank you, I'll take it neat. And a decent measure, please. That's better.'

Ruby accepts her glass with small enthusiasm. 'I don't really like whisky.'

'What do you drink?'

'Depends. Vodka and Red Bull?'

'What's that? I'm sure it's disgusting. I don't have anything of the kind anyway, so you'll have to make do with Scotch.'

We both laugh and Mamdooh peers at us in surprise.

When we are alone again she draws up a stool and sits close to my chair. The sun has set, the street outside is noisy once again with shouts and music as people prepare the *iftar*. It is already twenty-four hours since Ruby arrived.

As I taste my drink – rolling the unaccustomed spirit in my mouth – I am thinking about Lesley.

It is some time since I have spoken to my daughter, I can't remember how long exactly, but it must be months. Whenever we do talk there are always polite words that fail to build a bridge. And the space between us, that has always been there. From the very beginning.

Lesley was born in the middle of a grey, sad English winter. My pregnancy had been unplanned, my husband and I hastily bought a house to be a home for our unexpected family. From the windows there were views of sodden fields, and ponds mirroring the weeping skies. In this house, the baby and I spent long days alone together while my husband was working in the City.

Lesley cried unceasingly, for no reason that I could discern. I had completed my medical training by that time, and raw as I was as a doctor I knew for certain that she was not ill or even failing to thrive. I couldn't feed her myself, although I persevered for almost a month, but she accepted a bottle. She gained weight and passed the developmental milestones at the right times, but she was never a placid or contented baby.

I don't deny the probability that she absorbed my unhappiness and reflected it back at me. I tried to hold the infant close, tried to soothe her yelling by rocking her in my arms as I paced through the silent house, but she would not be pacified. Her tiny body went rigid and her screams were like scalpel blades slitting my skin. When Gordon came home he would take her from me and she would whimper and nuzzle and then fall asleep, exhausted. The silence came like a blessing.

As soon as I could, I found a nurse for her and took a job at the local hospital.

And from there we have gone on.

'Well?' Ruby demands. 'Can I stay?'

I turn my glass, looking at the dimples of light trapped within it.

'*Can* I?' she repeats.

'What did your mother say to you?'

An exasperated sigh and a shrug. 'She said she was about to call the police and report me missing. She said I am irresponsible, and thoughtless, and if I can't think of her I could perhaps consider my little brother, who was worried sick about me. I don't think he *was*, by the way. Worrying about people's so not Ed's thing. She said I should go home and behave better and get a job and dah dahdah, be a different person. Get a personality transplant maybe. I've heard it all before, about five zillion times.'

'She was worried,' I repeat.

I'm on unsafe ground here, caught between what I know I ought to say and what I feel. Which is recognition and a certain amount of sympathy.

We look at each other over our whisky glasses.

'You see, the trouble is that I'm crap at everything,' Ruby quietly says. 'At least, all the things that Lesley and Andrew rate. Not that I'd admit that to very many people, actually.'

'I don't think you are,' I tell her.

'Thanks.' Her tone is dismissive but her eyes implore me.

'All right,' I say slowly, because it is dawning on me that I do rather want her to stay. At least, I don't want her to go right now. It's not that I am lonely, but I would like to hear her talk some more. 'I will telephone Lesley again, and ask if you may have her permission to spend a few days with me.'

She hugs her knees and rocks on the stool. 'Fantastic.' She grins.

I finish my whisky first. My hands are steady now.

Lesley answers the telephone. 'Hello?'

'It's Iris,' I repeat.

'Mummy, tell me what's really going on?'

I never felt comfortable with *mummy*; it was Lesley who always insisted on it.

Into the space I say careful sentences about it being a

60

pleasure to meet Ruby, how Lesley would be doing a favour to me if she were to allow her to stay for a few days in Cairo. Now that she's here, I say, we might as well turn it to advantage. The Egyptian Museum. An outing to the Pyramids at Giza. Maybe even further afield, ancient history, archaeology. And so on.

Although nowadays I hardly leave the house, I find myself almost believing that Ruby and I will make these excursions together.

'If you agree, that is, Lesley. You and . . .'

Her husband; second husband, not Ruby's father. I have met this one two or three times but I find that I can remember nothing about him, not even his name. It's impossible to work out whether it is my forgetfulness that is to blame, or his unmemorableness.

'Mummy, what are you laughing at?'

'I'm not laughing.'

She sounds uncertain. 'Are you sure it won't be too much for you, having Ruby there?'

'I don't think so. If it turns out to be, I promise I'll say so.'

'Well . . . it's kind of you to do this for her. Thank you. After she's just turned up like that, uninvited. Andrew and I had no idea, one minute she was here and the next she'd vanished. It never occurred to me . . . she bought an air ticket, just like that, took her passport . . .'

'Enterprising of her. But she's not a baby, is she? Young people skip around all over the world these days. And as I said, she'll come to no harm here. Boredom will set in before too long and then you'll have her home again.'

'I expect so. We'll see.' I can hear that Lesley badly wants Ruby to go home, but she knows better than to insist on it. I find myself admiring her adroitness. 'Thanks again for taking her in.'

'What else would I have done?'

'I don't know, Mummy.'

The bridge of careful words begins to creak and sway, and we both step hastily backwards.

'I'll make sure she behaves herself,' I say.

'I'll call again tomorrow,' Lesley insists.

We quickly end the conversation. Now, and for the next few days, I am responsible for Ruby. When I return to the other room she is holding up the bottle that Mamdooh left on the tray.

'Top-up?' she asks.

Lesley looked around the quiet, lamplit room. Andrew was working on his laptop, Ed was upstairs in his bedroom.

'She said Ruby's not a baby anymore.'

'Quite right.'

She wanted to explain to him something about how, in one corner of her mother's heart, Ruby would always be an infant. That was how mothers functioned. She believed, too, that in some recess deep within themselves, daughters also yearned for childhood again.

But Andrew would not be interested in her theories about mother love. He might put his work aside to discuss the new electronic chart plotter to be installed in his boat, but not much else.

'Are we going down to the Hamble at the weekend?' she asked.

'Depends on whether I get this report finished.'

Lesley put down her unopened book and wandered into the kitchen. She polished two water glasses that had been left on the sink drainer and put them away in the glass-fronted cupboard. She checked the fridge to make sure there was enough juice and milk for breakfast, and glanced at Ed's homework diary pinned to the noticeboard. The kitchen was a warm, ordered space which she had planned and laid out in every detail.

Yet she felt superfluous in it.

She wondered where Iris and Ruby were sitting now, trying to imagine the room and its decoration. It took on a Moroccan flavour, inevitably. Lesley had never been to Cairo, but in the 1970s she had run a business that imported fabrics and furniture from North Africa, mostly from Marrakesh. In those days, however, Iris had been working elsewhere and when the two of them met it was during Iris's brief visits to England, or once or twice elsewhere in Europe. Iris travelled wherever and whenever she could, usually alone, usually with the minimum of luggage and complete disregard for her own comfort. She didn't mind sleeping on airport benches and riding in the backs of trucks. Living as she did, in African villages where she provided basic medical care for the poorest women and children, being comfortable didn't have as many complicated factors as it did for most people.

Lesley remembered how they had once met up in a hotel in Rome. The doorman had looked askance at Iris when she walked into the lobby. Her clothes were not dirty, but they were worn and unmatching. She carried a couple of African woven bags, her face was bare and her feet were splayed in flat leather sandals. She walked straight across the marble floor to where Lesley was waiting, and the smartly dressed Italian crowd fell back to make way for her. Nobody knew who she was, but everyone knew she was somebody.

And it was Lesley, in her Armani and Ferragamo, who felt overdressed.

On a whim, she had ordered champagne cocktails for them both. Iris seized and drank hers with such delight ('how heavenly! Oh, what a taste of the lovely wicked world') that Lesley suddenly understood why her mother chose a life in which a drink in a hotel bar could deliver so much pleasure.

Of course, her imagined Moroccan-style interior was probably much too elaborate and over-designed to come anywhere close to reality. Iris's actual house would be bare, verging on uncomfortable.

Now Ruby was there with her. They had taken a distinct liking to each other, the two of them. Lesley had understood that from the telephone conversations, although no one had mentioned it.

What were they talking about? What were they telling each other?

Jealousy fluttered in her, and she did her best to ignore it.

The quiet of her own house was oppressive. It was a long time since she had spoken to Ruby's father, Lesley realised. She resolved to give him a call.

Iris and Ruby ate dinner together, in a small room through an archway off the double-height hall. Auntie rubbed a grey veil of dust off the table and Mamdooh lit a pair of tall candles, so Ruby understood that this was an occasion. As she gazed upwards into the dim, cobwebbed heights Iris briefly explained to her that the celebration hall was where important male guests would have been entertained. The musicians would have taken their places on the dais at the end and there might also have been a belly-dancer. The women of the household would have watched the party from the upper gallery, hidden from the men's view behind the pierced screens.

'Why?'

Iris frowned. 'Do you know nothing about Islamic culture?'

'Not really.'

'The women occupy the *haramlek*, a part of the house reserved for them, where men may enter only by invitation. There is a separate staircase, a whole suite of rooms including the one where you sleep. And the other half, where the men may move freely, where visitors come, is the *salamlek*. Respectable women and men do not mingle as they do in the West.'

Ruby wondered, is she talking about then – the past – or today?

She listened, and ate hungrily. The meal was a simple affair of flat bread and spiced beans cooked with tomatoes and onions, of which Iris hardly touched anything. Ruby noted that her skin was stretched like paper tissue over her wrists, with tea-coloured stains spilt all over the knobs and cords of her hands. She wore no rings.

Mamdooh and Auntie came softly back to remove the remains of the meal.

'*Ya*, Mamdooh, Auntie. We have decided that Ruby will be staying here with us for a few days, before she goes back to her mother in England. We must make her welcome to Cairo.'

Mamdooh's expression did not change as he nodded his head, but Auntie's walnut face cracked into a smile that revealed inches of bare gum and a few isolated teeth.

After the shuffle of their slippers had died away Ruby sighed. 'Mamdooh's got a problem with me, hasn't he?'

Iris folded her napkin and slipped it into a worn silver ring. Ruby hastily uncrumpled hers and copied her.

'He is set in his ways, that's all. We both are. Do you know, when I was about your age, Mamdooh's father was our house *suffragi*? He looked after us. Sarah, Faria and me. The three flowers of Garden City. I remember our Mamdooh when he was a plump little boy who followed his father to work. So we have known each other for sixty years.'

Ruby waited for more, but Iris semed to have lost herself. At last she shook her head.

'We are set in our ways. It will do us good to have a

change in our routine. Give me your arm, please. I think I will go to bed now.'

With Iris leaning on her, Ruby walked slowly through the dim rooms to the *haramlek* staircase. Iris was explaining that during Ramadan the faithful did not eat or drink between sun-up and sunset, and it was tiring for the old people. If Ruby wouldn't mind helping her to bed, they could eat their meal and have an evening's rest.

'Sure,' Ruby agreed.

In Iris's bedroom she drew the white curtains and turned down the covers. She helped her grandmother to take off the striped robe and the old-fashioned camisole beneath. The creased-paper skin of her shoulders and upper arms was blotted with the same pale stains as her hands and her shoulder blades protruded sharply, like folded wings. She was as fragile as a child but at the same time there was a lack of concern in her, a disregard for her body that impressed Ruby with its simple strength. Ruby herself was prudishly modest. She hated exposing more than a calculated and obvious few inches of her own flesh. Doctors' visits were torture, even sex was less of a major essential than it was cracked up to be. That was one of the reasons why she liked Jas. He was just as happy to lie down and hug and whisper. Without being like . . . like two dogs behind a wheelie bin.

They had once seen a pair of dogs at it, and although they had laughed Ruby had been disgusted.

'Thank you,' Iris said coolly once she was in bed. It was only eight o'clock. Ruby lingered, not knowing what she was going to do with herself for the rest of the evening. Her glance fell on the framed photograph on the bedside table. A young woman, certainly Iris herself, stood with a tall man in an army shirt. Her back curved against him, his arm circled her waist. Their bodies seemed to fit one against the other, like a carving or a sculpture. She was just going to ask about him when she saw Iris's face and the surprising fierce flash of warning in it. She took a step away from the bedside.

'You can turn out the light by the door,' Iris told her.

Ruby mumbled goodnight.

In her own bedroom she knelt at the window and pressed her face to the glass. Down in the darkness she thought she saw a figure looking up, but she didn't like the idea of anyone being able to see into her room and moved hastily aside. She sat down on the edge of the bed instead and took stock.

The upside was that she had got away, from home and Lesley and Andrew, and from London and Will and all that, and from thinking about Jas all the time. She could stay here and chill out and there would be nobody to ask her every five minutes what her plans were. She wouldn't have to pretend that she was fine about not having any.

The downside was being here.

The house was intriguing, in its way, but it was also quite creepy. It was weird to be on her own with just three old people: one who didn't like her, one who didn't seem to speak a word of English, and her disconcerting grandmother who must be kept happy or she'd get sent home.

The city outside was like nowhere she'd ever been. She'd go out and see more of it when she'd consolidated herself in the house, but at this minute its crowds and its strangeness were intimidating.

Tomorrow, she told herself. It'll feel different tomorrow.

Ruby picked absently at the piercing in her nose that was itching and weeping a little. To flatten a wave of loneliness, she went out and prowled along the corridor and looked down into the hallway through the screens that protected the *haramlek*. There was nothing to see except that in a bookcase against the opposite wall there was a row of books. She lifted them out one by one. They were about history and they smelled musty.

After a while she went back to her room and took out her Walkman. She found the CD that Nafouz had brought back, the one that Jas had made for her, put in her earphones and lay down on the bed.

I lie still, watching the various textures of the darkness. If I turn my head, I can just see the glint of reflected moonlight on the corner of the silver picture frame.

On the evening of his first telephone call, I scrambled to finish dressing for dinner before he arrived to pick me up. The dress was one I had had in London before the war, dark coral-pink silk with a full skirt and a low bodice. I had just enough time to pin up my hair and paint my mouth before the doorbell clanged. I looked at myself in the dressing-table mirror as Mamdooh went to answer it. My eyes looked wide and startled.

The most important time in my life was about to begin. I knew that, even if I didn't know anything else.

Mamdooh had shown him into the dimly lit drawing room. Xan was standing with one hand on the back of a sofa, staring through the part-open shutters into the fading sunlight. He was wearing uniform, his face was deeply sunburned. He turned round when he heard me come in.

He said, 'I came as soon as I could.'

'I'm glad.'

Then he took my hand and led me to the window so we could see each other's faces. I remember a Cairo sunset, a grey-green sky fading into apricot barred with indigo and gold. My heart was banging like a drum. There was a second's silence when everything in the world seemed to stop and wait. Xan very slowly lifted my hand to his mouth and kissed it.

As I looked at him his eyebrows drew up into amused peaks. 'Where shall we begin, Miss Black?'

I had thought I remembered everything, every single thing about him, but the fun in him struck me afresh.

I pretended to consider. 'Let's think. You have to ask me whether I would prefer dinner at Le Petit Coin de France or Fleurent's. Um . . . then you say something about maybe looking in afterwards at the Kit Kat Club.'

'Of course. Out in the desert, one forgets these essentials.'

'So we might have a drink here first, while I try to make up my mind. I'll probably decide to change my outfit at least once before we leave.'

Xan grinned. 'I am at your service.'

I mixed gin and tonics from the tray Mamdooh always left ready for the three of us and our dates. We sat down together on the sofa and I raised my glass.

'To wherever it is you have been, and to having come back.'

His face clouded for a moment and he took a long swallow of the gin.

'I will tell you about it, but not this evening. Do you mind?'

'No, don't let's talk about the war this evening.'

I knew nothing, then, about what he had seen or had to do, but even in my naïveté I understood that what Xan needed tonight was to forget, to be made to laugh, to put down the weight of wartime.

I said, 'So. What will happen is that by the time I am dressed, and have decided on Fleurent's, and we have got there in a taxi, they will have given our table away to a brigadier. Of course it's now the only place at which I can bear to think of eating, but in any case there will be at least two tables packed with people we know, and so we will squeeze up with them. There will be a lot of laughing and even more drinking, and then we will all decide that we are having so much fun that we must go on somewhere else. We will pile into taxis with all sorts of people, losing half of the party and joining up with half of another, and in the confusion you will be in the taxi behind. When we arrive at wherever it is we are going we will be unable to find each other for at least an hour. By which time I shall be very tired and will probably insist on being taken straight home as soon as we do stumble across each other.'

Xan laughed. 'You lead a rackety life, Miss Black. It's not a very convincing plan of action in any case. I shall not let you get into a taxi without me, and I will not let you out of my sight for one minute, let alone a whole hour. And we are not going to Fleurent's, or anywhere near the bloody Kit Kat Club. Why should I share you with every soldier in Cairo?'

'Then where are we going?'

He took the glass out of my hand and set it on the red and black marble table top. 'Wait and see.'

Mamdooh brought my Indian shawl and wished us a very good evening as we went out together.

The sky was almost dark, a heavy velvet blue with the first stars showing. I stood on the familiar Garden City street, under the thick canopy of dusty rubber leaves, and let Xan lead me. There was a car waiting a few steps away, with a driver who got out quickly and opened the door for us. He was tall and hawk-faced, dressed in Western clothes but still looking like one of the Bedouin tribesmen who lived in the desert.

'This is my friend Hassan,' Xan said quietly.

'Good evening, Hassan.'

The man nodded at me.

We sat in the back of the car and I watched the shuttered streets gliding by. Excitement and anticipation chased through me and I found that I had to remind myself to breathe. But it was easy to be with Xan; he didn't talk for the sake of it and he didn't make me feel that I should

70

chatter and gossip in an attempt to be entertaining.

'I live there,' Xan said, pointing up at some balconied windows.

I craned my neck in an effort to see more. 'Alone?' I asked.

He laughed. 'With some other men. You never know quite who's going to be there. When someone comes back from a picnic in the desert it's a matter of taking a look around to see if there's a bed that looks more or less unoccupied. You dump your kitbag and hope for the best. It's pretty empty at the moment, actually. Not all that surprising, if you know what I mean.'

I knew what he meant by a picnic. We were both quiet as we thought about the recent Allied defeats in Crete and Greece as well as Cyrenaica.

'Does Jessie James live there too?'

I had liked Captain James and wanted to know what was happening to him.

'Jess? Yes, when he's in town. But the Cherry Pickers are away now.'

Jessie's famous cavalry regiment had charged with the Light Brigade at Balaclava. Now, with armoured vehicles instead of horses and cannon, they were in the line east of Tobruk.

I nodded.

Xan glanced at me as we crossed the English Bridge. We were heading towards Giza and the desert.

'You're at GHQ, aren't you? Who do you work for?'

'Lieutenant-Colonel Boyce.'

Xan's smile broadened. 'Small world, the army. May I drop in and see you in the office one of these days?'

'I'll make you a cup of HQ tea. It's a treat not to be missed.'

His finger rested on my wrist for a second. 'I'll hold you to that.'

71

We were passing through the fields and scrubby mud-brick settlements and lines of palms that marked the western edge of the delta. There was almost no traffic out here, and ahead lay the flat pans and low wind-blown dunes of the desert's margin. Even at the height of summer the desert nights are bitterly cold, and thinking about it made me draw my shawl closer round my shoulders.

'Don't worry,' Xan said.

I had thought perhaps we were heading for the Mena House Hotel, a popular destination near the Pyramids, but then the car turned in an unfamiliar direction down a narrow unmade track. There were no lights here at all and we drove with only the headlights slicing through the soft darkness. I gave up trying to work out what our destination might be and sat back instead, watching Xan's dark head outlined against the darkness outside and letting the currents of happiness wash through me.

After a while Xan leaned forward and murmured something in Arabic to Hassan. I was surprised that he knew the language, and yet not surprised.

'We're nearly there.'

Directly ahead of us I could make out the smoky glow of a fire, and the black silhouettes of a handful of palm trees. There were some tents and a few people moving between us and the fire. Camels were tethered in a line. We were coming to a tiny oasis.

Hassan brought the car to a halt. Xan and I stepped out where the shingle-and-sand camel track petered out in a sea of fine, soft ripples.

'Welcome,' Hassan said to me. '*Mahubbah*. These are my people.'

A circle of men sat close to the fire on upturned oil drums. Through the smoke I could smell the rich scent of food and realised that I was hungrier than I had ever been on arriving at Fleurent's. One of the men stood up and came towards us. He was old and had a white beard. He was wrapped in a coarse woven blanket.

'*Mahubbah*,' he murmured. He touched his forehead to Xan who returned the salute, then the two men embraced each other.

'Abu Hassan,' Xan said respectfully.

I stood in the sand, and fine cool trickles ran into my shoes. I felt strange in my coral-pink silk evening dress with the chill desert breeze blowing strands of hair across my face.

The old man bowed to me and Xan took my arm. He murmured in my ear, 'Hassan and his father welcome you. They would like you to know that their house is your house, and they are your servants.'

I didn't know the proper phrases to offer in return for this formal welcome and I tightened my grip on Xan's arm.

'Will you tell them I am unworthy of their generosity, but I am proud to be their guest?'

'Exactly,' he said warmly, and I listened again to the clicking of unfamiliar Arabic.

Hassan and his father bowed once more and retreated towards the circle of seats and the firelight, leaving Xan and me standing alone.

'This way,' he said, pointing away into the darkness. 'Wait a minute, though.'

He reached into the boot of the car and produced a bag that he slung over his shoulder, and an army greatcoat which he held out to me.

'Wear this for a moment or two, in case the cold gets too much. Will you take my hand?'

I did so and the warmth of his fingers enveloped mine.

The ghost of a path curved round a swelling dune, the path's margin marked by low thorny bushes. I stumbled a little in my dancing shoes, but Xan held me tightly. After a

73

few more yards I saw a dark smudge ahead of us, then the glow of lights caught within it.

The shape resolved itself into a tent, a little square structure made of some kind of woven animal hair. There were long tassels hanging from the four corner poles, their filaments lifting in the breeze. We plunged hand in hand through the heavy sand, and Xan drew back the tent flap and stood aside to let me in. The tent was lined with hangings in broad strips of green, black, cream and maroon, and the floor was covered with rugs and piled with embroidered cushions. Lit candles on flat stones burned everywhere, and in the centre of the little room, under a hole in the roof, stood a rough metal brazier full of glowing embers. It was as warm inside the tent as in Lady Gibson Pasha's ballroom, and in the flickering candlelight it was a hundred times more beautiful.

I caught my breath in a sharp *oh* of surprise and delight, but then Xan came close behind me and put his big hands over my eyes.

'Are you ready?' he murmured, and his breath was warm against my ear. He turned me through a half-circle again, so that I was facing the way we had come in.

'Ready,' I answered and his hands lifted.

I blinked, and stared. Ahead of us, framed and cut off from the rest of the world by the dunes, lay the Pyramids. I had never seen them from this viewpoint and it was as if the three great tombs with the prickling sky unrolled behind them were ours alone. Their mass, pinned between the stars and the shapeless desert, was rendered two-dimensional and even more mysterious by the darkness. Silence shrouded the desert as time slipped out of gear and the great wheels of the universe spun free around us. I tilted my head to try to catch a whisper beyond audible range, but all I could hear was the camels coughing as they shifted in their line.

Xan took the greatcoat from my shoulders. The fire was warm on my ankles and bare arms.

'Do you like it?' he asked.

I turned my head from the view, meeting his eyes, trying to find a word. 'Yes,' I whispered.

He undid the canvas bag he had brought with him and took out a bottle of champagne tied up in an ice bag. He peeled off the foil and eased the cork. Then he burrowed in the bag again, produced two tin mugs and handed them to me. I held them out as he popped the cork and the silvery froth ran into the mugs. We clinked them together.

'I'm sorry about the glasses. But this *is* the desert, not Shepheard's Hotel.'

'I would rather be here with you, looking at the Pyramids and drinking champagne from a tin mug, than anywhere else in the world.'

'Really?' His face suddenly glowed in the candlelight.

'Yes.'

I was amazed that Xan had taken such pains to surprise me, and that this evening was so important to him. He had planned it so that we stepped straight from the Cairo cocktail circuit into another world, and in my limited experience no one had ever done anything so deft, or so perfectly judged. At the same time he was as eager for my approval as a young boy.

In actual years Xan couldn't have been more than twenty-five or -six, just three or four years older than me, and I guessed that in other important ways we were contemporaries.

He was probably more experienced with women than I was with men, but neither of us had ever felt anything as dazzling, as momentous as this.

We were not-quite children together. And we were also immortal.

How could we not be?

I lifted the tin mug to my lips. 'Here's to us,' I said and drank my champagne.

'Here's to us,' he echoed.

He took my arm and drew me to the heap of cushions next to the brazier. 'Are you warm enough? Are you comfortable?'

Ripples of coral-pink silk were crushed between us. I rested my head partly against the cushions and partly against Xan's shoulder, and saw how the Great Pyramid of Cheops sliced an angle of pitch blackness out of the desert sky.

'Yes.'

'Good. Iris?'

This was the first time he had spoken my name, rather than teasingly calling me Miss Black.

'Mm.'

'Talk to me. Tell me. Let me listen to your voice.'

This moment was a part of Xan's dreams. Perhaps when he lay in a scraped shelter in the desert, hungry and cold and suspended between remembered horrors and stalking danger, with a pair of boots for a pillow and the butt of his handgun close against his ribs, this was what he had allowed himself to imagine. It was the intimacy of talking with nothing held back, the sharp pang of desire mingled with the sweetness of trust. It was a dream that had become real tonight for both of us.

I reached up and touched his temple. A thin blue vein was just visible beneath the sun-darkened skin.

I told him about growing up as a diplomat's daughter, shuttled between embassies around the world with loving but distant parents who insisted, when the time came, that boarding school back home was best for me and that home-sickness – for a home that I couldn't quite locate – was to be overcome by people like us, never yielded to.

In his turn, Xan told me about his father who had been a distinguished and decorated commander in the first war. In the years afterwards he had come out to Egypt to expand the family textiles empire, but business had never been his strong point and the Molyneux family set-up had been an eccentric one. Xan had spent much of his boyhood playing with the children of the family servants.

'So that's how you know Arabic so well.'

'Kitchen Arabic, yes. Then I was sent home to school, and after that on to Sandhurst. My father insisted that I was going to be a regular soldier and I was commissioned in 1938. Until I was eighteen or so I used to come out to Alexandria or Cairo for summer holidays. My family weren't nearly enough the thing to be invited to embassy parties, but maybe you and I saw each other somewhere else? Maybe I sat at the next table to you at Groppi's one afternoon and envied your ice cream.'

'You wouldn't have spared me a glance. I was a plump child and my mother made me wear tussore pinafore dresses and hair ribbons.'

Xan spluttered with laughter. 'And look at you now.'

'Where d'you call home?' I asked.

It was a question that I asked myself often enough, without ever being able to supply a proper answer. It wasn't the Hampshire village where my parents had lived since my father was invalided out of the Diplomatic Service, or the London that I hardly knew and which in any case was now being flattened by the *Luftwaffe*. Nor was it the Middle East, and the starchy embassy compounds of my childhood.

Home was a strange, evanescent complex of spicy cooking smells and my mother's French perfume, the brown arms of my nursemaids, shimmering heat hazes, and jacaranda blooms outlined against a sun-bleached sky.

It was dreams, mostly.

'Home?' Xan mused. The candle flames were reflected in his eyes. 'It's here,' he said at length.

'Cairo?'

'No, *here*.'

I understood that he meant our tent with its coloured hangings, the starry night outside and the two of us. I explored the significance of this, allowing it to swell and flower in my mind. I wanted the exact same thing but I was afraid that it was too much to ask. I had lived all my life effectively alone and the prospect of not being alone, the *luxury* of it, made me feel giddy.

'Why?' I ventured to ask and hated the break in my voice. A burning log broke up in the brazier and a shower of powdery sparks flew into the air.

Xan propped himself on one elbow, his face just two inches from mine. 'Don't you know why, Iris?'

'I am not sure. I want to hear you say it.'

He smiled then, lazily confident of us. 'I saw you walking under the trees at that party, with Sandy Allardyce. I looked at you and I thought that I would give anything to be in Sandy's place. Then Faria Amman brought you across to our table and I felt so damned triumphant, as if it was the sheer force of my will-power that had brought you there.

'When I heard your voice, it was exactly how I knew it would be. Your smile was familiar too. It's not that I think I know you – that would be presumptuous – it's more that I have dreamed you. You have stepped straight out of a fantasy and become real. Does that sound idiotic? I expect every man who takes you out to dinner says the same thing.'

'No, they don't.'

I wanted to tell him that I understood what he meant, if I could have found a way of saying it that didn't sound conceited. And I wanted to be Xan's dream.

The night was so perfect, I even believed that I could be.

'And now I see you aren't a phantom. It turns out that you have warm skin, and eyes brighter than stars. Your hair' – he twisted a lock of it round his finger – 'smells of flowers. So this is where I want to be. This is what I want home to mean.'

His mouth was almost touching mine. As I closed my eyes, I heard several sets of footsteps scuffing through the sand outside the tent.

Xan sat up, grinning, and poured more champagne into the tin mugs.

'Sayyid Xan?' a voice said, and Hassan's head appeared at the tent flap. I sat up straighter and smoothed my skirt over the cushions.

Two young boys followed Hassan into the tent, and they began setting out dishes and bowls. Hassan lifted the earthenware lid of the biggest pot and a cloud of fragrant steam escaped.

'Are you hungry?' Xan asked me and I remembered that I was ravenous.

After the men had withdrawn again, bowing and smiling, Xan put a bowl into my hands and ladled out the food. It was a thick stew of lamb with beans and tomato, and we sat turned towards each other on our bank of cushions and devoured it. I tore up chunks of bread and mopped the spicy sauce, then Xan took hold of my wrist and licked my fingers clean for me. He kissed each knuckle in turn and I noticed how his hair grew in different directions at the crown of his head. This tiny detail, more than anything else, made me want to touch him. And want him to touch me. I was almost frightened by how much I wanted it.

'Who is Hassan?' I asked. 'What is this place?'

'We played together when we were boys. His father taught me to ride. Now we work together, if you understand what I mean. Hassan knows the desert better than anyone else in Egypt.'

One of Xan's eyebrows lifted as he told me this.

'Work', I guessed, would probably be for one of the secret commando raiding groups that operated between and behind enemy lines. In my months with Roddy Boy I had glimpsed a few reports of their missions.

'That's very dangerous, isn't it?'

'This is a war.'

Both statements were true. There was nothing either of us could add, so we just looked at each other in the candle-light.

Then Xan leaned forward. 'I'm here now,' he whispered. 'We are here.'

I put my hand to his head as he kissed me, drawing him closer, and the whorl of unruly hair felt springy under the flat of my hand.

'We weren't going to talk about the war,' I said at last.

'It would be a mistake to do so. It would be a mistake of profound dimensions. It would even be a blunder of historic proportion and therefore I candidly advise against it. Most certainly I advise against it.'

I spluttered with surprised laughter. The voice was Roddy Boy's, his plump circumlocutions captured to perfection.

'And I concur. What's more, the ambassador agrees with me.'

This time it was Sandy Allardyce's faintly self-important drawl. I laughed even harder. Xan was an excellent mimic.

'Good.' Xan smiled. 'That's better.' He knelt upright and rummaged among the dishes. 'What have we got here?'

There was a glazed bowl of dates, and a little dish of plump shelled almonds. He made me open my mouth and popped the food in piece by piece.

'Stop. I'll explode.'

In an old Thermos flask there was strong black coffee, and when everything else was finished we drank that from our tin mugs. I saw Xan glance at his watch and I felt a cold draught at the back of my neck. I shivered a little and immediately he put his arm round me.

'Hassan and I have to leave again very early in the morning. I'll take you home now.'

I smiled at him, pushing the meaning of tomorrow out of my thoughts, then leaned forward and gave him a lingering kiss. It took a serious effort of will to pull back again.

'That was the very best evening of my life,' I said.

'Was it? Do you mean that?'

Once again, his eagerness touched my heart.

'I do.'

'There will be more,' he promised. 'Hundreds, no, thousands more. A lifetime of evenings, and mornings and nights.'

I touched my fingers to his lips, stalling him for now. I couldn't ask where he was going, or when he would be back. All I could do was to send him off with the certainty that I would wait for him.

We blew out the candles together and untied the tent flap. We stood side by side and looked across to the Pyramids. And then we turned away from the tent and the view, and walked back hand in hand to the tiny oasis. The men who had been sitting around the fire were gone and the fire itself had burned down to a heap of ash with a heart of dull red embers. Hassan was waiting for us, sitting with his back against the trunk of a palm tree.

We drove back into the City. At the door to the apartment Xan touched my face. 'I will be back soon,' he promised.

'I will be here,' I said.

My eyes hurt from staring into the darkness.

My body aches, deep in the bones, and I am shivering as if with a fever. A little while ago I heard the child wandering

81

about, but the street outside and the house are silent now. She must have fallen asleep. I long for the same but instead there is the patchy, piebald mockery of recall, and fear of losing even that much.

Always fear. Not of death, but of the other, a living death.

I think of Ruby's offer to help me, innocent and calculating, and instead of finding her interesting I am suddenly overwhelmed with irritation, discomfort at the invasion of my solitude, longing for peace and silence.

The shivering makes my teeth rattle.

CHAPTER FOUR

When Ruby woke, her low mood of the previous night had lifted.

She swung her legs out of bed at once and went to the window. The view of the street was already becoming familiar.

Humming as she turned back again, she picked up a T-shirt and a pair of trousers from yesterday's heap that she had tipped out of her rucksack. She pulled on the clothes, then opened a drawer and scooped the remaining garments into it. The absolute bareness of the room was beginning to appeal to her; it looked much better without a bird's nest of belongings occupying the floor. She even straightened the covers on the bed before hurrying down the passageway to her grandmother's room. Her head was full of how she would start helping Iris to record her memories. Maybe after all she could try to write them down for her. The *way* they were written wouldn't matter, surely? No one would be marking them or anything like that, not like school or college.

They could start talking this morning, while they were eating their breakfast.

Ruby was looking forward to figs and yoghurt and honey.

The door to Iris's room stood open. She skipped up to it, ready to call out a greeting, then stopped in her tracks. The window was shuttered and the only light came from a lamp beside the bed. Iris was lying on her back and Auntie was reaching over her to mop her forehead with a cloth. The air smelled sour, with a strong tang of disinfectant. When Auntie moved aside Ruby saw that Iris's face was wax-pale, and the cheeks were sunken. Her nose looked too big for the rest of her face and her eyes were closed. It was as if she had died in the night.

Ruby's cheerful words dried up. She hovered in the doorway until Auntie half turned and saw her. At once she came at Ruby, making a shooing movement with her hands. Iris lay motionless.

'What's the matter? What's happened? Is she ill?'

The answer was a few mumbled words in Arabic and a push away from the door. Ruby could only retreat and head downstairs in search of Mamdooh. She found him in the kitchen at the back of the house.

'Is my grandmother very ill?'

Mamdooh pressed his fig-coloured lips together. 'Mum-reese has fever.'

'What does that mean?'

They glared at each other.

'Fever,' he repeated. And then, making a concession by way of further information, 'Doctor is coming. Now she must sleep.' He didn't actually push her, but he made it as clear as Auntie had done that Ruby was in the way.

'Will she be all right?'

'*Inshallah*,' Mamdooh mumured, flicking his eyes towards the ceiling.

'Is there anything I can do to help?'

'Nothing, Miss.'

Ruby glanced around the kitchen. The walls were painted

a shiny, old-fashioned cream colour and the cupboards had perforated metal doors. There was a table covered with an oilcloth, an old-fashioned metal draining board at the side of the chipped enamel sink. There was a smell of paraffin and boiled laundry.

'All right.' She sighed. She knew something about sudden death but she had no idea about illness; it had never played any part in her life.

Iris wasn't going to die right now, was she? What would happen to her, Ruby, if she did?

There was no answer to this. She would just have to wait for the doctor to come.

She wandered out into the courtyard and sat for a few minutes on the stool next to Iris's empty chair, watching the way that sunlight turned the trickling water into a rivulet of diamonds. Soon she realised that she was very hungry indeed, and decided that it would be simpler to go out and buy herself something to eat rather than trying to negotiate Mamdooh and the kitchen. She checked that she had money in her trouser pocket and let herself out of the front door.

As soon as she started walking the heat enveloped her, and sweat prickled at the nape of her neck and in the hollow of her back. She kept to the shady side of the alleyway. There was an exhausted dog panting in a patch of deeper shade beside a flight of stone steps. He lifted his head as she passed and showed his pink tongue, and Ruby unthinkingly stooped to pet him. The dog cringed, lifting his legs at the same time to reveal a mass of sores on his belly. Flies rose in a buzzing black squadron.

Ruby shuddered and snatched her hand away.

She marched onwards, following the route to the busy street that Mamdooh had taken the day before. She had noticed plenty of little bakery and coffee shops in the bazaar, she would buy some breakfast there.

The underpass led her to the edge of the maze. She hesitated, looking back over her shoulder as if someone might be tailing her, then hurried into the nearest alley where coffee was one of the stronger elements in the thick tangle of smells. But the narrow shops and piled barrows here were all crammed with plastic toys and knick-knacks. Dolls' pink faces leered at her and dented boxes containing teasets and miniature cars were piled in teetering pyramids. Two men had a tray of toy dogs that yapped and turned somersaults and emitted tinny barking noises. As Ruby tried to squeeze past, two of the toys fell off the tray and landed on their backs with their plastic feet still pawing the air. A trio of small boys bobbed in front of her, shouting hello and holding up fistfuls of biros. 'Very good, nice pens,' they insisted, jumping in front of her when she tried to dodge them. The crowd was dense, choking the alley in both directions. The stallholders began calling out and holding up their goods for her attention.

A man blocked her path. 'This way. Just looking, very cheap.' When she tried to edge past him he caught her elbow and she had to shake him off. He yelled after her, 'Just looking, why not?'

She felt like shouting back that she didn't want a plastic teaset, that was why not, but the effort semed too great. Music pulsing from a tier of plastic and gilt transistor radios was so loud it was like walking into a solid wall. She pushed past the people immediately in front and a wave of protests washed after her. She turned hastily right and then just as quickly left, at random, trying to get away from the toy vendors and the people she had just trampled.

In this area of the market the stallholders and shopkeepers were selling clothes and shoes. Barrows were stacked high with Adidas nylon tracksuits and white trainers, and the walls were festooned with racks of shiny blouses and pairs of huge pink knickers and bras with bucket-sized cups. There were more women shoppers now, all with their heads and throats swathed in grey or white scarves, all with long-sleeved tops and skirts that hid their legs. The tourists she had noticed yesterday were conspicuously absent. Ruby was sure that everyone was staring at her. She felt increasingly grotesque. Her hair obscenely sprouted and frizzed in the damp heat and her arms and breasts seemed to swell and bulge out of her tight T-shirt and her sweaty trousers bit into her waist and hips. She was too tall. Her skin was too pale and she was clammy with heat and rising panic.

She was also very thirsty but there was nothing as far as the eye could see except mounds of shirts and shoes, and bolts of synthetic fabric that made her drip with sweat just to look at them. She pushed forward, telling herself that somewhere not too far away there would be someone selling bottles of water. The shouts of the vendors and chipped quarter-tones of loud fuzzy music banged in her head.

She was gasping for breath as she stumbled out into a square that looked familiar. It was familiar – it was where Mamdooh had come yesterday, to meet his friends. There was the same coarse, dusty foliage and a pair of sun umbrellas rooted in pitted concrete cubes.

A group of men was gathered at an empty tin table. They weren't eating or drinking – that was because of Ramadan, Ruby knew that now. But they weren't talking either. They just sat in a horseshoe, looking out into the hot white light. Looking at her.

She walked forward, thinking she could ask for help because they had seen her with Mamdooh. But none of the faces betrayed even a flicker of recognition. She hesitated, not sure now whether these really were Mamdooh's friends. Maybe it wasn't even the same square. She detoured a few steps to the murky door of the café, intent on buying some water, but when she peered inside she saw only men's faces turning blankly towards her. A waiter wearing an apron looked on, absolutely unwelcoming.

Ruby turned tail, even though her throat was now painfully dry. She paced back into the sunlight in the middle of the square and turned full circle, trying to work out which of a half-dozen alley mouths to make for. She had no idea.

Her glance passed across someone leaning against a wall a few yards away, then jerked back again.

Here was a face she recognised. Where and when had she seen it before?

Yesterday, that was it. It was Nafouz's younger, handsomer brother.

He was slouching, one knee bent with the foot pressed against the wall behind him. He was also openly watching her.

Ruby marched up to him.

'I'm fucking glad to see you,' she said, trying to hide just how relieved she actually was. 'I'm completely, totally bloody lost.'

He looked slightly shocked at her language, but also pleased and – surprisingly – rather shy.

'I think you are lost,' he agreed, his nice smile showing his good teeth.

'Are you *following* me?'

'Why would I do that?'

He was still smiling so that she didn't know whether it was a straight question or a mocking one.

'How the fuck should I know?'

'You swear very much for an English girl, Ruby.'

'D'you have a problem with it?'

'It is not problem for me, no.'

'Right. Look, now you're here, can we go somewhere and buy a drink? I'm really thirsty.'

He pushed himself away from the wall. 'Of course. Please come with me this way.'

They made their way together down a thin passageway with the old walls on either side leaning inwards so they seemed almost to touch at the top.

Ruby said, 'Um, I'm really sorry. I've forgotten your name.'

'It is Ashraf. You can call me Ash.'

'OK, then, Ash. Where are we going?'

'To a place the tourists like.' His smile flashed at her over his shoulder. He was definitely mocking her now, but she was too thirsty to bother with a response. They walked in silence for a few minutes. The gathering threat had subsided, Ruby noticed. Either she had been overreacting, or she had become less conspicuous because she had an escort.

After a few more corners of the maze she was about to protest, but then they came to an entire lane that was filled with rickety chairs and tables, spilling out of the open doors of a café. Waiters with trays held at shoulder height threaded between the tables, plonking down cups and bottles and bills. Ash had been right about the tourists, because almost all of the people crammed into the alley were Westerners with cameras and bags of bazaar purchases. Mucus-faced urchins and Egyptian women with dark faces and glittering eyes worked the tables, trying to sell purses and lighters and packets of tissues. Ash took Ruby's hand and towed her through the crowd to a just-vacated table, well-placed on the threshold of the café itself. Peering into the gloom inside, Ruby saw the glint of huge, fogged mirrors covering the walls.

A waiter was already looming over them as she sank into a chair. She asked for a bottle of water and a cup of coffee and some yoghurt and then gestured to Ash.

He shook his head without speaking.

'Sorry. Forgot,' Ruby sighed.

When the water came she tore off the plastic top and downed half of it.

'Why are you in Khan on your own?'

Ruby told him.

'I am sorry for your grandmother's illness,' he said. 'She will be well soon, *inshallah*.'

'Yeah. I hope so.'

Once she had quenched her thirst and spooned up some yoghurt, Ruby sat back and looked around. Ash was watching the crowds, with his face in profile. He was very good-looking, with fine, almost feminine features and thick, long eyelashes. She reached out to the pack of Marlboro that showed in the pocket of his shirt.

'Can I bum one of these?'

'You are a woman. It is better not smoke in public.'

Ruby snorted, then clicked Ash's lighter to the cigarette. After inhaling deeply she said, 'So. No swearing or smoking. What am I allowed to do, according to you?'

Ash raised one eyebrow. 'Maybe come for a ride with me?'

'You've got a car?' It was an entrancing idea. She was dying to see Cairo beyond this isthmus of ancient streets but after her experience in the bazaar she would have preferred not to try it alone.

Rather stiffly Ash said, 'I have my moby. You can be pillion passenger.'

'Moby? Oh, one of those bikes with engines. OK then.' Ruby scraped the last of the yoghurt out of the jar.

'You are still hungry I think.'

'Yeah, I am, actually.'

Ash stopped the waiter and asked him for something. While they waited they smoked and watched the tourists come and go. Because she was with Ash and because Iris actually lived here, Ruby now felt superior to mere holiday-makers.

A plate was put down in front of her. There were two fried eggs and a basket of flat bread.

'Perfect,' she crowed, and Ash looked pleased.

While she devoured the food he told her that he worked at night as a telephonist in a big hospital. 'Very good job,' he said.

He was also trying to improve his English, and saving up to pay for a computer study course. Nafouz was helping him, but they had to give money to their mother and younger brothers and sisters. Their father had died more than two years ago.

'May he rest with God,' Ash added.

Ruby put her knife and fork down on a clean plate, and picked up the bill the waiter had brought. She frowned at the blurry blue numerals.

'I would like to pay for you, but this place is not cheap,' Ash said awkwardly.

'Why should you pay for me?'

'Because I am a man.'

'I can pay for myself. For now, anyway,' Ruby said. 'And you haven't eaten anything. Shall we go?'

They left the café and Ash led the way back to the underpass. It was surprisingly and disorientatingly close at hand.

Ash's bike was locked to a grille in the wall at the end of the narrow street leading straight to Iris's house and the big mosque.

'What's it doing parked right here? You *are* following me,' Ruby accused. 'Did you tail me all the way round that bloody bazaar?'

He only grinned and straddled the machine's seat, sliding his hips forward to make room for Ruby on the pillion. 'You are coming?'

'I suppose so. Just for half an hour. Then you've got to bring me back to check how my grandmother is, right?'

She sat primly upright at first, but then the little machine shot forward and she had to grab Ash round the waist in order not to fall off the back. He sped into the traffic, weaving in and out of taxis and buses. Ruby ducked her face behind his shoulder, too afraid to look where they were going. The dusty sides of cars flashed past an inch from her thigh and clouds of gritty blue exhaust fumes made her eyes sting. When they stopped at traffic lights she put her feet on solid ground with a gulp of relief, but only a second later they would lurch forward again in a surge of metal and revving engines. Cairo appeared to be one solid mass of overheated chrome and steel.

'You like?' Ash howled at her over his shoulder.

'I hate,' she screamed back, but he only laughed.

They emerged into a vast square set about with tall buildings and with an inferno of endlessly revolving traffic trapped within it.

'Midan Tahrir,' Ash mouthed at her.

'Is that so?'

He waved a reckless arm at a low pink block. 'Egyptian Museum. Very famous, I take you soon.'

'Can't wait. Are we going to stop?'

'Maybe.'

A moment later they shot out into slightly clearer air. Ruby saw branches and leaves against open sky as Ash swung the bike in a flashy circle and cut the engine to bring them coasting up against the kerb. Ruby sprang off, coughing and rubbing her eyes, and Ash locked the bike to a puny sapling rooted in the wide pavement. They were in a boulevard lined with trees. On the other side, beyond several lanes of traffic, was a low wall and then seemingly empty air.

'Come,' Ash commanded. He took her wrist and they darted into a gap between thundering buses.

Below and beyond the wall, there was water. It was a

wide, swirling, grey-brown river and on it sailed a dozen little boats with slanting masts and graceful sails like unfurled handkerchiefs. Ruby leaned far out over the wall, looking at the vista of bridges spanning the water, towers and distant trees.

'Nile river,' Ash said at her side. She gazed at the ripples and reflections. Tall buildings on the opposite bank and humid grey clouds swam on the moving surface.

'That way' – he gestured – 'Alexandria. Then Europe. And that way' – he swept his left arm in a stately arc along the river – 'Egypt.' For Ash, it seemed, the name was enough to convey the magnificence of his country. He took her hand to emphasise the importance of what he was showing her.

'Yeah.'

Her unwillingness to be impressed annoyed him. He began jabbing his finger towards nearby landmarks. 'See, Cairo Tower. El Tahrir Bridge, up there 26 July Bridge. Gezira island. *Sheraton Hotel*.' The last was a hideous cylinder on the tip of a tongue of land opposite.

'No, really? Amazing.'

He jerked her wrist sharply and she stood upright, startled and defensive.

'Watch it,' Ruby snapped.

They faced each other, glaring. The breeze off the unfamiliar river was humid, and the sprawl of an unknown and hostile city stretched away on every side. Suddenly Ruby missed the clatter and roll of skateboarders under the concrete spans of the South Bank, and the smell of hot dogs, and all the damp, foggy chill of London. She heard Lesley's voice and shut that off inside her head.

It was important not to piss Ash off because he was the only friend she had here.

But it was Ash who began laughing first.

'You make a frown like a monkey,' he told her.

She corrugated her face even more elaborately and crossed her eyes until they were both laughing. Then she nodded at the river. 'It's beautiful. I like the boats.'

'One evening I take you sailing in a felucca. At sunset. Very romantic.'

'Great. I'd rather that than the fucking museum.'

'Ruby,' he sighed.

'Sorry. Gimme another brown?'

'What?'

'A ciggie. A cigarette, for God's sake. I'll buy some if you show me where, if that's the problem.'

'No problem,' he said politely.

They began walking, their hands occasionally brushing together. Ruby noticed the top of a grand pillared building behind a high wall guarded by a couple of armed and uniformed men. She was surprised to see the Union flag hanging limply from a central flagpole.

'What's that place?'

He shrugged. 'British embassy.'

'Oh.' Ruby wasn't very interested.

They passed beneath a huge, ancient-looking tree, its trunk a mass of writhing tendrils for all the world like dun-coloured snakes. In its thick shade the air was almost cool.

'Banyan tree.'

They stopped and looked up into the canopy of coarse leaves. Taxis cruised and honked a few feet away, a couple of passers-by glanced incuriously at them. Ash's throat was smooth, his skin pale brown. Ruby stepped up close, put her hands behind his head and pulled his mouth down to hers. She kissed him hard, flicking her tongue between his lips.

She saw the flash of dismay and disbelief in his eyes before he stepped sharply backwards.

'Why you do that?' he demanded.

94

She had done it without thinking, just because she felt like it.

'Didn't you like it?'

He had liked it, of course, but it was not what he had planned.

Ash had intended to make a play for the English girl, that went without saying, but he had expected to chase her until she was cornered and when she finally gave way the triumph would all have been his. Now she had taken the initiative and he felt diminished. He had no idea what to expect next.

They were now both aware of the breadth of experience and expectation that separated them, and they were uncomfortable.

'You have boyfriends,' Ash said flatly.

Ruby tried to give a careless laugh, but it came out sounding harsh.

'Yeah. What do you expect? Yes, I do. Have had.'

He nodded. 'I see.'

She didn't like his disapproval and tried to startle him back into sympathy with her. 'No, you don't. My boyfriend died. In an accident.'

Ash's eyes were very dark brown and the whites were so white they looked blue.

'What? Accident in a car?'

'No. He fell. He fell off the balcony of someone's flat. It was late at night, a party. He had been drinking and taking stuff. I didn't see how he fell. Maybe he jumped, I don't know. He was a bit fucked up. His name was Jas.'

Ash shook his head. This information was almost too much for him, but he took her hand gently and led her a few steps to a bench facing the river wall. They sat down with their backs to the traffic and stared at the ugly cylinder hotel across the water.

'Did you love him, this Jas? Did he love you?'

He asked this so simply and tenderly, and his directness seemed to flick a switch in Ruby. She almost heard the click. Without any warning tears welled up in her eyes and poured down her face, scalding her cheeks as they ran.

'Maybe. Yes. It wasn't like you think.'

'I think nothing,' Ash said.

Ruby knuckled her eyes and sniffed hard. She tried not to cry, as a general rule. Not about Jas, or anything else. She usually tried not to think about Jas being dead either, except as a bare fact, but now she couldn't stop the thoughts – or the images that came with them.

The flat had been on the ninth floor of a stumpy tower block on the edge of a no man's land of railway sidings and warehouses with broken windows that looked like cartoon eyes in the darkness. It was a rain-smeared late night that had begun in a pub with Jas and some of his friends, and ended in a boxy room with a couple of mattresses on the floor. There were quite a lot of people in the flat. Not the ones who had been there at the beginning, they had melted away and different faces had bobbed up. Two girls had been arguing about the music that was raggedly playing, and one of them had snatched a CD and flung it at the wall. Her boyfriend had given her a shaking and her head wobbled disconcertingly. When he pushed her away from him she fell sideways on one of the mattresses.

Ruby was sitting on the other, with her knees drawn up to her chest like a shield. She had been wanting to go home for a while, or at least somewhere that wasn't this place, and wondering how to negotiate an exit. She was dimly aware that Jas had moved away but she felt too out of it herself to pay any attention to what he might be doing. The next thing was a shout, and a ripple of movement in the room that pushed the girl on the next mattress into a sitting position and sent several others stumbling towards the door onto a balcony.

Ruby found herself walking towards the door. Cold air blew towards her, and the few steps seemed to take a long time. There were one or two voices, high-pitched with alarm, but most of all she could hear a huge silence. She knew at once that something very bad had happened.

The balcony was small. There was a flowerpot in a corner with the brown stalks of a dead plant sticking up, and a scatter of cigarette butts and roaches. The walls were brick, topped with gritty stone. A white-faced bloke was holding on to the stone as if he was on a ship in a bad storm, and a girl was half turned away with her hand over her mouth. Ruby walked very slowly to the wall and looked over.

A long way down, Jas was lying on his side with his head and his arms and his legs all at weird angles. There was a dark pool spreading round his head. He was dead. Just in one glance you could tell that much.

The girl took her hand from her mouth and started to babble.

'I just saw his feet and legs going. His shoe caught on the edge. I wasn't looking, I just sort of turned. I saw his legs and his feet, falling.'

The sick-looking man put his arms round her. 'OK,' he said. Ruby wondered why, when it wasn't OK at all.

'Who is he?' someone else muttered. She realised now that she hadn't set eyes on any of these people before tonight. Jas had been her connection. He made friends easily, but never tried to keep them. They had drifted along together, Ruby and he, without asking themselves or each other any questions.

When the police arrived, there wasn't much she could tell them. It was that that shocked her, really. She knew his name, and the address of the house where he squatted. He came from Sunderland, and he liked curry and Massive Attack. He had made her a CD compilation and decorated the insert with red biro swirls.

It wasn't very much. It wasn't very much for a life that was now over.

The police drove her back from the police station to Will and Fiona's house in Camden. It was already light and people were going to work in their neat clothes. A policewoman offered to come in with her and explain what had happened but Ruby shook her head. She scrambled out of the car as quickly as she could and bolted inside. She hoped that no one would be awake yet so she could slide into her bedroom without being seen.

But Will was up. He was coming down the stairs, wearing a suit and a blue shirt and a dark-red tie, his cheeks and jaw shiny from his morning shave. In the kitchen there were kids' drawings on the pinboard and a bunch of flowers in a milkjug on the table, the same as yesterday.

'Fi's still asleep. Where have you been all night?'

He was in a position to ask the question because he was her stepfather's brother, so she was part family as well as part lodger. But they were also conspirators because when they were alone Will didn't always treat her like family. Or at least, the way families were supposed to treat each other. Ruby thought he was rather pathetic, but she had taken advantage of the situation in the past. Being in a conspiracy with Will meant she could get away with things that he and Fiona, as a fully united front, would never have allowed.

But not any longer. Not after this night.

She blinked, and her eyes burned with the image of Jas lying at the foot of the stumpy high-rise.

'Um. I went to a party.'

Will looked angry, in his plump way.

'What are you like? What sort of behaviour do you call

98

this? It's five to six in the morning and you're supposed to go to college today.'

Ruby glanced away, down at the floor. She was thinking if she could just get away quickly, upstairs to her bedroom, she could keep all the spinning and churning bits of misery inside and not let Will see them.

'I know,' she mumbled. 'Sorry.'

He sighed. Then he came round the table and took hold of her. He put his hand under her chin and tilted her face so he could examine it. She felt too numb to break away from him, or to do anything but stand there. Will sighed again and then his hand slid over her bottom but he gently pushed her away at the same time, as if it were she who had come on to him. He was very good at making things appear the opposite of what they really were. A long time ago – yesterday – she used to think it must be one of the number of things he had a first-class degree in.

But there was no place this morning for any of those old notions. They seemed to belong to a different person.

'Go on, then. Go upstairs and get into bed, before Fi catches you. I've got to get to the airport.'

He was fussing with his briefcase, snapping the locks.

Ruby went up the stairs, very slowly. Her feet felt as if they had rocks tied to them.

In her bedroom she took off her clothes and then stood holding them in a bundle against her chest, very tightly, as if she were hugging a baby. She even made a little crooning noise, out loud, and the disembodied sound made her jump. When she buried her face in the clothes she realised that they stank of sweat and smoke and sick. She had thrown up in a green-painted toilet cubicle at the police station.

She put the bundle down on the velvet-upholstered button-backed chair and covered it with a cushion. Then she crawled under the bedcovers and pulled them over her.

As soon as she closed her eyes he was lying there with the black puddle spreading round his head.

She told Ash briefly about Jas. It wasn't right, she realised as soon as she had begun, to use it as a way of getting his sympathy. Then she gave him a flat smile. Her tears were drying up, leaving her eyes feeling sticky in the heat.

'Anyway,' she said, and shrugged. She stood up quickly, pulling at her clothes where they were glued to her skin. After a second he got up too, still looking at her with gentle concern.

'That is very sad. I am sorry,' he said. 'What would you like to do now? Do you want to go back to your grand-mother's house?'

She didn't want to cry again, for one thing, didn't even want to think about crying. It was all too dangerous.

'Can we just go on with what we were doing before?'

They walked on, under the dusty leaves, in and out of patches of shade. Ash waited for what she would do or say next.

'Don't you have a girlfriend?'

He considered carefully. 'Of course, there are some girls I like. But it is not quite the same thing, I think.'

His solemnity made Ruby laugh. She still wanted to make him like her and the wish surprised her.

'It was only a quick kiss, back there, you know? I just did it, I thought it would be nice. Sorry if it was totally the wrong thing. I get things wrong all the time, it's the way I am. You'll have to get used to it if we're going to be friends. That was one of the good things about Jas. He kind of didn't mind anything. He'd say things like, we are each the person we are and we should try to be that person to the full, not someone else. I liked that a lot.'

Ash stopped again. He looked over his shoulder at the

traffic and at the passers-by, then he steered Ruby into an angled niche in the river wall where an ornate street lamp sprouted.

'*I* would like to kiss *you*, now, please.'

She leaned back. The stone was hot against her ribs and spine.

'Go on, then.'

'Wait. To me, these things have importance. They are not just a quick this, or for nothing that. Perhaps you think to be this way is funny?'

'No,' Ruby said humbly. 'I think it's lovely.'

'All right.' He came nearer. Close up, there were all kinds of different textures and colours visible in the dark-brown irises.

He kissed her, an experimental meeting of mouths that seemed, to Ruby, very tentative. Then he pulled back again.

'Good,' he said.

'Thank you.'

Feeling rather pleasingly chaste, she resumed her walk at his side. After a little way they turned aside from the river and wandered through a quiet area of curving streets with enclosed gardens thick with greenery. It was much quieter here. The tall brown and cream buildings looked sleepy and well-protected. Some of the gates had guards in little wooden sentry boxes, or stationed in chairs on the pavement where they could watch everyone who went by. Ash and Ruby let their hands brush more often as they walked.

'This is Garden City. Nice place, for rich people.'

'Where do you live? Is it near here?'

Ash laughed, a little awkwardly.

'What do you think? It is not like this, my home.'

'I don't know anything about Cairo.'

'I will show you.'

Later they came out alongside the river again. An island,

separated from the mainland only by a narrow channel, lay directly opposite. Ash told her it was called Rhoda, pointing out the landmarks and telling her little pieces of history. Ruby nodded dutifully. They had been walking for a long time and the sky was already fading from blue to pale grey. There were more feluccas with their sails like birds' wings on the water.

'It's time I went back,' she said.

They turned north, walking towards the Tahrir Bridge. When they reached the place where Ash had left the bike, lights were beginning to twinkle on the bridges and the buildings across the river. The sunset sky was streaked with gold and pale green.

'It's beautiful,' Ruby sighed.

Ash took her arm. 'I have an idea. A special, very special Cairo view, just for you. You have to tell a small lie, but I think you can do that?'

She gave him a warning look. 'Maybe.'

He was marching her through the torrent of traffic and through a gateway into some gardens. A huge hotel with hundreds of balconies and lit-up windows loomed over them, and a line of shiny cars snaked up to the doors.

'You stay in places like this?'

'I have done,' she admitted.

'So you know what to do.'

As the revolving door disgorged them into a glass-and-marble lobby, a doorman in a tarboosh and white baggy trousers worn with a sash and a red waistcoat stepped in front of them.

'I am staying in the hotel. Room 806,' Ruby said firmly.

'Good evening,' he murmured and stepped back again.

Heads up, they walked past the brocade armchairs and the fountain to the lifts. Ash was chuckling.

'Are we nicking something?' she demanded as the lift doors closed.

'What is that?'

'Stealing.'

'Of course not. A view is free, belonging to everyone.'

They swept up to the top floor and stepped out into a mirrored lobby. There was a murmur of voices, tinkling piano music and glasses.

'Please close your eyes,' Ash ordered.

He took her hand and led her from carpet to paving. They were outside again, with a breeze fanning Ruby's face. A little spasm of fear ran down her spine as she wondered how close the edge was.

'You are safe,' Ash breathed in her ear. He steered her a few more steps, then halted. 'Now, open.'

She looked. They were in a garden on the roof of the hotel. Below them, far below, was the dusk-blue higgledy-piggledy mass of Cairo. Lights shone in the crowded tower blocks, chains of traffic lights blinked and neon signs flashed all the way to the western horizon. The sun had set but the sky was blazing gold and orange.

'Do you see?' Ash murmured. His arm was round her shoulders, she could smell his skin.

'Yes.' She thought he meant just the view. But then, at the exact point where the dusty glitter of the city met the fiery sky, she saw three sharp triangular cut-outs pasted against the glow. '*Oh.*'

Ruby leaned forward, hands on the rooftop rail, taking in her first glimpse of the Pyramids. They looked so close, almost part of the city itself. It made her think of how these buildings and domes and streets had crept from the banks of the Nile all the way out into the desert. She had always imagined the Pyramids surrounded by empty seas of sand, but seeing them like this made them seem even stranger and more unreal.

'You like it?'

103

'Yes. I like it very much.'

The sky was fading. The pianist in the rooftop bar played more loudly and guests in evening dress drifted out to look at the view.

'We have to go,' Ash muttered. A man in a black tailcoat headed briskly towards them.

'Hello.' Ruby grinned at him.

'I am afraid this is a private party, Madam.'

'Sorry. Lost our way. We're just leaving.'

As they reached the lobby a waiter carrying a silver tray of drinks passed them and with a smooth movement, flashing him a smile at the same time, Ruby helped herself to a tall glass. In the lift, they leaned back against the padded wall. The glass was beaded with condensation, decorated with a straw and mint and rattling with chunks of ice. She handed it with a flourish to Ash. He gave it a longing stare and then the day's thirst overcame him. He sucked down two-thirds of the Coca-Cola with a single swallow, then politely handed the glass back to Ruby.

'No. It's all for you,' she told him.

Outside again, it was night-time. Darkness descended here like a curtain falling.

Hand in hand, Ruby and Ash walked back to the bike. She felt quite comfortable this time, sitting close up to Ash with her arms tight round his waist, as they swooped through the traffic on the way home.

He stopped where Nafouz had drawn up in the taxi, only forty-eight hours ago.

'Thank you for a nice day,' Ruby said, realising with a shock just how long she had been out.

He touched her cheek with his fingers.

'I will come again?'

'Yeah. I mean yes, I'd like you to.'

'I am your Cairo boyfriend?'

When Nafouz made the same suggestion she had laughed at him. But Ash's wanting to set out the terms in this way made Ruby feel modest, and also shy in a way that she hadn't done since she was twelve.

'If you want to be.' I am *blushing*, she realised.

He leaned over and kissed her in the same tentative way. As if she might break.

'How will I hear from you?' she asked.

His eyes widened. 'I will be here. I find you.'

'See you, then.'

She rapped hard on the sun-blistered door of Iris's house, and heard Ash accelerating away.

The door swung open.

At the sight of her Mamdooh moved fast. He propelled Ruby into the house and locked the door, dropping the key out of sight in the pocket of his *galabiyeh*.

'Miss. You have been away many hours.'

'Sorry. I . . .'

'Sorry not good enough. You make Mum-reese worry, Auntie worry, and myself.'

He was breathless with anger.

'I . . .'

'Cairo people not bad, but you are young woman, know nothing. Some places dangerous for you.'

He didn't know anything either, Ruby thought. She couldn't deal with being treated as if she were ten years old. London wasn't a safe place, but she knew how to look after herself. She was here, wasn't she? It was Jas who had gone under, Jas who was kind and friendly to everyone, and just a bit fucked up.

Auntie came down the inner staircase and darted straight at Ruby. Ruby braced herself for another rebuke, but Auntie took her hands and lifted them, pressing the knuckles to her own mouth. Her eyes were almost hidden in the fans of wrinkles but there were tears at the corners. Awkwardly, Ruby detached one of her hands and put it on Auntie's shoulder. She was so small, it was like comforting a child.

'I'm really sorry,' Ruby began.

She had said the same words often enough before, but Auntie's tears made her feel something different. Or maybe it was remembering Jas, or all the impressions of the day piling up inside her. Without warning she started crying again herself, beginning with a dry sob and then with her face puckering and the tears breaking out as if something hard had burst inside her.

Instantly, Auntie gathered her in her arms. She held Ruby like an infant, murmuring in Arabic and patting her hands and rubbing her arms. Mamdooh put a very big, clean and folded handkerchief into her hand.

'You have had trouble today? Someone has tried to hurt you?'

'No, no. I made a friend. His name is Ashraf, his brother is the taxi driver, and he . . . he works in the Bab al-Futuh Hospital. He showed me Garden City and a view of the Pyramids from the top of a hotel. I didn't mean to stay out so long. How is my grandmother? What did the doctor say?'

Auntie said something in Arabic and Mamdooh nodded.

'She is resting.'

'Can I go up and see her?'

The old people held her between them now, one on either side.

'First you must have food. After, you can take some tea for her. It is better you are not crying.'

Ruby understood the sense of that. And the breakfast of two eggs she had eaten in Khan al-Khalili was a long time ago.

The kitchen was quite cosy in the light from a pair of oil lamps, and there was a good smell of food. Ruby noticed how Mamdooh and Auntie moved between the table and a wood-fired oven as wordlessly as if they were part of the same organism. Mamdooh laid out spoons and three brown bowls, Auntie brought out a blackened pot from the oven. Flat bread was laid on a wooden platter, and coarse salt in a smaller bowl. They must have lived and worked together for so many years they didn't need to discuss anything, certainly not to make bargains and score points the way Lesley and Andrew or Will and Fiona endlessly did.

They all sat down together. Ruby reached for the bread at once, then realised that the two old people were watching her, waiting for something. She wondered blankly what it could be, and then it struck her. She cast about in her mind. Her first school, the first of many, had been a Church primary.

'Forwhatweareabouttoreceive,' she mumbled, 'maytheLord-makeustrulythankful.'

This seemed to fit the bill. They were being respectful of her religion. Mamdooh nodded gravely, then lifted the lid off the pot.

It had been quite a day, one way and another, Ruby thought. She had been kissed as if she had been playing Spin the Bottle at a kids' party, and she had said grace.

Mamdooh noticed the smile that transformed her. 'That is better. Now please eat some of this very good food.'

It was good. Chick peas and tomatoes, and some thick but tender meat. In reply to Mamdooh's questions she told them a little about Ash and where they had spent the day.

Afterwards, Ruby carried the plates to the big old sink and Auntie showed her how they were to be washed and dried, and where to put them away.

Mamdooh prepared a tray. There was the little silver teapot and a bunch of fresh mint leaves, sugar and a glass cup in a worn silver holder. There was also a medicine bottle, a glass and some pills.

107

'You like to come up now, Miss, to Mum-reese?'

'Please call me Ruby, you know? Shall I carry that?'

'It is for me to do, thank you.'

Ruby said goodnight to Auntie, who wrapped her arms round her again and showed her few remaining teeth in a wide smile. Ruby guessed that they had both forgiven her.

The lamp was on beside Iris's bed, but the rest of the room was dim. Her eyes had been closed, but as soon as Mamdooh came in with Ruby behind him she opened them. At first, the expression was blank. If there was anything in the depths, it was bewilderment. But then Iris saw Ruby. Her lips moved and she tried to sit up against the pillows.

'There you are,' she said.

How long have I been ill this time?

I have had the lurid, monstrous dreams of a high fever, but not so many of them. I am sure it was only this morning that the doctor came, the young Frenchman called Nicolas Grosseteste. His senior partner was my doctor for many years, although I rarely needed his opinion. But poor Alphonse is dead now and Doctor Nicolas is capable enough, in his superior way. He thinks I am old and frail, but I am not quite as frail as he believes. I have had malaria and another bout would probably finish me off, but it is not malaria this time. My immune system is weakened from many years of living in equatorial climates and I am susceptible to fevers. But I feel better tonight. Seeing the child makes me feel better.

Mamdooh gives me a glass of tea.

'Shall I hold it for you?' Ruby asks.

'I am not paralysed.'

'I'll just sit here, then.'

Mamdooh rattles the medicine bottle. I take it from him and read the label, and then the bottle of pills. There is a broad-spectrum antibiotic, and linctus for my chest. So Nicolas doesn't think that I am about to die either.

'Thank you. Ruby will sit with me, Mamdooh. She can help me to get ready for bed.'

He wishes us goodnight and goes away, closing the door. I sip my tea. Ruby looks less sulky than she did – when – yesterday?

'Talk to me,' I order. And then it comes over me, warm, loosening my limbs like a shot of pethidine, the luxury of it.

Talk to me. How long since I have said that to a living soul?

'Um. What about?'

'Whatever you like.'

'Well. You know what? I saw the *Pyramids* today.'

'You went out to Giza?'

'No. I don't think so. From the top of a hotel by the Nile.'

'Ah, yes. What did you think?'

'Amazing. I didn't know they were in the middle of all the houses, though.'

She looks so pleased with this adventure. I reach for her hand and at once she sandwiches mine between hers.

'They're not, not really. When I am on my feet again, we'll go out to Giza. I'll show you a different view.'

'That'll be cool.'

We sit here, hands linked, considering our different visions of the pharaohs' tombs.

CHAPTER FIVE

There is light sliding into the room and for the moment I am disorientated.

But a second afterwards I realise that I have slept much later than I usually do, and the unfamiliar brightness is mid-morning sunshine. There is an associated feeling that I take longer to identify, but then I look down at my fingers on the bedsheet and I can remember Ruby's hand curled in mine. She was holding my hand when I fell asleep and I must have slept so deeply that I have hardly stirred all night. The dent in the covers left by her resting elbow is still there. The un-familiar sensation is happiness.

This morning the chambers of my head all seem to stand open, with their contents reassuringly accessible. I feel weak after the fever, but better than I have done for a long time. I sit up and put my bare feet to the floor.

Ruby is in the inner garden with Auntie. They are looking at the plants together and Auntie is rubbing a scented leaf in the palm of her hand for Ruby to have a sniff. Their backs are turned, but then Ruby looks sideways over her shoulder and sees me and her face breaks into a smile. I think she needs company and a measure of affection. Perhaps we both do.

Auntie brings a tray of tea, and when we are settled in the shade Ruby tells me that she has already had breakfast in the kitchen with Mamdooh and Auntie.

'And supper last night, as well. Auntie's been showing me things, she's been making fruit jelly for you with pomegranates and a special jelly bag. I always thought jelly just came in cubes that you pour boiling water on.'

'Do you cook at home?'

Ruby considers. 'A bit, I suppose. Easy stuff. Mum's a good cook, though. I'll never be as good as her. She's brilliant at all those things, like food and gardening, and making elegant Christmas decorations. Well, you know that.'

I don't, not really. Lesley is my daughter and I don't know when we last cooked for each other. I didn't know about her expertise with holly and fir cones, and I have never been to her present house so I haven't admired the roses. I acknowledge that these failures are my fault and not Lesley's. Of course I acknowledge it. For her whole life, right from the beginning, I wanted to be somewhere else. It was not because of who she was, but because her presence – and her father's – intensified such a sense of loss in me. I wished it otherwise, but wishing made no difference.

I thought, and still think, that life is a cruel affair.

'Iris?'

'Yes. I am listening.'

But a glance at the child's face shows that I must have lost track of what she was saying for longer than I realised.

I was thinking, and the train of thought led back to Xan.

'Ruby, do you remember we talked about you helping me to collect some of my old memories?'

'Yes.'

'I think it's a good idea. I think we should start today.'

'Right. Yeah, absolutely. But you remember what I said

about . . . you know, not being all that great at spelling et cetera?'

The sound of trickling water fills the garden.

'What? Yes, you did tell me. We'll find a way.'

I am eager to begin. Ruby's idea has thrown me a lifeline.

Hastily, I finish my breakfast. I call for Mamdooh and ask him to bring the key to my study. It is a rather dark little room at the rear of the house, hardly ever used and dignified only by the name of study because it had to be called something.

'Yes, Mum-reese.' Without moving he looks from Ruby to me.

'Ruby is going to help me catalogue some of my papers,' I say grandly. There are no papers. Or if there are I cannot recall where and what they would be.

'Yes,' Mamdooh says again, without conviction, but at least he goes off for the key.

The three of us make our way there and he unlocks the door and stands aside. Ruby and I file in and Mamdooh follows, opening a shutter to let in the daylight.

There is an old desk and a chair that I am sure I have never set eyes on before. But I do remember the typewriter. I take off the cover, blowing away the dust, and there is the Olivetti portable I bought in – where? In Rome, probably, when I was visiting Salvatore. (I have not lived without sex for all these years. Love is a different matter.)

The typewriter. I turn to Ruby. 'You could use this.'

The child stares at it. Then she prods the q key with her forefinger so it strikes the platen with a dull click. It is as if she has never seen a typewriter in her life before.

'Can you type?' I ask her. 'I can only use three fingers but it always seemed fast enough. You could make some notes while we talk and then perhaps type them up when it's convenient?'

She looks up from pressing the keys.

112

'I did a word-processing course once. You know. Using a computer?'

'A computer?'

Fifteen years ago, when I retired and left the hospital in Namibia where I worked, computers were just starting to appear. The medical director, a suave young South African, had one of the first. Laurence Austin, that was his name. I'm pleased to retrieve this piece of long-buried data.

Mamdooh says, 'In Midan Talaat Harb and other places there are cybercafés. I have seen young people using computers there.'

I have no idea what a cybercafé might be, but Ruby is nodding her head in acknowledgement.

'We could ask Nicolas,' I suggest.

'Doctor Nicolas was visiting Mum-reese yesterday, when you were out of the house so many hours,' Mamdooh explains to Ruby.

The child's cheeks have flushed and she looks unhappy so I try to reassure her. 'Don't worry. I don't even know what will be worth writing down. Maybe nothing.'

'I'd like to help,' she mutters, still eyeing the typewriter like an adversary.

So we find ourselves, later when the day is beginning to cool, sitting in our places in the garden. Ruby has a note-book in her lap and she grips a pencil so tightly that the knuckle of her thumb is white.

Silence stretches between us, then stretches again.

Anyway, now that I have come to it I realise that the whole idea is absurd.

Memory is not a recipe or a shopping list. Memory is the scent of clear water at an oasis, the brush of lips on naked skin, a plangent chord. I cannot capture these things and dictate them to another person. I am a doctor, not a poet. There is nothing I can say.

After more silence Ruby's eyes meet mine.

'Are you stuck? What about starting with a day? Just pick a random day that you remember. How old were you?'

'Twenty-two,' I say without thinking.

'What happened?'

Only a week after our dinner overlooking the Pyramids, Xan took me to a fancy dress party. We had seen each other every day, for swimming at the Gezira Club and cocktails at Shepheard's, and for dinners in restaurants that we both agreed came nowhere near our tent in the desert for food or ambience. We went dancing, and we met one another's friends who turned out either to know each other already or to know people who knew them. We also sat for hours in quiet corners, holding hands and telling each other our histories.

Everything happened very quickly in those days. We were young and it was wartime. Within a week I was Xan Molyneux's acknowledged girl.

Sarah Walker-Wilson pursed her lips. 'Who is he? Does anyone at home know him?'

Sarah's and Faria's opinions meant nothing to me. I was in love with Xan and I was drunk with happiness, spinning with it, whirling like a cork caught in an eddy.

Xan and I decided to go to the costume party as Paris and Helen of Troy. Xan went to the toy department at Cicurel's and acquired a tin breastplate, a shield and a helmet with a stiff red horsehair plume. They were more Roman than Greek and they were far too small for him. The spectacle of the little helmet perched on his black hair, the shield dangling from his wrist and the breastplate barely covering his diaphragm was irresistibly funny. He completed the outfit with sandals, a toga made from a bedsheet and a cavalryman's dress sword. He put his hands on his hips, striking a pose with the hardware clanking, and demanded to know how classical and heroic he looked.

My costume was a white strapless evening gown borrowed from Faria and accessorised with the long metal pole that Mamdooh used to open the top shutters in our flat. From one end of the pole I hung a little carved wooden ship with the number 1 painted on either side. At the other end was a much bigger model launch, also borrowed via Faria from one of her numerous nephews and labelled 999. I wore a huge hat made of two cardboard cut-outs of the *Queen Mary* that Xan had spotted in the window of a travel agent's near Shepheard's, with 1000 painted on the sides.

Every time we looked at each other we almost collapsed with laughter. Xan collected me from Garden City in a taxi and when he tried to kiss me the *Queen Mary* knocked off his tin helmet. He pushed the thousandth ship out of the way and our mouths met. His profile was dark and then lit by the street lights, and his hair was standing up in a crest where the helmet had dragged on it. I ran my fingers through it as I pulled him greedily closer.

The party was given by three of his friends in a flat in Zamalek, quite near where Xan himself lived. It was a tall, awkwardly shaped apartment in which the sparse furniture had been pushed back into the corners. The walls were stained where people had leaned or rested their heads against them, and one was almost covered with scribbled names and telephone numbers and cryptic messages. The packed rooms heaved with Caesars and Charlie Chaplins and Clara Bows, there was a lot of drink and, just as at most Cairo parties, there was kissing and shouting, no food at all and very loud music from a gramophone on a sideboard forested with bottles. Xan took my hand as we were swept into the thick of it.

We were surrounded by familiar faces. Sarah was there, dressed as Little Bo Peep with her blonde hair in ringlets and ribbons, and brandishing a shepherd's crook adorned with a blue satin bow. Sandy Allardyce wore a cardinal's robes and I wondered whether they were hired or if he had simply borrowed them from a passing monsignor. In Cairo anything was possible. Even Roddy Boy loomed into view, wearing an eyepatch and with one arm tucked inside an admiral's coat that had probably belonged to his great-grandfather who had almost certainly been with Nelson at Trafalgar.

'Hello, there,' my boss greeted me, dodging the shutter pole and the dangling ships, and wedging his telescope down the front of his coat so he could kiss my hand. 'Most appropriate costume, Miss Black, if I may be so bold.'

'Thank you, Colonel.'

If I may be so bold was the way my boss actually talked. Xan's meticulous imitations of him came into my head and I chewed the corners of my mouth to contain the laughter, so unsuccessfully that I choked into my champagne glass and sent froth spilling over Faria's gown. Roddy Boy was drunk enough not to notice.

'Are you a friend of David's?' he boomed. David was one of our hosts, an associate of Xan's with a mysterious war job. I had heard about Major David and tonight Xan had briefly introduced us.

'I've only just met him. Xan Molyneux brought me along.'

Roddy Boy's eyes flicked over me. He wasn't so very drunk, then. 'Ah. Yes,' was all he said.

Jessie James floated up.

From somewhere, somehow, in the middle of Cairo in the midst of a war, he had acquired a choirboy's white surplice and starched ruff. His pale yellow hair was parted and plastered flat to his head and he was carrying *Hymns Ancient and Modern*. Looking at him, you could almost hear an English cathedral choir singing the 'Coventry Carol'.

'Darling, beautiful Helen of the thousand ships. Can't we

run away together and leave that bastard Molyneux behind? Or at least come and dance with me to this vile music?'

'Evening, James,' Roddy Boy said.

'Hello, there,' Jessie murmured as he swept me away. We propped my pole of dangling ships in the corner and edged into the throng of dancers.

So Xan and I were surrounded by friends and people we knew, but we were in another place too. It was a small, sweet, vivid and waiting world that contained only the two of us. As the party separated us and then washed us together again, we would catch one another's eyes and everything else faded into monochrome.

Once, when I had battled my way to the kitchen for a glass of water – the locally made gin and whisky ran like rivers, but quenching your thirst with anything else was more of a problem – Xan came up behind me. His hands slid down on my hips and his breath fanned my neck.

'I want to touch you all over. I want to taste every inch of you. Are you going to make me wait, Iris?' He was a little drunk, too.

I turned round to face him, stretching on tiptoe to bring our eyes level. 'No,' I said. 'I can't wait.'

But we did wait, just a few hours longer, teasing ourselves with the anticipation of what we both knew would happen.

I danced again with Jessie, then with Sandy Allardyce who had forgiven me for the night at Lady Gibson Pasha's. Faria arrived very late, wearing one of her Paris evening gowns and not the smallest attempt at fancy dress, with her faithful poet in tow. At the end of the evening we sat in the kitchen with the soldiers and the Cairene beauties and the men from the British Council, drinking whisky and playing silly games as if nothing mattered in the world.

This was what Xan and the other officers wanted: to wipe out one existence for just a few days or hours, and substitute

117

another that was ripe with noisy laughter and perfume and girls.

Xan and I were almost the last to leave. We emerged into the short-lived, dewy cool of pre-dawn and walked hand in hand through the deserted streets to his flat. The place was empty and silent. It was the first time I had been there and I took in its temporary, makeshift atmosphere. It was a staging post; somewhere to take a brief respite, not to settle in. There were boots in the hallway with the shape of strangers' feet in them, a handgun on a shelf in the living room.

'Except for Jessie, everyone is away at the moment,' Xan said.

We touched our fingertips together, briefly, superstitiously.

Then he took me in his arms.

His bedroom was bare, almost monastic, the bed itself narrow and hard.

He knelt above me and I smiled up at him.

'It's not the first time, is it?'

'No,' I said.

His tongue traced a course from my mouth to the hollow of my collarbone, lingered there and then moved downwards. 'That's good.'

I had had several lovers, Xan more than several, but for both of us this was a first of its own kind.

The *last* first time, the first of many. That was how certain we both were of what we wanted and believed. And for me what followed was nothing like sex with the polite, awkward boys I had half enjoyed in London. It was unlike anything I had ever known, and it was wonderful. I didn't know you could laugh and cry at the same time, and feel that strangeness of another body within yours and yet love and trust every fibre of it.

Afterwards Xan gathered me against him and we looked

118

a long way into each other's eyes. We were sweaty, exhausted, and my whole body felt as if a hundred thousand new nerve endings had just been connected.

'I love you, Iris Black,' he said.

'Xan Molyneux, I love you too.'

'Is it too soon for us to say that? If it's the truth?'

'It's not too soon and I know it's the truth because I feel the same way.'

Neither of us said so, but we both knew that if we left it too long to speak of it, that might be too late. I laughed, to hide a shiver.

'Anyway, how can you work out how many days would be proper? Is there a formula? Twenty or fifty?'

'I have known you for more than twenty days. It's thirty-eight, to be precise.'

The precision touched my heart. I had totalled up the days too, like pearls.

I put my hand to his face and drew his head to rest against my shoulder. 'We will be happy,' I whispered.

I could see, through the uncurtained window, that dawn was breaking.

The memory flashes through my head, as richly textured and vivid as my fever dreams, and just as evanescent.

What I begin falteringly to describe to my granddaughter is a shop window in a Cairo street. The shop was called Sidiq Travel, the name painted across the chocolate-brown fascia in faded art nouveau lettering. In the window were two posters, one of the Eiffel Tower and the other of an improbably golden Beirut beach complete with waving palms and a white-jacketed waiter with a silver tray of cocktails balanced at shoulder height. There was also a propped-up double-sided cut-out of the *Queen Mary*. Everything was coated with the grey-white gritty dust of Cairo.

Ruby's head is bent and she is writing in her notebook. I can't see her face.

'Mr Sidiq sold me the ship from his window display,' I say. 'To make a hat.'

Ruby's shoulders hunch and it now seems that there is desperation in her posture. My voice trails away until the silence is broken only by the tiny splash of the fountain.

What am I trying to say?

'Go on,' Ruby says at last, miserably. 'About the *Queen Mary*.'

I can't catch the memory. A moment ago it was there, I'm sure of it, and now I'm left with its absence. What were we talking about?

'It doesn't matter.' My forgetfulness seeds a sudden rage in me. 'It doesn't matter,' I say again, much louder.

She is still writing, then crossing something out and rewriting it. The pencil seems to gouge the page.

'Let me have a look.'

'No.' The notebook snapped shut and held against her chest.

What have I said, that's now being withheld?

'Hand it over.'

'I won't fucking hand it over,' she yelps at me, jumps to her feet and looks around the garden for an escape route. There's nowhere to run to.

I lever myself to my feet, painfully, and we confront each other.

My anger fades; what is the point of it? I hold out my arms instead and Ruby hesitates, chewing her bottom lip, then shuffles forward with her head hanging. I put my arm round her, seeing how smooth and lustrous the skin of her forearm is. I have forgotten the silky charge of young flesh. Gently, I take the notebook out of her hands and when I look at her face again I see that she is on the point of tears.

'Ruby?'

'What?' she wails.

I put my hand out to the arm of my chair, searching for some support, and lower myself again. Then I open the notebook and look at what she has written. It is only a few sentences and I can hardly decipher them.

The letters are childishly formed, the words uneven and the letters jumbled. She has written *qunen* for *queen*.

'I told you, didn't I, but you didn't fucking listen.'

'Don't swear like that. It's monotonous, apart from anything else.'

She did tell me she was dyslexic, and I heard her but I wasn't listening. I am so wound up in my own history, in my frailty and fear.

I feel ashamed of myself. 'Come here.'

She stoops down by the chair and tries to take back the notebook, but I keep a firm hold on it.

'I am very sorry, Ruby. You wanted to do something for me, and you were honest about what you thought you could do. Whereas I was impatient and thoroughly selfish. Will you forgive me?'

A sigh. 'Yeah.'

'I spend too much time thinking about myself. It happens, when you've been alone for a long time. Can you understand that?'

'Yeah, I s'pose.'

The mulishness is melting out of her.

There is something else I should say, while I am being honest.

'I am very glad you came,' I tell her. Then the absurdity of what we have just tried to do strikes me all over again and I start to laugh. 'It's very funny. I am the memoirist who can't remember.'

'And I'm the am . . . the ama . . . *shit*. The writer who can't write.'

121

Her eyes are still bright with tears but she begins to laugh too. The laughter is spiked with sadness for both of us, but it fills the garden and drowns out the trickle of water.

Mamdooh appears in the archway that leads into the house and stares at us in mystification. I have to blow my nose and wipe my eyes.

'Mum-reese, there is a visitor.'

'Who can that be? Doctor Nicolas?'

'It is a visitor for Miss.' He tells Ruby frostily, 'He is your friend you are seeing yesterday.'

I tell Ruby, 'Go on, then, don't keep your friend waiting, whoever he is.'

She skips away.

I have been the focus of Mamdooh's censure myself. 'My granddaughter is a young girl,' I remind him.

'Indeed.'

Ruby opened the front door, which had been firmly closed by Mamdooh, and found Ash and Nafouz waiting at the foot of the house steps. They were wearing their white shirts and new-looking trainers.

'Ruby, hello.'

'Hi.'

Ash walked up the steps like a suitor. 'We come with my brother's car. We take you for a tour, you know?'

'We-ell . . .' Ruby longed to go, but then she thought of leaving Iris sitting in the garden on her own and reluctantly shook her head. 'I can't. My grandmother kind of needs me right now.'

'I am sorry. Your grandmother is ill today also?'

'No, she's much better. But she should have some company.'

Ash smiled. He really was good-looking, Ruby thought again.

'Then this is not a problem. Nafouz?' He beckoned his brother forward. 'Nafouz and I, we like to take you *and* the lady for a nice ride.'

Ruby blinked at this. It was certainly the first time any of her boyfriends had offered to double-date with her grandmother.

'We-ell,' she said again.

'Please to ask her,' Nafouz joined in.

'OK, then. Hang on here. I'll go and find out if she wants to.'

Iris was sitting with the closed notebook still on her lap.

'You probably won't want to do this,' Ruby began, but Iris tilted her head and looked sharply at her.

'Whatever it is, I think you should let me decide for myself.'

Ruby told her about Ash and Nafouz and the taxi. Iris listened carefully and then her face split into a smile. When she smiled like that her wrinkles seemed to vanish and she could have been any age, even the same age as Ruby herself.

'A very good idea,' she said briskly. 'I shall certainly come. Will you call Auntie for me?'

Five minutes later, with her head swathed in a white scarf and a pair of black sunglasses hiding half her face, Iris declared that she was ready.

'You look like somebody,' Ruby said, meaning a face or a style that she had seen maybe in a magazine, but couldn't place.

'I am somebody,' Iris retorted. The prospect of the outing had noticeably lifted her spirits. She was almost giggly.

Auntie and Mamdooh came out with them. Auntie mumbled to herself and tugged at Iris's clothes and scarf, settling them around her. Mamdooh had put his tarboosh on his head to walk down the steps, and was trying to get Iris to lean on him for support.

'I can walk,' Iris insisted.

123

Ash and Nafouz had been lounging against the wall opposite, but when they saw Iris and her retinue they stood respectfully upright. Mamdooh loomed over them.

'How do you do?' Iris said clearly, sounding rather like
the Queen and making Ruby begin a cringe. But the two
boys bowed and murmured their names and pointed to the
black-and-white taxi.

'Please to come this way, Madam,' Nafouz said.

'We shall be back later, Mamdooh, thank you,' Iris said.
She let Nafouz escort her to the car. She sat up in the front
seat beside him, without seeming to notice the splits in the
plastic upholstery and the way tongues of decayed sponge
stuffing stuck out. Ash and Ruby scrambled into the back
seat, where Ash raked his hands through his wing of black
hair and gave Ruby a half-wink.

'Where would you like to go?' Nafouz asked Iris.

'Downtown, I think,' she answered. She settled back in
her seat and drew her scarf round her throat.

The traffic, Ruby noted, was just about as bad as always.

Iris craned her head at the shop windows and the towering
buildings. She was talking Arabic to Nafouz, and laughing
and pointing. Ash's hand crept across the seat and took hold
of Ruby's.

'Cairo has changed very much,' Iris said in English after
a while.

Ash nodded vigorously. 'Now modern city,' he agreed.

I do leave the house of course, once in a while, but this time
feels different. There is the charming but no doubt oppor-
tunist brother beside me, Ruby and her beau whispering in
the back seat, the air thick with the speculative negotiations
of youthful sexual activity. This should make me feel old,
but it has the opposite effect.

As we turn into Sharia el Bustan I am thinking that I must

discuss contraception with Ruby. I never had such a conversation with Lesley. Or if I did I have forgotten it, along with everything else. Maybe I can be a better grandmother than I was a mother.

Maybe it is the recognition that there is still something I can learn how to be that makes me suddenly feel so buoyant.

The shop windows glitter with clothes and furnishings exactly like those in shopping streets in every other city in the world. These boys – what were they called? – are proud of Cairo's modernity, but I miss the horse-drawn caleches, the plodding donkeys, old smells of animal dung and diesel fumes and dust roughly laid with water. Just down the next street was Sidiq Travel. Xan and I carried our *Queen Mary* trophy along this road.

As we pass out into Talaat Harb the lights are coming on in the government buildings. Avoiding the feeder road for the Tahrir Bridge the boy swings the car left down the Corniche and a minute later we pass in front of the walls of the embassy. Once, the gardens stretched down to the bank of the Nile. Here are the trees that shaded the afternoon tea parties of my childhood. I half turn to tell Ruby this but she and the boy are murmuring together, deaf to everything else.

Now we turn left again. I know these shuttered, curving streets so well.

The boy raises one eyebrow at me and I nod.

He has me neatly pigeon-holed. He knows Garden City is where I lived, it is where most of us British lived in those days. Tended gardens, elaborate wrought-iron gates and grilles, ceiling fans turning the humid air in the afternoons. The car rolls slowly past the ghosts, past the blind windows that shield more recent histories.

I am glad when we emerge again into Qasr el Aini and this time head over the bridge. The sun is going down, and

125

coloured lights glimmer in the river water as we reach the island.

The big trees still shade the club grounds, and the racetrack and the polo ground, but now the branches only partly obscure the light-pocked cubes and rectangles of drab apartment blocks on the western bank. Sixty years ago there were fields and canals on the far side, with ploughs drawn by gaunt buffalo, and villages of mud houses. Now the sprawl reaches almost all the way to Giza.

'I have forgotten your name. Forgive me?' I say to the driver.

He flips me a smile. A flirtatious smile, for God's sake. 'Nafouz. What is yours?'

'Doctor Black.'

'You are medical doctor?'

'I was. I am retired now.'

Nafouz purses his lips to show me that he is impressed. 'I am taxi driver only but my brother Ash is working in hospital, operating switchboard.'

'You both speak good English.'

'We try,' Nafouz agrees. 'We learn.'

The layout of these Gezira streets is familiar, the buildings less so. The ugly lattice of the Cairo Tower looms on one side, on the other is the wall of lush trees that shade the club grounds. Nafouz turns left and we approach the gates. Sixty years drop away and I am in a taxi on my way to meet Xan.

'Stop. I want to get out for a minute.'

I step out into the dusk. The gates are the same but there is a gatekeeper in a kiosk now and a striped pole to be raised and lowered. A long line of cars stretches back from the barrier, mostly shiny German-made cars; members of today's Gezira Club are queueing up for admission. I remember cotton sundresses and shady hats, uniforms and cocktails and the

126

plock of tennis balls, Xan waiting for me in the bar as I arrived from a day's work at my desk in Roddy Boy's outer office.

Xan saying, 'Darling, let's have a drink. I've got to go away again tomorrow. It's a bit of a bore, isn't it?'

'Yes, Madam?'

The gatekeeper calls out to me, and a man in a dark business suit raises the electric window of his BMW as it glides through the gates. The next car in line rolls forward.

'Yes, Madam?'

'I . . . nothing. I'm sorry. A mistake.'

What was I looking for? All the businessmen and chic women and obedient children in these cars are Egyptian. The enclave of empire that I knew, the shady mown-grass sanctuary of British assumptions and attitudes, vanished long ago. The people are all dead. I am still here but I am as much of an anachronism as tea dances and air raid warnings.

I am still here.

Instead of making me sad, the thought fills me with a sudden reckless appetite. Through the window of the taxi I can see the white oval of Ruby's face, watching me.

It's getting dark. I pull off my sunglasses and settle myself back in my seat.

'Let's go to Groppi's,' I say, slapping my hands on the plastic dashboard so that everybody jumps.

Nafouz asks, 'Are you sure, Doctor?'

I insist, very brightly, 'Certainly I am sure.'

So the four of us find ourselves sitting at a table in the little café garden of Groppi's.

Once, everyone in Cairo who could afford it came here. Vine tendrils smothering the walls and strings of coloured lights made it seem far removed from the city's white glare. Ladies in furs sat at these little round tables drinking tea with men with silky moustaches, and officers ordered cream cakes for their girls.

It's dusty and neglected now, with an unswept floor and waiters in dirty jackets. The two boys are hungry and Ruby looks bored.

'What would you all like? What shall we order?' I say encouragingly, but no one seems to know. We make a strange foursome. 'We must have ice cream.' I remember the ice creams, mint-green and luscious pink with stripes of coffee-brown, all with tiny crystals of ice bedded in them. They were served in cut-glass coupes, decorated with furled wafers.

Ruby is eyeing me. No one seems to want ice cream.

'I'm sorry. It's different.' I can feel the suck and swirl of time past, rocking and pulling at my feet like a vicious current. I'm looking at the menu, a dreary plastic-laminated affair sticky with fingerprints. The two boys are smoking, giving each other looks out of the corners of their liquid eyes. Ruby leans forward to help herself from one of the packs on the table.

'Does Lesley let you do that?'

She gives a sharp cough of laughter and smoke pours from between her teeth. Her odd mixture of childishness and bravado tickles me, and I find myself laughing too. The atmosphere changes and we order toasted sandwiches, far too many, and coffees and pastries and bottles of Coca-Cola. It is after sundown so the boys break their Ramadan fast with gusto and the strange meal somehow becomes what I wanted, a celebration.

'Go on,' I urge them, over the plates of food that the waiters slap down on the table. 'Go on, eat up.'

They tell me about their family. Father dead, several younger siblings whom they must help their mother to support. Ruby's beau is the clever one, the one they are banking on. He looks very young to carry such a weight of responsibility.

'I learn to speak English, and also some computer studies. But it is not easy to pay for teaching.'

And he meets my eyes. They have seen where I live and they probably think I am rich. In fact I am poor, certainly by European standards. I murmur in Arabic, a conventional piety. Ruby is looking away, thinking her own thoughts.

The table top is pooled with coffee and there are still sandwiches and little cakes glistening with fat and sugar to be eaten but Nafouz is tapping his watch.

'Time for work. We are both night shift.'

Ash wraps a sandwich in a paper napkin and holds it out to me. 'You have eaten nothing.'

'I don't want it. Take it with you, for later.'

'I may?'

'Of course.'

I call for, and pay, the enormous bill. It is a long time since I have been to a café, much longer since I have paid for four people at once. Before everyone stands up I say, 'Thank you for this evening, Nafouz. Thank you, Ash. I enjoyed it very much.'

This is the truth. It has helped me to see the today versions of yesterday's places. Memory is a little like découpage, I think, a harmless activity that I was encouraged to practise when I was ill as a child, involving pasting cut-out views and scenes to build up a picture in layers. The build-up creates a kind of depth. It adds perspective. Of course the base layers are fading and partially obscured. The old Groppi's I knew, like Cairo itself, has been overlaid by the present version. Because I am here, seeing it as it is now, I realise that there is nothing mysterious or fearful in this. Of course I can't catch and keep everything. I can only strive for what is important; my memories of Xan.

Ruby is standing up, looking at me, a little perplexed. 'Iris?'

I collect myself. 'Yes? What is it?'

'We've got to go. Ash is late.'

They are waiting in the doorway. On the way back to the taxi the boys take my arms, as if I am their own grandmother. I am glad of the support because I am very tired. On the way home, I look out at the lights and the thick crowds in the streets. Nafouz has yet another cigarette clenched between his teeth.

Behind me, I can hear Ruby and Ash whispering on the back seat. When we reach the house they say goodbye to each other offhandedly, in the way that the young do, not making another arrangement because they don't need to. It's understood that they will meet again just as soon as possible. I feel a thin stab of envy, and then amusement at the nonsense of this.

Mamdooh and Auntie seem actually to have been waiting in the hallway for our return. At any rate, they spring from nowhere as soon as Ruby and I come in.

With the afternoon's change of perspective I notice how we have become interdependent, the three of us, over the years. I need them and they need me to need them.

'We have had an excellent outing. A drive, then Groppi's.'

An idea has just formed in my head and I keep it fixed there as I unpin my headscarf and hand it to Auntie. 'We'll have some tea later, upstairs. Ruby, Mamdooh, will you come with me?'

Ruby shuffled in their wake back down the passageway to Iris's study. Mamdooh was trying to insist that Mum-reese should rest, Iris sailed ahead with the absent but intent look on her face that Ruby was beginning to recognise.

'I think there is a box in there.' Iris pointed to a pair of cupboard doors painted with faded white birds and garlands of leaves.

'A box?' Mamdooh frowned.

'Exactly. If you open the doors for me?'

130

Ruby yawned. It had been OK, going out in the car with Iris, but now Ash had gone to work and she wouldn't see him until tomorrow. She would have liked to spend a bit more time on her own with him.

'There it is.' Iris pointed.

Mamdooh lifted a pile of dusty books, some sheaves of printed music and an old-fashioned clothes brush off the lid of a dark-green tin box. It had handles on the sides and he stooped and puffed a little as he hauled it off the shelf. The dust that rose when he dumped it on the desk next to the old typewriter indicated that it hadn't been disturbed for a very long time.

Iris undid a bolt and threw back the lid. Ruby glanced at the disappointing jumble inside. Among brittle newspapers and tattered books here were some playing cards and a box of dice, a couple of tarnished metal cups, a big bunch of keys and a brown envelope. There was a musty smell of forgotten times.

'Can you carry it upstairs, or is it too heavy?' Iris asked, turning her face up to Mamdooh.

'I can carry,' he said at once.

Mamdooh put the box on a low wooden table in Iris's sitting room and closed the shutters, then turned to see that Iris was already burrowing through the contents. He gave Ruby a look that suggested she was responsible for all this disruption and backed out through the door.

Ruby settled herself among the cushions on the divan and picked up the manila envelope. A handful of curling black-and-white snapshots fell out and she examined them eagerly. This was more like it. They weren't very interesting, though. In one, a group of white men stood in front of a low mud-brick building. In another some black men were putting a roof on what looked like the same building. In a third, two men wearing long baggy shorts with knee-length socks were

131

shaking hands. Ruby looked a little more carefully at a picture of a young Iris in a cotton sundress. She was sitting on a low wall in front of some stone carvings with a man in an open-necked shirt. The skirt of her dress billowed over his knee, not quite hiding their linked hands.

'Who's this?' Ruby asked.

'That's the Trevi Fountain. In Rome.'

'Who is *he*?'

'His name is Doctor Salvatore Andreotti. We worked together many years ago on a medical project in Africa.'

'Just good friends.' Ruby smirked.

Iris glanced up from her excavations in the box. 'We were lovers for a time.'

'Oh. Right. Were you? Um, what are all these others?'

'Let me have a look. That is Nyasaland in, I suppose, nineteen fifty-eight. That building is a clinic, and those two men are the district commissioner and the regional medical director. I worked in the clinic for five, maybe six years.'

'Lesley was four. She told me.'

Iris collected up the scattered pack of cards, snapped them with a practised hand. 'Yes. She was born in fifty-four.'

Ruby had heard Lesley talk about how she was brought up by her father and nannies, while her mother 'looked after black kids in Africa'. When she mentioned her childhood, which wasn't very often, Lesley tended to look brave and cheerful.

Ruby felt suddenly curious about an aspect of her family history that had never interested her before. 'Why did you go to work in Africa when you had a husband and a daughter in England?'

'It was my job,' Iris said. 'A job that I felt very privileged to have. And I believe that I was good at it.'

'But didn't you miss them?'

'I had home leave. And once she was old enough Lesley

would come out to stay with me in the school holidays.'

'She told me about that. She said her friends would be going to like Cornwall, or maybe Brittany, while she would have to make this huge journey with about three changes of plane and at the end there would be a bush village and terrible heat and bugs, and not much to do.'

'That sounds like it, yes.'

It occurred to Ruby then that there was an unbending quality about Iris that being old hadn't mellowed at all. She would always have been like this. Uncompromising, was that the word?

'You remember everything,' Ruby said, softly but accusingly.

Iris seemed to have found whatever it was she had been looking for in the depths of the tin box. She pounced and her fingers closed over something. Then she lifted her head and Ruby saw the distant expression that meant she was looking inside herself. Her pale blue eyes were foggy.

'Do I?'

'Nyasaland, the what'sit fountain, men and dates, everything.'

Now Ruby saw in her grandmother's face the grey shadow of fear.

'Those things are only . . . Like so many plain cups or plates, on shelves. You can reach for them, use them without thinking. Most of them don't matter, like what I remember of those photographs. Sometimes you lose your grip on one of them and it falls and smashes to pieces, and you shrug and say to yourself, what a pity.

'Then you reach for a cup or a bowl that you use every day, one that you love and use so often that as you stretch out your hand it is already making the shape that fits its curve. You are certain that yesterday it was in its proper place, but now there is nothing. Just air. You have lost something that was so familiar, so much a part of your life that

133

you were not even looking for it. Just expecting it to be there, as always.

'That's the way the important memory feels, the one you don't want to lose. And it's the fragment of your past that explains why you have lived your life the way you have done.'

When she spoke again Iris's voice had sunk so low that Ruby could hardly hear her. 'And made the mistakes that you have made. Do you understand any of this?'

Ruby hesitated. 'A little. Maybe.'

'You are very young. There's not much on your shelves and you don't know what's going to be precious. It's not until you're old that you find yourself hugging the bowl all day long. Afraid to put it down.'

That's what she's doing, Ruby thought, when she goes into a trance and doesn't hear what you're saying to her.

She's holding on to the precious bowl, in case it's not there the next time she goes to look for it.

'Yes,' Iris said to herself. Her voice was no more than a whisper now.

Ruby suddenly stood up. She left the room, and Iris seemed too wrapped in her own reverie even to notice. Her head lifted in surprise when Ruby came noisily back, as if she had actually forgotten she had ever been there.

Ruby held out the framed photograph that she had taken from its place beside Iris's bed. 'Who is this?'

She was half expecting another reprimand or at least an evasion, because whoever he was, the man in the photograph was important. Most definitely he wasn't Iris's husband, Ruby's grandfather Gordon.

Instead, something remarkable happened. Iris's face completely changed. When she thought about it later Ruby described it to herself as melting. All the little lines round her grandmother's mouth loosened, and the fog in her eyes vanished and left them clear blue and as sharp as a girl's.

Warm colour swelled under her crêpey skin and flushed her throat as she held out one hand for the picture. The other fist was still closed round whatever she had taken from the tin box.

Very carefully, so that there was no chance of either of them letting it fall, Ruby passed the photograph to her. Iris gazed down into the man's face.

A long minute passed.

'Who?' Ruby persisted.

'His name?'

'Yes, you could start by telling me his name.'

Iris said nothing.

'Do you want me to help?'

Instead of answering Iris opened her hand, the one that didn't hold the picture. In the palm lay a toy ship carved from some dark wood. On the side a white numeral 1 was painted.

'The first of a thousand ships.' Iris smiled. Now even her voice sounded softer and younger, with the vinegary snap gone out of it.

Ruby had no idea what she was talking about. She knelt down and examined the ship as it lay in her grandmother's palm. It was old, but it didn't look remarkable. She picked it up and placed it carefully on the arm of Iris's chair. Then she took the photograph back, noticing how Iris gave it up with infinite reluctance. She studied the two young faces and saw that they were dazzled with happiness.

Iris said slowly, in her different voice, 'His name was Alexander Napier Molyneux, Captain in the Third Hussars, on secondment to Tellforce. That picture was taken in October 1941, on the day that Xan asked me to marry him.'

Ruby was delighted with this information.

'Really? Did he? Did you say yes?'

'I did.'

She waited for more, but Iris was silent. Gently Ruby put the photograph aside and folded Iris's hands in hers. The old fingers were like twigs, the tendons rigid against Ruby's smooth palms.

'Are you afraid of forgetting him?'

'I never kept diaries, you see. I was so certain of my mind. And now it's going. Sometimes I reach and there is nothing there. In the accustomed place. Most of the pieces don't matter. But if this one breaks, there will be nothing left.'

Ruby understood that she meant nothing of value. If the precious bowl was missing or shattered, what remained was rendered worthless.

She tightened her grip on Iris's hands, suddenly understanding what they must do together.

'You *can* remember. I know you can, because of the photographs and the fountain and the ship and the travel agents. You told me about those without even thinking. You've just told me about Xan Molyneux, haven't you? It's there, Iris, I know it is. And I know what we have to do. It's just *talking*. You have to tell me the stories and I will remember them for you. I'm really good at that, my friend Jas told me. I remembered all kinds of things about people we used to know back in London, and he was always amazed. But I did it automatically. I told him it was like collecting anything. I used to have these collections, you know, when I was a kid. Shells, insects. Hundreds of them. I used to know exactly what they all were and where to find them in my room, although Lesley was always going on about mess. All you have to do is tell me.

'I'll keep it all in my mind. And then, if you do forget, I can tell your memories back to you, like a story.'

She massaged Iris's cold hands, trying to rub warmth and certainty into them.

'Do you see?'

136

Iris's colour had faded and the tight lines pursed her mouth again. 'Maybe,' she said uncertainly.

Ruby smiled. Confidence and an idea of her own value swept through her, and she leaned up to kiss her grandmother's cheek.

'Definitely,' she insisted.

CHAPTER SIX

Before the war Colonel Boyce's office at GHQ had been a spacious bedroom in a substantial villa. By the time I came to work there the room had been partitioned into three cubbyholes, each with one-third of a window giving a thin vertical view of the untended gardens and a checkpoint where a couple of soldiers guarded a gate in the perimeter fencing. Roddy Boy had one cubbyhole, and as his typist I occupied a walled-off slice of the corridor outside the bedroom. My desk was wedged between a pair of tall tin cabinets in which I filed the endless succession of pinks generated by inter-departmental communications.

Roddy's head poked out of his office. 'Miss Black? Could you take this along to Brigadier Denselow?'

I took the sealed folder marked *Secret* and walked down two sets of stairs and through a pair of temporary doors into what had once been the villa's kitchens. The GHQ buildings were a warren of stairways and cramped offices, packed with sweating staff officers who ploughed through mounds of paperwork and vied with each other for access to bigger fiefdoms. It was a swamp of bureaucracy, rumour and competitiveness as Headquarters expanded and the prospect of fast-track promotions encouraged ambitious officers to try to outsmart each other. Roddy Boy was always in the thick of some piece of intrigue designed to thwart his rivals.

Brigadier Denselow and his staff had four adjacent offices that opened through the servants' back door into the villa garden, so there was daylight and fresh air. This empire was jealously guarded against all comers. Denselow's assistant, Captain Martin Frobisher, was sitting with his feet on his desk reading a novel from the Anglo-Egyptian Club library.

'Hullo, light of my life,' he greeted me routinely.

I handed over the folder and Martin signed the docket for it. In answer to his entreaty I told him that no, I wasn't free for dinner.

'You never are,' he sighed. 'What's wrong with me?'

'Nothing. But I am in love with another man.' Whom I had not seen, nor even heard from, in seventeen and a half days. Each of those days was a glassy structure of routine within which I contained – as patiently as I could – my longing for Xan and my constant fears for his safety. I was only one of millions of women in similar circumstances.

'He's a lucky devil. Lunch, then?'

I had a pile of memos composed in Roddy's trademark verbose style to type and circulate. I shook my head, smiling at him. I liked Martin. He had been welcoming when I first arrived in the military maze of Headquarters. 'Pressure of work,' I explained and threaded my way back past the first-floor salon where shifts of cipherenes worked twenty-four hours a day, to my own office.

When I reached my desk I saw that Roddy's door was firmly closed and the hand-made 'Do not disturb' sign hanging from the knob indicated that he was busy.

There was no window in my segment of corridor, so I worked under a metal-shaded desk lamp that gave off an acrid smell of burning dust. I switched it on and took the cover off my typewriter.

I had been painstakingly typing for perhaps half an hour before Roddy's door opened again. I saw my boss's knife-creased trousers emerge first. Even in the hottest weather Roddy always wore immaculate service dress, including tunic, Sam Browne, tie and long trousers.

'Matter of morale,' he would mutter. 'This is GHQ. Notwithstanding, some chaps around here are reprehensibly sloppy.'

He was followed by a pair of sunburned legs in khaki shorts, very stained and dusty.

My heart lurched in my chest. I looked up at the owner of the legs and Xan smiled down at me. Behind the smile he looked exhausted.

'You promised me a cup of GHQ tea, remember?'

'So I did. Milk and sugar?' I laughed because I knew perfectly well how he took his tea.

'Let me think. Do you know, maybe it isn't tea I want at all? Perhaps a drink instead? At Shepheard's?'

Roddy gave us his pop-eyed stare. 'Ah, yes. You two know each other, don't you?'

'We have met,' I said demurely. The last time I had seen Xan was as he was leaving my bed, at dawn, before heading away into the desert on one of his mysterious sorties. After the first relief at seeing him alive and unhurt, I could hardly think of anything except how much I wanted us to be back in bed together.

'It is lunchtime,' Xan said, consulting his watch. 'Colonel Boyce, may I take Miss Black away from you for an hour?'

Roddy could hardly say no, although it was obvious that he would have preferred to do so.

'Hurrrmph. Well, yes, all right. Only an hour. We are extremely pressed at the moment, you know.' He turned to

140

me, eyes bulging. 'Have you heard from your father lately, by the way?'

This was a not very oblique reminder that, through his acquaintance with my father, Roddy considered himself to have a paternal role to play.

'Yes, I had a letter about two weeks ago. He's living very quietly these days, down in Hampshire. My mother hasn't been very well lately. He did ask to be remembered to you. I think he's quite envious of you, Sir, being so much in the thick of the war out here.'

A reminder of his importance never went amiss with the Colonel. He tipped his head back and the shiny flesh of his jowls wobbled. 'Yes. Please give him my regards, won't you?' The green telephone on his desk rang. 'Ahhhm. The Brigadier. Excuse me, please.'

The door closed behind him and Xan immediately seized my hands and kissed the knuckles. 'Christ. Come on, let's get out of here.'

We went out into the thick, hot blanket of the afternoon heat. It was the beginning of October 1941, but there was no sign as yet of cooler weather. The buildings of Garden City looked dark, cut out in two dimensions against the blazing sky.

'Xan . . .'

He held me back a little. 'Wait. Are you free this evening?'

I pretended to consider. 'Let me think. I was planning to go to the cinema with Faria . . .'

'Oh, in that case . . .'

'But maybe I could chuck her. What do you suggest instead?'

He raised one eyebrow. 'Bed. Followed by dinner, and then bed again.'

'Do you know what? I find that I am free tonight, tomorrow night and every evening for the rest of the year.'

We had been walking in a flood-tide of khaki. Fore-and-aft caps bobbed all around us, with a sprinkling of Australian broad-brimmed hats and French kepis. Xan took my elbow and we stopped at the kerbside, letting the current flow past. My apartment was only a few minutes' walk from here and it would be empty except for Mamdooh taking his siesta in his room next to the front door.

We looked the immediate question at each other, but now I could see a haze of something like suffering as well as weariness in Xan's eyes.

'Let's do what you suggested. Let's go to Shepheard's,' I said.

'Good,' he said softly. 'I only got in about two hours ago and I'd like a beer after dealing with GHQ.'

A horse-drawn caleche came plodding up behind us. The horse was a bag of bones, its coat dark with sweat and foam-flecked under the ancient harness. Its blinkered head drooped in a nosebag. The driver spotted us and whipped up the horse to bring him alongside.

'Sir, lady? Nice ride. Very private, no seeing, eh?' A curtain could be drawn across the front of the carriage to make a little hideaway from the seething streets. The vehicles were known as love taxis.

'Thanks. No,' Xan said, but he gave the driver a coin. The man returned a broad wink and a wave of his whip as the horse clopped onwards. We walked on to Shepheard's, past the beggars and amputees and ragged children who held out their hands to the Cairo grandees passing up and down the steps of the hotel.

Shepheard's was out of bounds to other ranks. The bars and terraces swarmed with a lunchtime crowd of fashionably dressed civilians and officers of all the nations who had forces in Egypt. We found a table on the veranda overlooking the street and ordered buffalo steak sandwiches and Stella beer from one of the waiters, then sat back in our wicker chairs without immediate expectation. The service at Shepheard's was even slower than the bureaucratic processes at GHQ.

From two tables away Martin Frobisher lifted his hand to us in an ironic greeting. Xan gave him a nod and I studied Xan's face from behind the shield of my sunglasses. He had shaved this morning, but he had missed several patches and the stubble glinted in the sun. I imagined him in the dawn light, somewhere between here and the wire, with a tin bowl of warm water and a tiny mirror balanced on the bonnet of a truck. The faint white rims of old sweat stains marked his khaki shirt and dust caked in the eyelets of his boots. When he took off his socks and underclothes, a miniature sand shower would patter round his feet. I had seen that happen.

It felt strange to be sitting on the veranda at Shepheard's with him, patiently waiting for our beer, when only an hour ago I had no way of knowing even if he was alive or dead.

And if it was strange for me, I reflected, how much more disorientating must it be for him?

I said quietly, 'Am I allowed to ask where you have been?'

He jumped, as if his thoughts had been a long way off. He did smile at me, then rubbed his jaw with one hand. 'On a patrol.'

'Was it bad?'

'I have had better experiences.' He spoke lightly but the taut muscles round his mouth revealed his distress.

Surprisingly, the waiter was back with us. He put the beers down and Xan's had hardly touched the table before he swept it up and finished it in two long gulps. The desert left your mouth parched and your skin so leached of moisture that it felt as stiff as paper. And yet here was Xan now, surrounded by chic French and Egyptian women, and the pink-faced, well-fed officers from GHQ who directed the background to war operations from behind their desks.

I couldn't know what he had seen in the course of the last seventeen days but the likely images gnawed at me, jarring with the cosmopolitan scenes on the veranda.

'Sorry,' Xan said after a moment. 'I promise I'll liven up once I've had something to eat.'

I leaned forward and touched his hand. 'It's all right.'

He did revive when he had eaten his sandwich and most of mine. He sat back again in his chair and grinned at me. 'Now all I need is a bath and some sleep, and you.'

'All three shall be yours. Xan, it wasn't a social call you were paying on Roddy Boy this morning, was it?'

In the weeks that I had known him I had tried not to press Xan with too many questions. Up until now we had done our best to live in the present, and the present was always parties and joking and a blind determination to have fun. But today I found it very hard to accept that I should know so little. I also knew that he wasn't volunteering any more information because he didn't want to make me afraid for him.

He looked around at the nearest tables before answering. Everyone was talking and gesticulating or trying to catch the attention of the waiters. No one was taking any notice of us.

'No, it wasn't.' And then, after a pause, 'How much do you actually know about what he does?'

In theory, I was only supposed to handle routine typing, filing and administration. All confidential signals and memos were dealt with by army personnel, and collected and delivered by me in sealed folders marked *Secret*. But Roddy had long ago decided that I was trustworthy and he also liked to impress me by letting drop how key his role was. Quite often, he asked me to collect or deliver signals in clear to the cipher clerks because the junior staff officer whose job it should have been was inclined to be too busy for this menial task.

I had lately started reading everything that passed through my hands, greedy for the smallest crumb of information, good or bad, that might have anything to do with Xan. So I now knew the names and quite often the general where-abouts of most of the commando forces who supplied us with intelligence from deep behind enemy lines. I was almost certain that he was with one of these highly secret groups, criss-crossing the remote desert in order to pick up informa-tion on enemy troop and supply movements.

'A fair amount,' I said cautiously.

'And so you have heard of Tellforce.'

The sun struck splinters of light off Xan's empty glass and cast hard shadows over the white field of the tablecloth.

A child with sores all over his scalp had been leaning against the steps and grasping imploringly at the legs that went up and down in front of his eyes, but now one of the waiters went over and pushed him roughly aside. A thick wash of panic and dismay and revulsion rose in my throat, against Egypt and against the war.

'Iris?'

'Yes. Yes, I have heard of Tellforce.'

Another shadow fell across the table. We both looked up and there was Jessie James.

The two men exchanged a glance that excluded me.

'I didn't know you were back,' Jessie murmured.

'I got in a couple of hours ago.'

Then Xan was on his feet and they exchanged a brief handshake. Jessie hauled over a chair and sat down beside me, telling me that I shouldn't hide myself away just because Xan was always off fooling around in the desert.

The sombre mood that had descended on Xan and me lifted again. Xan and Jessie drank more beer and I ordered a tiny thimbleful of thick, sweet coffee. Jessie was full of the latest gossip and funny stories about people we knew. One of his fellow Cherry Pickers had won a mule in a poker game with a group of Egyptian traders. He had ridden the mule home from the card game and installed it in the garden of his rented house, and now insisted that the mule thought it was a human being and therefore he had to humour it. He had bought it a straw hat with a hatband in the regimental colours, and he took the animal and its hat with him to polo games and race meetings at the Gezira Club. Whenever he smoked one of his Sobranie cigarettes he lit another for the mule and blew the smoke up the animal's nostrils.

'No,' I protested.

Xan laughed and Jessie blinked at me. 'D'you think he should make the mule smoke Woodbines? The two of them are very happy together. I'd call it a marriage made in heaven.'

I finished my coffee and looked at my watch. Roddy might have gone off for one of his prolonged lunches, but he might equally be sitting at his desk and waiting for me to reappear.

'I'd better go,' I said reluctantly.

Xan lightly touched my wrist. 'What time will you be free?'

'About eight.'

The two men stood up and Jessie drew back my chair. I kissed them both on the cheek and left them.

I walked slowly back to GHQ through the stale mid-afternoon heat. Dogs lay beneath carpets of flies in the bands of slate-grey shade at the foot of high walls, and beggars slept with their *galabiyehs* tucked between their scrawny legs. I was remembering what I knew about Tellforce.

Later that day, after we had made love, Xan and I lay in my bed. My head rested on his chest and I listened to the slow rhythm of his breathing. Faria had gone to a big dinner that was being given by Ali's parents for some cousins from Alexandria, and Sarah was in her room. Lately she had shown

146

less energy and enthusiasm for her social life. She had been ill a month earlier with one of the debilitating stomach complaints that were Cairo's special weapon, and was taking a long time to recover. Her skin looked yellow and she complained that the heat was relentless. Faria and I were worried about her.

It was dark outside. I could hear dance music being played on a gramophone somewhere nearby.

'Are you awake?' Xan murmured. His voice set up minute vibrations inside the drum of his chest.

'Yes.'

He sighed and shifted position, combing his fingers through my hair and adjusting the position of my head so that it rested more comfortably in the hollow of his shoulder. I felt the weight of happiness, almost tangible, defined even more sharply by the constant counter of anxiety and by the certainty that we would have to part again very soon.

'I love you,' he said simply.

I smiled dazedly, my mouth moving against his skin. We lay and listened to the tinny scratching of the music, the small noises of the apartment.

'Before Jessie arrived this afternoon you mentioned Tellforce,' I began at last.

The name of the secret force had been in my head all afternoon. I didn't want to hear how closely Xan was associated with it, but I couldn't unlearn what I already knew. Once we had acknowledged his involvement, I reasoned, maybe we could jointly put the thought of it aside until it was time for him to leave again. And if I knew more, it might be easier for me to help Xan to forget it as far as possible.

'This is between us,' Xan murmured.

I twisted my head so I could look into his eyes. 'I swear.'

'Do you know what we do?'

From what he told me that night, which was only the bare

facts, together with what I knew already, I was able to put together the picture.

Tellforce was an irregular group of officers and men who had been recruited for their knowledge of the desert and the ways of the desert. They knew the shifting contours of the sand seas, and the extreme heat and cold, and the brutal force of sandstorms. Before the war the officers might have been mining engineers or hydrologists or Arabists, but now their job was one of the most demanding of all the special operations. They drove patrols of heavy specially adapted trucks deep into the desert, moving far behind enemy lines and spying on their manoeuvres. They kept twenty-four-hour roadside watches from the sparse shelter of wadis or patches of scrub, and from these uncomfortable hideouts they counted every single truck, tank and car that passed, noted their numbers, and estimated the numbers of occupants. Collecting these snippets of information meant that Tellforce patrols were always at risk of being spotted by enemy convoys or aircraft.

They were also known as the desert taxis because they delivered commando raiders to their targets and then searched for the survivors and brought them out again. And they made their own lightning strikes on trucks, fuel and supply dumps and parked aircraft whenever an opportunity for sabotage presented itself.

'I see,' I said at last.

I had always understood that Xan must be involved in special ops of some kind, but the reality was even more daunting. The desert taxi service was always busy, and by definition in the most dangerous places. I passed my tongue over my lips, feeling them as dry and cracked as if we were out in the desert now.

'Don't worry,' Xan said.

'I won't,' I lied.

148

'Hassan is always with me.'

I remembered the impassive tribesman who had driven us out to the oasis beyond Giza, and instead of the car I pictured him and Xan perched in the cab of one of Tellforce's 30 cwt Ford trucks.

I imagined the truck driving full tilt at a wall of yellow sand and ploughing up the face of the dune above a bow wave of dust, then rocking for an instant on the sharp crest. The monochrome immensity of the Libyan desert would stretch ahead, maybe with a tell-tale flash of sun reflected off metal or the dust plume of an enemy convoy in the distance, before the truck plunged under its own momentum down the cliff on the other side. There would always be the risk that the vehicle might tip over itself and cartwheel to the bottom.

'We have been at Kufra,' Xan continued.

'We were out on a patrol alongside the Palificata and we happened to spot some unexpected enemy tank movements. Mark III Panzers. They just materialised out of nowhere, fifteen of them.'

I listened, keeping my breathing even to counter the swell of apprehension.

'We were a half-patrol, just five trucks and a command car. We had been moving mostly at night and were about to leaguer under camouflage for the day when the forward vehicle signalled a halt. Luckily we had dune cover so we held up and watched them go by.'

Xan slid his arm from under my head and fumbled for a pack of cigarettes from the pocket of his discarded shirt. He lit one and leaned back against the pillows. I waited for what seemed like a long time.

'That was what I had to tell Boyce.'

Relevant SIGINT and HUMINT, information gleaned from enemy signals traffic or human intelligence reports from reconnaissance patrols like Xan's were Roddy's raw materials. It was his job to assess and collate them, then build up a picture for the central command of our section of Intelligence. The work was done as quickly and as efficiently as possible. Eventually the information was passed for encoding and onward transmission to commanders in the field.

'Yes. Then what happened?'

Xan exhaled.

'We watched them go by,' he repeated. The lines drawn in his face told me that wasn't all.

'We waited. I started to hope that they must have missed the other half of the patrol too, even though they were in a much more exposed section than we were. Then after fifteen or twenty minutes we heard the Panzer cannons start up.'

I understood, then. Tellforce trucks and a command car would stand no chance against the armoured tanks' high explosives and armour-piercing shells.

'I gave the order to the men to hold off. We could have pushed forward after the tanks and done what we could, but . . .'

The silence uncurled between us. Doing what they could would have meant only one possible outcome.

'The firing stopped after a few minutes and then we did move in.'

Xan described the scene in only the barest and most unemotive words. At first it was impossible to see anything through the smoke and churned-up dust. Then, as his little convoy crawled in the tank tracks, they came upon all that was left of the second half of the Tellforce patrol. Three of the trucks were on fire, the incinerated occupants spilling out of the doors or lying huddled in the sand. Most of the men were dead, the others badly wounded. The tank commanders probably assumed that they were coming up to

150

the outposts of a more significant force. They had smashed straight through the isolated patrol and rolled on in search of bigger objectives.

The dust began to settle and the sun appeared as a pale disc above the eastern horizon. Xan left one detachment of men to dig graves for their dead companions and with Hassan and the wounded survivors he set off towards the distant first aid outpost at Kufra. Among the injured was the captain, whose legs had been blown off at the knees.

'Burke and I were commissioned on the same day. He was a cotton trader before the war. There was nothing he didn't know about the desert. I sat in the back of the truck with him, giving him sips of water from my bottle. He kept saying, "damn nuisance, Molyneux. Damn nuisance. I need feet in this game. Damn nuisance." Over and over again. He died with the truck bumping and skidding over the sand. Bled to death.'

Xan stubbed out his cigarette with little jabbing movements. When I was sure that he had finished I put my arms round him and made him lie down again beside me.

'I drove back to Cairo with two other badly wounded men who needed surgery. Somehow Hassan kept them alive until we got them to hospital here.' It was five hundred miles. 'Then I came straight in to see Boyce.

'Boyce said the Mark IIIs couldn't have been where they were. There was no Intelligence relating to them, therefore they can't have existed. All the Axis supply movements are going the other way, up towards Tobruk. It's quite straightforward, he kept insisting. Tapping his fingers on the folders on his desk. They know we're going to make the big push for Cyrenaica, they're preparing for it.

'So in the view of GHQ, half of my patrol was wiped out by a mirage, eh?'

I had never seen Xan angry like this before. But in fact

151

he was angry not with GHQ or Roddy Boy, but with the war itself.

I held him, trying to draw some of the rage out of him. 'I'm sorry,' I murmured, but I was only trying to fill the silence with the reassurance of words. There was nothing I could say that would really mean anything. 'It will be over one day. It will be done, and it will have been worth doing.'

He closed his eyes, then forced them open again, as if he didn't want to contemplate what lay behind the lids.

'Will it? Will it have been worth it?'

The dance music was still playing. That, and the clatter of my typewriter, the twin sounds of my Cairo life. I felt suddenly choked with disgust at the meaninglessness of so much death and washed with grief for the men in Xan's patrol whom I had never even known.

'I don't know,' I heard myself admit.

After a moment I realised that Xan had fallen asleep, just in a second. I hadn't realised the depth of his exhaustion. The music stopped with a sudden squawk, as if someone had irritably pushed the arm off the record.

He slept for twenty minutes, stirred in my arms, then jerked awake again. As soon as he remembered where he was a smile of pure relief broke across his face and he looked like the Xan I knew.

'I've been asleep. Bloody awful manners, darling. Will you forgive me?'

I kissed his nose, then his mouth. 'Yes.'

'I feel better. I'm sorry about before. What's the time? Come on, let's go out to dinner. How about Zazie's?'

It was ten thirty. Most of us in Cairo kept eastern Mediterranean late hours although some of the British still insisted on dining at seven thirty, as if they were at home in Surrey. I was already scrambling into my dressing gown and heading for the bathroom. If Xan wanted to go out drinking and dancing, that was exactly what we would do.

I put on the coral-pink silk I had worn for our dinner at Hassan's oasis camp and picked up my Indian shawl.

'You look beautiful,' Xan breathed. 'And you smell like heaven.'

Sarah was sitting in a corner of one of the sofas in the living room. She was wearing an old cashmere cardigan, badly pilled under the arms and down the sides, and there was a blanket drawn over her knees as if it were cold.

She smiled determinedly at us. 'Hello, you two. Where are you off to?'

'We thought we'd try Zazie's.'

I glanced quickly at Xan. 'Sare, why don't you come with us? It'll be fun.'

'Yes, come with us,' he said warmly.

She lifted one hand and twisted the strand of pearls she always wore.

'Thanks, that's sweet of you. I won't, not tonight. I still feel a bit rotten.'

Her cheeks looked hollow and the rusty-looking dry ends of her hair spiked round her face.

'Are you sure?'

''Course. And I've already eaten. Mamdooh made me boiled eggs and soldiers.'

'Ah.' We smiled at each other, without needing to acknowledge that eggs in Egypt were small and had an odd, musty flavour.

'Xan, you're just back?'

Just back was what we all said. As if the men had strolled into a Cairo drawing room from a day's hunting or golf.

'Yes.'

'The news is good, isn't it? General Auchinleck's going to relieve Tobruk and take back Cyrenaica. Any day now, that's what I hear.'

Cairo was full of rumours of an imminent Allied attack under the new C.-in-C. Middle East. The besieged garrison at Tobruk would certainly be relieved. Sarah gazed imploringly at Xan, her face full of longing for a victory, for fresh news, or just for a change that would help her out of the heat and the social round and her stubborn illness. I wondered where all the eager men were who had swarmed round her when she was well.

'Maybe,' Xan said.

'Are you certain you won't come?' I repeated.

Sarah nodded quickly, biting her lip. 'Have a good time.'

In the hallway, on the silver salver that stood on top of a hideous carved wood and inlay-work chest, I saw a thin blue airmail letter addressed to me in my mother's handwriting. I took it quickly and folded it into my bag to read later. Xan found a taxi to take us to Zazie's.

The nightclub was packed, as it always was. Xan had to slip several notes into the palm of the maître d' to secure us a table. We chose our food from the elaborate menu that came in a leather folder complete with silk tassels, and Xan ordered a bottle of champagne. French champagne was getting scarce in Cairo now, and it was brought to the table in a silver ice bucket and served with a considerable flourish. We lifted our glasses to each other in a toast that contained no words, only wishes. A pianist had been playing through the din of the club, but now he crashed out a final chord and the lights dimmed even further.

A single spot came up on the stage in the corner of the room, the dusty red velvet curtains parted and the floor show belly-dancer shimmered between them. Everyone clapped and whistled as she began a slow gyration that set her sequins flashing. The lower half of her face was veiled but her enormous almond-shaped eyes were instantly recognisable, as were the lustrous expanses of dark honey-coloured skin revealed by her diaphanous chiffon costume. Elvira Mursi was the most famous dancer in the city. She kept her real identity secret but there was a rumour that she had been born in Croydon, and was as English as Sarah Walker-Wilson.

Xan watched the dance, occasionally turning to me with a flash of amusement. When the champagne was finished we started drinking whisky. He was determined to enjoy the evening to the utmost. He clapped Elvira to the last rippling bow, then kept up a flow of talk that made me laugh so much that I forgot the day. That was his intention for both of us.

By 1 a.m. the club was a hot, smoky mass of people who had come in from dinners and other more sedate parties. Xan and I shuffled in the crowd packed onto the tiny dance floor. I spotted Sandy Allardyce at a table with a handsome much older woman. She fitted a cigarette into a long holder and as he lit it for her her heavily ringed fingers rested on the sleeve of his coat.

'Who is that with Sandy?' I murmured in Xan's ear.

'Haven't you met her? That's Mrs Kimmig-Gertsch. She is Swiss, or claims to be. A widow. Her husband was in armaments, I believe.'

'What does she do in Cairo?'

'Oh, she lives here. She has a lovely house in the old city, right beside the al-Azhar mosque.'

'And what is she doing with Sandy?'

Xan grinned.

There was a small commotion in the crowd at my shoulder and a girl's loud laughter. I turned in Xan's arms and saw Betty Hopwood. She had fallen over and was now being helped to her feet by her partner, who was one of Jessie's fellow Cherry Pickers. Betty caught sight of me, tottered back to the more or less vertical on her high heels and waved extravagantly.

'Cooeee, Iris. Hello, Xan. Come and join us.'

Betty was an immensely tall South African girl with cotton-ball white-blonde hair. She was an ambulance driver with the Motorised Transport Corps. After these women drivers had worked five consecutive days of twenty-four-hour shifts meeting ambulance trains and transporting wounded men, they were entitled to one precious day off. And all they wanted on that day, after they had slept and been to the hairdresser's, was to cram in as much fun as possible. Xan and I found ourselves being hustled to Betty's table where our glasses were refilled with whisky. The Cherry Picker Major winked at Xan.

'What a scream,' Betty yelled at me. 'Look at my dress.'

She was wearing a tight sheath of silver lamé and she swivelled to show me the back of it where a long rent in the fabric was roughly fastened with safety pins. The MTC girls were required to live in barracks, and as late passes were impossible to obtain they were all experts at breaking and entering.

'I hitched my frock up under my khaki, but the barbed wire came down so low that I had to take off my coat to squirm underneath and then *rrrrip*!'

Betty found this so funny that we all dissolved into laughter in sympathy with her. Another bottle of local whisky materialised on the table. While the men were talking Betty leaned over and rested a hot hand on my arm. 'He's rather heaven, isn't he?'

I looked in slight surprise at the Major, but Betty nudged me sharply.

'No, I mean your Captain Molyneux.'

'Yes, he is,' was all I could think of to say.

Those endless hot, scented Cairo nights. The men never wanted the parties to end. For them, going to sleep just meant that the desert was one day closer. Betty and I and all the women we knew had learned to keep dancing and laughing long past the moment when we should have dropped with exhaustion.

At 2 a.m., when we emerged from Zazie's, the night air was full of the reedy smell of the Nile. Taxi and caleche drivers jostled for a fare. My head spun and I leaned on Xan's arm, watching the reflections of lights swaying in the black water. We were now part of a big, laughing group of people that contained Sandy Allardyce and his widowed lady, and it soon became apparent that we were heading back to the widow's house to continue the party. Betty and the Major and Xan and I squeezed up in the back of a taxi and we sped through the dark streets. When we stepped out again I looked up and saw three fine minarets like black needles against the stars.

We streamed up some worn stone steps, following behind Sandy and Mrs Kimmig-Gertsch. An anonymous door in a blank wall swung open and an immense Nubian in a snow-white *galabiyeh* with a royal-blue sash bowed to us as we marched in.

Xan had been right, the house was beautiful.

Most of the rich people's houses I had visited in Cairo belonged to people like Faria's family, or to British and French hostesses like Lady Gibson. They tended either to be decorated with heavy, dark family antiques, or to be theatrically done up in the modern style with white carpets and grand pianos and too much Venetian glass. But Mrs Kimmig-Gertsch's house was left to speak for itself.

It was very old. The windows were set in deep embrasures that revealed the thickness of the walls, and the stone floors were gently hollowed by centuries of slippered footfalls. We were shown by bowing servants into a grand double-height hall, panelled in wood. Between the arched roof beams, the ceiling was painted dark blue with silver and gold suns and moons and signs of the Zodiac scattered across it. A huge wrought-metal and crimson glass lamp in the Moorish style hung on chains from the central boss of the roof. Way above our heads a gallery circled the upper part of the hall, with exquisitely carved and pierced hinged wooden screens that would have shielded the women of the household from the eyes of male visitors. The room was simply furnished with low carved tables and divans piled with kelims and embroidered velvet cushions.

The party spread itself out and settled on the cushions, with Mrs Kimmig-Gertsch sitting in a slightly higher chair at the end of the room. Someone found a gramophone behind a door in the panelling and put on a recording of a plaintive Arabic love song that rose and fell as a background to the talk and laughter. The servants brought in silver pots of mint tea and little brass cylinders of Turkish coffee, and set them out beside crystal decanters of whisky and brandy.

Sandy led me across to Mrs Kimmig-Gertsch and formally introduced me.

'How do you do, Miss Black?'

She held out her hand for me to shake, the diamond and sapphire rings cold and sharp against my fingers. In perfect English with a heavy Swiss-German accent she told me that I was very welcome and I must make myself at home in her house.

Her eyes were hooded, but her gaze was very sharp and quick. I didn't think Sandy's friend missed much.

I thanked her and went back to my seat next to Xan.

After a while, I wandered out of the room in search of a bathroom. None of the servants was in sight so I chose a likely doorway, but found that it led out into a little loggia that gave in turn onto a courtyard garden. There was a scent of flowers and damp earth, and the sound of trickling water. By the light from the open doorway behind me I could just see the turquoise and emerald tiles lining the walls. Above was a quadrilateral of dark velvet sky, and the triple towers of the mosque. It was the most perfect and peaceful little garden I had ever seen.

I stood there, admiring and – yes – coveting it, until one of the servants coughed discreetly behind me and asked in Arabic if I was in need of anything. I murmured my request and was shown the way.

When I returned to the party, cards had been brought out. Xan and I were commanded to make up a four for bridge with Sandy and our hostess.

My head was swimming with champagne followed by too much whisky, and I wanted to go to bed with Xan much more than I wanted to play any card game, let alone bridge. As we played I answered gently probing questions about what I did, who I was acquainted with in Cairo. I didn't distinguish myself either in the conversation or at cards, and Sandy and Mrs Kimmig-Gertsch won ten shillings from us. Judging by the final glance that the widow gave me from under her heavy eyelids, I had been weighed up and dismissed.

It was four in the morning when the Nubian major-domo ushered Xan and me out into the grey pre-dawn. I didn't think about the time; I just wanted to get home again to the apartment and lie down with my lover.

Xan slept for just an hour, then slid away from me. 'Go back to sleep. I'll telephone you later,' he whispered.

At seven thirty I was making myself a cup of tea and swallowing aspirin for my headache when Faria appeared in her cream silk robe, grimacing at the earliness of the hour. She did a little voluntary work for her mother, who with two other Cairo society ladies ran a charitable club for servicemen. This must have been one of Faria's mornings for buttering toast or distributing tickets for the ENSA concert.

She took the aspirin bottle out of my hand and shook two pills into her mouth, but she wasn't too exhausted to ask questions about where I had been the night before.

I told her and she raised her eyebrows.

'What did you think of Mrs Kimmig-Gertsch?'

'Formidable.'

'There is a rumour that she is a German spy.'

'Why is Sandy running around with her?'

Faria gave me a look. 'He is a British spy. Didn't you know that?'

In spite of our headaches we both laughed. The idea of the two of them, an incongruous couple locked in a steely pas de deux of espionage and counter-espionage over cocktails and card tables, was irresistibly funny.

On my way out of the flat I met Sarah. She had a small suitcase in her hand and she told me that she was going to Beirut for the weekend. I said that I was pleased she was feeling better, ordered her to have a good time and kissed her goodbye. Then I walked to work with the hundreds of soldiers and civilians heading to their desks in GHQ.

It was eleven o'clock before I remembered my mother's letter.

I had just made Roddy Boy a cup of tea and taken it in to him with two Huntley & Palmers custard creams placed in the saucer, which was exactly what he required every morning. I swallowed another aspirin with my own tea, then carefully slit open the thin folder.

My dear Iris,

I hope so much that you are well and that the heat has not been too disagreeable. By the time this reaches you there should be some relief from it.

During all my father's Middle Eastern and African postings my mother had suffered badly from the heat. She had thin, pale skin lightly dusted with tiny freckles and hair the colour of unripened apricots, and she lived in huge hats and layers of muslin veiling and linen drapes. Then in the mid thirties they were posted to Finland, and in the middle of the first harsh winter there she developed bronchial pneumonia and nearly died. The first I heard of it was when my housemistress at school called me into her study and told me that it had been touch and go, but the doctors were now almost certain that she would pull through.

I begged them to let me go straight to Helsinki but everyone including my father declared that would not be necessary, and so it had turned out.

After that, though, my mother's health was always fragile.

There is so little news to tell you, darling. I had a nasty cold that lingered stupidly on and on, but now I am quite well and I have been doing a little work in the garden. The day lilies were quite heavenly this year, I so wish you could have seen them.

There followed some details about our cats, and the neighbours, then about the shortages.

No eggs or sugar, and butter and meat hardly exist. Your father and I don't find it so bad but it is very hard for young families like Evie's.

Evie was the much younger wife of my father's younger brother, who was away on active service. She had three children under six and had brought them down to live in a little house in the same village as my parents.

161

Michael and Eleanor are still in London, I don't know how on earth they manage but of course Michael's job keeps him there. Every night the bombs, and the blackout all the time, and everyone so careworn and anxious and exhausted.

Eleanor was my mother's oldest friend and her husband was something important in the Ministry of Supply. My mother was not an ambitious letter writer and didn't go in either for elaborate descriptions or – of course not – complaints, but these sparse words conjured up for me a London disfigured with smoke and rubble, trembling under the Blitz and yet still populated by determined people who were quietly and bravely doing their best. In Cairo, too much rich food and drink was taken for granted, we danced in frocks run up by local dressmakers and congratulated ourselves on being thrifty, and bought our silk stockings over the counter in Cicurel's. This contrast made me feel my champagne headache even more sharply.

My mother signed off, as she always did,

God bless, darling. From your loving Ma

I checked the date before I refolded the blue paper. The letter had been written six weeks earlier and had come by ship the long way, round the Cape and through the Suez Canal to Port Said, the same way that I had travelled out to Cairo myself more than six months ago. I finished my tea and biscuits, and resumed typing.

It was a long day. When I emerged at eight o'clock there was the usual crowd of boyfriends and hopefuls waiting to meet their girls. To my delight, Xan's black head was among them. I ran and he caught me in his arms and whirled me off the ground.

'Come with me?' he begged, after we had kissed.

I asked where, expecting that he would say Shepheard's or another bar for a cocktail before I went home to change for dinner. But he tucked my hand under his arm and led me to the car, the same one in which Hassan had driven us out to Giza. He handed me into the passenger seat.

As we drove out into Qasr el Aini, Xan said, 'I'm going to look in at the Scottish Hospital to see one of the men I brought in yesterday. Is that all right?'

'Of course it is.'

The Scottish Military was just one of the places where wounded men were taken when the hospital trains and ambulance convoys finally reached Cairo. Xan parked the car and ran up the steps, and I hurried behind him. The hallways and stairwells were crowded with soldiers, bandaged and on crutches or in wheelchairs, and the wards we passed were crammed with long rows of beds. On the first floor we found a ward where most of the occupants lay prone, what was visible of their faces like sections of pale carved masks, as motionless as if they were already dead.

Xan stopped beside a bed in the middle of a row, then leaned over the man who lay in it. 'Hullo, old chap. You look quite a bit better than you did this morning,' I heard him say.

There was no answer. There could hardly have been, because the lower half of the soldier's face and his neck were a white carapace of dressings. A tube led from where his mouth would have been. Xan sat down on the edge of the bed and talked in his ordinary voice, about how another soldier called Ridley had made it too, and how there was a cinema just down the road from the hospital that was air-conditioned, cool as a winter morning Xan said, with padded seats, and they would go and see a picture, the three of them, and have a gallon of iced beer afterwards.

I don't know if the soldier understood or even heard him, because he gave no sign. Xan just went on talking.

I looked at the chipped cream paint on the metal-framed bed, and the floor that was made of mottled stone with pink and brown slabs in it like a slice of veal-and-ham pie. There was a strong, sweetish smell in the ward with a whiff of suppuration in it. At the far end of the line of beds a man began moaning, a sound that rose and fell, and seemed to drown out the rattle of metal trolleys and the swish of foot-steps.

Sweat broke coldly on my forehead. It occurred to me that I was going to faint, or maybe to vomit.

I walked quickly away, heading down the ward without any idea where. I passed several nurses who were busy with dressings trays, and another who was sitting at a man's bedside. She was holding a cigarette to his ragged mouth and he was inhaling as if the smoke were life itself. I pushed blindly through a pair of swing doors into a sluice room, past a row of sinks and into a lavatory cubicle.

When I came out again, wiping my face with my hand-kerchief, the cigarette nurse was there rinsing out a kidney bowl at one of the sinks. Her cuffed sleeves revealed pale arms and reddened hands with prominent wrist bones.

'Are you all right?' she asked.

'Yes. Thank you.' What I felt now was shame for having responded like a swooning Victorian maiden to the spectacle of other people's suffering.

The nurse briskly set down her metal bowl, took a glass out of a cupboard and poured water from a jug. She handed the glass to me and I sipped carefully from it.

'I'm sorry,' I said pointlessly. I meant that I was sorry for taking up her attention when there were so many demands beyond the swing doors.

To my surprise she smiled.

'It can take people that way at first. You get used to it, though.' Her voice was attractive, with a distinct Scottish burr. She was a trained nurse, not a VAD like some of my friends, with a crested badge to prove it pinned on her apron next to her watch. 'Do you want to sit down for a bit? Your friend's still talking to Corporal Noake.'

The sluice room was relatively cool. Water groaned in the pipes and dripped from the faucets.

'I'm fine. I will be, in a minute.'

'I've seen you around town,' the nurse said. She was taking packages of dressings out of a box and talking to me over her shoulder.

'Me? How come?'

She laughed. 'You're the kind of person people do notice.'

I couldn't remember having seen the nurse at the Gezira Club or Groppi's, or dancing at Zazie's. Her starched, folded cap came down low over her forehead and hid her hair.

She held out her hand, the other still clutching a pack of bandages.

'I'm Ruth Macnamara.'

'Iris Black.'

We shook.

'If you're sure you're all right, I'd better get back to work. Sister's got a down on me. See you around, eh?'

'Yes,' I said to her departing back. 'I hope so.'

I walked slowly back up the ward. Xan was still talking to his corporal. I went round to the other side of the bed and looked down into the soldier's eyes.

'Hullo, there. I'm Iris, Xan's friend.'

I didn't know how much was left of the lower part of his face but the man himself was still there. His eyes flickered, moved, then fixed on mine. Just perceptibly, he nodded. I took his hand and sandwiched it between my two and he clung to me with his eyes.

After a minute, Xan said easily, 'We'll be getting along now, Noake. You get some sleep. I'll look in again tomorrow, if they haven't packed us off by then.'

We left him among the other carved men.

When we reached the car again we sat and lit cigarettes and stared out at the darkening sky.

'Will you really be going tomorrow?' I asked.

'I don't know for sure. It won't be long, though. There's the big push coming.'

We all knew that. The Germans and Italians knew it too, and were waiting.

'What happened to Corporal Noake, exactly?'

'He was shot in the neck and jaw. His lower jawbone was partly blown away.'

'Poor man.'

'He was luckier than Reggie Burke,' Xan said grimly.

'Yes.'

We finished our cigarettes and the last of the daylight drained out of the western horizon as if the desert sand were drinking it up.

'Where would you like to have dinner?'

I didn't want food, or whisky or dancing. I wanted Xan, and Xan safe, and the end of the war.

'Let's go home,' I said.

He leaned forward at once to the ignition and we drove back through the Cairo streets to Garden City.

CHAPTER SEVEN

'Will you?' Xan repeated.

It wasn't that I didn't want to answer, just that happiness momentarily flooded my throat and turned me mute. White light swelled behind my eyes, spilling inside my skull and half blinding me.

We were reclining on a rug in the shade of a tree, and the high sun shining through the chinks in the leaves made them black as carved ebony. We had been watching a polo match. As well as Xan's low voice I could hear shouting and ponies' hooves drumming on the turf and then the sharp crack of a stick on the ball.

I turned my dazzled face to his. His head was propped on one hand and he leaned over me, waiting.

'Yes,' I managed to say. 'Yes, yes, yes. I will. More than anything. For ever and ever.'

So, incoherently, I promised to marry Xan Molyneux. The leaves and the chinks of light and all the rest of the world were blotted out as he lowered his head and kissed me.

Jessie James was the first person we told. He came to meet us still in his white breeches and shirt soaked with sweat

167

from the match, stalking over the grass with his face flushed with exertion and success.

'Did you see that?' he called.

'No,' Xan said bluntly.

'But it was the very best goal I've ever scored. What kind of friend are you, Molyneux?'

'A very happy one, you oaf. Iris says she'll marry me. Can you believe that?'

Jessie stopped in his tracks. A smile split his face, but he pretended to be dismayed. 'Oh, no. This is a mistake. Iris is going to marry *me*, once she's realised what a hopeless apology you are. Tell him that's so, Iris, won't you?'

I put my hands out and grasped his. He was hot and our palms glued together as I danced around him. 'Wish us luck, Jessie.'

His smile faded into seriousness then. 'I do. I wish you both all the happiness and all the good luck in the world.' There was a tiny beat of silence as he kissed my cheek. 'You're a lucky man, Molyneux.'

'D'you think I don't know it?'

But I knew that I was the lucky one.

Later that afternoon Jessie took a photograph of us, using a camera airily borrowed from a man called Gordon Foxbridge who had been watching and taking pictures of the polo match. Major Foxbridge was a staff officer I saw from time to time in the rabbit-warren corridors of GHQ, and he was an enthusiastic amateur photographer. His sombre pictures of Arab tribesmen in the desert were later published as a book.

'Gordon, old chap, I want to record a momentous day,' Jessie insisted.

Major Foxbridge offered to take the photograph himself, but Jessie wanted to do it and so the Major obligingly handed over his Leica, and Xan and I stood at the edge of the Gezira

Club polo ground where the baked earth had been scraped and scored by ponies' hooves. With Xan's arms wrapped round my waist I let my head fall back against his shoulder and laughed into the lens.

'Watch the birdie!' Jessie sang.

It was Gordon Foxbridge, though, who developed the picture in his own darkroom and then delivered it to my desk in a brown manila envelope marked '*The engagement of Miss Iris Black and Captain Molyneux*' as if we were in the *Tatler*.

It showed the two of us exactly as we were but it also enlarged us. That day, Xan's glamour obliterated his assumed anonymity and my dazed happiness lent me a beauty I didn't really possess.

Wherever I have travelled since, through all the years, the photograph has come with me.

And this is the picture that Ruby asked me about.

What answer did I give? I can't remember.

How can I find the words to tell her, my grandchild, all this history? I can't even catch hold of it myself. If I try to stalk it, it floats away out of reach and leaves me with the featureless sand, the empty place on the shelf. So I have to be patient and let the memories and the dreams come, then try to distinguish them.

But I have never been a patient woman.

Ruby's quaint offer touched me, and so did the way she set it out with assurances about her shells and beetles. I can imagine her as a smaller child, dark-browed and serious, walled up in a bedroom decorated by Lesley and poring over her collections. Lining up objects, probably in an attempt to fix an unwieldy universe.

She is an unusual creature. Her coming is an unlooked-for blessing.

*   *   *

That same evening we went back to the Scottish Military Hospital to see Corporal Noake once more. Jessie James wanted us all to go out to dinner, he wanted to set in train one of the long evenings of Cairo celebration, but Xan insisted that first he must go to see his men.

From the medical staff we learned that the news of the other soldier, Private Ridley, wasn't good. As a result of his injuries a severe infection had set in and he was in a deeper coma, but Xan didn't tell Noake about this. He just sat there on the edge of the bed, talking cheerfully about going to the pictures and drinking beer, then laughing about the desert and some place they had been to where the flies swarmed so thickly that they couldn't put food in their mouths without swallowing dozens of them. Noake's response was to grasp Xan's wrist and give the ghost of a nod.

I saw Ruth Macnamara moving screens and bending over the inanimate men. She didn't appear to hurry but everything she did looked quick and deft. I wanted to talk to her again so I left Xan to his monologue and followed her the length of the ward.

At the opposite end from the sluice room was a kind of loggia, open to the air on one long side. Two or three men sat in chairs and there were two beds parked against the wall. Ruth was bending over one of the beds, examining the occupant.

'Hullo, Miss,' a young man in one of the chairs called out. 'Looking for me?'

It was a relief to hear a strong voice.

'Not exactly. But now I'm here, is there anything I can do for you?'

The man grinned. 'How about a dance?'

I was going to say something about finding a gramophone or maybe he could sing, but then my eyes travelled downwards and I saw that the folds of blanket below the humps of his knees were flat and empty.

The young soldier added softly, 'Well, perhaps not. Another time, eh?'

Ruth straightened up. 'Come on, Doug. They'll fix you up with some falsies and you'll be dancing like Fred Astaire. Hello again, Iris.'

'She's right,' I said to Doug.

'Medical, are you?' he asked.

'No,' I admitted. I wished I were. I wished I could do something – anything – for these maimed men and for the prone, silent ones who lay in their rows in the ward. I wished I could do anything useful at all, instead of just typing Roddy Boy's memoranda and placing two custard cream biscuits in his china saucer at precisely eleven every morning.

'Ah. Well, you're pretty enough just to stand there and be admired.'

Ruth swung round. 'That's enough of that. Iris, can you give me a hand here? Round the other side of the bed.'

I stood opposite her, with the wounded man's body between us.

'He needs turning,' she said. The man's eyes fixed on her face, then on mine. His chest was heavily bandaged, and curled edges of antiseptic yellow dressing protruded. I concentrated on not imagining the shattered muscle and bone within.

'Sorry about this,' he gasped.

'It's all right,' Ruth said briskly and I wasn't sure whether she was talking to the soldier or me. We slid our forearms under the man's body and grasped each other's wrists.

'Now, one two three, lift.'

He was hot, and quite light. Ruth and I shuffled our arms and as we hoisted him I saw the shadow trapped in the vulnerable hollow beside the crest of his pelvic bone. Gently, we let him down again in a slightly different position.

171

'Better. Thanks,' he said.

'Is your assistant coming again tomorrow, Nurse Mac?' one of Doug's companions called out.

'I'll try to,' I said.

Ruth raised an eyebrow. 'Volunteering, are you?' She was moving on and I was sharply aware that she had a lot to do. She made me feel superfluous and rather clumsy.

'I've got a job already.'

'What do you do?'

'Typist. GHQ. Very humble.'

'Oh, well. You must get asked out a lot, all those officers. Look, your friend's coming.'

Xan was walking towards us along the ward.

'Fiancé.' The word was out before I considered it, with all the pride and satisfaction that I should have kept to myself.

Ruth's glance flicked over me. She was amused. 'Really? Congratulations. When's the wedding?'

'Oh, we haven't fixed that yet. We . . . we only decided today. Let me introduce you. This is Captain Xan Molyneux. Xan, Ruth Macnamara.'

They shook hands as a rigid-looking senior nurse in a dark-blue uniform appeared in a doorway.

'Oh God, here's the old battleaxe. Look, where do you live?'

I told her and Ruth smiled briefly.

'What about you?'

'Out on the Heliopolis road. It's cheap. I've got to get a move on now. Leave me your phone number?'

'I'll come in again. Won't we, Xan?'

We. Would I ever get used to the luxury of using one little word?

'Good. 'Bye, then.' Ruth fled away down the ward.

'You've made a friend,' Xan said.

'I hope so.' I wanted to know Ruth Macnamara better.

172

And although the hospital was a sad and fearful place it drew me back. It was full of people who were doing what they could, certain in the knowledge that what they did made a difference.

We did go out to celebrate our engagement. We started with cocktails at Shepheard's and then dinner on a boat moored on the Nile, where Jessie proposed a toast and a circle of faces glimmered at us over the rims of champagne glasses. Faria was there, with the poet who was looking more mournful and whose clothes were even more crumpled and dusted in cigarette ash than usual. Sarah was still not back from her trip, but there were some of the Cherry Pickers and Xan's friend the mysterious Major David, and Betty Hopwood in a new dress of some iridescent greeny-black material that Faria whispered made her look like a giant beetle.

'How heavenly for you both,' Betty shrieked. 'When's the wedding?'

Everything did happen very quickly in Cairo. There was no reason to put anything off even until tomorrow or indeed to deny ourselves any of life's pleasures, because there was always the likelihood that the war would intervene, but I murmured that we hadn't decided yet. I wanted to tell my mother, and Xan's parents would need to hear the news. It was odd to think that there were all the relatives on both sides, and the lives we had lived in other places and our separate histories, as well as just Xan and me and the immediate chaotic present and the way we had fallen in love. But the war and Egypt made a separate realm, and for the time being the world outside was a shadowy place.

There was another reason too why Xan and I had not talked about a wedding day. He was going back to the desert and we both knew it would be very soon. Perhaps in only a few hours' time.

'I'll be in Cairo again by Christmas, darling, at the latest.'

'Promise?'

'Cross my heart. We're going to drive Rommel all the way out of Africa, I know we are. And after that you and I can make our plans.' He was optimistic for my sake and I tried to believe him.

Betty leaned across now and tapped my arm.

'Don't leave it too long.' She fluffed up her cottonball hair and winked at me. She had already told me the story of one of her MTC colleagues who carried a crumpled white satin wedding dress at the bottom of her kitbag, so as to be ready as soon as a husband came into sight.

'James? Where's that bloody Jessie?' one of the Cherry Pickers shouted. 'Some of us haven't found ourselves a girl yet. Where are we going now?'

To begin with Jessie obligingly orchestrated the evening, but as the hours went by our party gathered momentum until it rolled under its own impetus through the Cairo nightspots. By two in the morning we were at Zazie's again. Xan and I danced and I felt the heat of him through my satin dress, but drink and exhilaration distorted the normal sequence of minutes and hours, and we both convinced ourselves that the night was endless. There was time to laugh with our friends and time to dance, and there would still be time and time for one another. Leaving for the desert was no more than a little dark unwinking eye at the vanishing point of a long avenue of happiness.

Elvira Mursi came on and blew us both a kiss at the end of her spot.

Sandy Allardyce materialised. He held my hand, rather damply, and sat close to me on one of the little gold seats in a velvet alcove. His round red face was very serious and I realised only belatedly that he was making a confession of love.

174

'. . . a good man. Reckless, if you like, but a fine field officer. Yes. Choice. Of course. 'S what every woman has as her *privilege*. But, you know, wish it could have been different. Iris. Just wanted to tell you, you know?'

I shook my head, confusion and sympathy and a shaming desire to laugh mounting in my throat.

'Sandy. I *didn't* know, honestly. Had no idea. I never . . . let you believe anything I shouldn't have done, did I?'

'No. Never a single thing. Perfect lady, always.'

I couldn't speak now. It was the idea of myself as a perfect lady. Sandy took my hand as if it were the Koh-i-noor diamond and pressed his mouth to the knuckles.

'Never a word. Ssssh. Won't speak of it again. Rest of my life. Promise you, on my honour.'

From her front-row table Mrs Kimmig-Gertsch glowered at us.

The night did end, at last, with Xan and me in a taxi going back to his flat. The sun was up and the street sweepers were working, and donkey carts loaded with vegetables plodded to the markets. I was beyond being drunk and I wasn't tired, and the light had a hard, white, absolute brightness to it that suggested that this day was a crystallisation of everything that had gone before. I already knew that it was one of the days I would remember all my life.

Try to remember. Holding it, cupping my hands to mould the shape of it.

There was a cavalry officer in boots complete with spurs asleep on the dingy sofa.

The kitchen was a swamp of bottles and spilled drink.

The door to one of the bathrooms was jammed. I squeezed into the other, regarded my face for an instant in the clouded mirror, then hastily brushed my teeth with Xan's toothbrush. He was already unfastening the satin-covered buttons and loops down the back of my dress.

It is the memory of making love on that airless Cairo morning, when we had drunk and danced ourselves sober again, that I hold most close. We were so sweet and shameless, and so powerful in our innocence.

Even now, when I am eighty-two and losing my mind, the recollection of it can catch me unawares and turn my limbs to water.

Xan fell asleep in the end, and I lay and watched the impression of his dreams. He twitched and winced a little and to soothe him I put my hand over the bony place where his ribs fused, feeling the slow rise and fall of his breath.

I didn't go to work. I called Roddy Boy and told him I had Gyppy tummy, and bore the sarcastic slice in his voice when he told me that he hoped I would feel very much better before too long, and that he also hoped Captain Molyneux was taking good care of me.

In the afternoon, after we had eaten some recuperative pastries and drunk coffee in the shady garden at Groppi's, Xan took me to a jeweller's in the old quarter to buy a ring.

'There is a rather pompous family diamond, actually, that belongs to my mother. I'm the only son so she'll want you to wear it. D'you think you can bear that? But I want you to have something in the meantime. What would you like?'

We wandered hand in hand past the tiny doorways of the gem merchants. Copts and Jews called out to us, trying to urge us inside their shops. We reached an angle of a cobbled street where the way was too narrow for us to walk abreast, and Xan glanced up at a sign.

'This is the place.'

'I don't need a ring, Xan. I've got you.'

'It's only a symbol, darling. But I want you to wear it.'

The merchant unlocked the safe and brought out his velvet trays for us and we let the raw stones trickle in cold droplets through our fingers. In the end, under duress, I chose a smoky purple amethyst and ordered a plain claw setting for it. Xan led me out of the shop again and tucked my hand under his arm.

'There. Now, what would you like to do?'

'Where is Hassan?'

'At home with his family, I should think. Why?'

We hadn't spoken of it but we both suspected that this might be our last day and night together before Xan was called away again. In our Garden City apartment Mamdooh would be performing some domestic routine with polishing cloths or caustic soda and at Xan's there would be hung-over officers and the same debris of hard living that we had escaped three hours ago. We could have tried to find a hotel room, but with the endless flux of visitors and diplomats and officers washing through Cairo these were hard to come by. And I thought how perfect it would be to go out to the Pyramids again, and watch the sun setting behind Hassan's hidden oasis.

As soon as I told Xan he smiled at me.

'You have only to command. But I'll have to go and beg for a car.'

We walked back towards GHQ through baked afternoon streets. We passed a crowd of Australian soldiers with huge thighs and meaty fists, sweating under full packs, and a smaller band of British squaddies who looked undersized and pale in comparison with their Antipodean counterparts. They were all recently arrived because they gazed in bewilderment at the tide of refuse and dung in the gutters, and the unread-able street signs, and the old men in rags sleeping in the shade of peeling walls. The city was full of men in transit, on their way to camps in advance of the big battle. I only knew that it was coming, I had no idea where or when. Xan almost certainly knew much more.

We came to a tall, anonymous house in a neglected street that ran westwards towards el Rhoda. I was just reaching the conclusion that this must be a headquarters of some kind for Tellforce when a figure detached itself from the shadow of the broken buildings opposite and ran towards Xan. A brown hand caught Xan's khaki shirtsleeve and some quick words of Arabic followed. It was Hassan.

Xan gave me a glance and then moved a little to one side, listening to what Hassan had to tell him. I waited, feeling the sun burning the top of my head, knowing that whatever was to come would not be good news. Hassan stepped back again, briefly inclining his head towards me.

I could already tell from Xan's face what was coming.

'I have to go,' he said.

'When?'

'Now. I've got to be in place beside the road out of el Agheila with my patrol, tonight.'

By my half-informed reckoning this was about four hundred miles west behind the enemy front line, which was then on the Libyan border.

'*Tonight*? How? Isn't it . . . a long way?'

'Wainwright's here with the WACO.'

Tellforce had a small two-seater aircraft, usually piloted by the Tellforce commander himself, Lieutenant-Colonel Gus Wainwright.

'He's waiting at the airfield.' Xan took my face between his hands. Hassan had turned away and stood like a stone statue, guarding the steps and the dingy house and – I saw – Xan himself. I also saw that a glitter of excited anticipation had kindled behind Xan's eyes. Now it was here he was ready to go. He *wanted* to go, he was already rushing towards the adventure, whatever was waiting for him. I felt cold, even with the afternoon's humid weight pressing against the nape of my neck. But somehow I smiled, my mouth curling against his as he kissed me.

'I'm sorry,' he murmured.

Against all the impulses, which were to cling to him like an importunate child and beg him to stay, I pressed the flat of my hands against his shirt. Somehow, as the kiss ended I stepped out of his arms and put a tiny distance between us. Hassan edged closer by the same amount. First and most importantly it was the two of them now, and Xan's Yeomanry patrol, and the desert; not Xan and me. I would have plenty of time in the coming weeks to get used to that order of priority, before he came back to Cairo again.

'Come back when you can,' I whispered. 'Go on, go now.'

Hassan was already moving towards the Tellforce staff car that I saw parked under the shade of a tree. Xan turned away, then swung back and roughly pulled me into his arms again, and there was the raw bite of his mouth against mine and a blur of his black hair, and the buttons of his shirt gouged into my skin.

'I love you,' he said.

'I know.' The smile that I had forced into existence was real now, breaking out of me like a flower from a bud. 'And I love you. I'll be here. Just go.'

Hassan reached the car and slid into the driver's seat. Xan sprinted after him, then slowed again and shouted back over his shoulder, 'Will you go and visit Noake for me?'

I had already decided that I must do this. 'Of course I will.'

He wrenched open the passenger door and sketched a salute. With one hand I shaded my eyes against the sun, and I touched the fingers of the other to my lips and blew him a kiss. The skidding car tyres raised little puffs of dust that hung in the air like a whitish mist for long seconds after the car itself had vanished.

When I reached the hospital I went first to ask after Private Ridley. I was directed to a voluntary aid supervisor in an

179

unventilated ground-floor office that reminded me of my own slice of working corridor. The woman was French but she explained in neutral English that the soldier had died early that morning without regaining consciousness.

'I'm sorry. Was he a relative? Or a friend, perhaps?' She was looking at me curiously.

'Neither. A friend of mine is, was, his commanding officer.'

'I see.' She gathered together several sheets of paper closely typed with names, and patted them so their edges were aligned. She had well-manicured nails, a plain gold wedding band. Private Ridley had died probably while Xan and I were lying in each other's arms. Their loss running parallel with our happiness, somewhere in England there was a mother, a family waiting, perhaps a fiancée or a wife who didn't yet know that he was dead. I frowned, trying to line up these separate unwieldy facts like the supervisor's sheets of paper, and failing. Xan and I were alive, today, with blood thrilling in our veins. Another man was dead, and others had lost half a face, two strong legs. These particular known individuals suddenly seemed to stand at the head of an immense army.

As they marched in my head the living were outnumbered and overpowered by the slaughtered and the maimed, and the hollow skulls and shattered limbs snuffed out hope and happiness: not just Xan's and mine, perhaps, and that of Private Ridley's family and Ruth Macnamara's patient who couldn't dance any more, but all the world's. Zazie's and Shepheard's and the Gezira Club were dark, and crowded to the doors with dead men.

I sat in silence, shivering a little.

'I'm sorry,' the Frenchwoman said again. 'Can I help you with any other thing, maybe?' She had work to do, perhaps the same news to convey about dozens more men.

I managed to say, 'No. Thank you.'

I left the office and found my way up to the ward.

Noake was lying propped against his pillows, the lower half of his face masked with fresh dressings, but when he saw me he lifted his hand in a little flourish of greeting. I sat down in Xan's place, intending to talk cheerfully to him in the same way that Xan had done. I wouldn't tell him about Ridley's death, not yet.

'Hello, there. How do you feel? You've only got me tonight, Mr Noake, I'm afraid. Captain Molyneux's been whisked back to the desert, by *air*. Colonel Wainwright flew in today to get him, what d'you think of that?'

I could see what he thought of it. Beneath the bruised and puffy lids his eyes glimmered with interest and amusement, but there was also the ghost of a cheeky wink that acknowledged that officers and commanders flew. Everyone in Tellforce sweated in trucks across the endless dunes, digging out embedded vehicles and dragging the heavy steel channels that were laid under the wheels to give them purchase, but other ranks didn't get many variations to this routine. But I thought that it must also have been a welcome sight for patrols buried deep in the desert when the little single-engined plane came humming out of the sky and touched down on an impromptu runway levelled in the sand.

'I don't know when he'll be back,' I blurted out.

To my surprise, Noake's hand crawled across the sheet, found mine and grasped it tightly. I looked down at our linked fingers, and the tubes running into his arm through which they must be feeding him.

Noake had seen Xan and me together. He couldn't speak, his shattered mouth couldn't form the words, but he was letting me know that he sympathised with the lucky anguish that I suffered on parting from my lover.

For a moment, I had to keep my head bent.

Corporal Noake's hand was large and heavy. The nails

were torn and blackened, and there were deep fissures round the nail margins and across the knuckles. Xan had told me that he was a mechanic, gifted at coaxing new leases of life out of their battered trucks.

'Back for Christmas, that's what he said,' I murmured.

I didn't know how much I was supposed to know, or how much Noake should know that I knew. But he wasn't going to be able to tell anyone and I longed to talk about Xan.

'I've no idea what the real chances of that are. I don't suppose anyone does, do you? But there's a big push coming, everyone's talking about it, aren't they? I'm concerned for him, because I know a bit about what Tellforce does. But Xan's got to do his job like everyone else, like *you* did, Mr Noake.'

And like Private Ridley did. I sat up straighter and looked into the injured man's eyes, remembering the involuntary kindling of excitement I had seen in Xan. 'It must be hard for you, to miss what's going to happen.'

Noake nodded, his fingers still tight over mine.

'We'll have to keep each other company,' I said. 'And you will have to get better quickly.'

A starched apron came into view on the other side of the bed. Ruth was standing there with an armful of fresh bedding.

'Here you are again. Can't stay away from us, Albie, can she?'

I was glad to know his first name. 'Albie? May I call you that, too? I'm Iris, d'you remember?'

He blinked his agreement.

Ruth asked me, 'Where's your friend tonight? *Fiancé*, I mean.'

'I was just telling Albie. Gone. Called back to the desert in a hurry.'

'Oh. Oh, look, d'you want to have a cup of coffee or something after I finish work? I'm off shift in half an hour.'

'Yes, let's do that.'

She hurried away and I went on talking to Albie Noake. I had no idea what he wanted to hear but I told him about Faria and Sarah and the apartment in Garden City, and about Mamdooh and his son who followed him to work and sat on a stool in the corner of Mamdooh's cubbyhole near the front door, sucking on the bon-bons that Faria insisted on feeding him. I talked about Zazie's and Elvira Mursi and Mrs Kimmig-Gertsch's house, and Roddy Boy and my segment of corridor at GHQ, and what I remembered of Cairo in the days long before the war when my father was at the embassy. I held on to Albie's hand, smoothing it between my own. Once or twice his eyelids closed and I thought he had fallen asleep, but as soon as my murmuring stopped they snapped open again.

'She can talk enough for both of you, can't she?' Ruth demanded when she came back.

I disengaged my hand gently from Albie's and stood up.

'Shall I come back another day?' I asked him. As well as a nod there was a sound in his throat, part gargle and part rising groan. It was meant as a yes.

'You can always tell me to go away.' I smiled. 'Good night, Albie.'

I followed Ruth out of the ward and down some stone steps. Outside a door marked 'Nursing Staff' she said briskly, 'Wait here.'

Three or four minutes later she re-emerged and I blinked at her. The nurse's starched cap had always hidden her hair, and now I saw for the first time that it was a rich, dark red. It turned her pale skin translucent and took the slightly pinched severity out of her face. Ruth looked as if she was not much more than a year or so older than me. She had taken off her apron and wore a thin coat on over her uniform dress. Without the starched outer layer she didn't rustle or crackle when she walked. We nodded at each other, with a touch of wariness now that we were on neutral ground.

When I was driving with Xan I had noticed a small café on a street corner, within walking distance but far enough away not to be crowded with people from the hospital. I suggested that we might go there and Ruth nodded briefly.

'Anywhere we can get something to eat. I'm pretty hungry.'

The café had split and cracked clay tiles for a floor, and a tall mirror suspended at an angle above the counter that reflected the tops of our heads and foreshortened bodies. There were only a handful of other customers, but there was a good scent of coffee and spicy cooking.

Ruth ordered eggs and *fuul*, and I asked for a plate of fruit. We drank mint tea while we waited for our food and as soon as a basket of *'aish baladi* was placed in front of us Ruth tore off a chunk of the warm, coarse bread and chewed ravenously.

'Sorry. I don't get much time to eat during the day. Usually I like to get the bus straight home from work and have a meal. The person I live with cooks, or if I'm on my own I throw a few ingredients together.' She made a self-deprecating face, and then laughed. 'I'd *like* to be able to cook, but it's not exactly one of my gifts.'

Sarah, Faria and I didn't cook either. Mamdooh left covered dishes for us, or we might boil an egg or carve up a sandwich. But mostly we were taken out for dinner.

I felt the width of a divide between Ruth Macnamara and me, and I knew that she was just as aware of it. Ruth wouldn't miss anything, I guessed.

'Do you share with another nurse?'

'A doctor.'

'Where does he work?'

Ruth lifted an eyebrow. 'She.'

Then she named one of the other military hospitals.

I was blushing crimson at my own assumption. 'That was stupid,' I said.

'No, it wasn't. How many female surgical anaesthetists do any of us know? But Daphne is one. She's pretty good.' Ruth was proud of her friend, I could tell that much.

'I'd like to meet her.'

Ruth didn't say anything to that. A hot pan full of eggs and chopped peppers arrived and she dug her fork into it. I ate slices of melon and mango and watched her eat. When rather more than half of Ruth's plate was empty, she finally looked up again.

'That's better. So. Your *fiancé* is Albie Noake's commanding officer, is that right?'

'You don't have to keep calling him my fiancé. Just say Xan.'

She laughed then. 'OK. Xan.'

'Yes, he is. And when he was called back to his . . . unit, this afternoon, I said I'd go on visiting Albie instead of him.'

'That's good. The men get medical attention, of course, the best we can provide, but they don't get many of the other things that they need. Company, especially women's company, and non-medical encouragement, and diversion, and anything, really, that's outside hospital routine. Although the VADs and the other voluntary organisations do what they can. Albie's lucky.'

I understood what she meant. The ward was so big, and so overcrowded with suffering, it would be hard to provide individual support or even as little as a few minutes' unhurried talk for each of them. And they were all so far from their own families and friends.

'What will happen to him?'

'Short term, or longer?'

'Both.'

'Mine is an acute trauma ward. He'll stay there until he

is stable and his recovery is predictable. Then he'll be moved to a longer-stay ward, where I should think they'll start trying to repair his mouth and reconstruct his jaw. Or maybe that will be too complicated and he'll be sent by ship back to England for the work to be done there.'

'Will he be able to speak again?'

Ruth's own lips twisted a little. 'In a way. It will be a manner of speaking.' He was perhaps twenty-eight years old.

'Poor Albie.'

She went on eating. 'At least he's alive.'

Ruth was unsentimental and I could see how the work she did would absolutely require that, or else it would be unbearable. And as well as being distressing I could also guess how fascinating and even noble it must be, compared with what I did. I envied her.

'Xan brought in another of his men who was badly injured at the same time. He died this morning, but I didn't tell Albie. Maybe I should have done, though.'

The way that Ruth talked – everything about her, her matter-of-fact dry manner and her precise way of moving as well as speaking – was changing my perspectives. The truth was the truth. There was no point in trying to hide or to soften it, perhaps especially from men who had been so severely wounded. I suddenly thought that to do so might be to belittle them.

'Yes, I think you should,' Ruth agreed. Her glance flicked over me. 'Would you like me to do it, as your Xan isn't here? What was the man's name?'

'Private Ridley. No, thank you. I'll tell Albie myself when I visit him tomorrow.'

The food was finished. Ruth and I sat facing each other across the rickety wooden table. 'So I'll see you then,' she said.

'Do you ever get a day off?'

'Three full days and two halves out of fourteen. Subject to cancellation if we're busy.'

If the hospital trains and ambulances brought extra cargoes of men from the front. Uncomfortably I thought of my long lunches spent lazing beside the swimming pool at the Gezira Club, and my games of tennis with Sarah, and all the cocktails I had drunk and rich dinners I had eaten since coming to Cairo.

'I'd like to do some work in the hospital. Anything useful. I've got plenty of spare time.'

'There are women who come in with library books and magazines for the men, and they read to them. One lady has been teaching the convalescents to sew and knit.'

Ruth must have seen my face because she added, 'And there are the VADs, of course.'

The Voluntary Aid Detachment provided nursing auxiliaries. I knew two or three of them; they were mostly young women from backgrounds similar to mine, and they were nothing like Ruth. Again, she followed my thoughts.

'I am a trained nurse', she said, quite patiently.

'Where did you train?'

'Glasgow Royal Infirmary.'

'And your friend Daphne?' The doctor. The *surgical anaesthetist*. I imagined Ruth's slightly older sister.

'Yes, she studied at Glasgow University and did her medical training at the Infirmary.'

I took a piece of paper out of my handbag and scribbled my telephone number on it, then passed the slip across to Ruth. She took the pen out of my hand, folded my slip of paper and tore it very neatly along the fold line, then wrote her number in return.

'Maybe if Daphne and I ever get the same day off, you could come and have something to eat with us,' she said, without sounding convinced of either likelihood.

187

'I'd love to,' I said, my response sounding much too enthusiastic. But I was drawn to Ruth Macnamara. I hadn't met anyone quite like her before.

'I'd better go.'

I offered to pay for Ruth's dinner but she wouldn't let me. She took her own money out of a small brown leather purse and counted out a tidy heap of coins, the exact sum required. Then we walked out together into the twilight. I wondered if Xan was reunited with his patrol, and if they were already dug into a wadi within sight of the el Agheila road.

'Here's my bus.' It was one of the ancient dirty-blue Cairene boneshakers, crowded to suffocation point with Egyptians heading home to the city outskirts. Ruth climbed onto the step and somehow melted into the solid mass of humanity within. A second later I saw her face pressed against the murky glass of the nearest window. She gave me a smile that seemed to hang in the air after the bus had trundled on its way.

I started to walk penitentially towards Garden City but the day had begun to seem like a very long tunnel. Riding home through the dawn with Xan felt like a week ago. A taxi loomed towards me and I flagged it down.

'Yes, Madam, Shepheard's Hotel?'

'No.' I gave the man the address, fell inside and dozed until we jerked to a stop outside the apartment.

As I came in I noticed for the first time in months how opulent Faria's parents' furniture was, and how overstuffed the rooms felt.

Sarah was sitting in a circle of lamplight, her knees drawn up and her bare feet on the crimson sofa cushions. She looked pale, but her hair was freshly washed and there was a slick of lipstick on her mouth.

'Sarah! You're back. Did you have a good time? You look much better.'

Sarah held out her arms to me. 'Here I am. And *you*. Faria told me your news. I'm so happy for you, Iris. I'm really happy. Come on, give me a hug.'

I sat down beside her and we hugged and kissed each other. Sarah smelled of her favourite perfume but the bones in her shoulders and arms seemed much more prominent, and there was a veil of sadness in her face.

'Are you really all right?' I asked.

''Course. And you're going to be Mrs Alexander Molyneux. *How* exciting. Are you completely thrilled?'

'I am.'

'Can I be your bridesmaid?'

Thinking about Ruth Macnamara I said, 'Of course. You and Faria.'

'What heaven. Not pink, please don't say pink. Maybe palest mint green, what do you think?'

'Where is Faria?'

'Oh, out.'

'Ali?'

'Jeremy, I think,' Sarah said. She must have bitten her lips from inside because they went pale under the lipstick. Then she stretched out her legs and jumped up with a little laugh. 'Let's have a drink. A drink to you and Xan.'

She poured us a significant measure of gin apiece and tilted her glass.

'To the two of you. Happy for ever,' she called, and drank.

CHAPTER EIGHT

In the restaurant, waiting for Sebastian, Lesley ranged her cutlery so that the pieces lay perfectly parallel and with the tails exactly half an inch from the table edge. The napkin's white cone stood in the centre of the rectangle created by the knife and fork, and the autumn sun striking through the plate-glass window was reflected in a starry prism from the blade of her knife.

'Don't play with your knife and fork.'

Lesley had been thinking of Iris and the voice in her head was hers. Her mother had been strict about table manners; suddenly Lesley felt her as close as if she were sitting in the opposite chair. Then she looked up and saw her ex-husband. He came across the restaurant, jacket flapping and a scarf trailing, arms out as if to catch the wind.

'Lesley, hello, hello. Am I late? You're looking fabulous.'

'Am I? Thank you.'

Sebastian aimed a kiss at her cheek before taking his seat opposite her, allowing a waiter to retrieve his scarf and carry off his battered leather briefcase, which was the size of a small suitcase.

'Have you been here long? It's one, oh God, twenty past.

The bloody phone rang just as I was walking out of the door. An author having a *crise*. I had to deal with it.'

'It's all right.'

He leaned forward and put his hands over hers. The table rocked slightly.

'Good. That's good. Here we are, then.'

She slid her hands away and replaced them in her lap. Sebastian glanced around the room, checking to see if he knew anyone.

'Look at this old place. It's changed a bit since our time, eh?'

When they had first met each other, a year or more before they were married, Sebastian Sawyer used to bring her here for dinner. The restaurant was round the corner from his flat and he had been a regular, with whoever the current girl-friend happened to be. In those days it had been a checked-tablecloth French bistro, with the menu chalked up on a blackboard, and she had hardly noticed anything because she was in love with him. Now it was all blond wood and brown suede. Off-the-shelf restaurant design, Lesley noted critically, professionally.

'You're frowning.'

'What?'

'Is something wrong?' Sebastian asked.

'No, nothing. Well, except that I'm worried about Ruby, of course. You know that. It's why I wanted us to have this lunch together. You are her father, and . . .'

He held up his hand. 'Don't worry. We're going to have a good long talk. Let's order first, shall we?'

Lesley picked two things off the menu at random. Sebastian asked the waiter where the beef was from and peered for long moments at the wine list. At last he folded away his reading glasses, took a mouthful of wine when it arrived and appeared to be chewing on it, then leaned back with a rich sigh.

'Now then,' he said encouragingly. 'Ruby.'

'Have you talked to her?'

'As a matter of fact I have. Since you and I were going to meet today, I gave our daughter a call last night.' Sebastian twinkled at her. As a senior publisher with a large staff of young, attractive women, the twinkle was a well-used weapon in his armoury. 'I couldn't get her mobile, of course, so I tried the number you gave me and lo and behold, my ex-mother-in-law answered.'

'What did she say?'

'To be perfectly honest, I don't think she had a clue who I was.'

Lesley made a quick reckoning. Sebastian and Iris had met only a handful of times. Iris had come home from Africa for the wedding, and during the eight years before Ruby was born there had been maybe four or five other encounters. Iris came to London again soon after Ruby arrived, she was sure of that; there was a photograph of her holding the new baby and gazing unsmilingly into the camera lens.

Family life hadn't really suited Sebastian. When Ruby was three, he left home and moved in with a youngish novelist with a growing literary reputation. There had been a succession of other women since then, getting younger and younger. Ruby had resented this. 'This one's not much older than me. It's pathetic, that's what it is.'

So far, Ruby was his only child. 'Doesn't need to *have* kids, does he? He just goes out with them,' she sneered.

'Iris's memory isn't good,' Lesley said now.

'Anyway, I asked to speak to Ruby and she came on the line.'

Their starters were placed in front of them and Sebastian immediately broke off and dug a fork into his. Lesley looked out of the window at the crowds of shoppers and the buses trundling like giant logs in a slow current. It was odd to be sitting across the table from a plump, routinely genial stranger who had once been her husband. A man with whom she had had a child. But then she quite often looked up and saw Andrew and he seemed to be no less of a stranger, and they were also joint parents and she was still married to him. Much of her life, it seemed to Lesley, now had a flimsy, two-dimensional quality to it, as if you might walk round to take a look behind the painted flats and see another world altogether.

The only real, solid, unshakeable constant was her love for Ruby. She loved Ed too, of course, but Ed was entirely knowable. He did what he was supposed to do and took pleasure in that, like his father.

But Ruby . . .

Lesley ached with longing for her missing daughter. Her shoulders bowed, curving inwards on the dart of pain that pierced her ribcage.

She had to hold on to the leg of the table to stop herself flying out of her seat and rushing to Heathrow for the first plane to Cairo. The only thing that held her was the mental picture of herself arriving at Iris's house, and the flat, baffled stares – one mirroring the other – that Ruby and Iris would give her.

She cleared her throat. 'Er, how did she seem?'

Sebastian put down his fork, dabbed his mouth with his napkin. 'She seemed perfectly fine.'

Lesley waited.

'She shouldn't have run off. She shouldn't have worried you like that. But she did get herself all the way to Cairo. She's going to museums, she said, seeing the sights. She's made friends with some people of her own age, they're showing her the city. What's the real problem with that? She's with her . . .' Even unctuous Sebastian couldn't quite bring himself to say *Granny*, where Iris was concerned. '. . . With your mother.'

And there you have it, Lesley thought.

My mother, my daughter.

I don't think my mother ever loved me, otherwise she wouldn't have left my father and me.

I love Ruby more than anything and she doesn't want my love. It chafes her, just like when she was a little girl and I took her to have her hair cut. The tiny ends of her hair worked their way inside her vest and itched and itched. Even though I undressed her and gave her fresh clothes, the memory of the itching still made her scream. I am the cut hairs, for Ruby. Part of her but not part of her, and an irritation.

Iris and Ruby.

Motherhood, or actually the denial of it, is the thread that connects all three of us. I wanted to spin a better, finer filament for Ruby and me, a gossamer link that wouldn't drag between us and trip us up the way that Iris's and mine always has done. But all I seem to have created is a different kind of unwelcome tie.

Or look at it another way: perhaps we are like the same poles of a magnet, Ruby and me and Iris and me, always driven apart. And by the same analogy Ruby and Iris have leapt together, irresistibly attracted.

Lesley was familiar with all the images of repelling and chafing and restraining. She had no need to ask herself what an analyst would make of them, she already knew the answer. Over and over again, whichever way she entered the circle, everything led back to Iris.

Rejection has become my pattern, my expectation. Sebastian and Ruby have made their own flamboyant rejections. Andrew and even Ed, in their invisible and within-bounds way, make their own smaller gestures.

'What is the problem?' Sebastian asked. He was looking hard at her.

Despair rose in Lesley. The food she was trying to chew turned to a thick paste on her tongue.

What was to be done? Leave Andrew, dismember their son's life, because her husband preferred his work and his boat and his yachting magazines to her company?

What *was* there to do, except go on living and working and being grateful for all the benefits in her life?

'Lesley?'

She forced herself to swallow and then took a deep breath. She wanted to cry, but that was impossible.

'I miss her,' she said. It was only the thinnest, icy sliver of the vast glacier of truth, but she was offering it to Sebastian.

He leaned back in his chair and let out a laugh.

'Les, poor old Les. Of course you miss her. It's what happens, it's perfectly natural. We have kids, we give them everything we can, just to enable them to grow up and not to need us anymore. It's harsh, but it's the way it goes. Isn't it the same for all your friends? Would you rather Ruby was some dependent little creature who didn't want to take a step away from us?'

Lesley lifted her eyes. What did he know? She saw Sebastian's plump, well-fed face through a fog of rage. It was as if all the capillaries suddenly burst inside her skull, flooding her brain with black blood and madness.

She picked up the knife from her plate. With a single swoop of her arm she lunged across the table and with all the weight of her body behind it she stabbed the point of the blade deep into her ex-husband's left eye.

Then she blinked and looked again. The knife still lay on her plate, Sebastian was still smiling broadly at her. Her hands shook.

195

When she finally spoke, her voice came out as a croak. 'We? Us?'

Sebastian's smile moderated, crimping inwards into a rueful, amused moue of roguish culpability.

'I know. Of course. You're quite right. I haven't been much of a dad to her. I said so, you know, on the phone, and we promised each other that when she's back in England we'll spend some more time together. I've got to make a trip to New York before Christmas, seeing a couple of my opposite numbers over there. Maybe Ruby could come with me. She'll have to amuse herself a bit during the day because I'll have meetings, but she's proved that she's old enough to do that.'

Taken with this idea, Sebastian hooked his arm over the back of his chair and regarded his ex-wife.

She was broadening a little in the hips and her hair looked as if it was discreetly coloured to blot out the grey, but she was well-dressed and her jewellery was subtle but expensive. She looked exactly what she was, a prosperous wife and mother with her own business, who had driven up to London from the country to have lunch. With her ex-husband. She was a woman with a history.

'What do you think?'

'I think . . .' Lesley began.

The blood still hammered in her head, and the knife lay on her plate. She jerked her eyes away from it and they settled on his glass of wine, just refilled by the waiter. She eased herself out of her seat and slid her thighs into the narrow space between their table and its neighbour. Then she bent down so her mouth was close to his ear.

'I think you are a selfish, self-satisfied, pompous idiot. You are a pathetic father and you were a lousy husband. *Fuck* you.'

Then she snatched up the wineglass and tipped the contents into his lap.

Even as he exclaimed and rocked backwards with wine cascading between his legs, she was stalking away across the restaurant.

Waiters and napkins descended on Sebastian. He let them swab him down and as he was attended to he raised his eyes to the two men at the next table. They exchanged the briefest glances that said *Women*, and *She always was a nightmare*, before his neighbours discreetly resumed their conversation.

Lesley walked out into the street. She was disorientated; for a moment she couldn't even remember where she was. She turned away, wanting to get as far from the restaurant and Sebastian as possible, and stumbled for several blocks before she realised that she was heading in the opposite direction from the car park. She stopped and made herself think, and slowly the familiar geography closed around her again. She retraced her steps, taking a parallel back street to avoid having to pass the plate-glass window of the restaurant. She was sure that Sebastian would still be sitting there, sluicing down the rest of the wine and enjoying his beef and the certainty of its provenance.

She reached the underground car park where she had left the car, and plunged into the reeking depths. Her heels clicked, pit-pat, on the gum-blotched floor.

When she was inside her car, and had made sure that the windows were closed and the central locking was activated, she lowered her head to rest on the steering wheel. She thought she would cry, here where there was no one to see her, but as she waited for the relief of tears she suddenly realised that she felt better.

The picture of Sebastian with the red arc of wine falling towards his lap came back to her. She could see his face quite clearly, transfigured with shock and disbelief. She hadn't stayed around for long enough to catch the fury that would have followed, but that was quite easy to imagine.

Instead of crying she laughed. She lifted her head and stretched her arms as if she were just waking up from a long sleep.

She sat in the car park for a little while longer, reliving the scene in the restaurant. After that she repaired her make-up and drove home.

Ed was already back from school. He was sprawled in front of the television with a bowl of cereal balanced on his chest, milk dribbling from the spoon as he lifted it to his mouth.

'Ed?'

'Yeah, hi, Mum.'

'Ed?'

'Yeah?'

Lesley waited but his eyes didn't move from the television screen.

'How was your day?' she asked.

'OK,' he answered at length. Another milky spoonful followed a sloppy trajectory towards his open mouth.

She crossed the room in two steps and snatched the bowl from his hand. An arc of white droplets sprayed through the air and spattered the cushions.

Ed sat upright and stared at her. 'Mu-um,' he complained.

'Look at me when you talk to me.'

'I *am* looking. What's up?'

'Don't ignore me. I'm your mother. Don't sit there gaping at the TV and dribbling food, just answer me. Maybe even ask me a question in return.'

'What's *happened*? Just calm down, Mum.'

Lesley had never struck either of her children. Now she was too angry to stop herself. She aimed a wild slap at the side of Edward's head, the dish wobbling in her other hand and spilling more milk down her skirt and on the floor. The

198

blow hardly connected but it made her fingertips tingle and burn. Ed gaped, his eyes and mouth forming three shocked circles. She turned off the television and silence seeped between them. Lesley's throat felt as if it was full of sand.

'Now. Pick up your things. Put them away where they belong. Then go upstairs and start your homework.'

He stood up and swept his coat and school bag off the table. Then he marched out of the room without looking at her.

She mopped up the puddles of milk, rinsed the bowl and put it in the dishwasher. In the household diary she read that Andrew would be out that evening at a dinner with clients, so that would mean a simple supper just for Ed and herself. She opened the freezer, took out a labelled plastic box of her own pasta sauce and left it on the draining board. Checking that there were bags of salad leaves in the chiller drawer of the refrigerator, she saw a bottle of Andrew's good Sancerre. She lifted out the bottle, poured herself a full glass and took a long swig. Then, holding the chilled curve of the glass against her cheek, she walked out into the garden.

Late roses lingered on the bushes, the outer petals faintly bruised with the chill of autumn. It seemed to Lesley that everything she looked at, every leaf and twig, the stone bird bath and the diamonds of latticed trellis, had grown a bright, hard margin. There was an extra cold clarity to the world, each painfully intricate detail thrown into relief by her despair. A white butterfly settled on a furled spike of lavender, its powdery wings closing as the stalk shivered in the breeze.

A stronger gust of wind shook the bush and the butterfly was blown away.

Ruby and Iris sat in the garden, the trickle of the little fountain loud in the stillness. The late afternoons were now beginning to be touched with a chill as the sun faded. Iris's feet were propped on a padded stool and Auntie had draped a thin blanket over her legs.

'That was my dad on the phone,' Ruby remarked.

They had fallen into one of the silences that Ruby now understood to be companionable, able to be broken if one or other of them had anything they wanted to say, or equally to be left to stretch into a long chain of minutes. At first she had felt uncomfortable and had tried to talk – about anything, any nonsense that came into her head – just to fill the vacuum. Then she had noticed that Iris didn't hear anyway. Her eyes went absent.

Sometimes her head fell back and her mouth dropped open, and Ruby knew that she was asleep, but at other times she was awake and lost in herself.

Iris stirred. 'Who?'

'My dad. On the phone.'

'When?'

Ruby was growing accustomed to this too. Now and again, Iris would forget something that had just happened. Mamdooh would carry in the tray of mint tea and Iris would drink hers and when he had taken the tray away she would say sharply, 'Where's Mamdooh with that tea?'

'We've already had tea,' Ruby would tell her. 'Do you want some more?'

This time she said, 'Just now. You spoke to him and then you called me to the phone.'

Iris's mouth moved as if she was trying out the proper response, and the furrows radiating from her lips deepened as she found her place back in the present. 'Oh yes.'

'Mum must have been on to him. He never usually phones just for a chat. He's more of a "not now, sweetheart" kind of a person, really.'

'He's not the one she's married to now?'

'No. That's Andrew.'

200

Iris sighed. 'I really cannot keep up with Lesley's husbands. What's the difference between them?'

Ruby started to laugh. The laughter took hold until she was coughing and shaking with it, and it infected Iris too. They wheezed and wiped their eyes and finally Iris sank back against her cushions. 'Oh dear. Well, *is* there a difference?'

'Yes. Totally. Sebastian, that's my real dad, thinks he's quite cool. He knows lots of well-known writers and people, and although he's quite fat these days he wears sort of *youthful* clothing. Not quite bad enough to be embarrassing or anything, but always with a nod to what's in, if you know what I mean?'

'I'm afraid not.'

'Uh, wacky scarves. Logo T-shirts. Beanie in the winter. And in the week, designery suits and no tie.'

It was plain that Iris understood almost none of this, but she was enjoying the faces that Ruby made and the way her hands fluttered and nipped to describe the outlines of her father's clothes. Ruby liked it when Iris was amused because it made her feel that she was welcome, and maybe even useful.

Their idea of Ruby capturing Iris's memories had made little progress so far. Whenever Iris did start to talk, the stories seemed to be just that – stories, about ancient night-clubs and games of polo and the army. It was quite hard trying to memorise the details of such unfamiliar things. And then Iris's voice would slow down and grow vague, and Ruby would look into her eyes and see that she had gone missing again. Now she talked to her as if she were the one who was telling a story.

'Dad and Mum separated when I was three. He'd come to take me out at the weekends and we'd go to the park and things. I was little, so I can't remember what it was like when he did live with us. Anyway, he had a girlfriend, quite young, and she didn't like kids so I didn't see that much of the two of them together. It was just Sebastian and me, and even I could tell that was pretty boring for him.

'Then, after quite a long time – it seemed a long time – suddenly Mum started going out with Andrew. They got married, I was a bridesmaid. I had to wear pink stuff, a whole matching outfit, a dress with puffed sleeves and fake rosebuds in my hair. I hated it and at the reception I picked all the flowers off the headband and threw them at people. When I was eight and a half, my brother was born.'

Iris nodded. 'Did you mind?'

Ruby shrugged. 'I don't know. I suppose so, but it was happening to plenty of other people as well. Most of my friends, you know.'

'Was it? And this one, Andrew, what does he wear?'

Now Ruby's hands chopped a series of straight lines and boxes.

'Ah, I see.'

They were laughing again.

'He's a businessman. Management, accountancy. That sort of thing. And he likes sailing, he's got a boat.'

'Go on.'

Ruby looked at Iris. Her head was resting against the cushions but her eyes were bright. When she laughed she did look younger, as though she could have been any age at all.

'It's not boring? Really? Let me think. OK, when I was about . . . eleven, when Ed was getting to the age when he wasn't a baby anymore and was always climbing into everything and being a pain, and I was supposed to be working for exams to get into a *good school* but I was doing really badly, Andrew started thinking that he and I should be doing some bonding. So he decided that he'd teach me to sail, right? There was one weekend, we went off down to the boat together, just the two of us.'

202

Now Ruby stretched her face, rolled her eyes and pressed her fingertips into the hollows of her cheeks.

'Oh dear,' Iris murmured again.

'God, it was worse than *oh dear*. It was quite rough and windy, and the Solent seemed to me it was like the Pacific Ocean or something. Andrew could sail the fucking boat quite well on his own, OK, but he was doing this big pantomime number about how he needed a crew and we had to work as a team and rely on each other. So it was all this yelling and splashing, and me tripping over the ropes and him shouting *Ready* and *Going about*, and the boom banging above my head and the sails flapping and cracking. Wherever I put myself I was always in the wrong place. There's this big sail like a parachute that goes at the front, and I really liked it because it was bright colours, but when we tried to put it up it got wrapped round the forestay and we had to sail round in circles in the opposite direction to try to unwrap it. Andrew was yelling *No, no, no* and I was completely certain we were going to capsize and drown.'

Ruby was taken up with the momentum of telling this story. She jumped to her feet and mimed the frantic winding of winches and stumbling from side to side of the cockpit under her stepfather's command.

'What happened?'

She undulated her hand sharply to indicate the height of the waves.

'I got seasick and puked everywhere. Andrew turned the boat round and we sailed back to the marina, and as far as bonding goes the glue didn't work. He never suggested doing it again, anyway. Not that I'd have gone, I hate sailing. Wouldn't you? He and Lesley go quite a lot, but actually I don't think Mum likes it much either.'

Iris nodded. There was still a smile in her eyes. 'No, it

doesn't sound particularly enjoyable. I enjoyed hearing about it, though.'

Ruby sat down again and took her grandmother's hand. 'Now it's your turn.'

Slowly Iris tapped her fingers against her mouth, as if memories were about to spill into words. Ruby waited patiently, saying nothing. She had already learned that trying to prompt her only interrupted the ghost train of her grandmother's thoughts. A minute passed, then another, liquid with the small splash of the fountain. They both lost track of time.

'Amethyst,' Iris said softly at last.

Nothing followed and when Ruby looked up from watching the patterns of silvery drops she saw that she had fallen asleep. She unlaced their fingers and settled Iris's hand back in her lap, then adjusted the rug over her knees and stood up. It was as if Iris were a child, she thought suddenly, and she were the mother.

This idea took root and grew, casting a shadow like a dark finger pointing right across the garden and up the turquoise tiles lining the opposite wall. Ruby felt afraid of what she couldn't quite understand. She wished she knew where she was going or what would happen next month, or even next week.

She would have liked to talk to Jas about being disorientated and not knowing where you stood, but Jas was dead.

Ruby left Iris to sleep and wandered through the dim spaces of the house.

In the hall she trailed her fingertips over the table and raked faintly shining lines in the dust veil. Away from the sound of the water, the thick walls trapped silence and the smoky scent of incense that must live in the cracks of the stonework because she never saw Auntie or Mamdooh burning it.

Her aimless wandering brought her to the door of the kitchen. She put her hand to the heavy panelling and pushed.

Auntie looked up at once. 'Mum-reese?' she asked, pillowing her cheek against her folded hands.

'Yes, she's sleeping.'

'Ah.' The old woman put down the knife she had been using to slice vegetables and came round the table to Ruby. She reached up and pinched her cheek, gently, shaking her head and smiling at the same time so that her pale gums and isolated teeth were all on show. She murmured something in Arabic, the tone of her voice so soft with sympathy that Ruby's eyes stung with sudden tears of self-pity. She sniffed furiously and pulled out of Auntie's grasp.

Auntie pointed to the comfortable chair near the stove. It was padded with cushions made out of worn carpet strips in shades of faded garnet and copper, and it seemed to hold the substantial print of Mamdooh's body.

'Me?' Ruby asked, and Auntie nodded so she sat down.

It was peaceful in the kitchen, with the click of the knife blade on scrubbed wood and the sharp scent of cut leaves. After a while, starting with a drawn-out note that still made Ruby jump, the chanting of the muezzin poured in through the screened windows. That was where Mamdooh had gone, to prayer.

Auntie took a pomegranate out of a woven rush basket and sliced it in half. With the sharp point of her knife she cut the jewelled beads of fruit away from the creamy pith and let them fall into a bowl. Next she took an earthenware pitcher, ladled a couple of spoonfuls of yoghurt onto the fruit and handed the bowl and a spoon to Ruby with a series of small encouraging nods.

Ruby dipped the spoon, and tasted. Tiny sharp globes burst against the roof of her mouth and her tongue was thick with velvety yoghurt. To be fed made her feel that she was back in a warm, familiar place again. For now; for the time being.

'It's nice.' She smiled. 'Thank you.'

When the call to prayer died away, Auntie began singing to herself as she worked. The sad chain of notes seemed to come from somewhere between her throat and the back of her nose, ululating in half and quarter-tones, with no beginning or end. Ruby listened and ate her pomegranate. Tomorrow was Ash's day off. He had promised to come on the moby and take her out somewhere.

'Where?' Iris asked sharply. This morning she was wearing her silky striped gown and her hair was caught up at the sides of her head with turquoise and coral-headed combs. Ruby and Ash shuffled a little awkwardly under her gaze. 'Where are you taking her?'

'To al-Qalaa. To Citadel, Ma'am,' Ash answered politely.

To *where*? Ruby was going to protest, but decided that she would save it until they were alone together.

'I see. You will tell her some of the history?'

'Of course. I am proud of this.'

'Good.' Iris approved of Ash, and even Mamdooh had opened the front door and shown him through into Iris's garden without any noticeable signs of objection. 'Go on. Off you go. Make sure you bring her back here by six o'clock on the dot.'

'Of course.' This time, Ash even bowed.

'*Creep*,' Ruby whispered under her breath.

The moby was outside. Ash pulled his sunglasses down over his eyes, flicked back his hair and gestured to the pillion. He was wearing his white shirt and dark-blue nylon Adidas tracksuit bottoms.

'Where *are* we going?'

'Didn't you hear? To Citadel.'

'Don't I even get consulted? Maybe I don't want to go there.'

He frowned at her. 'Why not?'

Ash never backed down and Ruby liked that. He was also looking particularly fit today. She flicked a grin at him and bounced onto the pillion seat.

'Oh, come on then. Let's get going.'

He kicked the starter and they plunged out into the traffic. By now, Ruby was quite confident on the back of the bike. She pulled a scarf across her mouth and nose to filter out the dust and fumes, as she had seen other women passengers do, and wound her arm round Ash's waist. Above them, monopolising the skyline, were the sand-coloured walls and turrets of the old Citadel. The way to it curved upwards along a series of wide, sun-baked avenues, past gaudy tents and littered fairgrounds on Midan Salah al-Din. When they reached the entrance at Bab al-Gabal they left the bike padlocked to the trunk of a struggling sapling and continued on foot, into a walled and crenellated maze of turrets and domes separated by glaring empty spaces that trapped the afternoon's heat. Treading over hot stone and dust-lapped patches of lawn, Ruby began to lag behind Ash.

'Why are we here?' she demanded irritably.

'History. First fort built here, nine hundred years old. By Salah al-Din.'

'Yeah?'

'You know who this is?'

'Should I?'

He frowned at her again. 'You are educated English woman and you know nothing, it seems. He is a great leader and warrior against your Christian Crusaders. You have heard of *Saladin*?'

She sighed. This did ring a faint bell. 'Yeah. Look, I'm crap at history, always was. And geography and maths and biology, you name it. But I'm not at school anymore so it really doesn't matter, does it?'

Ash looked dubious. 'Learning is important. It is a way to make a life better for yourself and your family. You don't believe this?'

Ruby squinted against the light. There was a weight inside these walls that made her feel uncomfortable and Ash's crowding insistence made it worse.

'Yes, I believe it, but that doesn't mean I have to do it.'

He gave her his white crescent of a smile. 'You are funny. And you are very pretty today.'

That was better. 'Am I?'

Ruby had stopped making up her eyes with black lines and dark smudges, and she had also stopped gelling her hair into spikes because she had run out of gel with which to do it. It flopped over her forehead now in a shiny fringe that she clipped on one side to leave her pale forehead bare.

'Yes,' he said. He took her hand and turned it over to look at the veins on the inner side of her wrist. He glanced round to make sure that no one was watching them, then touched the tip of his tongue to the place where her pulse beat.

A second's giddiness made Ruby close her eyes.

'Come on,' Ash whispered at last. 'I show you something.'

The enormous mosque enclosed at the heart of the Citadel could be seen from almost every corner of the city, but from close at hand Ruby thought it was disappointing. The domes were covered in dull tin and the pale walls were stained, and a fat snake of tourist visitors lethargically coiled in front of the huge doors.

'What are we looking at?'

'This, the Mosque of Mohammed Ali.'

Ruby was going to make a rejoinder, but she thought better of it. 'It's pretty big. Who was he?'

'Two hundred years ago, he ruled this country. He made

208

Egypt modern, and he is also responsible for the great massacre of the Mamluks.'

'OK. Tell me. I suppose you will anyway, whether I want you to or not.'

They passed into the parallelogram of purple shade in front of the mosque. Ash stood with one foot up on a broken block of stone.

'The Mamluks were soldiers, born as slaves, with no families, made to gain power by the fight and scheming for the sultan. Mohammed Ali when he came to rule knew he must defeat them, or they will kill him instead. So he is giving a great banquet over there, in the Citadel Palace, and to be his guests five hundred of the most powerful Mamluks come, in their fine robes, up inside the walls here. There is feasting and dancing and everyone is happy. Then the day is ended, and the Mamluks mount their horses and make a procession back down the narrow road, between tall walls, to the al-Azab gate. But Mohammed Ali has ordered the gate to be locked and from the walls above his soldiers fire guns on the Mamluks, and when the men and horses and swords and fine clothes and coloured banners are all fallen in a mess of bodies, the soldiers come in and finish off each one so that a river of blood, from men and horses, runs down like a wave under the gate. Only one of all those fierce Mamluks escapes, by leaping his great horse over the wall and flying away.'

'How horrible.' Ruby could hear the terrified whinnying of horses and the screams of dying men, and the rattle of gunfire in the rocky defile. 'I don't like it here.'

Ash touched her wrist again. 'I feel it too. We will go, but first I must go inside to pray.'

At the mosque doors there were guardians policing the tribes of tourists. Ash and Ruby exchanged their shoes for felt slippers and Ash lightly twitched the sleeves of her shirt to cover her arms. He lifted the folds of her scarf and draped her head, and then they passed inside.

The domes and half-domes soared above them, like the insides of a giant's eggshells studded with thousands of precious stones. Chandeliers and huge glass globes hung from the dim heights, and there were screens of latticed metal and borders of scalloped gold. Ruby stood with her feet together and her hands pressed against her sides.

Ash stepped forward onto the intricate patchwork of rugs that scrolled away in front of them. He knelt and pressed his hands and then his forehead to the floor.

As she waited Ruby felt an absence inside herself, a strange whisper of sensation that was more a negative balance than a physical reality. Surreptitiously she rested the flat of one hand against her belly, but that made no difference. It wasn't hunger. It was more like being thirsty, while knowing at the same time that a river of water wouldn't quench the thirst. Her only belief, ever since she had been old enough to reach for one, and which had been later thoroughly agreed with Jas, was that she didn't want to believe in anything. And yet now she found herself parched with the need for whatever Ash had, for whatever kept his head bowed to the dusty rug.

A pair of tourists passed close beside her, a man and a woman in their fifties, European or even British. The woman had her finger folded as a bookmark inside her guidebook. Something about her, maybe her clothes or a just-perceived hint of perfume, or even the unexpectant set of her features, made Ruby think of her mother. She felt another small pang, an indicator of absence, and she acknowledged that she missed her.

Ash's narrow back arched like a cat's and then he unfolded himself to the vertical once more. They walked out of the mosque and reversed the shoe procedure. In the few minutes that they had been inside, the sun had dropped behind a bank of pale lavender cloud on the western horizon.

'I'm thirsty,' Ruby said.

Across a square paved with uneven blocks of stone, polished by centuries of footsteps, a drinks vendor's little metal cart stood against a low wall. From the child vendor Ash bought two cans of cold Coke, ripped the ring-pull from one and handed it to Ruby. He drank from his. Ramadan was over now.

Ruby cooled her cheek with the beads of condensation from the can and wandered towards the wall. She had been expecting a view, but what she saw made her eyes widen in surprise. Cairo lay spread out beneath them. From this height and distance the jungles of apartment blocks looked desolate and deserted, leaning inwards to each other, concrete towers with empty windows, threaded with twisted metal. The only colours were grey, sand, brown and khaki, with scoops of purple and indigo where the shadows lay. In the far, far distance three tiny triangles toothed the cloud horizon. It was another view of the Pyramids, separated by most of the city from the one Ash had shown her from the top of the hotel. She stared across at them, trying and failing to fit herself into the warp of distance and history. She felt Ash close behind her and turned. Their faces almost collided and she pressed awkwardly against him, finding his mouth with hers.

'Go on, you can kiss me.'

Ash moved an inch away. 'Perhaps not a good place.'

Groups of tourists were being marshalled by their guides. Smaller knots of young Egyptians took photographs of one another and the European couple drifted past, the wife two steps behind her husband. Ruby glanced at the needle minarets against the subsiding sky. In an hour it would begin to get dark.

211

'Do you believe in God, then? Allah, whatever?'

'It is what I must do.'

She was left in doubt whether the compulsion was from piety or social pressure or as an insurance policy.

'Must?'

'Yes, Ruby. This is simple for me, more easy than you think.'

Ash took her arm and they followed the angle of the perimeter wall. To the east of them were the brown ribs of the Muqqatam hills and ahead, stretching north, another landscape of brown diggings and ragged buildings, blistered with a few domes, a low-rise reflection in miniature of the other city.

'What's that?'

'Shall we visit something else?' His face was serious.

Ruby sighed. What she would have liked was to sit or lie down with Ash somewhere quiet and private and have him put his arms round her and press their foreheads together, not even needing to talk, as she and Jas used to do. Since that plainly wasn't going to happen, they might as well pass the time in some other way. She felt out of sympathy with the brutal scale of the day, and no longer disposed to enjoy whatever it brought.

'If you want.'

They went back and unchained the moby. It was a short ride to the sepia walls of the low-rise mirror city they had seen from the heights of the Citadel.

The bike threaded on a narrow dirt road between what looked like very small square-built houses, with arched open doorways and lattice-screened windows. A line of children skipped across in front of them and Ash called a warning, then they came into a paved yard where a flock of long-haired white and brown sheep bumped at a wooden feed trough. Between a pair of dusty acacia trees Ruby saw a high

212

domed canopy sheltering a pair of stone tombs, and to the side of the pillars supporting the canopy there were more stone blocks, the same shape as the houses but smaller, just big enough for one person to lie within. A child's ball and a pink plastic doll, legs askew, lay in the dirt in front of the bike wheel.

'What is this place?' she murmured.

Ash shrugged, carelessness only partly masking an evident anxiety.

'Cities of the Dead.' He grinned, flicking an eyebrow at her. Ruby looked at a broken wall of pink-tinged plaster that was printed all over with child-sized dark-blue hand prints, a charm to ward off the djinns.

All the little houses were tombs. But the whole place was busy with the living, too. There was an old man in a blue *galabiyeh* and a white headcloth, minding the sheep. A little boy sat on a step, stirring the dust with a stick, and his mother looked out of the doorway behind him and tipped a bowl of dirty water into the gutter. There was a tap on the wall beside her and she refilled the bowl and went inside again.

'A place to live,' Ash added.

Ruby kept quiet, waiting and half guessing why he had brought her here.

'My family. You can meet them. Not Nafouz, of course, he is with the taxi.'

He wheeled the bike and they walked down an uneven street of tomb houses. The departing sun left an ash-grey light filtering through the feathery acacia leaves.

They reached an ochre-painted building with a single stone step, none of it very old-looking. Ash led the way and she followed, ducking her head beneath the lintel. Inside there was light from a single electric bulb, a table with an oilcloth, a very old woman sitting with a child in her lap. Ruby stared,

213

trying to make sense of what seemed so unlikely. In the middle of the small space was a raised stone covered with incised inscriptions. It was unmistakably a tomb, and above and around it lived Ash's family.

The old woman and the half-dressed child both held out their hands to Ash.

'Misa' al-khairat' (evening of many good things). The woman beamed and the child scrambled off its grandmother's lap and ran to him. Ash swung it up by the hands and kissed its brown cheeks.

'Habib, habib.'

Then everyone's eyes slid towards Ruby.

Ash said her name and added, my friend. Ruby carefully skirted the tomb, and went to stand in front of Ash's grandmother. Her head was wrapped in a dark cloth, her skin was seamed with wrinkles and as brown as a walnut.

'Ahlan w-sahlan,' she said, with her bird-eyes on Ruby.

'Ahlan biki,' Ruby muttered, as Ash had taught her. She was rewarded with a string of Arabic exclamations and a wide smile. Ash's grandmother folded Ruby's hands between her own two. It was all right, Ruby thought. She couldn't look quite as disconcerted as she felt. Holding the child in one arm, Ash was hunting among the jars and packets that stood on a shelf. Like Jas, she thought, or Ed – searching for something to eat as soon as he came home. This was a home, but the grave drew her eyes. She wanted to stare at it, but thought it would be better to pretend it wasn't there.

A woman came in with a thin blue plastic carrier bag in either hand. There were shops too, then, in the Cities of the Dead.

'Ummi,' Ash said. He went to her and kissed her, and unwound the handles of the plastic bags from her fingers. He dumped the shopping on top of the grave.

Ash's mother was small and thin, with the same dark eyes

as her sons. Ash introduced Ruby and they went through the same greeting, but *Umm* Nafouz (Ruby knew she must call her by the name of her oldest child, Ash had told her that too) was busier and less cordial than the grandmother had been. She turned away quite quickly and began to take bags of flour and tinned food out of the shopping bags. Ash scolded her and moved her to one side, so that he could do it. The child ran between them, laughing and exclaiming.

No one was looking at her now, so Ruby gazed at the room's centrepiece. It had plain stone walls and a slab on top with all the lettering. How many people were buried within, and how long ago? The dead were too close. She looked quickly away again.

Ash's mother was laying out pans and food, preparing to make a meal. There was a gas bottle with two ring burners beside the table, a radio and cassette player on a shelf, and a curtained doorway at the back of the room that must lead to where the family slept.

There was warmth in this place that more logically should have felt cold and gloomy. The child wriggled between her legs and Ash's, and put its hands over its eyes, then lowered them just far enough to be able to peep over the fingertips. She was inviting Ruby to play the game.

Ruby hid her own eyes briefly then exposed them again. 'Boo,' she said and the child laughed. Ruby was quite surprised by this. Usually little kids disliked her.

It was dark outside. She looked quickly at her watch.

'It's half past five. I told Iris six o'clock, remember?'

Ash said, 'You are right. I will take you home.'

Ruby put her hands together and bowed to Ash's mother and grandmother. '*Masa' il-kheer*,' she said. Ash nodded as if he were her schoolteacher.

'*Masa' in-nur*,' the two women replied. The grandmother lifted her hand in a blessing.

215

The child wrapped its arms round Ash's leg and shouted a protest at him. He bent down and whispered something, then took a sweet out of his pocket and popped it into its mouth.

'*Yalla*. Let's go.'

The shepherd and his sheep had gone. Ash wheeled the bike and Ruby walked beside him, unsure what to say. There were lights in many windows of the little houses, people walking by with bags of shopping like *Umm* Nafouz's, and in a beam of light from a doorway a couple of children intently playing a game with a handful of stones. Other tombs had barred doors, windows protected by metal screens. They were dark, guarding their secrets. Crooked alleyways led away in all directions. Ruby remembered how vast the burial areas had looked from up at the Citadel. You could get lost in here, among the dead houses, and never be found again.

He said, 'You are quiet.'

'Yes.'

'You think it is a strange thing.'

'It's only strange . . . to me. That doesn't mean it *is* strange.'

'It is my family tomb. When we were young we came here once every week to visit, to have picnic among our dead, to celebrate the *moulid*. It is not a place of fear for us, but of memory and respect. Then after my father died . . .' Ash shrugged. 'It is a home to live in. And the dead and not-yet dead, we are company all together. Why not? The dead do not harm us, only the alive.'

A much bigger structure loomed ahead of them, a dome and finial outlined against the navy-blue sky.

'See in here,' Ash breathed. He took her by the wrist and they glided through heavy doors into a cold, close atmosphere. It was quiet enough in here, Ruby thought, to hear the dust settle. A shiver began beneath her hairline and ran the length of her spine. Ash clicked his cigarette lighter and a fragile nimbus of light spread around them. There were more tombs here, but these were built in tier upon tier up to an invisible ceiling, carved and decorated over every inch with patterns and lettering and painted in red ochre and cerulean blue. Here and there, in the flicker of the lighter, was a glint of gold.

'Mamluk tombs,' Ash said. He traced the line of a stone wreath. 'The stone carver, once he finished . . . kkkk.' He mimed a chop at the wrist of the hand holding the lighter. 'This work done, finish, no more carving for other masters.'

Their eyes travelled upwards, over the wealth of pattern. High above was a flattened arch picked out in flaking gold.

The flame died and left them standing hip to hip in the blackness. Ash's hands cupped Ruby's face and his lips brushed her cheek as he whispered to her, 'You were polite to my family. Like a good Egyptian girl. My mother will not be so unhappy.'

They stood close together. Ash was warm and he tasted of cigarettes and spearmint chewing gum. Light spilled inside Ruby, a brightness so easy and careless that she wanted to laugh. It was partly to do with wanting Ash and his narrow, brown body, of course it was, and she was surprised by how much she did want him, but it was also the opposite of the negative balance that had troubled her in the mosque of Mohammed Ali. There was a positive here, glimpsed in the tomb house of Ash's family and in the way that life continued among the remains of other lives. It was very strong in Ash himself.

'Was this what you meant, when I asked you if you believed in God and you said *it is what I must do*?'

Ruby's hand travelled through an unseen arc, to take in the Mamluk tombs and the Dead Cities and the people who had to live there.

To believe would be an explanation, a system, and a life-line. Otherwise there was only dust.

217

'God is good. He takes care of each of us.'

'I wish I believed that.'

Ash laughed. 'Infidel.'

Ruby pressed her head against his shoulder, ran her hands down the curve of his back to the hollow above his hip bones. He was beautiful.

'Sit down here. We will smoke one cigarette and then I take you back to your grandmother's house.'

He guided her to a ledge that ran around the base of the nearest tomb. The lighter clicked again.

'But, you know, it is not a free ride. God does not do that. I work hard and go to school, English, and I hope I will learn computers. I told you this, learning is important. Nafouz and I, we must look after our mother and brothers and sisters and we will live in a better place. But for now . . .' His shoulder twitched against hers. '. . . For now, we can enjoy too sometimes. Why not?'

Ruby laughed. She still felt the lightness inside her. 'Yeah.'

Ash was vital, springing with energy. He wasn't bored or disgusted with everything, as she quite often felt in London, and he was different from Jas. Jas used to lie on his bed for days at a time, smoking weed and listening to music.

'So now you have made a tour, eh? Citadel, Mamluk tomb, my family.'

'Yeah.' The shock of the tomb houses still reverberated. She needed some time to absorb what she had seen.

'Ruby, it is not possible for everyone to live in a house the same as your grandmother.'

'I know that,' Ruby said.

'Now. It is time. I take you back.'

'Will we go out again soon?'

'Of course we will.'

They rode back to Iris's door. When she looked up at the high wall, with not a light showing anywhere, Ruby thought

218

of Iris sitting alone inside with only the two old people to look after her. Ash's grandmother seemed the luckier, with her children and grandchildren around her and the dead too, everyone together.

Why was Iris cut off from her own daughter, and Lesley from her mother?

She would ask, Ruby decided. She would find out.

She scrambled off the bike and kissed Ash goodnight.

'*Ma' as salama*,' she said. *Go in safety*.

'Good,' he crowed. 'Soon you speak Arabic as well as me.'

CHAPTER NINE

The child has been to the cemeteries. As we are drinking our tea together she tells me about it and I can see that the experience has shocked her.

'People live right on top of the graves. In the little tomb houses. There are sinks and electric lights and kids' toys, just like anywhere else.'

Ruby's appearance is changing. This morning her face is bare of the black paint and most of the studs and metalwork, and without this angry disguise she is becoming more familiar, as if history is seeping under her skin and bringing family contours to the surface. I can see something of my mother in the set of her mouth, and I notice for the first time that she has Lesley's hazel eyes. She still tries to be hardboiled, but I am beginning to see more of the underlying innocence. She is even swearing less than she did when she first came.

I tell her, 'The cemeteries are poor areas, but they are quite respectable. There are schools, sewerage, clinics. Further on towards Muqqatam are real slums. Don't go there, please.'

'Ash said the one they live in is his family tomb.'

'That's right, it would be.'

'But . . .' She shivers a little. 'All the dead people.'

'Are you afraid of the dead? Of death?'

Of course she is; she is young.

'No. Well, not of ghosts or . . . djinns. But I wouldn't like to sleep the night in a cemetery.' Her face changes, a shiver passing over it like wind across still water. 'I don't want to die.'

'Someone close to you has, haven't they?'

I was expecting to hear about a family dog, or perhaps even a school friend in a car accident. Her answer surprises me.

Ruby tells the story quickly, without embellishment, but her mechanical delivery hardly disguises the depths of horror. The last image of the crumpled boy with his head in a pool of dark blood will stay with me, too. I am filled with concern for her.

'Ruby, who knows about this?'

'I told Ash. But then I felt bad, like I was using Jas's death to get sympathy or attention or something.'

'No one else? Not your mother or father?'

'No.'

'Why not?'

'Why didn't I tell them that Jas was on one then fell off a balcony and died?'

'That would be the normal expectation, I suppose. You witness a tragedy, the violent death of a young man who is a close friend. Your mother would comfort you, wouldn't she? She would want to do that.'

Ruby looks me straight in the eye.

'You didn't.'

She is very sharp, and I deserve that stinging observation.

'No.'

'The thing is, Lesley and Andrew didn't really know about Jas. He wasn't the kind of person they would go for. Don't get me wrong, there wasn't anything bad about him. He was kind, never wanted to do anything to hurt people, and he was funny, but he wasn't plugged in to things most people care about, like money and jobs. I suppose some people might have thought he was a bit messed up. Lesley would have done.'

Ruby sighs. 'She's my mother and all that, and you know how that works.'

Her expressive hands sketch in the air, miming a smooth ball and then suddenly turning into claws, raking the layer of space trapped between them.

'Lesley likes everything to be in order. She's really controlling. I suppose it's partly her way of keeping us safe, looking after us. But it can be a real pain. For example we've got some glass shelves in the kitchen at home, and all the mugs and milk jugs and stuff are kept there. But they have to be in a straight line and they have to be *plain white*. You know? They're just mugs for drinking tea out of, but if there's a patterned or coloured one it has to be kept out of sight in a cupboard. You can't really drop someone like Jas in the middle of a world like that.

'So I kept him separate. I liked having him all to myself, anyway. I'd just go off from Will and Fiona's place and stay with him. He had a room in a squatted house, but he'd made it nice. He'd decorated it with postcards and pictures of flowers and leaves and trees, cut out of magazines, stuck all over the walls, on top of each other, so the whole room looked like a garden that had exploded. We'd just lie and look at it. He used to say, "It's just the two of us, babe. Just you and me. This is our Garden of Eden." I loved that. But then, after he . . . died, it was like he'd never been there. That was really hard. I didn't want to think that he was so close to nothing.' Her voice sinks to a whisper. 'As if I was the only memorial he had.'

Now I can see the shape of ideas crossing her mind. I am sad to think that Ruby might have been allowed to believe that she is stupid, because she is anything but.

'Are you afraid of death?' she asks.

'No. Nor will you be, I hope, when you get to my age. But I am afraid of what might intervene between now and then.'

Her hands move, trying to catch a slippery shape in the air.

'I know. Of forgetting.' Her eyes flick briefly towards the open door of my bedroom where Xan's photograph stands on the table next to the bed. 'Has anyone close to you died?'

'Almost everyone,' I say drily.

She laughs and then guiltily catches herself, reckoning that amusement is inappropriate in this context. What she is trying to do, as gently as she knows how, is to give me the opportunity to talk about Xan. She's curious about him on her own behalf, but it's also part of our odd bargain. I am supposed to reminisce and she will remember for me.

But it is *hard*.

Ruby put it well. I wanted to be the memorial, not to Xan himself because his family and his friends and his regiment remembered him too, but to our love. I had nothing else of him, and for a long time looked for nothing else.

For sixty years, the best part of a lifetime, I have jealously guarded these memories. I never spoke of them to my husband, or to my daughter, and I am aware that that was an act of selfishness. Lesley always knew, with the inarticulate, visceral intuition of a child, that I withheld myself from her. Even by the time she had learned to speak, the distance between us was almost palpable.

And if I believed that I might be punished for what I have failed to do, or believed in anything except the random cruelty of life, I would agree that the slow burial of my memories

223

under the desert sand of forgetful old age is an exquisitely appropriate form of punishment.

Ruby is watching me, trying to work out where I am, waiting for me to say something. I have forgotten what we were talking about a minute ago.

In the end she prompts me, 'I met Ash's mother and his grandmother.'

Yes. The cemeteries.

'Ash's grandfather must be buried there,' she adds.

'Perhaps.'

Silence falls again while we separately speculate.

The desert is one immense tomb, unmarked.

'I can see in a way that must be quite comforting. You know, having everyone really close around you, dead and alive, the family all together. With no – what's the word – taboo about it, like we have. And I suppose you don't feel lonely, either.'

She is making a direct comparison, Ash's grandmother with her own. Yes, I have been lonely. And I am so used to it that it is only the lessening of loneliness, through her company, that has made me aware of it. I have not always been so brusque, in my words or in my judgements: this is what too much solitude does. You forget how to be tactful and gentle. But Ruby doesn't seem to mind and I'm glad of this.

She leans forward, tilting her chair closer to mine. 'Iris? What happened? Why don't you and Lesley get along?'

I want to answer her, but the words and reasons and recollections jumble together and then swirl away, out of my reach . . .

. . . No. That won't do. It would be easier to take refuge in the windy spaces of forgetfulness, but this truth is still sharp enough in my memory and I have to admit it: I didn't want to be a mother. Not then, not to Gordon's child, not to Lesley.

Maybe I never was cut out to be anyone's mother. Even if everything else had been different, my lack of maternal inclination might have been the same.

I was a good doctor. I loved my work and surely I must have been good at it. To one or two people, maybe, I was a good friend. Can't that be enough?

'I think Lesley and I respect each other,' I say.

Ruby feels rebuffed, I can tell. Silence spreads through the room as I try to work out a way to undo this.

Outside, the sky is overcast. Winter is coming, and it brings a damp chill that seeps through Cairo like mist off the Nile. I don't mind the heat of summer, spending the days as I do within these thick walls or in the tiled shade of the garden, but nowadays I am like Faria – I feel the cold.

I try to ward off the automatic shiver. Ruby is here, and I can imagine how the silence in this old house must be dispiriting for her. Ideas suddenly jostle in my head and I clap my hands, making her jump.

'When did you get here?'

She looks startled. 'What? Do you mean, when did I arrive? Um, it was twelve days ago.'

'Is that all? It seems longer than that.'

'Does it? I mean, I don't want to get in the way or anything, just say if I am.'

'In the way? Of course you are not in the way. I am only thinking that you have been in my house for nearly two weeks and I haven't taken you anywhere, or shown you anything except for that one outing with your friends, and it is high time that I did. I promised your mother that I would educate you.'

I clap my hands again, louder this time.

'We'll go out now. We'll have an excursion. I know, we'll go to Giza.' The idea develops its own momentum. I am overtaken by a longing to leave the house and walk a different

225

route, away from the repetitive circuit of my thoughts. 'We'll drive out there, visit the Pyramids and then watch the sun set over the desert. What do you think?'

'Drive out there? Nafouz and Ash aren't here today. That was last week, when we went to Groppi's, remember?'

I stand up. Ruby picks up the blanket as it falls from my knees and folds it over the back of my chair.

'Will you call Mamdooh? Tell him I will need the car.'

She follows me into my bedroom. In the cupboard hangs my warm deerskin coat.

'You have a car?'

I am thinking of the sky fading to the colour of amethysts and the way that you have to steer a car when the wheels turn wayward in loose sand.

'Of course I do. Hurry up, or we will miss the sunset.'

Mamdooh's face was dark.

'Mum'reese, it is not a good idea. For Miss, I can arrange to make a visit with a guide who will speak English. Tomorrow, or even better the next day.'

Ruby followed Mamdooh through the kitchen, both of them in Iris's wake. He had given her one furious glare, indicating that all this must be her fault, and Ruby had done her best to signal back that it was nothing to do with her.

'Where is the key? Mamdooh?'

'It is here.' Auntie stood aside and Mamdooh took a set of keys out of a drawer in one of the old cream-painted cupboards.

'Very good. Come on.'

Auntie picked up a duster and polishing rag. In a small procession, with Ruby at the back, they passed through a door she had never seen opened before. It led from the kitchen into a small scullery, very small but high, with a tiny window let into the thick wall far above their heads. Mamdooh slid

226

several bolts and opened another door. Ruby saw that it led into a cobbled alley at the back of the house. The blank walls out here were scabbed and blistered, and a thin trickle of grey water ran down the central gutter. The smell of sewage was powerful.

Iris stepped over the gutter and stood expectantly beside a pair of wooden doors secured with a chain and padlocks. Mamdooh very slowly went about the business of unlocking and withdrawing the chain. Finally he folded back the doors.

There was faint scurry in the dim interior, unmistakably a rat making for safety in the darker recesses of what must once have been a barn. There were wooden feed troughs along one wall, and a cobwebbed harness hanging from a peg.

And there was a car.

Auntie moved first. With her bunched-up duster she made a little swipe over the bonnet. Under the thick coat of Cairo dust and gritty sand, it was just possible to tell that the car had once upon a time been black.

Iris looked mystified. She opened the driver's door and leaned into the interior, dust rising in little puffs under her fingers as she twisted the steering wheel.

'Not any insurance, not any service, oil, *benzene*,' Mamdooh muttered. 'Look, tyres all flat.'

Ruby wandered round to the back and rubbed the rear insignia plate clean. Even though it was ancient, the car seemed quite familiar. It was a Volkswagen Beetle, not so very different from the new one owned by Lesley in which Ruby had learned to drive.

'Mum had one of these.' She smiled as she came round to the front again.

'What?'

'A Beetle. Until last year, then she got an Audi.'

Now Mamdooh stood back with his fists clenched on his hips. 'It is not possible to drive this car.'

227

Iris gently closed the door again. 'I bought it in the seventies, when I was living in Swakopmund, from a German dentist called Werner Esch. He was going back to live in Europe but he didn't want to ship the car home, and he gave me a good price. When I moved up here to Cairo I drove all the way, and everything I wanted to bring with me fitted into here.' Absently she patted the hood, her fingertips leaving little marks like the blurred footprints of birds.

Auntie had been rubbing the chrome door handle but her eyes were watering from the dust and she coughed into a fold of her white headscarf. Reluctantly Iris stepped away from the car although her hand still stretched out as if she didn't want to relinquish the memory and promise of adventure that went with it.

'We'll get a taxi instead.'

'Mum-reese, it is too late today. When you get to Giza it is dark.'

'I have been out after dark in my life, you know.'

'Miss will not see anything.'

Iris's eyes glittered. He had outflanked her, but she wouldn't be deflected. 'We'll go somewhere else, then. Ruby, tell me, where would you like to go?'

Without waiting for an answer she clicked her fingers. 'The museum. We'll go to the museum and that will give you some history before we go out to Giza. I don't suppose you know any, do you? We'd better be quick about it.'

Within half an hour a black-and-white taxi, much newer than Nafouz's, circled the vast traffic roundabout of Midan Tahrir and drew up outside the dark-pink block of the museum. Iris sat up in the front next to the driver and Mamdooh, who had insisted on coming with them, was squeezed in the back next to Ruby.

In the mornings the front of the building was choked with

228

tourists and their guides and buses, but at the end of the day there was only a handful of stragglers and postcard sellers loitering in the dusk. As they swept through the gates they made an unusual threesome, but it was Iris with her stiff back and profile like a face on a coin who drew the attention. Ruby slouched with her hands in her trouser pockets. She didn't care for the wholesome, family-day-out aspect of most of the museums she had been dragged to at home, but at least this outing was a diversion. As they reached the doors she was even experiencing a flutter of mild interest.

Mamdooh negotiated for tickets, then they walked inside.

Ruby tilted her head to look upwards. Dim galleries rose round a central well crowned with a span of murky glass. Radiating away from where she stood were tall wooden cases filled, heaped, overflowing with a wild profusion of exhibits. She drifted down the wood-and-glass avenues, gazing at the displays. There were tiny carved wooden figures from tombs and huge imperious pharaonic statues. There were primitive boats and earthenware pots, broken shards and scratched hieroglyphs and curled papyrus, massive jewellery in gold and cornelian and glass, amulets and bracelets, and humble leather sandals that looked as if they had been discarded only a day ago. The artefacts were all dusty and most of the labels were written in scratchy, faded Arabic, but for Ruby this only added to the appeal. This was a museum, not a museum experience. It was rich and darkly disordered and abundant, and tantalising because she didn't know enough to begin to comprehend it. It was a vast collection of innumerable collections, a multi-magnification of her own one-time passion that made her hungry and awestruck at the same time.

Her breath fogged the glass as she stared at a swarm of bizarre brooches in the shape of golden flies.

Mamdooh shuffled and huffed at her shoulder.

'Miss, to come this way please.'

Go away, she wanted to shout. But Iris was beckoning to her too. At the far end of a long vista of columns and crammed niches a phalanx of cleaning women with buckets and mops were swilling the stone floors.

'Where are we going?' Ruby asked.

'Upstairs.'

Reluctantly she followed them up shallow stone steps to the first-floor gallery, all the time wishing that she could have this treasury to herself without the distraction of Mamdooh and Iris.

There was a crowd of visitors in one room, and past the craning heads she caught one brief glimpse of the serene funerary mask of the boy king.

'Here?' she pointed.

Iris shook her head. They came to a side gallery, with rows of polished wooden benches in the ante-room.

'I will wait here,' Mamdooh announced.

The room beyond was hushed and dimly lit. The mummified remains of the royal pharaohs lay in sealed glass boxes.

Ruby crept along the line, lingering beside each enclosed mummy. Here were a queen's dark ringlets and hooked nose, here was a skull showing through skin like dried leather, long yellow teeth bedded in the jawbone, a withered arm circled with a coil of gold. Iris moved in step with her, murmuring the names: *Seti I, Ramses II, Tuthmosis IV.* Some of them looked as if they were merely asleep, others were withered and collapsed, a bundle of remains more touching than macabre. What struck Ruby most was that these were just people, with wrists and nostrils and fingernails. Outside in the halls were the decorated sarcophagi and tomb ornaments, but here were men and women. They had lived and known glory, and then they were dead. She was alive and they were not, and nothing but a heartbeat separated her from them.

She murmured to herself, *the skull beneath the skin*. She

didn't know where the line came from, but she had heard or read it somewhere.

She understood why Iris had brought her here. The dead were just the dead, neither awful nor remarkable. History separated out these individuals and preserved their names where others were obliterated forever, but there was no real difference between this hushed room and the tomb house where Ash's family lived.

I watch Ruby as she tiptoes past the glass cases.

This is death in formal guise, like in the Cities of the Dead. Inevitably it makes me think of its antithesis, tumbled and shocking and finally forgotten in the sand.

Xan was away, out of my reach. As I had promised I would, I went to the hospital and up the stairs to the ward full of carved men.

'Hello,' I said quietly to Albie Noake. The upper half of his face had more colour in it now and he was propped higher against his pillows. Within his reach lay a notepad with a pencil attached to it by a piece of string. His eyes followed me as I moved a chair to the head of the bed, where I could sit with my mouth close to his ear. By the time I put my hand over his where it rested on the bedsheet I knew that he knew what I had come to say.

'Mr Ridley died without gaining consciousness. I'm so sorry. I wish Xan had been here to tell you.'

Briefly, his eyes closed. I wondered how much they had seen and been through together, Albie and Xan and Private Ridley.

Then Albie's hand twitched beneath mine and he indicated with a tilt of his head that I was to pass him the notepad. He wrote carefully and a bead of sweat appeared on his forehead, then ran slowly down his temple, like a tear that was otherwise denied.

Thank you for teling me, he had written. *Poor old Ridley.*

I lifted my head and met his eyes again. There was a look in them that begged me to stay and talk about life and hope, anything that was nothing to do with dying in the desert.

'I'll sit here and chat to you for a bit, shall I?'

At first I stammered and started down avenues that all seemed to lead back to the war, so I would have to retrace my steps and cast around for a different topic. In desperation I told him about the letter I had had from my mother, and that led on to Evie, my aunt by marriage, and her three small children who played in the afternoons among the hydrangea bushes in my mother's garden. Albie listened, nodding and looking past me as if he could see the billows of dead leaves whirled up and then trodden underneath skidding gumboots, and the footprints in mud whiskered with lank grass, and hear the rooks cawing in the elm trees along the wall of the churchyard. Maybe he came from a village not dissimilar to my parents', and my irrelevant mumbling helped him to remember it. Or maybe he came from the East End, and Hampshire meant nothing to him except a blanking-out of much worse.

I talked until I forgot he couldn't answer.

'Do you have children, Albie?'

He picked up the notepad. *No, not married.* And *Missed my chance with you! Mr Molynew beat me to it.*

'I bet there's a girl or two waiting for you at home.'

There sending me back soon on a hospital ship.

'When? Albie, that's good news. They'll repair your jaw, they can do all kinds of amazing surgery nowadays. You'll be as good as new.'

That was what Ruth had said to the soldier with no legs who wanted to dance.

We'll see. Will you come again before?

'Of course I will. I'll come every day, if you can bear it.'

I can. Thanks.

He looked tired, and he made no objection when I took the notepad out of his hand and awkwardly tried to settle his pillows.

'Good night, Albie. See you tomorrow.'

I hadn't seen Ruth, but she came up behind me as I left the ward. We stood at the top of the stairs, looking down at the comings and goings of nurses and visitors across the stone-floored entrance hall.

'I told Albie that his friend died.'

'How did he take it?'

'Stoically.'

Ruth nodded. 'They are almost always stoical. I wish sometimes that the men would cry or show their feelings in some way. Such terrible things have happened to them. They've been brave enough already.'

Thinking of the quiet ward full of men with their hideous wounds, I could only agree with her.

'At least you're doing something to help them.'

'It isn't much. Look, as it happens Daphne's off this afternoon and I'm going home in an hour. Would you like to come out to the flat and have some food with us? It won't be anything very grand, I'm afraid.'

It occurred to me that Ruth must think I was grand. I blushed and mumbled that I'd love to come.

'Fine. About half past eight?'

I told her that I would look forward to it very much.

When I was with Xan I felt utterly happy and complete, and there was something similar with Ruth Macnamara. In their company I felt the rightness of the world and of myself in it, more than I did with Sarah and Faria, far more than I had ever done at any other time in my life.

After their slow tour of the mummies they came back to the doorway. When Iris raised her eyebrows in enquiry Ruby

233

took one more glance back over her shoulder at the quiet figures.

'Thanks,' she said.

Mamdooh's bulk rose up from the bench. They made their way down the stairs once more. The women with mops had almost reached the main doorway and the floors behind them were shiny with damp. The museum was about to close for the night.

'I think we can go back home now,' Iris announced. Mamdooh summoned a taxi from the waiting line.

Back at Iris's house, Ruby helped her off with her coat. Iris's face had gone papery with fatigue, but there was a gleam in her eyes.

'You were interested in that, weren't you?'

'Yes.'

'I thought you would be,' she crowed.

On impulse, Ruby took her grandmother in her arms and hugged her. At first Iris held herself rigid, pulling away, but then she relaxed. Ruby felt how light she was, like a leaf, with the bones of her shoulders as tiny as a bird's.

'I loved it.' She planted a kiss on top of Iris's head. 'And death, after all, when it's right there it doesn't seem too huge and terrible to let into your mind. That was what you meant, wasn't it?'

Iris went to bed early, fussed away into her room by Auntie. Ruby wandered into her own bedroom and took out Jas's CD. She lay down on top of her covers and thought about him, and for the first time since the night at the top of the tower block it wasn't his crumpled shape in a halo of blood that superimposed itself over all the others. She saw him in his exploded garden of cut-out flowers instead, and heard his slow mumbling voice explaining to her just what the music meant.

The first ping of a pebble at the window startled her, at

the second she scrambled up and looked out. She could just make out the upturned oval of Ash's face framed in the white collar of his shirt.

She slipped silently down the stairs and palmed the heavy front door key from where Mamdooh always left it, on a little ledge concealed by a wall hanging. Catching her lip between her teeth with the effort of concentration, she slid the key into the lock and turned it, wincing at the way the silence amplified the smallest scrape and click. Mamdooh and Auntie were almost certainly already in their beds, but it was all too easy to imagine how Mamdooh might massively materialise in a doorway and catch her in the act of breaking out. The door swung slowly open, the ancient hinges faintly protesting, and there stood Ash, beckoning her out.

Grinning at him, Ruby put one finger to her lips. She pushed the door shut as carefully as she had opened it and locked it behind her. Then she linked hands with Ash and they ran away down the alley towards the open street. Once they had rounded the corner he nudged her up against a wall and kissed her, briefly sliding his hands inside her shirt. Catching her breath, she let her head fall back against the wall. The crescent moon at the top of a minaret lay like a black shadow of the real moon against the dark-blue sky.

'Nafouz is waiting for us,' he whispered.

'Where are we going?'

'To a club, just like you go to in London.'

Ruby's eyebrows peaked in surprise. 'Lead me to it,' she said and laughed.

The taxi was parked close to the bazaar. Nafouz nudged the door open and Ruby fell in beside him with Ash pressing close on the other side. The car skidded away. Nafouz's teeth flashed at her. He was wearing a leather jacket over a T-shirt with *Armani* written across the front.

'Hello, Ruby, my good friend.'

'Hello, Nafouz. I hear we are going clubbing.'

'You are right. How is your grandmother?'

'Asleep.'

They all laughed as the taxi sped eastwards, towards the low, solid line of the Muqqatam hills.

The club was housed in a nondescript slab of a concrete building overlooking the burnt-orange and neon-white glitter of the city. Inside was a packed crowd, dancing under a layer of cigarette smoke that fumed blue in the lights. Ash took Ruby's hand and drew her after him.

Ruby had seen nothing like this in Cairo. Here were throngs of made-up Egyptian girls in tiny spandex skirts and spangled tops that showed their midriffs and most of their breasts. There were boys in leather and backpackers in braids and combats and Jamaicans with dreads and singlets, and a DJ working the decks up on a low podium. There was the same smell as in all clubs; perfumed sweat and greasy hair and the mineral tang of adrenalin. It was utterly familiar and at the same time Ruby felt completely out of place with a naked face and the long-sleeved cotton shirt over loose jeans that had become her Cairo uniform.

'You might have *told* me,' she hissed in Ash's ear.

'You are most beautiful girl in the place, no competition.'

Nafouz's hands already spanned the bare milk-chocolate waist of a girl with her hair piled up on top of her head. She slid her hips up against him and at the same time craned her neck away as he tried to kiss her. Ash flicked a glance at Ruby and led her on through the crowd to the back of the room where there was a bar. He bought a bottle of Coca-Cola and put it into Ruby's hand, then from the deep pocket at his hip he produced a bottle identical except that it was uncapped, and had been temporarily resealed with a whittled cork. He bit the cork out and spat it aside, took a swig from the bottle and passed it to Ruby.

The gulp she took made her cough. It was neat whisky.

'Hey. I thought you were a good Muslim boy and didn't drink.'

'Every man is a contradiction.'

Ruby started laughing, and took another drink of whisky. The DJ was bringing the crowd up, and through the mass of dancers she saw Nafouz also tilting a Coke bottle to his mouth. With Ash, she merged willingly into the mass and the music. The noise and the press of unknown bodies swallowed them up.

Much later, with their hair sticking in thick hanks to their foreheads and their clothes soaking, they pushed their way up some steps and along a narrow concrete corridor, and emerged into the darkness. Out here the music was no more than a murmur of vibration in the skull and the fingertips, like the onset of pain. Ash stumbled and put his hand out to a fence post to steady himself. The first whisky-Coke bottle had been emptied and Nafouz had produced another. As he barged towards them it was clear that he had downed all of his first bottle.

'Let's sit,' Ash muttered. They walked a few yards and found an angle of broken wall enclosing some flat-topped rock. The ground was littered with cans and broken glass with shreds of plastic flagging the thorn bushes. The wind that sliced down the gully made Ruby shiver as the sweat cooled on her skin, and the shelter of the wall was welcome. They sat down on the rock with their backs propped against it and Ruby cupped her hands over Ash's as he flicked his lighter and lit a cigarette. She took it from him and he lit another for himself.

'Funny,' she said thoughtfully. 'It's like another place in there, a different city.'

'Like London?'

'Well, no. Not very.'

237

She didn't want it to be anything like London. The carpet of lights beneath them was Cairo, it was enticing and exotic, and the inside of a club banging with dance music was not. To cover the surprising, slight feeling of disillusionment she slid closer to Ash. She rested her mouth against his neck and her hand crept across his thigh, and after a second he shifted position and came closer, his mouth finding hers. There was whisky on his breath. Ruby closed her eyes and began to let go. It felt warm and consoling to be touched and stroked, Ash was beautiful and she liked him, and he had been kind to her. In a similar situation at home she would have expected to have had sex with him days ago. Of course she would.

She undid the zip of his trousers. Everything was fine there. When he didn't make the corresponding move she undid the buttons of her own jeans and lifted her hips, encouraging him.

Ash tilted upwards on his elbows, looked down at her and sighed.

'Ruby, I am not going to do this.'

Surprise made her jerk backwards and the back of her head hit the wall.

'Fuck,' she murmured and rubbed it with her free hand. 'Why not?'

'I think it is not right.'

'You don't fancy me.' This was startling. She was used to trading elements of herself as a powerful currency, the dollar standard, with everyone from boys she met in clubs to Will. She had been doing it since she was fifteen. Only Jas had been different.

'Yes, I do. Do not be stupid.'

'Well, come on then. *I* want to.' She tried to smile saucily at him, but her lips seemed to get stuck.

'No.'

'What's the matter with you?'

He seized her wrist, hard, then turned it over and with infinite gentleness kissed the thin skin where the pulse beat.

'I like you too much.'

'Right. Wasn't doing it with me what you were after, you and Nafouz, when we first met?'

Ash said angrily, 'Nafouz is not me. And yes, at first, all right. Everyone knows European girls, English girls, they will make love to Egyptian boys, it doesn't matter to them. Egyptian girls are not like that.'

Ruby stabbed a finger towards the concrete block. 'What about all of them?'

'They are not out here, are they? Most of them, their brothers are in there, their cousins, friends, people who know them all their lives. They come out, to dress up, dance, maybe have a drink or two, even, if they think their fathers will not know about it. But not to do this.'

'I see.'

'I think you do not.' He took her face between his hands, forced her to look at him. 'Before, you were just a tourist girl. Now I know you, you are Ruby to me. Better than rubies. Perhaps I love you.'

Ruby let out a disbelieving hiss of laughter from between her clenched teeth. She felt rejected, but at the same time another thought dawned on her.

Perhaps what he said was true.

It was possible that they were now dealing in another currency altogether and she didn't have to trade herself in the old one. Perhaps, like Jas, Ash was going to be different.

'Why do you not believe me, Ruby?'

'If you're saying it, OK, then I do believe you. I don't know why you would love me, that's all. Anyway, boys usually say that to get you to shag them, not as a reason for not doing it.'

'I took you to visit my family,' Ash said, hurt. 'Did you

not understand? My mother said to me, "Who is this girl?" and I tell her the truth, "I am not sure, but she is important" and so you are. Why would I not love you?'

She sat in the circle of Ash's arms and stared at the ground beyond their feet. The shards of glass had begun to reflect a cold grey glow like polished steel. The eastern quarter of the sky was turning grey too. In another hour it would be dawn.

'You can do what you want, I suppose,' she muttered. And then, because the lack of grace in that was so audible, she turned her face against the warmth of his neck and inhaled the scent of skin and whisky. 'I'm glad we went to your place, right? I've thought about it a lot. There's no reason why your mum should take to me on first sight, but she'll probably get used to it. If you want to go on seeing me, that is.'

'I do,' he said, as solemnly as a vow.

Ruby smiled. 'All right. If you're not going to shag me, we could just have a cuddle.'

'*Make love*,' he corrected her.

'Whatever, yeah.'

He took off his jacket and spread it over their shoulders, a shred of a blanket. Then they lay back with their arms round each other, Ruby's chin in the hollow of his shoulder, the length of their bodies pressed together. She made a small contented noise, deep in her throat, and let her eyes close.

'There,' Ash said softly.

When she opened her eyes again, the sky had turned from midnight blue to pearl grey. She sat up, swallowing a yawn and frowning at the taste in her mouth. The lights beneath them were dimming, and as she watched a whole orange ribbon was extinguished.

'We have to go,' Ash said. They stood up stiffly and linked their cold hands together.

The doors of the club were locked and only a handful of

cars and mopeds remained in the square of weed-burst asphalt that formed the car park. The taxi was there, but they had to make a tour between the other cars and then down the blank concrete side of the building before they found Nafouz. He was sitting on a rusty oil drum, his hands hanging loose between his knees and his head bent. A hank of his black hair fell forward like a dead animal's pelt.

Ash darted over and shook him roughly by the shoulder. Nafouz's head lolled like a puppet's before he managed to hoist it upright. It was obvious that he was very drunk. Ash shouted a stream of Arabic at him as Nafouz got uncertainly to his feet, and if they hadn't supported him by taking hold of an arm apiece he would have fallen over. They half dragged and half carried him across the waste ground to the taxi.

'He can't drive,' Ruby said. 'Get his keys. You'll have to.'

Ash staggered a little under his brother's weight as he fumbled through the pockets of his leather jacket. Nafouz's bloodshot eyes missed focusing on him. The keys emerged in Ash's fingers and between them they forced open the rear passenger door and bundled him inside. Nafouz tipped slowly sideways until his cheek rested on the torn plastic seat.

'I have not learned to drive a taxi,' Ash said.

'Why not?'

He angled his head, embarrassed. 'It takes money. For Nafouz, there is driving. For me, school.'

'I see. So we either leave him here and walk it, stay here with him until he sobers up, or I drive. Right?'

'You know how to drive?'

Just in time, she stopped herself just from saying *of course*. In fact, she wasn't certain that she could actually take this vehicle through the anarchy of Cairo traffic, but the opportunity had presented itself to save the situation and show Ash that she could do something. *Go on*, a voice murmured in her head. A voice she had heard often enough before.

'Yeah.' She held out her hand, and after a second he handed over the keys. 'You know the way? You'll have to direct me.'

'*Inshallah*.'

But they were already leaping into the front seats. Ruby prodded the key into the ignition, stirred the flabby gear-stick to check they were in neutral and started the engine. She reversed the car furiously in a spray of grit and then with a grinding of gears she searched for first, found it, and the car bucked forward. The metal fencing and the gates flew past them, and ahead the pale ribbon of road unwound down through the hills towards the city.

'Go slower,' Ash shouted.

By way of an answer Ruby straightened her arms, braced her hands on the wheel and trod hard on the accelerator. The first bend was sharp and turned sharper, doubling into a hairpin. She braked too hard on the crown and almost lost it, but by fighting with the wheel she kept the car on the road. They rounded the corner in a squeal of brakes and pinging gravel.

'Let's get back before we bump into the law.' She laughed at Ash.

'Let us just get back, please.'

It was easy enough where there was no traffic, but soon they were on a freeway mounted on concrete stilts where a steady flow of speeding trucks and cars built up. At a junction she forgot to drive on the right and a blare of horns made her jump and swerve so hard that the car rocked on its axles. Nafouz shifted and groaned in the back seat. It was almost daylight.

They came into the city, down avenues lined with tower blocks and measured out with huge advertisement hoardings. The drive she had made from the airport with Nafouz seemed long, long ago. Even in the dawn, the traffic here was the usual grinding, hooting maelstrom and Ruby hunched forward in her seat, trying to follow Ash's directions and

242

concentrating on not hitting anything. Or at least not too hard. At last they came down Sharia el Gheish and passed through the old city walls.

'I know where we are,' Ruby shouted. She banged one fist on the wheel. 'See? We made it.'

'Thanks be to Allah for all his goodness.'

Ahead of them were the impenetrable alleys of Khan al-Khalili.

'Where now? Which way?'

'Wait. Stop here. Here, in this place.' Ash jabbed his finger at a space across the kerb in front of a shuttered shop. 'This is my friend's. We will leave the car here.'

Ruby swung the wheel to the accompaniment of frenzied hooting and they bumped to a halt an inch from a concrete bollard. The taxi coughed and stalled.

'How did I do?' she beamed.

Ash passed a hand across his face, dragging his jaw downwards into a disbelieving gape. Then he very carefully got out. Nafouz roused himself and half sat up. His face had turned a strange, livid grey.

Ruby jumped out. 'He's going to throw up in a minute.'

Ash flung the door open and hauled at his brother's shoulders until his head hung out of the car. 'I am ashamed. I am very sorry that you see him this way.'

'Ash, it's not the first time I've seen someone drunk. Won't be the last, either. Does he often get like this?'

Ash sighed. 'Not very often. It is his way to leave his life behind him for few hours, you see? My father, sometimes the same. Now, we will walk home. I make him drink black coffee before my mother sees him. And you, Ruby? You know to go that way?' Ash pointed along the street to the busy intersection where Mamdooh had led her out on the first expedition to the bazaar.

'I know.' She had been up all night but her head felt

supernaturally clear and the blood hummed in her veins. The world was clean and new and full of possibilities.

'Go home now,' Ash ordered. Nafouz got out of the back of the car, his hands and knees appearing to bend in all the wrong directions. He rested his head on the roof of the old cab while his body gathered momentum, then he launched himself crabwise towards the driver's seat.

'Oh no, you don't.' Ruby skipped in front of him and whisked the keys out of the ignition. She dropped them into Ash's hand.

'You did very well. To drive the car and everything. I am proud, you know, to be your friend,' he murmured to her. The sidelong admiration in his eyes made Ruby's day seem even brighter.

'My friend? Aren't you my boyfriend?'

'Is that what you like?'

She saw that he was blushing. 'Yeah, I do like.'

Ash slammed and locked all the doors of the taxi and pocketed the keys. Then he put one arm round his brother and said something sharp to him. Nafouz responded by standing up and wagging his head as he stared around, trying to work out how they had got here.

'I am going to be late for work,' Ash groaned. The two of them started walking, shoulders colliding, one rigid and the other made of rubber. Ruby watched until they turned the corner, then she walked slowly towards where the three minarets pointed at the sky. The metal shutters of cafés and shops were rolling up, and there were smells of coffee and cinnamon and fresh bread mixed with diesel fumes and singed rubber. The street was flooded with people hurrying towards the day. Her steps led away from the busy road, down the narrow alley that grew narrower to the point where no cars could pass, almost to the great mosque itself, and to Iris's peeling and unmarked front door.

'Home again,' Ruby remarked aloud. The heavy key was still in her pocket, and now she unlocked the door, holding her breath as she pushed it open and praying that the household would be still asleep.

She trod silently up the dim wooden stairs and along the dusty length of the *haramlek* corridor. It was like creeping back into Will and Fiona's after a night out.

Then a sharp voice called, 'Ruby, come here.'

Iris was sitting among her kelim rugs and cushions. There was a book open on the low table, but her grandmother hadn't been reading; she wasn't wearing her reading glasses. Ruby took one step forward, raising her shoulders and clenching her fists, ready for the anticipated onslaught. This was familiar ground.

CHAPTER TEN

The child looks guilty, and therefore defensive. She pushes out her lower lip and glares at me.

I am relieved to see her safe: it has been a long night of waiting and imagining, watching the hands of the clock.

'Did you enjoy yourself?'

She reaches down with one long arm, scratches the back of her knee. There is a piece of blanched twig caught in her hair and her clothes are dirty and even more rumpled than usual. Her eyes look heavy and her mouth is swollen. She has been lying on the ground, no doubt wrapped in her young man's arms, and the memories of talk and kissing and the desert sky spattered with stars come flooding back to me. A lifetime and no time at all separates me from Ruby.

'Yes, I suppose so. It was a weird sort of night.'

She is looking aside and over her shoulder, checking to see if we are alone.

'You have been in your room, asleep, haven't you?'

Her eyes open wide, and then her shoulders and fists loosen. We are both occasionally obliged to disobey orders or practise mild deception with Mamdooh and Auntie, and the conspiracy strikes us suddenly as very funny. We both laugh as Ruby takes three steps and flings herself down beside my chair, knotting her fingers in mine.

'I'm sorry if you were worried about me. I thought you were asleep, I just went out for a bit, then one thing led to another.' She gives a gusty sigh. 'Story of my life, really.'

'From what I already know, I think you can take good enough care of yourself. I didn't always behave in the proper way either, when I was your age, and I can't say that I regret it.' I reach out and pick the twig out of her hair, separating it from the dark strands so as not to pull on them, and she takes it from me and thoughtfully cracks it between her fingers.

'Ruby? Will you reassure me that you are using contraception?'

A spot of red appears high on her cheekbone.

'Yes. Or no, actually. It's a bit ironic, you asking about that.'

'Sexual irony? I would like to hear more.'

Now she sits back on her heels. 'I've been on the Pill since I was fifteen. After Jas died, I . . . it seemed too casual to go on taking it. As if I was just waiting for the next shag to come along, you know? So now I don't. But you can always use a condom, can't you?'

'Is that ironic?'

'No, what I mean is, I wanted to, I mean I would, but Ash doesn't. He says I am more precious than rubies, and it's not what you do. It's religion, or culture, or something.' Now, without looking at me, she is confiding. 'And he said maybe he loves me.'

I can hear the whisper of sand, whistling, shifting.

'Good,' I say quietly.

'Iris?'

'Yes, I'm listening.'

'I really like being here with you. I loved the museum. I

like the way you're easy to talk to, as if there's nothing between us, as if we're just ordinary friends.'

Her hand is smooth, brown, with dirty fingers. Mine surprises me with its knotty veins and ugly liver spots.

'Thank you,' I say.

We are settled in our routine now, Ruby and me, and although the rhythm of my days is not much changed the house has a new life beating in it.

In the mornings when the sun has risen high enough to warm the air we sit in the garden and drink coffee together. Ruby cuts up fruit and passes the pieces to me one by one, or breaks off strips of flat bread and dips them in honey before arranging them on my plate. As if I am the child, she the attentive parent.

When she is at home I hear her moving about, her feet on the stairs and the small creaks and scraping of her bedroom furniture, or the snatches of song as she takes up some inaudible chorus through her headphones. Then there is the bleat of a motorcycle horn from down in the street and she is off with her friend. I don't insist on knowing where, although quite often she comes back and tells me anyway.

Ashraf took her out to see the Pyramids and she came home comically disappointed. So many people, she frowned, and queues and dusty souvenir shops and tour guides holding up umbrellas. As if the Pyramids themselves are somehow diminished by the surf of tourism lapping around their skirts.

'Was it like that in your day?'

'Not quite, it was wartime. But all the soldiers went out there to take a look, you could get a gharry at sunset when it was cooler, and there were young boys selling picture post-cards and camel rides. The British Army had padded the Sphinx's head with sandbags to protect it.'

'I wish I could have gone then instead of now. You were allowed to climb the Great Pyramid in those days. Did you?'

'No. But I know people who did.'

Ruby has also started making solitary visits to the museum, spending hours there at a time. She comes home to relate her discoveries, and to ask questions I can't always answer.

'Queen Nefertiti, right?'

'Yes?'

'She and the Pharaoh Akhenaten decreed a new religion, and built a whole new capital city at Amarna dedicated to one god, the Aten.'

'I think that's it.'

'There are huge statues of the god in the museum, with a sloping head and thick curving lips, but he's got a round stomach and thighs like a woman's. Maybe they were really worshipping a goddess, an earth-goddess, what do you think?'

'Ruby, I don't know. I've forgotten, even if I ever knew. You could find a book about it.'

Then she is off again, speculating about Nefertiti's beauty, wondering about the significance of the sphinxes, and telling me that a metre-long piece of the beard of the Sphinx at Giza is in the British Museum.

'I think we ought to give it back. Don't you think that would be satisfying, fitting it back on his chin like putting a piece in a puzzle?'

'Yes, it would, rather.'

We discuss the case of the Elgin Marbles, of which she has never heard. Lesley might even be pleased, I think, with the cultural content of some of our debates.

The child is also picking up some Arabic – a slow but steady accretion of basic words, *bread*, *water*, *scarf* and so on, and the phrases of polite greeting and thanks and blessing. When I compliment her on her quickness she looks surprised and pleased.

'Thanks. Ash teaches me, you know? I try to learn something new in Arabic each time to say to his mother, to keep
on the right side of her. She asked me to stay and eat some
food with them last night so it must be working.'

'Ruby . . .'

Her face changes, 'I know, I know. It's rude to say no,
and hospitality means that even if they haven't got much
they try to give everything to the guest and go hungry themselves. So I just had a mouthful or two and chewed for a
really, really long time.'

She mimes the effort of registering delighted appetite
and at the same time swallowing next to nothing, and I
laugh.

'I like being able to say a few words to Auntie, as well. I
come out with something in Arabic and it cracks her up, she
goes *tee hee hee* as if it's the best joke she's ever heard instead
of just me asking for more soup.'

'Auntie's very reserved and she doesn't take readily to
strangers, but she liked you straightaway.'

'Yeah? Did she? Pity about Mamdooh, then.'

'Mamdooh is just doing what he sees as his duty, which
is to look after us. He is the protective male in a house full
of weak and feeble women.'

'And that is such crap. You're not feeble, and neither am
I. Nor is Auntie, come to that. She does all the real work in
the house, you know.'

'Ruby, you don't have to take issue with every single thing.
Mamdooh is the way he is, just accept that and try not to
outrage him.'

She looks as if she is about to take issue with me, but she
bites her tongue and sighs instead. 'Mamdooh's OK. Hey,
you know your car?'

The sudden changes of conversational direction used to
irritate me because I thought she lacked mental discipline,

250

but now I accept that her mind leapfrogs faster than mine. There is so much she wants to absorb and make use of; just to watch and listen to her makes my blood surge. My feet and hands tingle as if I am about to jump up and chase off into a world that I have hardly considered for years. I catch myself looking to the window, and the floating fragments of delft-blue sky visible through the latticework of the *mashrabiya* screen.

'My car?'

'I was telling Ash about it, Ash and Nafouz. You know, about how it's just sitting there in the garage falling to pieces among the cobwebs, and Nafouz said he's got a friend who's a brilliant mechanic who could maybe look at it and get it going again? Then we could go out for drives together, what do you think? We could go to Alexandria or . . . or on a dune safari.'

She loves pomegranates and has been peeling one as we talk. The skin falls away in a neat coil to uncover pith that she slits to get at the glowing heart. I shake my head in answer to her silent offer; the seeds stick in my teeth.

'I have been to Alexandria, and into the desert. I'm sure they haven't improved lately. And of course Nafouz has a friend who will be interested in somehow turning my car into a few pounds of profit for himself. What did you expect?'

'It was just an idea.'

'I'll think about it.'

She nods, eating pomegranate off the blade of the fruit knife. Five minutes later she jumps up and kisses the top of my head and five minutes after that she has gone out. Silence seeps slowly through the house, filling the corners and the dark angles of stairways.

The sharp ringing of the telephone makes me jump. I receive very few calls nowadays; sometimes Doctor Nicolas telephones to ask if I am well or to pass on some snippet of local news that he thinks might interest me, otherwise it is just tradesmen or people trying to sell things, and once or twice an impertinent developer who wants to buy my house from me. And of course, just lately, I have been answering the telephone to Lesley.

'Mummy, is that you?'

'Yes.'

'How are you?'

'I am very well. I'm afraid you've just missed Ruby, she went out about five minutes ago.'

'Oh, I see.'

The disappointment in her voice comes through like the wind sighing in bare trees. I think Lesley adores the child, and her adoration scratches at Ruby like a barbed-wire vest. I also remember what Ruby told me about not taking a boy to visit her mother because Lesley will only allow a regiment of perfectly aligned white mugs to adorn her kitchen. Lesley needs to exert a serious measure of control over her environment because she fears what lies beyond the defended perimeters. All her curtains and hedges and roses and Christmas rituals and crockery arrangements are about creating a safe place within a threatening world.

And of course, that longing for security is what her ever-absent mother has bred in her. As always, my meditations about Lesley tread the same circuit of guilt.

'She'll be back later. She's gone to the Egyptian Museum, she seems to have developed a great interest in Egyptology.'

'Really? She always did have odd enthusiasms.'

A silence between us contains the minute crepitations of distance and technology.

'I wanted to ask you . . . do you think you could send her back home, please?'

I consider this. 'Truthfully, I don't think I can send her anywhere. Ruby is an adult as far as I am concerned. Only she can decide when she is ready to leave. Of course, as her mother you could try to order her back to England, but I'm not sure that would have the desired result.'

'She is staying with you. It's *your* house.'

'Yes. And it will always be open to her, if here is where she chooses to be.'

Lesley's voice rises; like a change in pressure in my inner ear I can almost feel the *whoosh* of her anger as it ignites.

'You're conspiring with her, against me.'

'No, I am not.'

But maybe I am.

'What has she actually been doing there, all this time?' The fluttery edge in Lesley's voice betrays just how close she is to tears.

'I've told you. Going to the museum, learning a little Arabic, sightseeing, making friends. There is a nice young man called Ashraf, I have met him two or three times. Ruby won't come to any harm with him.'

'How do you know?' Lesley's disbelief suggests what I have already realised, that Ruby can't have been an easy child to try to bring up.

'By trusting her? Have you tried that?'

'Believe me. I've tried everything.'

My sympathy for Lesley turns out to be short-lived, because what I now feel is exasperation. 'What do you actually want for her?'

'I want her to come home. Or to go travelling properly with a plan, a goal in mind. Then to go to university, or at least decide what she wants to do with her life. Not always to be at the back of the class, bunking off, running away, sticking up two fingers at authority and expectation and her parents.'

'In other words you want her to be exactly like your friends' children?'

My voice is perhaps drier than it might have been.

'What's wrong with that? Is it a bad thing to want? I am

253

doing the best I can for her, the only way I know how. I asked her father to get involved for once and his only suggestion was a bloody shopping trip to New York.'

That's the previous husband, Alan or Colin or whatever his name is, not the one she's married to now. Lesley is shouting at me and I have to hold the receiver away from my ear until she stops.

In the end I say, 'I don't know exactly what Ruby was running away from when she left London but she wasn't running to me, because she didn't know me. Now she's here I'd give her the opportunity to work matters out for herself. She's safe and she seems happy. I'm happy to have her here.'

I can hear Lesley's agitated breathing. 'What's she living on? I give her a monthly allowance, maybe I should stop that and see how she likes it.'

'My guess is that she will be resourceful enough to get money from somewhere else.'

'From you.'

'Not if you insist otherwise. But she doesn't need much to live here.'

'Maybe I should just fly out.'

We have reached the real point of the conversation.

I let the following pause build up while Lesley explores the possibility, now that she has given voice to it, and it goes on for so long that I wonder if she has hung up.

'No,' she whispers at last, finally. 'I won't do that.'

We are left with a stale sadness hanging between us. The truth that I don't quite confront is that I *would* like to see Lesley. I would like to talk to her, perhaps – this new development that we can't explore because it's locked behind barriers of suspicion and jealousy – even share something of Ruby with her. But Lesley doesn't want to see me.

Well, that is my pay-off.

'There is plenty of room here,' I say.

'There wasn't always.' The retort comes on a long, exhaled breath that has turned impatient. Lesley is recovering already, this has been a painful conversation but she will put it behind her and carry on.

'No,' I humbly agree.

'Tell her I called, won't you? And ask her to give me a ring back when she comes in. Reverse the charges, of course.'

'All right.' I happen to have overheard one of these conversations. Ruby sounds evasive, non-committal, murmuring *fine* and *not much* and *OK, whatever.*

''Bye, then,' Lesley says.

'Goodbye.'

I feel cold now, and the sky beyond the lattice screen has clouded over. I go back and sit in my chair, and pick up another thread.

After the visit to Albie Noake I went home to Garden City. As I turned the corner into the quiet, cocoa-brown street I was almost knocked over by Jeremy the poet, who was dashing through the twilight in the opposite direction.

'Sorry. Uh, I'm so sorry. Oh, hello, Iris, it's you.'

He was wearing his linen suit, which shone at the elbows and down the margins of the lapels, and a British Council tie with a shirt whose collar points tipped upwards like the ears of some small rodent.

'Hello, Jeremy. Have you been at the flat?'

His gaze flicked sideways, then he raked his hair off his sweaty forehead and looked longingly over my shoulder.

'Um, no, not really. Just popped in, you know.'

'Faria's at home, is she?'

'No, actually. I, er, just on the off-chance . . .'

Clearly I wasn't going to get any more information, and in any case I wasn't particularly interested in Jeremy's comings and goings.

'Well, nice to see you. I must go.'

''Bye, Iris.' He was off round the corner before I could call goodnight.

I let myself into the flat. It was quiet and I thought everyone must be out, but then the door to the drawing room opened and I saw Sarah standing in a shaft of lamplight. She was wearing her old cashmere cardigan pulled tightly round her and her fine hair was scraped back from her face and tied with a scarf.

'I thought it was Faria.'

'No. It's me.'

She went back to her usual corner of the sofa and I noticed there were two empty glasses on the drinks tray.

'I met the poet downstairs.'

'Did you? Yes, he dropped in.' Sarah didn't look at me. She pulled the ends of her scarf tighter and tucked them in, tucking in the corners of her mouth to match.

'Are you all right?' I asked.

'Me? Yes. Fine.'

The front door opened and closed again, and a moment later Faria appeared. Her dark slanting eyes were heavily outlined with kohl and she was wearing her diamond earrings and a little suit in jade-green soft tweed. She undid the wrist buttons of her kid gloves and peeled them off, then stalked across to the gin bottle waiting on the drinks tray. She said into the heavy atmosphere, 'I've been at an endless reception for some business people of Ali's. I don't know why I have to go to these things, smiling and talking nonsense. I thought I would die of boredom.'

Sarah was pale and quiet, and Faria was often irritable these days. The flat wasn't as much fun as it had been when I first came back to Cairo.

Faria flung herself into a chair. 'Well, you two, tell me. Have you both got divine dates lined up for tonight?'

'Not me,' Sarah murmured.

'I'm going to dinner with a nurse I met at the Scottish Military, and her flatmate who's a doctor.'

Faria yawned. This sounded almost as dull to her as the afternoon she had just endured, but Sarah looked up eagerly. 'A doctor? Is he nice?'

'She's a woman. I made exactly the same assumption.' I laughed, but Sarah didn't join in. She wasn't interested in women; Faria and I were both engaged and what Sarah wanted now was to bag a husband of her own. 'By the way, Iris, a package came for you. It must be something important, Mamdooh said the messenger made him sign a chit for it. It's on the hall tray.'

'Thanks. I'd better go and change if I'm not going to be late. Ruth and Daphne live halfway to Heliopolis.'

I knew what was in the package, but I didn't want to open it in front of Sarah and Faria. Faria would have held up the stone to judge the quality, wondering why it wasn't a diamond, and Sarah would have bitten her lip and told me that it was so beautiful, and I was terribly lucky to have met someone like Xan.

I took the little square box into my bedroom and closed the door. The window was open and I stood for a moment with my hand on the sill, looking out at the outline of my jacaranda and the thick leaves of a rubber tree splashed with light from the apartments overlooking the gardens. In the autumn the cocktail hour was cool, and scented with late jasmine and charcoal smoke and spices from the street food vendors. A pale-green line marked a sliver of the western horizon visible between two apartment blocks.

Xan's amethyst was opulent in its simple claw setting. I slipped it on to my third finger and held my hand up in happy amazement.

I was an engaged woman; I was going to marry Xan

Molyneux. I wanted nothing else in the world.

When I had finished admiring my ring I pressed my forehead against the window frame and stared towards the west and the desert. I prayed wordlessly for Xan and whatever road he was watching, wherever he was hiding from the enemy convoys and spotter planes.

A knock on my door shook me back to earth.

Faria called, 'Daddy's car is here. Can we drop you off anywhere?'

I imagined pulling up outside Ruth's flat in Amman Pasha's enormous black limousine with the chauffeur in his pale-fawn livery opening the door and bowing as I stepped out.

'No, thanks. I haven't changed yet.'

'Have a lovely time,' her voice floated back to me.

I caught the Heliopolis bus. It was packed like a sardine can and smelled of tired bodies, and when we finally reached Ruth's stop I clambered down with a puff of relief. The main road was busy with trucks and troop carriers and civilian cars but when I turned a corner, following Ruth's directions, I found myself in a nondescript enclave of low modern houses with concrete balconies and outside staircases. The upper windows of Ruth's house stood wide open and loud dance music boomed out. I stared in surprise, then realised that the concrete stairs led up to a separate apartment. Strips of yellow light shone between the drawn curtains downstairs. As I tapped the door knocker there was a crash and a bellow of laughter from above.

Ruth's face appeared. 'Sorry,' she murmured, opening the door wider. 'Some French officers live up there, they make a terrible racket at all hours. Come on in.'

Ruth was wearing loose khaki trousers and a white shirt. I had never seen her out of her nurse's uniform and she looked younger with her dark-red hair undone and pushed back over one shoulder.

Their sitting room was small, but they had made it look beautiful with handwoven rugs and Bedouin cushions in the colours of the desert, and unframed abstract paintings on the white walls. The calm simplicity made a sharp contrast with the oversized, carved and inlaid furnishings of our flat in Garden City.

'Hello,' a voice said from behind Ruth's shoulder. 'I'm Daphne Erdall.'

I shook hands with Daphne. She was older than I had expected, perhaps in her early forties. She had a tanned face with broad cheekbones, a wide mouth and clear grey eyes, and her fair hair was so thick it stood out almost horizontally from the crown of her head. She was one of those people you look at and think, this is *someone*.

I had brought a bottle of whisky, a real Scottish malt that had been a present to me from Sandy Allardyce who had access to such luxuries through the embassy, and now I gave it to Ruth.

Her face lit up. 'My God, Daph, look at this. Nectar from the god of the glens. Can we drink some, Iris?'

'That's pretty much what I brought it for.'

'You're very generous. We've only got local gutrot,' Daphne said. She poured us each a measure and we held up our glasses. 'To friendship,' Daphne proposed in her direct way. Pleased, I echoed the toast.

'It's a nice flat,' I said, looking around. Another crash sounded from above.

Daphne laughed. 'Apart from Gaston and his cronies, that is. Actually they're all right. Our hours don't overlap much. I'm going to see to the food for a minute; Ruth'll take care of you.'

'I'll show you the rest of the flat,' Ruth offered.

There wasn't much to see. In the kitchen a square table was already laid with three places and Daphne was at the stove stirring a pan of couscous. There was a narrow bathroom with a hip bath, and a bedroom with shuttered windows. And there was one double bed, smooth under a white cotton coverlet.

Belatedly, the penny dropped.

Ruth was leaning in the doorway. 'Are you surprised?'

I was, but I tried not to show it. 'No. Well, yes, a bit. I haven't met . . . But actually, it's none of my business, is it?'

She raised one eyebrow. 'You'd be surprised at how many people think it is their business. Either to be nosy or comical about.'

But her hand lightly grasped my arm as I passed, a gesture simply expressing warmth without sexual import. I understood that for some reason I was going to be accepted by Ruth and Daphne, and the realisation gave me a shock of satisfaction. The two of them seemed very glamorous to me, and free of all the conventions of upbringing and social expectation that held me in my place. I found myself wanting to be more like them and less like my conventional self.

'It's ready,' Daphne called from the kitchen.

When we sat down at the table with the candles lit and Daphne poured from a jug of dark-red Lebanese wine, there was an air of celebration.

'It's a special occasion. You are here, and Ruth and I hardly ever get a chance to sit down and eat a proper dinner together,' she explained.

We drank the raisin-flavoured wine, ate roast chicken and couscous spiked with fresh herbs, and we talked. My hosts were good company, but they were serious-minded. I quickly realised that I couldn't rely on the superficial cocktail chatter that did for the rest of my social circuit.

As at every cocktail party and around every dinner table in Cairo that night, we discussed the war. But even the familiar assumption that the war itself was right and justifiable, made automatically by all my circle, was called into question here. Although Ruth and Daphne didn't call themselves pacifists, that is effectively what they were. Every day they saw the damage that combat did to men like Albie Noake and Private Ridley, and they spent their working hours trying to repair it.

It was easy to understand why they were sceptical about the big battle that everyone else was waiting for with nervous anticipation that sometimes tipped into excitement.

'You've seen my ward,' Ruth said quietly. 'In a week's time, or whenever the push for Tobruk comes, we'll be caring for twice as many severely wounded. Or three, four, five times as many. The corridors will be full of stretchers. And it will be the same in Daphne's and every other hospital in Cairo. The trains and ambulances will come flooding in from the desert, packed to the roofs with maimed men from both sides. Is any strategic gain, any military advantage whatsoever, worth that amount of loss and suffering?'

'You think we should surrender to the fascists?'

'I think the generals should consider what it is they are likely to achieve, beyond a few hundred miles of empty desert, that is to be bought with so many men's lives.'

'If we don't attack, the Axis forces will push across the western desert and on to Cairo. We have to defend Egypt,' I said.

Daphne's clear eyes rested on my face. 'For our own ends, not Egypt's.'

From my father, who had worked for many years with the high commission towards the final goal of Egyptian independence, I had inherited the belief that British involvement in Egypt was largely benign.

Daphne leaned forward, pouring more wine into my glass. 'Your father was a diplomat? Iris, don't be offended, but we British don't have a legacy here to be proud of, do we? This

261

isn't our country, yet we behave exactly as if it were and as if the people are our servants and inferiors. Farouk is the King of Egypt, but our ambassador is the ruler. Given our history and our attitude, why should any Egyptian, from Farouk right down to the fellahin, have any regard for us?'

Even Xan, whose boyhood friend and desert ally was Hassan, was inclined to talk collectively about Gyppos. All the officers did, with an amused, exasperated superiority. I remembered the scene on the steps of Shepheard's Hotel, when the waiter had pushed the child beggar out of reach of all the masters who were striding in to enjoy lunch among their own kind.

'The Europeans dug the Suez Canal, laid railway lines, built hospitals and schools and colleges,' I said.

'Yes, de Lesseps built the Canal but Egypt paid for it, and for all the other modernisations as well. The country ended up a hundred million pounds in debt because the developments were financed by money borrowed from European banks at extortionate rates of interest, and the fellahin had to be taxed to the point of starvation in order to repay it. Then Disraeli took advantage of the economic crisis to buy the khedive's shares in the Suez Canal Company at a rock-bottom price. When there was an uprising the Royal Navy bombed the harbour at Alexandria, the army massacred the rebels at Tel el Kebir and occupied the country. You know the story since then.'

I did. The sovereign country that had finally emerged from fifty years of British control was still effectively occupied and ruled by the British.

'So why are you here?' I demanded.

Daphne suddenly smiled. She was formidable to the point of being alarming, I thought, but she also possessed a magnetic charm. I noticed how Ruth's eyes were continually drawn back to her.

'Because I love this country. I was here before the war, working with a village medical programme. When the war is over I'll go back to it. In the meantime I'm a surgical anaesthetist and I treat each individual on the operating table as a life we can save. There have been a lot of injured men, and you heard what Ruth said. There are soon going to be thousands more.'

Under the tablecloth, I twisted Xan's amethyst on my third finger.

I turned to Ruth, pushing away the thought of a dam about to break and release a tide of blood. 'What about you? Why are you here?'

'I love Egypt too. And I love Daphne. I want to be where she is.'

She said it simply, but Daphne quickly shook her head.

'That's a personal consideration, put that aside. You are an excellent nurse, and you're doing an important job.'

'I know she is, I've seen her,' I said.

Smiling again, Daphne refilled my glass with the last of the wine. Ruth stood up to collect the plates but she rested her cheek first on the top of Daphne's head, and Daphne briefly encircled her wrist with her fingers. Then Ruth straightened up and went on clearing the table. Her face looked as if a light had come on beneath the translucent skin, and I swallowed my wine and looked at the wall.

'And you?' Daphne asked me.

'I work at GHQ. Clerical administrator. I came from London at the beginning of the year.'

'Iris has just got engaged,' Ruth said mischievously.

Young women like me, as the cynical wisdom of Cairo put it, came out here either to find a husband or to escape from one. I hadn't been guilty of either intention, and Sarah and Faria had often teased me at the beginning for not being interested enough in having fun, yet in Daphne's and Ruth's

263

company I couldn't help feeling frivolous. I didn't seem to belong on either side, although at least I was now beginning to recognise where I wanted to be.

I was annoyed to feel my colour rising.

'Congratulations,' Daphne said. 'What is he doing?'

'He's a cavalryman, but he's seconded to one of the special ops groups.' I wanted – longed – to talk about Xan, but I couldn't say anything more about what he did.

'Ah.' There was warmth and sympathy in Daphne's shrewd look. She knew what special ops work was likely to entail, and she left it at that.

I cleared my throat. 'I've been thinking lately about what else I could do here. I don't feel much use any longer, pounding my typewriter in GHQ. I suppose I could try to get into uniform, ATS or MTC, but I've been wondering about hospital work too. Ruth suggested voluntary visiting, or maybe joining the VADs.'

Again, there was an appraising look. Ruth put the malt whisky bottle back on the table.

'You could do that.' There was a pause. 'Or I could ask the Director of Nursing at the QM, where I work, if she could find a niche for you. She's a friend of mine. It'd only be voluntary work, mind, but there might be something more interesting than reading to the men or rolling bandages.'

The Queen Mary was the biggest of the Cairo hospitals now taken over by the military.

'Would you? I'd like that very much.'

'Leave it to me,' Daphne said. I knew she would do exactly as she promised.

The three of us raised our whisky glasses and this time the toast was a silent one. Now not only did I have intimacy with Xan, I had the luxury of this congenial female company. Warmth, unconnected with whisky, ran through my veins. I had been lonely, I realised, and now suddenly I wasn't.

We sat at the table for another hour and I made the two of them laugh with stories about Roddy Boy and Sandy Allardyce and Mrs Kimmig-Gertsch, and the rest of my Cairo world.

'A chauffeur.' Ruth sighed enviously when I told them how I had recoiled from the idea of pulling up at their door with Amman Pasha's car and driver.

'Well, he's not waiting outside for me now. And so I'd better go, or I'll miss the last bus into town.'

Ruth and Daphne insisted that I mustn't walk to the main road on my own. We were at the front door when footsteps came smartly down the concrete steps from the upper floor.

'Bonsoir, Docteur Erdall, Mademoiselle Macnamara.'

There were three young Frenchmen with moustaches and evening clothes, smelling of cigarettes and brandy, heading out for a night on the town. They had a car, of course I must allow them to give me a lift home.

'Good night, and thank you,' I said to Ruth and Daphne. They stood in the light spilling from the doorway and Ruth tilted her head against Daphne's shoulder.

'Come and see us again,' Daphne called.

I sat in the front of the dusty Citroën next to the driver and the other two officers squeezed themselves into the back. We sped over the potholed road at high speed, the car's worn springs banging in protest. There was a lot of laughing and gallant offering of cigarette cases.

The driver looked sidelong at me, his profile briefly illuminated by the lights of a passing truck.

'Vous êtes une amie de ces mesdames?'

'Oui, certainement,' I said flatly.

There was an outbreak of coughing from behind my shoulder and the driver's upper lip twitched under his moustache. The tips of his fingers patted lightly, expressively, on the wheel.

'*Bien sûr*,' he murmured. He insisted on dropping me right at the door of our apartment, and came round and opened the car door for me. He even kissed my hand, bending low over it as he did so.

'*Merci, monsieur.*'

'*Un plaisir, Mademoiselle Black. Au revoir.*'

Sarah was climbing out of a taxi. Together we watched the tail lights of the Citroën rounding the corner.

'Who were they?'

'Some French staff officers who gave me a lift home.'

'You are leading an exciting life.'

'Not really. Where have you been?'

Sarah shrugged. 'Just to the Anglo-Egyptian for a drink. I thought I'd look in, see who was there. But it was very quiet.'

We let ourselves into the flat. Everywhere in Cairo was quiet, not just the bar of the Anglo-Egyptian Club. Everyone who was not in the desert was watching and waiting for the next big thing to happen.

'*My darling girl*,' my mother wrote. '*Your father and I were so excited to hear your big news, and we are so very pleased for you both.*'

I read her letter at my desk, in a brief lull. GHQ was in turmoil. The offensive had begun two days earlier as twenty-mile lines of Allied troops and armaments poured across the frontier towards Rommel's Panzer Group Africa, and Tobruk. Roddy Boy had been wearing the same shirt for twenty-four hours because he hadn't had time to go home and change.

And now, what do you plan to do? You won't think I'm too sentimental, I hope, if I tell you that I have once or twice dreamed of my girl's wedding in an English church on a midsummer's morning, with her

father to give her away and perhaps Evie's children as
her little attendants. And her mother shedding one tear
in the front pew. Of course this war has changed that
for everyone, not just you and your Alexander.

(By the way, my mother's cousin Wilfred married a
Miss Molyneux. Do you think there is already a family
connection?)

If pressed, my mother could usually unearth a remote
connection by marriage to almost anyone you cared to think
of.

You do not mention a date, and it may not be your
intention to wait at all. I know that 'quick' wartime
ceremonies are quite normal nowadays – but, darling,
I should so like to see you being married. Perhaps after
Christmas, or even in the spring (if it ever comes, this
dark winter seems to stretch ahead for ever), your father
and I could somehow find a passage out to Cairo to
be with you? What with coupons and everything in such
short supply here, it may even be easier to put together
your trousseau out there. What fun it would be to go
shopping together at Cicurel's. I wonder if my old
Lebanese dressmaker still lives in her little house by the
Bab al-Futuh?

What a lot there is to think about. Daddy is well,
and sends all his love, as do I. The vicar has asked me
to help out with the garden effort, we are turning some
of the park over to vegetables.

God bless you both. Ever your loving Ma.

I reread this letter several times during that week in late
November.

The original offensive by the three brigades of the Seventh

Armoured Division and supporting artillery and infantry had developed into the confusion and horror of the battle of Sidi Rezegh. Thirty thousand British, German and Italian tanks and other vehicles milled and circled in a flat, exposed desert landscape of dust, thorns, smoke, burned-out tanks and dead men covering three thousand square miles. On the ground, it was often impossible to tell friend from enemy. Every vehicle that loomed in sight could be a threat or a reinforcement. Signals trucks were captured and whole formations seemed to evaporate because the next link in the chain couldn't communicate with them. The transport systems of all three armies changed hands and then changed hands again, supply dumps and entire headquarters were lost, and men of different units formed up together and fought on in the whirling chaos of smoke and sand.

The news at GHQ changed every hour as the chaotic skirmishes were won or lost and then forgotten as the next reversal altered everything yet again.

Roddy Boy and the rest of the suave, gabardine cohorts of GHQ stripped to their shirtsleeves and worked round the clock. Roddy and his staff sweated to interpret and transmit back to the field commanders the Intelligence that poured in from the shattered forces, while the cups of tea I carried in to him turned cold and orange on his desk. A new admiration for him dawned in me.

In the midst of this, in the rare moments of relative calm, I read the word *trousseau* and the incongruity of it made me smile before Roddy Boy appeared in front of me with yet another sheaf of paper and the order snapped over his shoulder, 'As quick as you can, Miss Black.'

Then, on 24 November, Rommel suddenly gathered together the remaining Panzers of his army and broke eastwards towards the thickets of wire that separated Libya from Egypt. Beyond Egypt, only time and the conquests of Palestine and

Syria would separate him from the oilfields of Iraq and Persia.

During Rommel's dash for the wire, as the support echelons of the Allied armies fled ahead of his tanks and the front-line commanders struggled to marshal their forces, there was no time for letter reading, or even for leaving the glaring, littered GHQ offices to eat, bathe or change.

I had no idea where Xan might be. I tried to stop myself from fitting Tellforce operations into the floods of Intelligence that washed over me. All I could do was work, snatch an hour's sleep, and work again.

After two days of confusion, Intelligence confirmed that in Rommel's absence the British had taken the opportunity to attack Sidi Rezegh once more, so he reversed his momentum and pulled back to a point east of Tobruk. In his wake the Panzers rolled back from the wire to re-engage, but these were the last throes of the battle and it was hardly a victory for either side. Eighteen thousand British and Allied troops had been killed, wounded or captured. Rommel had lost all but forty of his tanks, and German shipping losses in the Mediterranean meant that it would probably be weeks before he could replace them.

GHQ drew breath.

Roddy sat with his pink hands loose on the desk in front of him. There were dark, grainy patches of skin under his eyes and his tight flesh now seemed to hang in creases.

'You had better go home, Miss Black. Your father will complain that I am overworking you.'

'I won't mention it to him.'

'Go on, off you go. Wait a minute, though. Iris?'

'Yes, Sir?'

'Thank you.'

On 7 December, Axis losses around Sidi Rezegh forced Rommel to withdraw to the west of Tobruk and the 242-

day siege of the harbour and garrison was lifted. On the same day Roddy came out of his office after a short telephone call and told me that the Japanese had bombed Pearl Harbor. 'Now the Americans will be in,' he said.

The next evening I went to the Scottish Military again. The entrance was blocked by a line of ambulances, as it had been for days, and in the distance I saw Betty Hopwood leaning against the side of her vehicle as she waited for her cargo of stretchers to be carried off. Inside the hospital the corridors and ante-rooms were packed with lines of walking wounded.

Albie Noake had been moved off Ruth's ward and into one where patients shuffled about on crutches and played cards at the centre table. A man in pyjamas with bandaged hands got up from the chair at Albie's bedside and nodded to me. 'Evening, Miss. Noake's the lucky one, isn't he?'

Yanks are in. All over soon? Albie wrote.

'I don't know. I hope so.'

Any news from Mr M?

'No. Not yet.'

Bet there having some fun, wherever they are. I bloody hate missing it, scuse languige.

I put my hand on his, trying to smile. 'I know you do. They'll be missing you too.'

Still coming to see me off?

Albie's place on the next hospital ship sailing for England via the Cape had been confirmed. He would be leaving in two days' time.

'I asked my boss for an hour off to come to the station. He acted as if I'd asked for a month at the seaside, but he said yes in the end. I'll be there.'

They need the beds. It's gone mad here.

Our eyes met. 'Yes.'

Daphne and Ruth would be working eighteen-hour shifts.

I envied them their ability to do something for all these damaged soldiers. After my visit to Albie I went home to Garden City and listened to the wireless news. Then I stood for a long time at my bedroom window, as if I might hear or glimpse something of Xan just by staring into the darkness.

The railway station was in chaos. Egyptian railway officials dashed up and down the platforms trying to direct the medical orderlies who surged through the metal gates carrying stretcher cases. Trains waited to ferry the injured to the ships waiting in the Gulf of Suez. There were wounded men everywhere, in wheelchairs and on crutches, or slowly limping in twos and threes through the engine smoke and stale hissing steam towards their numbered carriages. Peddlers and street boys ran around between them, hawking fruit and dirty magazines and cigarettes.

'Hey, Tommy! Going home? Nice pictures?'

I couldn't find Albie. I knew the number of the MTC transporter that would be bringing him from the hospital, but I couldn't see it in the line. Then I almost collided with one of Betty's friends who told me that the vehicle had broken down, but the mechanics had repaired it and it would soon be here. Five minutes later it trundled round the corner. Two orderlies jumped out and folded down a step, and the men began to emerge. Albie was walking now, unsteadily but unsupported. Waving my arms in the air so he would see me, I ran towards him.

'I thought you weren't coming, thought you'd decided to stay after all,' I panted.

His bandaged head nodded. I picked up his kitbag in one hand, gave him my other arm and we set off in a shuffle through the crowds.

Then, at the end of the platform, turning from side to side as he searched through the throng, I suddenly caught sight

271

of a man who looked like Xan. I was used to this. In every crowded street in Cairo I would catch sight of someone who resembled him, and my heart would jump into my throat. But this time, as we drew closer together, instead of the likeness disappearing he looked more and more like Xan. It was another ten seconds before I let myself believe that it really was him.

Then I gave a shout that made all the heads bobbing around us turn to look at me: 'Xan.'

Albie saw him now too, and made the squawk of vowels sound that was all the speech that was left to him.

Xan sprinted through the crowds. With one hand he caught hold of me, the other he held out to Albie.

'You're here,' I said stupidly.

'I flew up this morning with Colonel Wainwright. I heard that Corporal Noake was on the way home, so I raced across to wish him bon voyage. You look a bit better than you did when I last saw you,' he told Albie.

Albie gave him the double thumbs-up.

Xan looked just himself, tired and dirty but as happy and full of laughter as he always seemed. Gratitude washed through me. Xan took the bag from me and with one of us on either side we walked Albie on down the train until we found a carriage with an empty seat in it.

I stood back while Xan helped him up the steep step, hoisted his bag onto the luggage shelf and settled him into his place. His head bent close over Albie and he talked quickly into his ear. I knew that he was briefly telling him whatever it was he had missed, in the desert with Tellforce. Doors began slamming all down the train. A guard in a sweaty uniform held a green flag furled under his arm. I hopped quickly onto the step and leaned past the crammed soldiers to kiss the side of Albie's face that was still there.

'See you back in England,' I said.

The flag was being unfurled. Xan and I jumped back down onto the platform. The train clanked forward and we walked and then ran alongside the window of Albie's carriage, waving and calling goodbye until we couldn't keep up any longer.

We dropped back and fell into each other's arms.

'I've got to go back to work. Roddy's in a flap,' I said reluctantly as we threaded our way through the clamour of the station.

'I'll see you back to GHQ.'

His hand gripped mine and held it close against him.

'What was it like?' I asked.

Xan sighed. 'I don't know what to tell you. I took my patrol in to pick up some of David's men who had parachuted in over Mersa el Brega. It was a bit of a bold scheme to kidnap Rommel, but it didn't go to plan. Fifty-six of them were dropped, but we only got twenty-one out again. And then we were threading our way back across to the south of Sidi Rezegh, Hassan and me in the armoured car, and we came across a single man trudging through the scrub. You couldn't tell which side he belonged to. That was what it was like. You couldn't tell who was fighting whom. You couldn't see anything except smoke and dust.

'I wound down the window and shouted to him, "Are you Italian?" And he shouted back in English as good as mine, "I'm not bloody Italian, I'm German."

'He was wounded in the arm, so we gave him a lift. He handed over some cigarettes as payment for the ride, English Capstan, taken from one of our supply depots. After about ten miles we came on some German armoury so we stopped and let him walk across to them. He marched a few yards, turned back and called to us, "I'll see you in London, George.'

'And I yelled back, "No, it'll be Berlin."

273

'Hassan kept a rifle sight on him all the way back to his own side, but I told him not to shoot.'

Xan turned to me and laughed, his tired face all creases. 'That was what it was like,' he said.

CHAPTER ELEVEN

The car was repaired.

The work was done by Nafouz's friend Husain who was a garage mechanic, and when it was finished Nafouz and Ash returned the car to the alleyway behind Iris's house. The pitted chrome had been polished as far as possible and the patches of bodywork not consumed by rust were black again.

They stood in a row behind the car, Mamdooh and Auntie and Ruby flanking Iris, and peered at the oily interior. With the engine running the whole vehicle shuddered and coughed like a phthisic old man.

'Just as fine with engine, see?' Nafouz beamed.

'Ace,' Ruby said.

'This is not for driving, it is not secure,' Mamdooh tutted while Auntie stood with her veil drawn across the lower part of her face and her eyes turned down and away from the two boys.

Iris said nothing. Instead, she made a slow tour from the back to the front of the car, touching the door handles and running her fingertips over the blisters of rust that bubbled around the sills. She stroked the bonnet's slope and completed the circuit to rejoin the four of them. Then she looked Nafouz straight in the eye. 'I will put my car in the garage now. Then you may come into the house and speak to me.'

'Lady, Doctor, I will put away . . .'

'No thank you,' Iris snapped. She opened the driver's door and slid into the creaking seat, grasping the wheel with her freckled hands. She sat up straighter, craning her neck and lifting her chin so she could see ahead through the windscreen. Then with a crescendo of revs she stamped on the clutch and scraped the gearstick into first. The car strained until she remembered the handbrake, and then it sprang forward and Iris spun the wheel to bring it coasting into the garage. She switched off the engine and stepped out, pocketing the ignition key at the same time.

'Mamdooh will show you the way,' she told Ash and Nafouz.

Iris and Ruby reached the inner garden first. Iris took Ruby's arm and hung on to it. She was panting a little but her cheeks were flushed and she looked as excited as a child. 'You know, I wasn't sure I could do that.'

'You didn't have any trouble at all.'

'I didn't, did I? And it was fun. It's going to be fun.' She took the keys out of her pocket and flipped them into the air, just managing to catch them again. Ruby thought she was like a teenager who had coaxed the use of his car out of her father for a Saturday night, and the idea made her smile.

Mamdooh escorted the boys out into the garden and stood like a sentinel with his hands clasped in front of him. Ash and Nafouz shuffled a little, staring around them without wanting to stare. The pots of greenery gave off a warm scent of leaves and earth, and the water splashed into its glazed bowl. Above the tiled walls and the *haramlek* windows the minarets reared against a flat grey sky.

Iris sat down and indicated a bench facing her chair. Nafouz took his place but Ash hesitated, and Ruby hovered beside him instead of drawing her chair to its usual position close to Iris's. The tomb house was very clear in her mind's eye, and when she took a sideways glance at Ash she knew that he was making the comparison too. The extreme sharpness of the contrast made her uncomfortable.

'And so what do I owe you and your friend for servicing my car?' Iris asked pleasantly.

Nafouz leaned forward, making a deprecatory flat-palmed gesture. 'I would like to say nothing, this is done for friendship only.'

'Thank you. But?'

'My friend is a poor man. He has a wife, children.'

'Of course. Go on.'

Nafouz mentioned a large sum, in Egyptian pounds, with a mournful shrug.

Equally regretfully, Iris named a third of the price.

Ash and Ruby looked at each other and she saw that Ash was smiling. It was clear that Iris and Nafouz understood each other perfectly.

'Come with me?' she murmured to him, tilting her head the way they had come. Mamdooh frowned, but he couldn't follow them and stand guard over Iris at the same time. Auntie was presumably preparing the inevitable tray of mint tea and sweet pastries. Ash and Ruby slipped back into the house while the negotiations continued their elaborate course.

Ash walked through the celebration hall, gazing up at the carved panelling and painted ceilings and the pierced screens shielding the gallery.

'All this house belongs only to your grandmother?' he whispered.

Through his eyes, Ruby saw the grandeur of it instead of the dust and cobwebs. She answered awkwardly, her voice sounding much too loud in the shadowy space, 'I think so. I suppose so. I never really asked her.'

'Do you live in a house also like this in England?'

'No. God, no. Nothing like.' She laughed, again too loud, and then bit her lip. Nothing like the tomb house, either. There was suddenly a thin shaft of mystified envy splintered with embarrassment between herself and Ash, and she didn't know how to deal with it. It was as if Jas had been pitchforked into the middle of one of Lesley's dinner parties for Andrew's clients.

She grabbed Ash by the wrist. 'Come on.' Maybe in her room he would just look into her face and not see anything else.

At first he followed willingly, then he realised that they were heading for the inner stairway.

He stopped dead. 'I cannot.'

'I thought you were allowed if one of the women of the household *invited* you.'

'Even then it is only for brothers, cousins. Not for stranger.'

Ruby walked round to face him, but he held himself stiff. She reached up and cupped his face between her hands.

'You are not a stranger,' she whispered. 'You're my friend.'

He blinked, but didn't move.

Then she pulled his head down so that her mouth touched his.

'I'd say you were my brother. But actually I love you,' she said. At the same moment it occurred to her that this wasn't a blandishment or even a veiled threat. It was the truth, as close as she had ever got to it.

Ash looked amazed. His eyes widened and he pulled her closer as he kissed her. Afterwards he let her lead him up the stairs and along the gallery. He broke away once to lift open one of the screens and gaze down into the space beneath. Mamdooh swept across the hallway without an upward glance, his slippers swishing on the stone. Ash and Ruby stole to the door of her room and crept inside.

278

'My bedroom,' Ruby said superfluously.

He stood with his hand on the latch and looked at the austere space. There were two or three books on a chair, a small squared-off pile of CDs, the cover on the narrow divan was pulled straight. Everything else was tidied away into the chest. It was the way Ruby liked it, now.

Ash grinned, and she saw that he was recovering himself.

'I have not visited a girl's bedroom before. I did not think you would be so tidy, Ruby.'

She aimed a kick at his shin, and he caught her wrists to stop her punching him. They scuffled like puppies, laughing and puffing until they stumbled against the divan in the window arch, then they flopped onto their knees and peered down into the street, their breath making twin mist plumes on the glass.

'After the first time with Nafouz, I came back to see and I thought this was your window. I saw the light here, just the one, shining in all this big wall. I stood down in the street and looked up, trying to see you.'

'So you *were* spying on me. And that time in Khan al-Khalili you'd followed me all the way, hadn't you? Some people might think that was creepy, you know.'

'Creepy? What is that?'

Ruby hooked her fingers and distorted her face into an approximation of creepiness and Ash recoiled.

'I am not like that in any way,' he said seriously.

'I know that *now*. I told you what I feel now, didn't I?'

'Yes. I am surprised and I am also pleased of course. But, Ruby, it means that we are not playing any more.'

They knelt upright, facing each other.

'Is that bad?'

Gently he put his hand to her waist, stroked it upwards, splaying his fingers so they rested in the indentations between her ribs. 'I am Egyptian boy, you are English girl. I am poor

279

boy, you are rich girl. I am telephone worker, you are . . . *phhh*. I do not even know. You can be anything you want, I suppose.'

'I'm not anything very much. No . . . wait, Ash, don't contradict. It's the truth. I ran away from home to come here because Jas died and because my uncle really *is* a creep and my mother and her husband think I'm a failure and a waste of time, and I just woke up one morning in England and looked around me and I thought that if I didn't do something soon they'd be right.

'If I was someone like you I'd have gone straight out and got a job, any sort of job, just something to support myself instead of taking handouts from my mother and not going to college like I was supposed to. But being me, what did I do? I helped myself to my mother's credit card, went online and bought a plane ticket to Cairo. She'll have seen what I did, but she doesn't want to admit even to herself just how cunning and shitty I can be. And I came here to Iris's house, thinking it didn't really matter where I was just so long as it was a different place to feel nothing much in.

'Then I met you. You took me to the Cities of the Dead and I saw your house and family and you showed me places and . . . this is going to sound properly cheesy, but it made me understand some things I hadn't worked out before. I don't think you should feel sorry for yourself unless there's good reason, and I really haven't got one, but I was still feeling sorry for myself without properly acknowledging it. So I was angry as well. But being here with you and Iris and Auntie, and yeah, even Mamdooh, has made me feel different. I like going to the museum because there's so much history and it's gone on for so long, and it's been so . . . full. Is that what I mean?'

'I think maybe,' Ash said gently.

'. . . So it makes me feel small, and yet part of it all, like we all are, you and me and Iris and all the people in her history, and mine and yours and everyone in the Cities whether they're alive or dead, and that's really comforting.' Ruby sighed. 'What am I trying to say? I do want to do something now it's my turn, not be useless. I just don't know what it is, yet.'

Her face broke up into a smile that made Ash tighten his grip and draw her closer to him. Their faces were almost touching.

She whispered, 'What you were saying, about you being Egyptian and me English, rich girl and poor boy?'

'Yes.'

'I think the only words that matter out of all of them are *girl* and *boy*.'

'Perhaps you are right.'

Face to face and hip to hip they had begun to slide down onto the bed. A sharp rapping on the door jerked them upright again in a tangle of legs and arms.

'*Miss* Ruby?' Mamdooh shouted.

Ash exclaimed in Arabic and leapt to his feet, staring wildly around him for an escape route.

'It's OK', Ruby said. She strolled to the door and opened it, and Mamdooh loomed into the room.

'This is not correct,' he spluttered. Ash was already sidling past him in an attempt to get away but Mamdooh moved with surprising speed to cut him off, and Ash shot an imploring glance at Ruby.

'What's wrong?' Ruby innocently asked Mamdooh.

His big face was puffed with rage. 'You bring shame.'

Ash began a protestation but Ruby hushed him.

'Shame? What right do you have to say that?'

Mamdooh wouldn't look at her. 'You are Muslim boy,' he said to Ash.

Ruby darted round and stood next to Ash. 'Yes, he is, and

he has never done one thing wrong or *shameful* as you call it ever since I have known him. I might have, but he hasn't. You should apologise to him.'

'Ruby,' Ash miserably whispered.

Mamdooh frowned from one to the other. He pushed his lips out so they looked even more like dark fruit. 'Is this truth?'

'Yes.'

'In this country, in this house, it is not for boys to visit the bedroom of a young girl.'

'In England we figure that if people are going to do something they'll find somewhere, bedroom or not.'

'You are being rude,' Ash told her.

Ruby whirled round, ready to take him on too, but he held her gaze. After a long moment her shoulders dropped. 'All right. I'm sorry, Mamdooh, OK? I promise I won't bring any boy up to my bedroom ever again. Will that do?'

Majestically, he inclined his head and stood aside to let them file out of the door.

'Mum-reese waits for you.'

Iris and Nafouz were sitting in the garden, drinking mint tea and looking like the best of friends.

'There you are,' Iris called when she saw them. 'Did you say you were going out?'

Patiently, Ruby said no, they had just gone off while she and Nafouz were settling up about the car. Iris's face cleared. 'The car. That's right. Have some tea, both of you.'

Ash accepted the glass Ruby gave him but he would only sit on the edge of the bench.

'It is time for Nafouz and me to go. I am glad car is fixed, Madam Iris.'

Iris smiled gaily at him. 'You must come for a drive.'

As she saw them out, Ruby asked Ash when they were going to see each other again.

'Soon. I have to work, Ruby, you know this.'

She watched the two brothers until they reached the end of the street and disappeared in the direction of Khan al-Khalili. They had the same walk, the same watchful way of turning their heads, and their closeness made her feel excluded. Nothing had been said about the night at the club; Nafouz's charming smile was as wide and implacable as ever and when she asked Ash he shrugged and replied, 'Sometimes it happens. It is not good but it is not the worst thing.'

They protected and looked out for each other, the two of them. If it came to a test of loyalty, Ruby thought, there was no question where Ash's would lie.

The garden was deserted. Auntie had already cleared away the teapot and glasses.

Ruby found Iris in her room, wearing her outdoor coat.

'There you are. Are you ready?'

'Ready for what?' Ruby asked.

'For a ride in the car, of course. Come on, where do you want to go?'

'I don't know. Are you sure you want to do this right now? And don't you need . . . insurance, things like that?'

'My dear girl, this is Cairo not Tunbridge Wells. All that can be dealt with. I want to go. Look out there, you can see the sky.'

Through the window screens, you could. Ruby said, 'All right, if you're sure you're not too tired and if you promise you'll drive carefully.' Then she grinned. 'Ha ha, will you listen to me? I sound just like Lesley and Mamdooh, only not quite so much fun.'

She put her hand under her grandmother's arm and they went downstairs together, Iris jingling the keys in her pocket.

They were not to have an easy exit. Mamdooh darted out from the back of the house and saw at a glance where they were heading. He began by insisting that it was too late, the roads would be too busy, Mum-reese would be too tired.

Iris stepped round him.

Then he put his tarboosh on his head and made to follow them.

Iris held up her hand. 'Thank you, Mamdooh. But this afternoon Ruby and I are going to make an excursion together. You may accompany us another time.'

He still came all the way out into the alleyway with them, and almost tussled with Ruby as she tried to heave open the old wooden doors and he lent his considerable weight to holding them closed. He wouldn't look directly at Ruby, blaming her as always for bringing all this distraction and disruption into the peaceful household, but he kept up a stream of warnings and gloomy pronouncements to Iris.

She smiled briefly and batted him aside. 'Thank you. I was driving around this city sixty years ago, you know, when you were just a boy coming to Garden City with your father. Get in, Ruby.'

They settled themselves in their seats and Mamdooh planted himself a foot from the rear bumper, legs apart and fists on his hips.

'Are you going to run him over?' Ruby murmured.

'I shall try not to.' The Beetle's engine coughed and then roared, there was a scream from the gearbox as Iris attempted to find reverse gear without engaging the clutch, but then she seemed to remember something of what driving involved and began to back out of the garage. She rolled down her window and nodded to Mamdooh as he jumped aside. 'Don't worry about us,' she said breezily.

They almost slammed into the opposite wall of the alley. Ruby's head jerked as Iris stamped on the brakes just in time.

'Mamdooh's pissed off with me. He found me and Ash up in my room just now. We weren't doing anything.'

Iris clicked her tongue as they drove off. 'Really, Ruby. You have no idea how to behave. What you do is your business, but if you try not to offend people you will find life much simpler.'

Ruby shrank lower in her seat. 'Sorry,' she said humbly. '*Look out!*'

A headscarfed matron on a Vespa was crossing ahead of them as Iris shot straight out of a junction. The scooter wobbled as Iris braked and then accelerated, making a gesture of apology as she turned across a hooting stream of traffic.

'These people always were crazy drivers,' she said, heading downtown. She was looking at the crowds with curiosity and apparent enjoyment.

Ruby unclenched her fists and told herself that at least it was the end of the day and every street was jammed with vehicles. When the collision came, they wouldn't be travelling at anything more than a walking pace.

But Iris's embedded motor responses seemed to fire up again, erratically at first and then more reliably. Her hands loosened on the wheel and she accelerated and changed gear and braked in the right order, apparently without thinking about it. After a few more angry blasts from trucks and taxis she even began to use the indicators.

The traffic heaved and shuddered around them, carrying the Beetle forward like a pebble churning in a wave, then freezing again in a collective hiss of hydraulic brakes, bleating horns, tinny music from the open windows of mud-grey Fiats. Traffic lights suspended in a cat's-cradle of wires changed from green to red. Ruby looked out at the tall advertisment hoardings wedged between peeling concrete buildings, bright-lit little shops, and the press of people dashing for home or into the mouth of the nearest metro station.

It was the twilight half-hour when the flat sky took on a sudden dark-blue depth. In another half an hour the stars would begin to show. The women with mop buckets would be washing the day's last eddy of visitors towards the doors of the museum and then the statues and carvings would lie in silence for the night.

After a few minutes she roused herself, aware that she had been daydreaming. Iris had been taking a series of left and right turns further and further away from the main stream of traffic and now they were in a quiet street lined with mimosas and oleander. The lights of apartments were beginning to blink on.

'Where are we?' Ruby asked unthinkingly.

Then she saw that Iris was staring ahead through the windscreen. She let the car drift to the side of the road and the tyres struck the kerb at an angle. The car behind them hooted and swept past.

'Iris? Are you all right?'

There was no answer and Ruby put her hand over her grandmother's where it rested on the wheel. Iris turned off the ignition and there was silence broken only by the little ticks of cooling metal.

'It's all different.' She shook her head as if she was trying to clear it, and then turned towards Ruby. The street lamp five yards away had just come on and the pale acid glare shone into her face. 'I don't know where I'm going.'

'I'm not surprised; of course it's all different,' Ruby began.

But Iris was staring through her. Her mouth trembled and her eyes had lost their focus. She looked shocked, as if she were seeing the faded streets of sixty years ago and was disorientated by the brutal superimposition of modern buildings and the unfamiliar breadth of teeming new roads.

They sat for a moment in silence. A pair of men walking by in smart suits with camelhair coats slung over their shoulders glanced into the car with brief curiosity. At least they weren't in a dodgy area, Ruby thought. It even seemed vaguely familiar, now she looked at it. The apartment blocks looked prosperous and there were guard houses at some of the tall gates.

She squeezed Iris's hand in her own. 'Let's go home. Can you drive?'

But Iris was soundlessly weeping.

'Don't cry. It's all right, look, here.' From the pocket of her jeans Ruby produced a Kleenex and tried to dry her tears.

'It has all gone.' Iris's voice was like an abandoned child's, plangent with a terrible despair.

'No, it's still here, it's still Cairo. It's just time, doing what it does.'

'Doing what it does,' Iris forlornly echoed, the words themselves seeming to make no sense to her however much she longed to find comfort in them.

'That's right,' Ruby confirmed. The obvious thing to do was take Iris back home, to the reassurance of familiar surroundings. She detached her hand from Iris's although Iris tried to hang on to it, climbed out of the car and came round to the driver's side. Then she gently helped her out and into the passenger seat, Iris doing as she was prompted with child-like trust. The tears had stopped and she just looked smaller and frailer.

Ruby took the wheel and started up the car. If she could drive the taxi back from Muqattam, she reasoned, she could equally well find their way home from here. Given time.

The streets were curved, seeming to loop around gardens crammed with leafy darkness. She drove slowly, ignoring impatient hooting, searching for a clue to where they might be. There was a tall brown block on the next corner, projecting metal balconies outlined against the glare of light from a busier street and Ruby slowed even further as they came to the junction, craning left and right.

Iris stirred. 'What are you doing? Turn right,' she said

suddenly, in a louder voice quite unlike the lost child's.

Ruby did as she was told. The traffic was lighter now and they swept past gaudy shop windows. She darted a glance at Iris. 'You know, you could direct me. I'm not very sure of the way.'

With a touch of irritation Iris pointed ahead. 'Carry on until the end of Sharia Mawardi, then turn left.'

'OK'.

They rattled over tramlines and then in the distance Ruby saw the outline of the Citadel, two solid shades darker than the opaque eastern sky. Now she had a reference point. After a minute or two, they were out in the blare and rush of Sharia Port Said and she could almost relax. They had been in Iris's old neighbourhood, Garden City.

'Soon be home,' she said.

'Yes,' Iris agreed. 'Are you all right, driving this car?'

'I think so.'

Ten minutes later they nosed into the cobbled alleyway. Ruby left the engine running and got out to open the heavy wooden doors, then eased the Beetle into its space. She let her hands fall into her lap with a silent gasp of relief. Her hair was glued to her damp forehead.

'I am sorry,' Iris mumbled.

'What for?'

'For crying.'

'Because we were lost?'

There was a pause. 'I suppose that was the reason.'

Ruby had no idea how much of the past Iris actually remembered and could only guess at the terror that the periodic blankness must bring. She reached for the knob that controlled the headlights and darkness rushed around them as they blinked out.

She said firmly, 'We're not lost. We're in Cairo and we've got each other, haven't we?'

288

Iris gathered herself, pulling her coat round her and arranging her limbs ready for the effort of climbing out of the car. She was very tired. 'We've got each other.' The words were repeated in the same wondering way.

It struck Ruby afresh that her grandmother was lonely as well as confused. She said, 'Come on, let's go inside.'

'I *wanted* to go for a drive.' That it hadn't been a comfortable excursion didn't diminish the original longing.

'I know. And we can go for plenty more, whenever you like.' The memory project seemed to have come to nothing; she could do this much if that was what Iris wanted.

'Don't say anything,' Iris begged.

''Course not. What about, anyway?'

They entered the house through the back door, conspirators.

In the hall, there was a coat folded over the back of one of the gaunt chairs. Iris saw it and stopped, turning to Ruby with the silent question. Ruby only shrugged; evidently there was a visitor, but she had no idea who it might be.

He was waiting in Iris's sitting room. He had been reading a paper, but he stood up when he heard them coming up the stairs.

'*Bon soir. Excusez-moi*. Iris, how are you?'

The man was compact, dark-haired and olive-skinned, dressed conventionally enough but with a touch of flamboyance in the extra-bright blue of his shirt and the silky handkerchief trailing out of his side pocket.

'Nicolas.'

'I was making a visit to a patient nearby and I thought I would call in. Maybe it is not convenient?' His dark eyes rested on Ruby. 'We haven't met.'

'Nicolas, this is my granddaughter Ruby. Ruby, this my friend Doctor Nicolas Grosseteste. My physician.'

Mamdooh's called him in, Ruby thought.

'Hi.'

He smiled. 'How do you do? Mamdooh so kindly gave me a drink. I have been enjoying five minutes with the newspaper while I waited.'

He was very charming and good-looking.

'Will you stay another five minutes?'

'If I may, Iris. It's too long since we saw each other.'

'Ruby . . .'

'I'll go and tell Mamdooh and Auntie we're back.'

Ruby went down through the house and found the old people in the kitchen. Auntie was chopping vegetables, as usual, and Mamdooh was sitting in his chair beside the stove.

'We had a nice drive,' she told him. 'Mum-reese is with the doctor now.'

'Very good,' he answered flatly. Mamdooh wouldn't give any ground. Auntie set Iris's glass in its worn silver holder on a small tray, poured boiling water to make tea, wrapped some bread in a napkin and put it beside a little dish of honey. With her head on one side, like a little brown bird's, she asked Ruby a question in Arabic and Ruby said, 'Yes, thanks, Auntie, I'll take it up.' This was their way of talking to each other, through and across the languages.

From the upper hallway Ruby heard the doctor's voice and Iris's response followed, then they both laughed and Iris made another rejoinder.

'But that was long before you were born,' she was saying.

They looked up when Ruby came in with her tray.

Doctor Nicolas stayed to drink another glass of tea and then said he must be on his way. He bent over Iris and kissed her hand, and she patted his arm affectionately. Ruby led the way down the stairs to show him out. As he put on his overcoat in the hall the doctor said, 'Your grandmother seems well.'

'Does she?'

'You sound as though you disagree.' Again, the doctor's dark eyes rested on her.

Ruby hesitated, unsure of how much to say. 'She's forgetful. It worries her. I want to help but it's hard when she can only tell me little bits about her life, all disconnected. Sometimes she'll only say a word or two, and they're meaningless, but she'll look at me and I know she expects and wants them to say much more.'

Nicolas studied her for a moment, then he smiled. 'Iris is a very strong woman and has been so all her life. She fears a loss of control, in particular of herself or her faculties.'

Ruby nodded. For some reason a picture of her mother came into her mind, Lesley in the ordered, humming space of the kitchen at home. White mugs on the glass shelves. Ranks of jars and tins in the cupboards.

Guardedly, she said, 'She doesn't want to forget her history. I don't blame her. Your memories must be so precious, when you are old. They're what you've saved up, aren't they? More precious than money or houses or fame. Iris doesn't want to lose hers because once they've gone you've got nothing. You are nothing.'

'You know, I am not sure I entirely agree with that. A human being doesn't exist simply in his or her own consciousness. Each of us has an effect on those around us, and we have our being in their estimation also. In their appreciation or otherwise. In their memories as well as our own.'

Ruby nodded eagerly. 'We've talked about that. I had this idea I could kind of store up her memories for her, you know, like an oral history project. But it doesn't seem to happen. She can't get it into words.'

'Memory is complex, as well as fragile. It isn't just a list of dates and events. You might argue that it is much more to do with scents and textures, and less tangible elements even than those. The cadence of a voice uttering a single word. A bird's song at dawn on one significant day. All these things compact, as in a great poem. I don't know how you might set about capturing and then translating them for another, but then I am only a doctor, not a poet.'

Ruby decided that she liked Doctor Nicolas. 'I'm neither. Just Iris's granddaughter. I want to help, that's all.'

'I believe you are doing that already, Ruby. May I call you that?'

'Sure. How am I helping?'

Nicolas considered. 'Iris has been living alone for many years, and as she has become more physically frail and less able to go out into the world I think she has become isolated. As a result of that isolation a moderate depression has taken hold. It happens that some of the symptoms of depression mimic those of the early phases of dementia, and I think that her confusion and anxiety are attributable to the former. Quite possibly she is confusing the two afflictions herself, and this is increasing her anxiety.'

'Have you told her this?'

'Of course I have tried to. But as you know, Iris does not welcome what she regards as intrusion into her privacy. I can treat her physical ailments, but her mind is still her own. However, since your arrival I have noticed a change in her. She is much more alert, more positive in her responses to stimuli, her blood pressure is lower, she seems to eat and sleep better. You have lifted her spirits.'

'Do you think so?'

'Most definitely.'

Ruby's smile lit up her face. 'Result, then. So you think I should stay?'

The doctor picked up his medical bag. 'Can you? You are very young and you will have calls on your time.'

'I think you could say I'm at a crossroads. Iris and I went out for a drive today, by the way. Did Mamdooh tell you

292

that's where we were? We've got her old Beetle back on the road.'

'Excellent. I should think going out is precisely what she needs. I'll call back again in a few days, Ruby. You can tell me how you both are.'

Nicolas held out his dry, cool hand and Ruby shook it. She went with him to the door and after he had walked briskly away she stood on the top step and breathed in the thick night scents. Animals, diesel fumes, spices, pee.

It came to her that she liked Cairo.

When she went back upstairs she found that Iris had fallen asleep in her chair. She unfolded a shawl and tucked it carefully round her grandmother's shoulders.

After the battles for Sidi Rezegh and Rommel's withdrawal to the line at Mersa el Brega, there came a lull in the desert fighting. Many of the officers and men of the Eighth Army came back to Cairo on leave, and for Xan and me and our friends Christmas 1941 turned into a series of wild parties, mostly impromptu and held in someone's apartment where we danced to the gramophone and drank whatever we could lay our hands on.

Sometimes it would have been easy to forget there was a war on at all. Some days were officially meatless, even in the smart restaurants, because enemy control of the Mediterranean meant that meat could no longer be imported and local supplies were rationed, so we just ordered shellfish or cheese soufflé instead. Grain shortages drove the poor in Cairo to attack the bakeries in attempts to steal what they could no longer buy, while Faria's Coptic Christian parents gave a party in their house for two hundred guests with a jazz band, French champagne and a five-course dinner served by gloved servants at tables decorated with garlands of fresh flowers flown up from Southern Africa. I still enjoyed these pleasures, but the city was full of contrasts that seemed to grow sharper every day. I was beginning to see the world, and my privileged place in it, through Ruth's and Daphne's eyes.

At her parents' party Faria told me that her father and Ali's father had insisted on finalising a wedding date. We were repairing our make-up at the dressing-table glass in her girlhood bedroom.

'The 28th of May,' she said, painting her lips in an unsmiling dark-red slash. Her black hair was as smooth and shiny as if coated in shellac and her oval face was expressionless.

Over her head I glanced at my own overexcited pink-and-white reflection.

'Are you happy?' I asked.

'Happy? Darling, I have no idea. Should one be? Would you be?'

Thinking of Ali, and the contrast he made with Xan, I guessed not – but I wasn't Faria.

'Anyway, life will go on, won't it?' Faria snapped her lipstick back into its case and turned her head from side to side so her diamond earrings caught the light. 'What about you and Xan?'

'My mother wants to come out here.'

'Ah. The English church, the ambassador to read the lesson, a regimental guard of honour.'

'I suppose so.'

Faria leaned close to me and I breathed in her heavy perfume. Shalimar. 'If I were you, I would elope. Don't waste another hour.' She winked, put her arm through mine and led me back down to the dance floor where Xan was waiting.

He put his mouth to my ear and a shiver of pleasure ran all the way down my spine. 'You are beautiful, Iris Black, and I love you. Are we going to stay all night at this pompous party, or shall we go home to bed?'

'Bed,' I answered composedly. I would never have guessed, nor would the boys I had briefly encountered in London, that I could ever like sex as much as I did with Xan.

As she had promised, Daphne Erdall found me volunteer work at her hospital. It wasn't nursing, which was what I had naïvely hoped for, but at least it was something. For three evening sessions a week I sat at a desk in the almoner's office and filled in forms with the details of British casualties; name, number, rank, regiment, injuries, date of arrival, supervising MO, ward, notification of next of kin. I typed letters addressed to wives in the Home Counties and mothers in the Midlands and Yorkshire and Scotland, and passed them on to the proper authority for signature. My boss was Christina Tsatsas, a good-natured Greek woman whose forearms and upper lip were shadowed with soft dark hair. When I took my short break we would stand on the small concrete terrace outside the window and smoke a cigarette, looking down into the dark of the hospital garden.

'You want to be a nurse?' Christina asked.

'Yes.'

'You have to train.'

'Of course.'

But I couldn't afford to give up my job at GHQ and if I embarked on part-time training I would see even less of Xan than I did now.

'After the war,' I said, giving voice to an intention that had hardly begun to form itself in my mind. I could tell that Christina thought I lacked the proper degree of determination ever to make a useful nurse.

I saw Daphne sometimes, and although at first I was a little in awe of her we slowly began to be friends. When I met her around the hospital, by accident or by arrangement, she was usually alone but she trailed a distinct glamour in her wake. She was always pressed for time but she never seemed too busy to speak to whoever stopped her in a corridor, giving them her full, serious attention. She was friendly with her all-male surgical team, but it was an arm's-length friendliness that fell well short of intimacy. People glanced after her as she passed them, either wondering who she was or, like me when we first met, acknowledging that here was Someone. Daphne herself was quite unaware of the effect she created.

If I was early for work and she was finishing a shift, we would have a cup of tea together in the medical staff canteen. Daphne would tell me about her day's list of operations and if they had lost a badly wounded soldier on the table her eyes would darken with sadness and frustration. Once or twice we talked about Ruth. Daphne was affectionate, but I suspected that she might be too self-contained to acknowledge – perhaps even experience – love in the frank way that Ruth did.

I tried inviting them both to some of the parties we all went to that Christmas, but they were rarely off duty at the same time and when they were they preferred to be alone together.

But then, oddly enough, they appeared at Mrs Kimmig-Gertsch's New Year's Eve party.

The lovely panelled hall where we had once played cards was decorated with a pine tree that must have been fifteen feet tall. I have no idea where it came from; as we waited in a line to greet out hostess, Xan and I amused ourselves by imagining the tortuous route that it would have followed from a Swiss mountainside, across occupied Europe to some eastern Mediterranean seaport, and through the German naval blockades to the docks at Alexandria.

'Or maybe she just had it flown in. Perhaps Sandy arranged a convenient airdrop with the RAF,' Xan suggested.

The tree blazed with dozens of real wax candles and its sharp, resinous scent perfumed the whole house. Mrs Kimmig-Gertsch herself stood in front of it, shaking hands with an impressive turn-out of Cairo society. The ambassador and his lady were in Luxor for their Christmas break, but everyone else seemed to be present. Sir Guy and Lady Gibson Pasha were in the crowd of arrivals just ahead of Xan and me, and there was even a rumour that the King himself might put in an appearance.

Mrs Kimmig-Gertsch inclined her head to us when we reached her. She was wearing a white Grecian-style evening dress swathed and draped aross her stately bosom, and a diamond and sapphire cross rather larger than the Star of the Garter. 'Have you planned a wedding day?' she demanded, her eyes on my amethyst. She liked to know everything.

'Not yet,' we murmured.

'Don't leave it too long,' she ordered, echoing Faria's advice. Xan bowed just a shade too theatrically and I concentrated very hard on not giggling, at least until her unwinking stare moved on to the people behind us.

Xan put his hand under my arm as we turned into the room. 'Look at this,' he whispered. There were jewels and furs, pale or sun-flayed European faces and haughty, sallow Levantine ones, medals and moustaches and feathers and coiffures mixing with the dress uniforms of a dozen armies. 'And we are in the middle of a war.'

It was hard to believe.

Sandy Allardyce stood a little further on, smoking a cigarette in a jade holder and narrowly watching the servants as they circulated with trays of drinks. He was wearing new evening clothes of a slightly florid, non-European cut. We waved to him through the throng.

'How will he fit in at his London club in those?' Xan wondered.

'I shouldn't think he'll need to. His club would seem very faded after all this.'

It was then that I saw Ruth and Daphne. The screens of the upper gallery had all been opened up for the party and they were leaning side by side over the carved partition and looking down on the heads of the crowd.

I pointed them out to Xan. 'I'm surprised. I'd no idea they knew Mrs Kimmig-Gertsch. Would you like to come and meet them?'

'Yes, very much.'

We found the stairway that led up to the gallery and made our way towards them.

'Ruth? Daphne? May I introduce my *fiancé*, Xan Molyneux?'

We all laughed. Xan said, 'I've heard a lot about you both.'

'Likewise,' Ruth agreed.

'I wanted to say thank you for nursing Albie Noake. I heard from Iris how expertly.'

'It's my job,' Ruth said, but a faint blush on her pale skin betrayed her pleasure.

Two by two, we made a slow circuit of the gallery, Xan with Daphne and me with Ruth.

'How do you know her?' I asked, as we watched our hostess sketch a curtsy to an Egyptian royal princess.

'Not me, Daphne. There's a *lot* of money, as you know, and before the war she was involved in a charity that was considering a major donation to Daph's village medical project. The money never quite materialised, actually, but we seem to have made it onto the guest list anyway. What about you?'

I told her about Sandy.

'Anyway, it's all very decadent,' Ruth said in her crisp Scottish voice. Below us a group of young men in distinctive red trousers were dancing a noisy conga line through the crowd. It was the Cherry Pickers. At the head of the line was a conjurer dressed in an Arabian Nights costume topped with a sequinned turban. He was pulling silk handkerchiefs and posies of flowers out of the fronts of women's dresses, and from behind Mrs Kimmig-Gertsch's head he magicked a live white dove. The Cherry Pickers whooped and clapped, and the bird flew up out of the conjurer's hand and landed on the gallery partition a few feet away from us.

'Is Jessie here?' I asked Xan.

'Of course he is. I think he's marking the mule's dance card.'

My new friends and Xan liked each other at once. He could talk as fluently as Daphne did about the war and about bread rationing and the predicament of Cairo's poor but he also teased her, and Ruth, about their serious-mindedness.

'It's New Year's Eve. No irrigation project can be got under way tonight, can it?' He hoisted two glasses off a passing tray and put them into their hands. 'Let's concentrate on irrigating ourselves. Here's to 1942,' he said.

They echoed the toast and I looked at their bright faces outlined against the swirl of party guests. I was pleased and excited to be with the three of them and I drank to celebrate, keeping pace with Xan and feeling the hot gas of the party singeing my cheeks.

We danced, and I picked at some of the cold lobster and creamy gateaux laid out in the dining room, and danced and drank some more. I held on to Xan's wrist and he steered me through the crowds as familiar and half-recognised faces swam up and sank back again. Much later, I found myself following him and a crowd of other people through the kitchen regions of the house and out into a narrow cobbled alley somewhere at the back. The cool air made me stumble in my high heels and Jessie James put his arm round my waist. The famous poker game mule that had become the constant companion of one of his officer friends was patiently standing outside a pair of stable doors and his owner was tugging at the bridle.

'Come on, darling. Don't be coy, come and greet your public.'

The Cherry Pickers all cheered. The mule was wearing a sable wrap with the tails hanging round its fore-quarters and an orchid corsage was tucked into the bridle's headpiece. The mule lifted one hoof, stepped delicately forward and crossed the cobbles to the door that led into the house. The rest of us formed a ragged column behind it.

'What's happening?' I mumbled to Xan.

'He wants them to see in the New Year together.'

A little group of musicians had been playing on the low dais facing the giant Christmas tree. Sandy Allardyce was giving them instructions and now the leader stood up, tucked his violin under one arm and made a little bow. A noisy group led by Betty Hopwood was counting down the seconds to midnight. *Twelve, eleven, ten . . .* As the mule made its entry through the tall doors it was stricken by the bright lights and the surging crowd. Its legs splayed and its head reared back, setting the sable tails jiggling.

Five, four, three . . .

Everyone was shouting now. The bandleader sounded a long chord on his violin and the mule gave a terrified snort.

Two, one, hooray . . .

There was a popping of corks like gunfire. With Sandy conducting, the band scraped into an approximation of the first bars and the crowd swayed dangerously as everyone crossed arms in imitation of the Cherry Pickers and the British diplomats, and stumbled to link hands with their neighbours. Ruth and Daphne were singing, I could hear their voices through all the clamour.

Xan's arm was round my waist, holding me upright.

We'll take a cup of kindness yet, for . . . auld lang syne.

The mule broke free and dashed through the room, scattering women in satin and diamonds, and sending chairs crashing over. His owner chased behind and cornered it beside the Christmas tree.

'Dash it,' he cried 'don't you know the words?'

'Happy New Year, Iris, darling.' Xan laughed as his hands cupped my face. '1942 will be our year. We'll make it our year.'

The mule cowered against the panelling, shaking its poor head in terror as its owner patted its nose and murmured reassurance into its hairy ear.

Suddenly, out of nowhere, a wave of nameless, formless, ice-cold fear mounted and crashed over me. I shivered under the shock of it, my stomach heaving so that I was sure I would be sick. A cold sweat broke out on my forehead and the palms of my hands turned sticky.

'Xan.' He was right there, solid and familiar, his breath on my face. 'Xan, I'm frightened.' My lips felt frozen, I could hardly get the words out.

'Darling.'

The hall was a hubbub of kissing and shouting. The mule had lifted its tail and defecated on one of Mrs Kimmig-Gertsch's Persian rugs and Sandy was furiously ordering the Cherry Pickers to drag it outside. The band started to play another number.

Xan helped me away from the thick of the crowd. In the ante-room he sat me in a high-backed chair, gave me a glass of water and rubbed my hands. My teeth were chattering. The foreboding was still there, a dark poisonous fog of it, sweeping towards us.

'It's all right. It's just the drink, darling. You've had a lot to drink.'

'Yes.'

301

I wanted that to be it. I wished I were drunk, but I knew I wasn't.

'There's a cab waiting,' Jessie said at Xan's shoulder. 'Shall we get her into it?'

They each took one of my arms and they helped me out into the blue-black night.

That was the beginning of 1942.

CHAPTER TWELVE

As we leave the city behind the darkness thins.

There is never a precise moment in the desert when you can say *now it is dawn*, but the day comes swiftly and without drama. Suddenly the single-storey mud villages and irrigation canals stand out on either side of the road in the flat grey light, and rigid black silhouettes of date palms subdivide monochrome fields of crops. We overtake a buffalo cart, and an old man riding a donkey with empty paniers dragging at its haunches.

We are going to see the sun rise at the Pyramids, I remember that much, but now that we are on the road I'm afraid of the coming daylight and the threatening flat space of the delta with the desert so close at hand. I want to be back in my house, inside the familiar place. If we go on, the harsh sun and the wind over the dunes will obliterate me.

I turn to the driver. 'Daphne, stop.'

Ruby noticed a scruffy little café at the side of the road where the owner was putting out tin tables and his wife was sweeping dust off the concrete standing with a palm leaf brush. A cup of coffee might help, she thought. This excursion was already turning out to be a crap idea.

'I know. Let's stop here, shall we?' she said to Iris.

It was light, although the sun wasn't up yet. The driver of a white minibus full of tourists hooted as she braked in front of him, the blast of his horn changing pitch as the bus roared by. Iris nodded in apparent relief.

They sat down on metal chairs with the battered table shielding them from the road. The café owner swabbed the table top with a gritty cloth.

'I would like some hot coffee,' Iris said. She looked pale but calmer.

Ruby was hungry. She ordered bread and eggs and a dish of fruit while the man yawned and scraped his jaw with the back of his hand. It was still very early.

'Iris? Who's Daphne?'

Iris sat quite still, gazing along the road that led away from Cairo. At first, Ruby thought she hadn't heard the question. A tin pot of coffee and two thick white cups were banged down on the table in front of them, followed by a bowl containing slices of greyish bread. Ruby poured coffee and pushed one of the cups close to where Iris's clasped hands rested on the table top.

'Daphne Erdall,' Iris said clearly.

'Go on.'

There was no answer this time, but this was the technique, Ruby had learned, when Iris drifted into one of the lost places.

You kept prodding her with questions and disjointed answers were doled out in response. Then – not always, but sometimes – the fragments of response ran together and occasionally coalesced into whole chunks of intelligible narrative.

Only two days ago, when Ruby was following the advice of Doctor Nicolas Grosseteste and taking Iris out for a slow

304

walk in the sunshine, the sight of a mule outside in the street with a small boy patiently holding up its nosebag had made her stop short and give a little laugh that turned into a gasp and then a cough. She wouldn't say what was funny or painful, but she had clasped Ruby's hand more tightly as they made their slow turn to the end of the street and back.

But then, when they were inside the house once more, Iris had suddenly come out with a story about a mule being led into this hall because its owner wanted it to sing Auld Lang Syne at a New Year's party, and the animal had rewarded him by lifting its tail and doing its business on the Persian carpet.

'Were you living here then?' Ruby asked, puzzled.

'Oh no. That was the beginning of 1942. The house belonged to Gerti Kimmig-Gertsch in those days.'

'So did you buy it from her?'

Iris only smiled, tipping her nose upwards in a way that was almost flirtatious.

'Of course not. How could I have done? It's a much more interesting story than that.'

'I'm all ears,' Ruby said, but Iris only complained that she was tired and would Ruby please send Auntie upstairs to her.

Later, Mamdooh said, 'Mum-reese very tired, I think. It is not good, going out walking in afternoon sun.'

Ruby met his eye. 'It wasn't all that hot.' This was true. In late November the sun was often no more than a whitish disc riding behind a thin layer of cloud. When the sky was clear, the heat built up slowly towards the middle of the day and then quickly soaked away as the sun sank again.

'You are strong, young woman, miss.'

'The doctor told me that it is good for Mum-reese to get out of the house. We're going to be making a few more excursions, actually. Now we've, like, got the car going again.'

Mamdooh wrinkled his forehead. The moles and warts edged closer together, as if seeking each other's company. 'I think not a good idea.'

OK, Ruby thought to herself. I won't come asking for your permission.

Then yesterday afternoon Iris had suddenly had the idea that they should make a dawn excursion to the Pyramids.

'The museum, and the Pyramids. Essential for all visitors to Cairo. What would your mother say if I didn't take you out there?'

Ruby shrugged and said she had already been out there with Ash and Giza had been crowded with a million tourists and touts and taxis, but Iris dismissed her with an impatient wave of the hand. They would get up very early and go out to see the sun rise. Iris kept repeating this and in the end Ruby said, 'Whatever.' When Iris had an idea in her head there was no deflecting her.

Yesterday evening, out walking with Ash, she told him about the plan for the morning.

'No difference, early or late. Always many people.'

'Yeah. But my grandmother is thinking of sixty years ago, you know? She mixes things up.'

'You will take good care, Ruby. I would be coming with you, but I must go to work.'

Ash was working a midnight shift at the hospital switchboard. He came home at 9 a.m. and slept for two or three hours.

'It's fine. What can happen?'

'Going to Giza only, I suppose nothing. You will take Cairo taxi?'

'I'm going to drive the Beetle, seeing that Nafouz got it all fixed up for us.'

'This is not a good idea, I think.'

Ruby laughed. 'Where've I heard that before? And it's

306

better for me to drive than to let my grandmother do it, I can tell you.'

'Well, then, just so far as Giza.'

Ruby got up in the dark and went barefoot to knock on Iris's bedroom door.

Iris was already out of bed, standing in the middle of the room in her vest and waist slip. She looked at Ruby with the shadow of confusion in her eyes. 'I don't know what to wear. What do you think?'

'Put on a dress and a warm cardigan, and your flat leather sandals. Here they are.' Ruby found the shoes and Iris sat down heavily on her bed while Ruby lifted first one foot and then the other. Knotted blue veins and the hard ridges of tendons bulged under the flaking skin and Ruby cupped each heel in turn, protectively, before she slid on the shoes. It made her throat tighten to see that Iris's toenails needed cutting and she blinked quickly to clear her blurred vision. She decided that she would ask her later if she could do it.

'There. Bring your hat and some sunglasses as well.'

'Thank you,' Iris said sharply. When she didn't happen to need help she hated any suggestion that she might. 'Why don't you go round and get the car ready, and I will meet you at the front of the house?'

'All right. See you in five minutes.' Ruby went downstairs through the dark hallway. It was early, but she was disconcerted to discover that the lights were already on in the kitchen. She had planned to ease herself and Iris out of the house before Mamdooh could interrupt, and luckily it was only Auntie who was carrying a pan of water across to the old stove. Mamdooh's chair was empty; Ruby guessed that he wouldn't be stirring himself for an hour or so yet.

Auntie put down the pan and hurried across to seize Ruby's

307

arm, peering up into her face and asking quick questions. Ruby picked out *shai* and *'aish*, tea and bread – Auntie was asking if she wanted breakfast.

'Don't worry, Auntie, thanks very much. We're just, like going out for a bit of a drive. Just to see the sunrise, you know? We'll be back.'

There was another rattle of Arabic with a sprinking of words that she knew, all to do with food.

'I'll just take some fruit, OK?' Ruby helped herself to a couple of pomegranates and put them with some oranges into a straw bag that she lifted off a hook. Auntie beamed and added a tight package of dried apricots, chattering vehemently as she did so.

'*Shukran*, Auntie. Whoa, that's plenty. We'll see you later.' She lifted her free hand in a quick wave as she slid through the door that led towards the back alley.

'*Inshallah.*'

'*Inshallah,*' Ruby cheerfully echoed over her shoulder. She latched the kitchen door behind her.

The pungent alley was almost pitch dark. Ruby trod with care, trying not to hear the rustlings among the debris in the central gutter. She groped for the big padlock, found its cold weight and slid in the key. Once she was inside the car she threw the basket onto the back seat, the Beetle started up at once and the headlights cut a welcome yellow wedge in the blackness. Just on the margin, very briefly, there was the glimmer of several pairs of eyes.

Ruby drove round to the point where the street narrowed to become impassable to cars.

Iris was waiting for her. 'You took your time,' she said, as she settled into the passenger seat.

'Auntie was already up.' They rolled towards the river and the Giza road.

*   *   *

Now they sat at the roadside café watching the morning traffic build up. Iris finished her coffee and drank some water, dabbing her mouth afterwards with a folded handkerchief as Ruby chewed her way through bread and hard-boiled egg chopped up with onion.

'Have some breakfast.' She pushed the bowl of bread an inch closer but Iris ignored her. 'Or tell me about Daphne Erdall.'

Surprisingly, Iris responded at once. 'She was a doctor. A very good doctor, a surgical anaesthetist here in Cairo, and her friend Ruth Macnamara was a nurse. I was very young and silly but I learned a lot from the two of them. It was because of Daphne's example that I decided to study medicine myself, once the war was over. I married your father when I was coming to the end of my clinical practice at St Bartholomew's.'

'My grandfather, you mean.'

Iris glared at her. Her lips were pale, and compressed into a thin line emphasised by radiating creases. 'Don't tell me what I mean. Yes, your grandfather.'

Ruby thought of the soldier in the framed photograph beside Iris's bed, the only photograph on display in the whole house, the soldier who was definitely not Grandfather Gordon. Remembering the name that Iris had mentioned she asked, 'What happened to Captain Molyneux?'

Iris considered for a moment before answering. Then she cleared her throat and said precisely, 'He was killed in the desert. In May 1942.'

In the following silence Ruby did the arithmetic. Sixty-three years ago; remote history, almost. 'That's sad,' she said.

'Sad. Yes.'

Iris sat with her hands folded, looking straight ahead of her at what Ruby could not see. There was something practised and impenetrable about her absolute stillness.

As Ruby tried to think what to say next she noticed that the world had acquired colour. The walls of the café shack were sunflower yellow, the crops in the field across the road a pale, watered-down green. Somewhere behind them, beyond the Suez Canal, the sun had risen.

The opportunity for saying something, anything at all, seemed to have passed. Ruby shifted on her tin chair and stirred a small cloud of greyish dust. She put her hand out and covered Iris's folded ones.

'Would you like some more coffee? Or shall we move on?'

In the absence of any response she beckoned the surly café owner and asked for the bill. Then she followed him into the dingy interior and took two litre bottles of water out of the chiller cabinet, fumbling with worn and dirty pound notes as she paid for everything. Outside again, she took Iris by the arm and led her back to the car. They drove on towards Giza in what was now a steady flood of taxis and buses that hooted and slewed through flocks of brown and white sheep and plodding buffalo. By this time it was much too late for seeing the sunrise at the Pyramids, but they headed on anyway towards the dun-coloured jumble of wire fences and loop roads and coach parks that surrounded the Giza complex.

Then Ruby glanced at Iris and saw that she was weeping again.

Tears ran down her face and over her nose and into the seams round her mouth.

Ruby pulled in to the side of the road once more, causing further hooting. She stuck her fist out of the window in an angry gesture, then she put her arms round her grandmother and tried awkwardly to draw her close. The handbrake and gearstick got in the way.

'Iris, stop. Please stop. I don't know what to do when you cry like this.'

Iris felt so fragile, too small and brittle to contain such grief. Ruby could do nothing except hold her with the old car's workings prodding in between them, and wait for the tears to stop. She stroked her thin hair and murmured pointless words that were intended to be comforting, and at the same time she thought about Jas. He was often in her mind but she hadn't cried for him, hardly at all.

At last Iris's shuddering sobs petered out and she was quiet. Ruby propped her up by the shoulders and looked into her eyes, and Iris jerked up her chin and pressed the heels of her hands to her face. 'Ridiculous.' She sniffed. 'Give me a handkerchief, will you?'

Ruby didn't go in for keeping handkerchiefs tucked into her sleeve or folded into a pocket, the way Iris did, but after some rummaging she found Iris's own for her and put it into her hand. While Iris dried her eyes and blew her nose, Ruby stared ahead through the windscreen.

With Jas still in her thoughts, she asked, 'Were you crying because Captain Molyneux died?'

'After sixty years? No, I don't believe so. I've grieved enough for his life cut short and for mine for running on for so long with so little in it. It's weakness now, but I suppose I am crying out of a general sense of loss. Maybe I am mourning for the human condition.'

'That sounds a bit . . . what's the word? Grandiose, is that it?'

'Does it?'

To Ruby's relief, Iris laughed. 'Yes, you are probably right. On the other hand, wherever you look there is so much loss and folly to contemplate, and we are so frail in the face of it that it's hard to do anything other than mourn. But you're young, Ruby. You are invincible, and for you everything carries a twin charge of novelty and infinite possibility. Whatever novelty I shall experience is unlikely to be pleasant

311

and the possibilities that remain are more or less limited to various rates of decay.'

Ruby considered. 'Well, I turned up, didn't I? That was a novelty, and you said you were pleased about it.'

'Yes, Ruby. You did, and I am.'

'Thanks. Doctor Nicolas told me he thought you might be sort of depressed.'

'That is his theory, yes.'

'You don't believe it?'

Iris sighed. 'I have had a long life and I have been useful. I enjoyed my work, very much, for many years. I have a home and people to care for me, and I could have more company if I wished for it. I am afraid of losing what I have always valued . . .'

'The cup on the shelf?'

Iris looked startled. 'Did I say that to you?'

'Yes.'

'I had forgotten. You see? Yes, there is that, and there is also the sense that I have had a hole at the centre of my life. It has been there for a very long time. But I don't know that these various anxieties and shortcomings constitute depression. It's a catch-all term, in my opinion. Modern medical thinking, you know.'

Ruby pressed the flat of her hands against the steering wheel and arched her back. She was still looking at the road. 'This *hole* in the centre? It's not really Captain Molyneux, is it? Would I be right in thinking it's actually Mum?'

There was a pause. 'Lesley.'

'Yeah. Your daughter, my mother.'

Ruby was thinking, she's not going to answer and she won't say anything else.

But Iris did nod her head, very slowly, as if it hurt. 'Maybe.' She took a long breath, raised her chin again and glared out at the file of traffic. 'Where are we going?'

312

If she didn't want to talk, Ruby couldn't make her. 'To the bloody Pyramids, supposedly. Do you still want to?'

'I . . . would like to go for a drive. Out into the desert a little way. Can we do that instead?'

'Of course we can.'

They rejoined the column of traffic, but instead of being drawn with it towards the three triangles magnetically pasted against the whitish southern sky, they broke free and headed on, westwards, with the sun rising higher at their backs. The pale-green ribbon of irrigated fields that threaded along beside the Nile had been left far behind and out here there were only low sand dunes that glittered where the sun caught them and trapped broad scoops of donkey-brown shadow within their concave arms.

Ruby took a series of turnings at random, deliberately trying to leave behind what remained of the thinning traffic. Cairo and the suburbs were so crowded, it was a pleasure to shake off the hooting and screeching of brakes, and creep forward into space and emptiness. The road narrowed and took a southerly direction, and in places it was submerged under a thin layer of wind-blown sand.

'There is a tiny oasis out here somewhere,' Iris said. 'With a view of the Pyramids that you don't get from anywhere else.' She looked back over her shoulder, searching for a glimpse of it.

Ruby was watching the humpbacks of the dunes. They were like pieces of architecture, seeming too perfectly smooth and sculpted to be natural. The sudden empty monotony of the slow-motion scenery was hypnotic. The occasional vehicle darted along a distant road that skirted the dunes, looking like an angry insect against the vast tawny flanks.

'Do you want to turn back and try to find it?' she murmured.

'I only went there once.'

The Beetle hummed along, its tyres swishing through the

skim of sand on tarmac. Ruby and Iris both fell into a contented silence, watching the endless rise and fall of the empty landscape.

For the first three months of 1942 I worked at my GHQ job in Roddy Boy's office and spent whatever time I had to spare at the Queen Mary. I saw how the medical services dealt with the constant stream of casualties brought back from the front as Rommel recaptured Benghazi and pushed eastwards again, and my admiration for Daphne and the others who worked with her steadily grew. When we met outside working hours, I began to ask her and Ruth more and more questions about medical and nursing techniques.

Ruth used to tease me about it. 'Is this medical school? Why do you want to know all these details about barrier nursing and antisepsis and bone-setting?'

'It's interesting.'

Daphne agreed, in her brisk way. 'Acute medicine is more interesting than anything else.'

We had become friends, but however well I felt I was getting to know them, their company sometimes made me feel like an outsider. Daphne was absorbed in her work and Ruth was absorbed in Daphne, and I skirted between them. So I didn't confide to them what I had begun to plan for the future, although I did talk about it to Xan.

'After the war, when we're married and back in England . . .'

'Yes, darling. I'm going to buy myself out of the army and find a job. What do you think I could do? Stockbroking? Bowler hat, golf, Surrey, that sort of thing?'

'Oh, yes. I can just see it.'

'No? What about being a farmer? Some jolly pink pigs to fatten up. Would you like to be a farmer's wife? Or . . . I know, insurance salesman. I'm sure I could persuade people to buy lots of lovely life insurance. Anyway, whatever I do won't matter, will it, because we'll have each other?'

'What shall *I* do?'

'Have babies. Dozens of 'em.'

'Well, yes, but there's something else. I want to train to be a doctor.'

'Do you?' He stretched out his arm and hooked me closer to him, smoothing the corners of my mouth with his thumbs. 'My clever, ambitious wife-to-be. In that case I won't need a job at all.'

'Xan, be serious.'

Some of the playfulness faded out of his eyes. 'I don't want to be serious.'

I could have bitten my tongue. I had seen very little of him since New Year's Eve and when he did appear in Cairo, with Hassan or on occasional flying visits with Colonel Wainwright in the WACO, he was filthy and exhausted and he flatly deflected all my questions about what he had been doing or how difficult and dangerous it had been. Even more than when I had first known him, when he was away from the desert Xan wanted to laugh and make love and forget everything else.

We held each other tightly. After a moment he said, 'I'm sorry. It's hard, and it's getting harder, to move between . . . war and being with you. It's like walking a tightrope between hell and heaven.'

'I can only try to imagine.'

'Don't. I don't want you even to begin to imagine it. Iris, if you want to study medicine after the war, then of course you shall. We'll make it our priority.'

'Good.' I smiled at him. 'I like getting my own way, right from the beginning.'

'That's settled, then. What's the news from GHQ?'

'GHQ is the same as ever.'

'Unfortunately.'

Intelligence gathered by Roddy Boy's section had in the past been employed to assure field commanders that the enemy had not been reinforced with men or arms, and then the opposite had turned out to be true. As I well knew, last year Xan's patrol had run into a detachment of Panzers that was theoretically nowhere in the vicinity, and Captain Burke and Private Ridley and the others had died, and Albie Noake had lost half his face. Now, as Rommel advanced once more, the First Armoured Division fatally met a Panzer force that – it turned out – had been augmented by tanks brought in by German naval convoy to Tripoli. Even though the men on the ground had seen the armour with their own eyes, GHQ had difficulty believing what our Intelligence could not actually confirm.

'We can only know what we bloody well *do* know,' I overheard Roddy protest in exasperation.

Now I heard from Xan that there was more concern. Xan's Tellforce and some of the other commando groups were discovering that the enemy had developed an uncanny ability to predict when and where their raids were to take place. The commandos would be parachuted in over their secret objectives, the supply dumps or enemy airfields, or dropped off by Tellforce patrols on intricate sabotage missions, and time and again they would find enemy ground or air forces apparently lying in wait for them.

'What does that mean?' I asked, although I knew the answer.

'A security leak.'

'From GHQ? That's not possible, surely?' Officers in the field routinely complained that there were too many pampered senior staff officers with too little to do, but I couldn't imagine that Roddy Boy or anyone like him was guilty of breaching security, even accidentally.

'Maybe not. But who can say for certain? Or maybe it's the Americans. It seems only to have been happening since they came in.'

'How?'

Xan sighed. 'If I knew, it would be simpler, wouldn't it? I'm just a patrol commander working out in the desert and doing what I'm told, but it seems to me that it's more than unfortunate coincidence.'

We were sitting together on a rug spread under a mimosa tree at the club. I drew up my knees and wrapped my arms round them, and that small movement seemed to release a thick drift of the dry, potent scent of mimosa blossom into the hot air.

'Maybe it's Sandy Allardyce.'

'Trading military secrets while locked in the arms of Mrs K-G?'

Deliberately we both laughed but it was anxious laughter with a note of wildness in it.

'No, it's not them,' Xan said.

I took hold of his hand and he slowly rubbed his thumb over the amethyst on my ring finger.

'You will be careful, won't you?' Uttering the words made me feel weak and imploring, but I couldn't help myself.

'Yes,' Xan promised, because there was nothing else he could say. I could hear the lazy *plock* of tennis balls and voices calling out the score, *love-forty*. The afternoon was mazy with heat, thick with the layered smells of Cairo, and stretched into tiny, crystalline, mineral-hard seconds and minutes of waiting. The war continued at sea and in the air but in the desert, where spring had briefly carpeted the wadis with gaudy flowers, there was a long lull in the fighting. The forces were drawn up on either side of the heavily reinforced Gazala Line. But the interlude could not last much longer. Rommel was getting ready. General Auchinleck, so the cocktail gossip went, was hoping for the best and expecting the worst.

None of us really knew anything. Along with the

317

Commander-in-Chief Middle East, no one could do anything other than hope for the best.

Xan's arms slid round me and he drew me down to lie beside him on the rug. Then he propped himself up so his face blocked out the sky and the feather foliage of the mimosa. He was braver than I was, and better at dealing with the slow drip of time and anxiety. But then, when the time came Xan would be with his men and Hassan, doing what he was trained to do while I was only waiting and imagining. Often enough in those airless, merciless African spring and early-summer days, I wished I were a man. I wished I could do something other than typing and filling in forms and answering telephones. I thought more about Daphne, and medicine.

'Don't worry too much,' Xan said gently. He was smiling.

'Worry? What about?'

He kissed me and we rolled over, laughing at each other. Always laughing.

A few days later, when Xan had gone away again with Colonel Wainwright, I woke up with a flat taste of metal in my mouth. As soon as I sat up I felt sick, and I perched on the edge of the bed for a moment and rested my feet on the cool floor tiles until I could contemplate getting dressed. Sarah was sitting at the dining table with a magazine and a cup of coffee, and the smell of the coffee immediately made me feel worse.

'Are you all right?' she asked.

I made a face. Food in Cairo was becoming scarcer and restaurant fish was not always reliably fresh. I had eaten shellfish the night before. Quickly, I left the room.

I felt better once I had been sick. Sitting at the table with Sarah, I drank some weak tea and nibbled on a piece of toast, and we talked about what we should do once Faria was married. She would be living with Ali in his palatial apartment near the Gezira Club, and her parents would want to take possession of our flat again. Sarah and I agreed that we would have to find somewhere smaller and cheaper to share, and I wondered aloud if Daphne and Ruth might know somewhere near their place on the Heliopolis Road.

Faria appeared, yawning, with her white silk robe trailing behind her. She looked irritable and, unusually, there was a faint sheen of perspiration on her forehead. She picked up the coffee pot and scowled. 'There's none left. Have you drunk every drop?'

Sarah and I glanced at each other.

'I'll go and ask Mamdooh to make a fresh pot,' Sarah said gently.

Faria slumped down in a chair.

'What are you doing today?' I asked.

'Fittings. Endless fittings, and making lists with my mother. I am only getting married. Why is one made to feel like a prize animal? With a couture ribbon tied round its neck, being led to the slaughter?'

'Is that how it really feels?' I asked.

Faria shrugged impatiently. 'Wait until it's your turn and you'll see.'

The sickness continued into the next day and by the time a week had passed I was having to accept that there might be another explanation for it than a mild dose of shellfish poisoning.

I mentioned my suspicion to Ruth and Daphne.

Ruth raised one amused eyebrow and Daphne said, 'I'm not a gynaecologist but it sounds like pregnancy to me. Weren't you using anything?'

'Not invariably.' I coloured a little, remembering the urgency of some of the times.

'Well, there you are. I can arrange a test for you, at the hospital.'

319

'What do you want to do?' Ruth asked.

Before I could formulate the answer, I knew without any whisper of doubt what I wanted to do. I wanted to have Xan's child. Xan's son.

'Xan said he wanted babies, dozens of them. I'm going to have the child, of course.'

My face split into a smile and I felt my limbs lighten, my head lifting on my shoulders as if it might float away. The nausea was concentrated inside me, a heavy, welcome, yawning weight beneath my ribcage.

'Ah. Then there's no problem, is there?' Daphne tilted her head towards me and pressed her clean hand over mine. She looked pleased and slightly sad at the same time, and Ruth stood up at once and rested her hands on her shoulders, holding her in her place.

I was babbling now and grinning at them both. 'None. It's a bit early and it'll mean my mother probably won't get the big wedding she's been dreaming of, but Xan will be relieved about that, I should think, and I don't want to feel like some sacrificial beast either, the way Faria seems to. We'll just get married, with our friends around us, and I want you two to be godparents. Will you?'

Daphne and Ruth glanced at each other, and I couldn't read what was in their eyes.

Ruth spoke for them both in the end. 'Yes,' she said. 'We'd be proud to, if that's what you and Xan both want.'

'I think you should come in and see my colleague Esther Reisen,' Daphne said briskly. 'She is a gynaecologist. It might be a good idea to be positive before you actually appoint the godparents, don't you think?'

'I will. Then I can tell Xan it's definite.'

A few days after that I had the confirmation from Doctor Reisen. I was pregnant.

I had no idea how to contact Xan; in the past I had just

watched and waited for him to materialise. Now I called in at the Zamalek flat, pretending that it was just a spur-of-the-moment social visit, and surprised two exhausted-looking officers who had apparently been sound asleep at eight o'clock in the evening. They didn't know anything about Xan's present whereabouts.

'He'll turn up in a few days, always does,' one of them promised. 'Would you like a drink?'

Roddy Boy did not respond to my casual enquiries about the present movements of the various Tellforce patrols.

'I cannot discuss that with you, Miss Black, as you know full well. Like all the other service mothers, wives and fiancées you will simply have to wait for whatever happens.' His plump mouth tightened and he looked slightly hunted.

There was nothing in the Intelligence traffic – at least, none that I was party to – that gave me any clues either. In the end I wrote a brief note, saying in the most anonymous and general language that Xan should contact me as soon as he was able. I sealed it in an envelope and addressed it to Captain A. N. Molyneux, and walked from HQ to the run-down street across from el Rhoda. I picked out the house near where Hassan had been waiting when Xan and I came back from choosing my amethyst, and I strolled up and knocked on the door. It was opened by a smart-looking Indian NCO.

'Yes, Madam?'

'I have a message I would like to deliver.'

'Please?'

'I have a message. For a Tellforce officer.'

'What is this Tellforce?'

I looked rapidly up and down the deserted street, then stepped quickly past the NCO and into the house. It was quiet, and the interior was as featureless as the exterior. I produced my envelope and held it out to the soldier.

'This letter is for my friend, and fiancé. See, it's addressed to him? It's a personal matter, but it is urgent. I am going to give it to you, here . . .' I held it out and reluctantly he took it from my hand. '. . . and I hope very much that you'll be able to help. If there's a way of getting it to Captain Molyneux I will be very grateful, and so will he.'

I turned back to the door.

'I don't know, Madam', he said, but I thought his nod contradicted his words.

'Thank you, Corporal.' I went back out into the street, trying to look – in case anyone should happen to wonder what I was doing – as if I had mistaken the house of my dressmaker.

I told Faria and Sarah that I was going to have a baby.

Faria was dieting before the wedding in order to fit into the wedding dress that had already been made and stitched with thousands of seed pearls. She put down her cup of hot water in which floated a slice of lemon, the only aperitif she was allowed in place of the usual large gin and tonic, and sympathetically blinked at me.

'Oh, no. Poor darling. But you know, there are things you can do, I can tell you someone . . .'

'I'm pleased. I want the baby, I should think Xan and I will just get married a bit sooner.'

Faria looked doubtful. 'Are you sure?'

I thought her uncertainty was much more to do with the prospect of her own imminent marriage than with mine.

'Yes,' I said.

Sarah didn't say much. Once she understood that it was a welcome pregnancy, she murmured a word of congratulation, and jumped up and left the room. Faria shrugged and lit another Turkish cigarette, then went back to flicking through a magazine. When I went to look for her I found Sarah in her room, sitting at her dressing table and staring at her reflection in the vast greenish mirror. I thought she might have been crying, but she denied it.

'Don't be silly. It's so heavenly for you both. A baby, just imagine.'

It wasn't so easy to imagine what it would really mean. I had no idea what being a mother might entail; all I wanted was to see Xan and tell him the news.

Two nights later I lay awake in my bed. Faria was with Ali at some pre-marriage formal celebration and Sarah was out with the middle-aged French diplomat with whom she had recently started a half-hearted affair. It was a hot night and the ceiling fan stirred the air without cooling it. I heard a small click, and then what might have been the lightest footstep in the corridor outside. The hair prickled on my head and my eyes snapped wide open. As I held my breath the door silently cracked open and I saw a black profile against the blackness beyond. It was Xan.

'You're here,' I whispered exultantly and held out my arms. The bed springs creaked as he slid down beside me and his mouth was warm on my neck.

'I stink, darling, forgive me. Doesn't Mamdooh lock the door when he goes home at night?'

'Yes. No, I don't know. It doesn't matter. Did you get my message?'

'I did, this morning. Therefore I am here, but only for a couple of hours. Tell me.'

He did smell, of sweat and tobacco and oil and dust, and I buried my face against his battledress. In the darkness he seemed bigger and more solid than I remembered, full of recent events and escapades that I could only guess at, and keyed up in a way that made his arms and legs minutely vibrate with anticipation. He was ready to jump or shoot or run, and knowing this made me want to hold on to him even more tightly.

'I am going to have a baby.'

There was a small gasp of indrawn breath, a silence, then a whoosh of exhalation that swelled into a shout. It was a shout of pure happiness and my face creased into a quiet, relieved smile.

'Are you? Are you certain?'

I told him about Daphne's colleague, the methodical Doctor Esther Reisen at the Queen Mary.

His hand came to rest on my belly. 'How do you feel?'

'Not bad. Sick, some of the time, but that won't last more than another three or four weeks. Are you really pleased?'

He kissed my hands and my neck and my mouth.

'I can't believe it. Yes, I'm more pleased than you can imagine. Will it be a boy or a girl?'

'A boy,' I told him with absolute certainty.

'Let's get married. Straightaway. As soon as we can arrange it. Never mind the cathedral and the dress and the guard of honour and all that rubbish. I'll ask the colonel for two days.'

'Yes,' I agreed. 'Yes, yes. Now, put your arms round me. Here. Touch me. Take this off. Wait. I'll undo it . . .'

There was a tangle of his clothing and my nightgown, and the creak of his Sam Browne belt and a shocking clatter as his service revolver fell onto the floor, and then we were naked and enveloped in each other.

Afterwards he lay with his fingers tangled in my hair, holding my head against his heart.

'Do you have to go?' I whispered.

'In a minute or two, yes.'

'Where?'

'Back.'

'Can't you tell me anything?'

'Rommel's rearmed, he's going to strike for Tobruk and beyond. He'll be trying to push the Eighth Army right back, back as far as the frontier and into Egypt.'

This much I knew.

'Have you heard of the Qattara Depression?'

'No.'

'It's a huge hollow, thousands of square miles of it, scooped out of the desert floor about forty miles south of the coast and the railhead at a place called el Alamein. The northern sides of it are too steep for tanks to descend and the bed is treacherous soft sand. If Rommel advances that far, he'll be caught in a natural bottleneck between the sea and the Qattara and this will be the last, best place to try and hold him before the frontier.'

'How is Tellforce involved in this?'

Xan's mouth came close to my ear, as if even here in my bed we might be overheard. 'Hassan and I think there is a way through the Qattara. Not an easy way, but I believe it can be done. If we can somehow reconnoitre a route for the heavy armour, without the enemy knowing about it, we can hook around and come in at them from the south where they will never expect to be vulnerable. We're based at Siwa now and we're working on it. Solving the Qattara route.' Against the thin skin beneath my ear his mouth curved in a smile of anticipation, and I shivered.

'It's time,' he murmured now. Then he sat up and began to gather his clothes. I reached to turn on the light beside my bed and lay with my head propped on one hand, memorising the chain of bone that formed his spine, and the lean hips, and the shadow of his ribs showing through tanned skin. None of the men who fought in the desert carried any surplus flesh on them.

When he was dressed, Xan sat down again beside me and picked up my left hand. He kissed the knuckles and pressed his lips to the amethyst, and smiled as he held my face between his hands.

''Bye, darling. Will you find out what it takes to get us married with indecent haste?'

'I will.'

He kissed me on the lips. 'Look after yourself, and the baby. I love you both. I'll be back again soon.'

He knelt down and retrieved his revolver from under the bed, slid it back into its holster and stood up. The door opened, closed behind him with a swift click and he was gone.

After numerous thwarted attempts, I finally managed to telephone my mother in Hampshire. She sounded tired, as if just repeating their number cost her an effort, but her voice turned sharp with anxiety when she realised it was me.

'Iris? Iris, is that you? What's wrong? Quick, tell me what's happened . . .'

They were primed for bad news at home in England; it seemed that it was the only kind. And a telephone call from Cairo was a reasonable cause for alarm.

'Nothing's wrong, Mummy, nothing at all, I've just got something I want to tell you that won't wait for a letter.'

'What is it?'

'I'm going to have a baby.'

'Oh. Oh dear, are you quite sure?'

I couldn't help smiling.

'Certain. And I'm very happy, and so is Xan. It means that we'll get married right away. I'm just sorry that it will mean not having you and Daddy here, and no trousseau or ambassador or anything like that. Do you mind very much?'

'Goodness me. Mind? I don't know. I was so looking forward . . .'

'I know you were. But it's wartime, and Xan and I love each other, and after the war we'll come home with a grand-child for you. We can't be the only family in this position.'

'No. It's the war, I suppose. Everything is different these days. Evie was only saying last week that at least two of her friends, you know . . . It's all *quite* different from my day. But you can't think of having the baby in Cairo. You must come home as soon as possible. If you book a passage now . . .'

'No, Mummy. I'm staying here with Xan. I have a very good doctor, everything will be arranged.'

'Iris, really. You are very headstrong.'

'I don't know about that. I'm very happy. Shall I speak to Daddy?'

'Oh, oh dear, I don't think so. You'd better leave that to me.'

'All right.' I smiled again. 'What about you? How are you?'

'Darling, don't worry about me. My chest has been bothering me again, but Doctor Harris has given me some new linctus. I'll feel better as soon as the summer comes, it's been so cold.'

'It's very hot here. Mummy, I love you.'

My mother sounded so tired and frail.

'I love you too. Please do take care, Iris.'

We are heading into the desert and I am thinking about my mother. Even hearing her faltering voice, distorted by the long-distance telephone connection.

She was only in her fifties, even though she seemed almost an old woman to me, and I realise that Lesley is now exactly the age that she was then.

The road we are now travelling is unmade, it is a rough single track that draws us on into the dunes and the city seems a long way behind. The car tyres lose their purchase in the sand and the engine whines until they find a grip again.

Xan loved the desert. He knew it and understood it, and in the end it kept him. I don't know where he lies, but I feel as if this drive brings me closer to him. The hot, dry air sucks at my skin but I am happy. A snatch of an old song almost works its way out of me.

'Which way?' Ruby asked after a while.

Iris didn't say anything and Ruby drove a little further, wrestling with the wheel without knowing quite what to do when the steering broke away from her. The car's bonnet slewed disconcertingly across the snout of the dune ahead before she brought it under control again. The effort made her suddenly sweaty and she realised that the sun was hot on the black roof of the old car.

Iris was humming to herself.

It was time to turn back, Ruby decided. She checked automatically in the rear-view mirror and there was nothing there. Not only no other traffic: nothing except the dunes and the sky.

'Right. Home time.'

She braked and the car slithered. The reassuring road had dwindled into a rough track and even that was almost invisible; there was a wind blowing that sent a fine swirl of sand fuming over the ground and covering everything. Their tyre marks were already fading into twin blurred furrows. Ruby swung the steering wheel hard right and the car ploughed a slow half-circle. She estimated it was a half-circle, and that would mean that they were facing back in the direction they had come. She glanced up at the sun, a whitish disk behind a haze of heat. Was it still in the east, or had it already slid to the south?

She drove another hundred yards, but the track was gone. The veil of blown sand was chased and harried by the wind, and it was getting harder to keep the tyres turning. She would have to stop and get her bearings.

Iris turned her head. She was smiling disconnectedly. 'Why are we stopping?'

'I want to take a look, make sure of the way back.'

'Back?'

'Yes,' Ruby said loudly.

She opened the car door and stepped out, and the wind tugged at her. Blown sand stung her ankles. She scrambled to the low crest of the nearest dune, surprised by how steep it was and how deep her feet sank. From the top she had expected that she would see the main road heading out to the oasis, whatever it was called, and the insect progress of trucks and buses. But there was only a vista of close identical dunes, rippled by the rising wind.

She ploughed down the slope and back to the car. The floor and her seat were already thinly coated with sand. She slammed the door and wound up the window, then sat with her hands on the steering wheel.

Ruby said, 'I don't know where we are.'

CHAPTER THIRTEEN

The sun was now only visible as a dim eye, pale as wax, behind a thickening veil of greyish umber haze. The wind steadily rose, whipping sand off the crests of the dunes like spray off a breaking wave. The desert was shifting, unleashing itself.

Ruby crawled into the back of the car and yanked on the window winders, forcing them round as far they would go to lock the glass into the frames. The rubber of the seals was perished in places. She leaned across Iris and did the same thing to the passenger window, then checked that all the doors were properly shut. She pulled the handles into the locked position for good measure. The wind was scouring up sand and flinging it against the windscreen and the door panels, making a noise like tiny hailstones drumming on the metal. The floor and the seats were already coated with pale, gritty dust that forced its way through holes in the floor and the cracks in the door and window seals.

'It's a sandstorm,' Iris said wonderingly.

'Looks like it.' Ruby's throat was dry and tight, and her eyeballs still stung just from the quick dash she had made to the crest of the nearby dune. The air inside the car seemed smoky, thicker than it was comfortable to breathe, irrelevantly reminding her of the way dry ice fumed in a club.

'A desert sandstorm can be very dangerous, you know. We should turn round and drive straight home.'

Ruby leaned forward in the driver's seat, gripping the wheel as if that might anchor them. 'I think it's too late for that now.'

The sepia-freckled skin stretched over Iris's temples and cheekbones looked thin enough to tear. Her eyes were very wide and clear, innocent and without comprehension. 'What did you say?'

Ruby opened her mouth, ready to vent her anxiety as anger, but she stopped herself. Instead, she took one of Iris's hands and held it. 'We'll have to sit here until it blows itself out.'

'Sit here?'

'Yes.' Ruby formed the word crisply, raising her voice a little, lending herself a conviction that she was far from feeling. It might have been her imagination but the car seemed to rock and shudder under the force of the wind. Let's think, Ruby advised herself. Decide what to do for the best. She tried to be rational, but fear suddenly prickled down her spine.

At the same moment a huge gust of wind sliced the entire top off the nearest dune and flung it against the car and for a second they were in darkness. Then more wind stripped the sand from the car windows. The light when it did come back was clotted, yellow-brown, swirling like soup. There was nothing to think about, she realised, not until this storm was over. Driving even another metre was unthinkable. There was no visibility, no tracks, no sun by which to steer, nothing except gravity even to define up or down.

The air banged and thundered. It couldn't last, a wind like this, could it?

331

Surely it would die down as suddenly as it had risen.

'Are you all right?'

Iris slowly nodded. 'A desert sandstorm,' she repeated. 'The men used to fear them. Even Hassan.'

'I'm not surprised.'

Inside the partly sealed car it was now uncomfortable to breathe the dust-laden air and Iris coughed, gasped for breath, then coughed some more. Ruby burrowed in her grandmother's bag, brought out her white headscarf and wrapped it round the lower half of her face for her. She pulled up her own T-shirt to cover her mouth and nostrils.

How had they come to land in this predicament?

She thought back to leaving the house, heading for Giza, bypassing the tourist crowds, following the desert road and deliberately taking the turnings that led away from the oasis traffic. Stupid, all right. But the sequence of turns was clear enough in her head, and to fix them there she forced herself to run them through her mind's eye again and again. Once the wind had stopped howling and whipping the sand, she could reverse the sequence. When she had got her immediate bearings.

'Ruby?' Iris's voice was very quiet and muffled even further by the folds of her scarf.

'Yes. Here, give me your hand again. We can talk to pass the time, can't we?'

'I'd like a drink of water.'

There was an instant's panic when Ruby thought *we haven't got any*, then with relief she remembered the two bottles she had bought at the café. She reached into the back of the car for one, twisted off the cap and handed it to Iris. Iris pulled back her scarf and gulped thirstily, and some of the water ran down her chin and splashed on the front of her dress.

'That's better,' she said, like a child, and handed the bottle back to Ruby.

The car seats creaked as they both sank lower, covering their noses and mouths, and preparing for the wait against the wind.

'Hassan?' Ruby prompted, almost automatically now.

'Yes, Hassan. He was Bedouin. Xan used to say that he knew the desert in every season, every mood. He knew it as well as the smile in his mother's eyes. Even the Qattara Depression. That was the key to it. The route across. Everyone said it couldn't be done.'

'Why not?'

Ruby's eyes were fixed on the blank that the desert had become, a solid blank, wind-driven, more to be feared than fog, than snow, because it was so unknown. She felt uncomfortably thirsty, the silvery idea of water collecting in the margins of her thoughts wherever she tried to direct them.

'Soft sand, impassable to tanks. That's what the generals all thought. Xan showed them.'

'Did he? How did he do that?'

It was difficult to talk through the face coverings and harder still to hear what was said. The cracks and gaps in the old car were mouthpieces for the wind, and it sighed and blared and moaned across them. Iris didn't try to answer. Her chin drooped on her chest and after a little while Ruby saw that she had fallen asleep.

Ruby sat and stared at the opaque world. Her eyes still stung, and although she tried not to she couldn't stop swallowing and catching the dusty rasp in her throat. She made some mental calculations about the two bottles of water and the fruit that Auntie had pressed on her. That already seemed ages ago. How long would these minimal supplies last?

A day, two days at the very most.

But they wouldn't be here for anything like that long. Once the wind dropped, they would be on their way again.

It was a good thing that Iris was asleep, although in this

gale Ruby couldn't imagine how she did it. The sandstorm was beating against the car, trying to get inside, sending in the hot fingers of dust that clawed all over them. She shuddered and rubbed her face to dispel the image, finding that her fingers and cheeks and eyelids were painfully gritty.

Ignore this. Think about something else.

She began with Ash. His face, white teeth flashing in a smile, the way his eyes slanted, all came easily. But he was saying that it was not a good idea for her to take Iris out in the Beetle. And in the end agreeing the compromise – *Well, then, just so far as Giza.*

Ash thought they were visiting the Pyramids. He wouldn't guess that they had come all the way out here. But this was not a helpful line of thought, so she pictured the museum instead. It was comforting to recall the filtered light and the sepulchral halls. She took herself past the lines of wooden display cases and the fantastical assemblages of pots, shards, papyrus, scarabs, stone carvings and huge golden ornaments. Ancient civilisation. Much of it too remote for her to begin to comprehend, but it was still commanding the desert margin and drawing the tourist tides, and the durable bits and pieces of it were washed up in glass cases, labelled and left for her to speculate about.

This was the perspective she needed as a counter to the bald, threatening desert.

People had lived here for thousands of years. Hassan, whoever he was, had known it like he knew his mother's smile. Captain Molyneux had heroically plotted a way across some particularly treacherous stretch of it. Was that where he had been killed?

This was not a useful speculation either. Ruby drew her knees up to her chest and wrapped her arms round them to contain her anxiety, doing it quietly so as not to disturb Iris.

The museum. Go on thinking about the museum.

334

The Mummy Room and the quiet rows of long-dead pharaohs. Desiccated by time, and wind and sand . . .

No.

Collections. Inanimate objects, lined up, order among disorder, that was more like it. The glass cases. Her own bedroom at home, for that matter. Shoeboxes full of the scribbled names of pop stars and children's TV personalities. Shells, with grains of sand still trapped in their pearly crevices . . .

No.

The fucking wind. If only it would let up for a second she could think straight. Just let the car stop rocking and howling like some demented musical instrument.

Home. Matchboxes and polished wooden frames, giant cockchafer beetles and tiny spotted ladybirds, her best collection of all. Lesley had hated them.

And now Ruby was suddenly and deeply frightened, the fear coming at her like another gust of wind. The thought of home and Lesley made her almost double up, stabbed with the longing to be there, to be safe, to hear her mother telling her not to do something.

Lesley was a thousand miles away.

Iris was so old, and she didn't know what was happening half the time.

She couldn't look to Iris for help: the only person who could save them was herself.

But I can't save anyone, Ruby's voice yelled inside her head. I'm only a *child*, what am I supposed to do?

She rocked in her seat, clenching her fists until her fingernails dug so hard into the palms that the pain almost distracted her.

You're not a kid.

Stop it! What's the matter with you?

It's just a sandstorm. It will die down in the end, it has to. What would Jas do?

Probably roll one, smoke it and then fall asleep. Like Iris, except for the rolling and smoking part. Ruby realised that she was laughing only when her lower lip painfully cracked open. She ran the tip of her tongue over the raw place and tasted a tiny drop of blood.

Jas, think about Jas and his Garden of Eden cut out of magazines and pasted on the walls of his room, fat green leaves and wide-eyed daisies and trees and roses and dark pointed firs.

That's better.

When Ruby looked at her watch she was startled to see that it was two o'clock.

It was important to keep track of time, wasn't it? Maybe the violence of the wind was diminishing at last. Through the pall of driven sand she caught a glimpse of the dune she had climbed earlier, only it had shifted so it was now ahead of them instead of out to the left. No, that couldn't be right. Surely it was the car that must have been blown sideways, so that it had ended up facing in a slightly different direction?

But that was impossible too. They had been sitting in it all the time, sitting for so long that her legs and back ached. It must have been the dune that had moved. The wind had carved it into a different shape. This one, and its neighbours as well, probably. How different would the new landscape look from the one she had been fixing all morning in her mind's eye?

Ruby turned her head to look at Iris. Her eyes were open and she was also looking at the ghosts of the dunes as they swam in the hanging dust.

'You're awake,' Ruby murmured.

'Have I been asleep?'

*   *   *

336

We were going to look for Xan, driving deep into the desert in search of him: we had to hurry or he would be gone and I would never see him again. The anxiety was intense and my eyes stung and burned with the effort of searching the monotony for the smallest sign of him.

Either I imagined this, or I dreamed it. And now I am awake again and I remember that I am with the child, and we are caught in a sandstorm.

'Ruby, how much water have we got?'

Wide-eyed, she studies my face. 'Two litres, minus what you drank earlier. Some fresh fruit, some dried apricots.'

'You had better drink some. Go on. Let me see you do it.'

She opens the bottle and tilts it to her mouth. I see the muscles convulsively clutch in her pretty throat, and the effort it costs her to lower the bottle long before her thirst is quenched. She holds the bottle out to me and I take a few swallows. When I hand it back she screws the cap on very carefully and stows the bottle out of our sight on the back seat.

'Are we in trouble?' she asks in a flat voice.

'I don't think so.' I peer out of the windscreen. There is nothing to see but yellowish murk, but it seems to me that this is now dust hanging in the air rather than sand torn off the dune backs. In time it will settle. 'Mamdooh and Auntie will send someone to look for us.'

'But they don't know where we are. I avoided seeing Mamdooh this morning, I didn't want the hassle. You know? I talked to Auntie in the kitchen and she talked to me, but she didn't know what I was saying. She doesn't, does she? And I told Ash that we were just going to the Pyramids.' Her voice rises. 'No one knows we've come out here.'

I try to remember how we reached this place, but it has gone.

I can recall the exact layout of the rooms in our Garden

City apartment, remember how the sequins on the costume of Elvira Mursi the belly-dancer glittered under the spotlights at Zazie's, but to save my life I cannot remember this morning.

I'm very tired. I rest my head against the window and see how everything is coated in dust. The backs of my hands are grey, my lap, my knees, the metal curve of the dashboard.

If no one knows where we are, no one will be coming to look for us. There is an inevitability in this that does not particularly disturb me.

'Don't worry,' I say.

After Xan slipped into my room that night and then slipped away again, I began making preparations for our wedding. From the proper department at the embassy I found out what it would take to obtain a special licence for two British nationals to marry at short notice and made the application. Sandy Allardyce helped me with the formalities.

'Are you happy, Iris?'

'Happier than I have ever been in my whole life.' I was becoming almost used to saying this. But that it was true was still startling, and miraculous.

Just briefly a shadow of regret, or perhaps envy, showed in his plump, pink face. In all the times that we had met at parties or embassy functions we had never again referred to Sandy's feelings for me, real or imagined.

'What about you?' I asked. Even this conversation was a long way beyond the boundaries of our usual exchanges.

'Me?' He coughed and shuffled a little. 'It seems possible, ah, likely that Mrs Kimmig-Gertsch and I may make some, ah, formal arrangement.'

'How marvellous. That's wonderful. I hope you will both be very happy.'

The shadow was still in his face. 'I am sure that it will be useful for us.' I thought that useful was an odd word in the context. 'But happiness . . . I don't know. And now when I look at you, Iris, at your face at this minute, happy seems too mundane a concept to use for you. *Transfigured* is closer.'

There was a little silence. Outside the window of Sandy's office the tall trees of the embassy garden made an oasis of shade in the exhausting afternoon heat. He came round his desk and planted an awkward kiss on my cheek, then patted my shoulder to dismiss me.

Xan was in a camp at the fringe of the Qattara, although I deduced this by guesswork rather than from anything he told me. We communicated by letters. His scribbled, creased pages reached me erratically, dropped off by the Tellforce plane whenever it touched down in Cairo or carried by the infrequent messengers who travelled between GHQ and his patrol. The smart Indian NCO called at Garden City to deliver them, and there was always a batch of my letters waiting to be taken away. So Xan and I planned our wedding.

We would be married by an English chaplain in a side chapel at the cathedral, with a tiny handful of friends to witness the ceremony. Xan wanted Jessie to be his best man. Although I knew that the Cherry Pickers were up at the Gazala Line, Xan did not seem particularly concerned about this. Ruth and Sarah would be my attendants; Daphne was unlikely to be able to take the time off from the hospital and Faria would be on her honeymoon. It was comical that Xan's and my minimal preparations were being made neck and neck with the final elaborate arrangements for Faria's and Ali's huge wedding. Our marriage would take place just five days after theirs.

I would wear a simple white silk suit and a hat with a spotted tulle veil. We would have lunch with our little group of friends after the ceremony and give a drinks party for everyone we knew in the evening at the Garden City apartment. Faria's parents had told Sarah and me that we could stay there until we had made other arrangments.

Gus Wainwright has promised me at least twenty-four hours' leave, Xan wrote. *It may only be a short honeymoon, darling – but we will have a whole life together afterwards.*

A whole life. A very long time and it is no wonder that I am tired.

The child is twisting in her seat.

'It's four o'clock.'

'Is it?'

'Mamdooh and Auntie will be going mad.'

'Yes, they probably will.'

'It's going to be *dark* in an hour or so.'

'Yes.'

'You know that means we're probably going to have to spend the night here?'

The desert night; the sky a bowl of darkness, stars dimmed by the dust from the storm. Very cold at this time of year and as silent as space.

Xan's resting place.

'*Iris?*'

'Yes. I am listening.' Although her insistence irritates me.

'I can't just sit here. I'm going to have a look.'

'To see what?'

She clicks her tongue and pushes the door open. Cooler air swirls in, bringing rolling clouds of dust with it, but the wind has died down. Only an hour ago the force of it would have snatched the door away from her and slammed it against the car.

'To see how to get us out.'

Ruby's feet sank deep into the sand. The surface was cool, with warmth embedded further down. She started to run

340

towards the face of the altered dune, the blood in her head urgently pounding with the need for action after so many hours cooped up in the stuffy sealed car. But the blown sand swallowed her feet up to the ankles, and her knees had seized up with sitting for so long. She stumbled and fell forward, her hands plunging in the sand up to the wrists. She stood upright and began trudging more slowly up the steep brown slope. The dune was only twenty-five feet high, but the sand slid away from under her feet and she was carried back one step for every two of upward progress. Her tongue was swollen and coated with thirst, and her stomach distantly rumbled. The dune's face turned concave and the angle became still steeper. She couldn't get up this way.

Ruby plunged back down again in ten giant's strides that set off little avalanches of sand slipping all around her. She half ran to the arm of the dune and began to climb the ridge. This was easier, but she was still gasping for breath and her throat was burning as she laboured up to the summit.

The sky was leaden overhead and away to the left, what must be eastwards – where Cairo lay – it was the colour of an old bruise. In the west the sun was declining somewhere behind a smeared palette of orange and umber and purple cloud. Ruby took her bearings quickly, but it wasn't the sky she was looking at. Hunching her shoulders against the wind and protecting her eyes with cupped hands, she turned in a breathless circle to see what lay beyond the dune.

Nothing. It was still a landscape of monotonous undulations, dunes rolling away into the distance, rippled or blasted smooth by the force of the wind, but otherwise unmarked. There was no track, no vestige of tyre marks, no sign of a road or a moving creature. The horizon was darkening, but there wasn't the faintest glow of light over where the city should be. It was a completely empty world.

Down in its hollow the car looked like some pharaonic

relic. Grey with dust and bedded in the sand on the windward side up to its wheel arches, it might have been there for centuries. Ruby could just see the pale, floating oval of Iris's face, turned up to look at her.

The wind up on the ridge was sharp, and Ruby listened to its faint whistling and sighing over the nearby crests. It was a hostile sound and she was shivering.

She jumped and slid back down the steep face to the car. Just in the time that she had been away the sun must have set and now the desert darkness fell like a blanket extinguishing a candle. Twelve hours of a winter night before daylight would flood the world again.

'Well?' Iris demanded.

'I can't see anything. It can't be all that far to the road, can it? I mean, how long were we driving along that track? But there's nothing to see from up there. In the morning, as soon as it's light, I'll go a bit further and I'm sure to see it. Then we can head out of here. But we'll just have to make ourselves as comfortable as we can for tonight.'

Ruby sat in her seat again, telling herself that she must think straight. Her tongue seemed to cleave to the roof of her mouth.

'It's time for some more water.' The bottle was dusty, beaded with condensation inside. When they had both had what seemed like only a tiny drink, it was empty. She reached for the basket that she had impatiently grabbed in the kitchen this morning, aeons ago. 'And some fruit.'

They each ate an orange, sucking every drop of the juice, and gnawed at some dried apricots although the sweetness only made them more thirsty.

When they had finished they sat in the hollow darkness.

'I'm sorry,' Ruby said. 'It's my fault.'

'It's nothing of the kind. This is my car, my country and I promised your mother that I would take appropriate care

342

of you.' After a moment Iris added, 'I wish I hadn't finally let her down in that, as well as everything else.'

'It's not *finally*. It's not. It's just a night in the bloody car, tomorrow we'll be out of here, all right?' Ruby pounded her fist on the steering wheel. She was angry at how stupid and how easy it had been to travel in a straight line from this morning's safety to tonight's jeopardy.

'Yes,' Iris sighed. Ruby couldn't tell whether she believed this or not, or even whether she really wanted it. She resisted the urge to shake her grandmother and shout at her, this is about our *lives*. If we can't find a way out of this desert and nobody knows where the fuck we are, we could die right here . . .

She didn't say anything, though. To give voice to her fears would only lend them more substance.

It was steadily getting colder. They had no warm clothes to put on and as the time crept by the chill night air seeped into the car until they were both shivering.

'Let's get into the back seat. We can cuddle up,' Ruby said at last.

They moved into the cramped space and pressed close together. It was a comfort to hold her grandmother's light-boned body in her arms and hear her breathing. Ruby rested her cheek on the top of Iris's head and watched the slice of black sky visible through the rear window. The red and white lights of a jet descending to Cairo airport blinked in the distance and this vision of normality made Ruby forget their predicament for a second, but then it dawned again with renewed intensity. The planes were too high; to the crew and the passengers strapped in their seats ready for landing the Beetle would be just a speck in the limitless sand.

But she could see them and that meant the sky was clearing. Even as the thought came to her, she saw a pale prickle of stars.

Iris was dozing. Although her limbs ached with cramp and her throat and mouth were parched, eventually Ruby fell asleep too.

She woke up with a thirst like a high fever and shivering uncontrollably as if her bones would crack. Iris had been stirring and mumbling; it was the sound of her voice that woke Ruby.

'What did you say? Are you all right?'

'That was the day.'

'Never mind. God, your feet and hands and freezing. I'll rub them a bit.'

It was bitterly cold. She chafed Iris's icy claws between her own but she couldn't work any warmth into them.

'I'm going to turn the engine on and run the heater for a few minutes to warm us up. I should have thought of it before. Sit still.'

In the driver's seat, Ruby groped for the ignition key and turned it. There was a grinding noise, the strangled wail of the starter motor clogged with sand, then silence. Ruby let her hand fall into her lap. The silence spread, rippling away from the immobilised car. The Beetle might as well have been a pharaonic relic, she thought, or just a lump of rock sticking up out of the sand, for all the use it was going to be in getting them out of here. The only way that they were going to survive was by walking, or by waiting to be rescued.

What were the odds, either way, she wondered?

Then a flash of hot, white certainty shot through her brain. She didn't want to die. Life was too good, too precious and too untasted. It was clear to her that she loved everything about it. The garden at home, with all those dumb plants that used to yield her beetles. The girls she had been at school with, even though they were nearly all bitches. Camden Town and the music scene, Ed and Simon and even Andrew and

Will, and especially Lesley. There were uncounted things that she still wanted to do, an incoherent mass of them like fucking Ash and going to Ayers Rock and to that Inca place in Peru, and most of all saying to her mother that she was sorry they always quarrelled. Weirdly but definitely, most of all that.

'Are you awake?' she whispered into Iris's hair.

Iris nodded her head, but she didn't say anything and Ruby wasn't sure if she had really heard.

'I love you,' she said.

It was simple. In the morning she would go for help.

The rapid dawn briefly raised their spirits. After the darkness, even in the monochrome light, even the empty dunes were reassuring. Soon the sun would flood warmth into the world.

They drank some of the second litre of water, trying to hold the blessing of it in their mouths for as long as possible. Then they clambered stiffly out of the car and eased their joints by stretching out in the sand. Iris looked frighteningly pale and shaky, and Ruby peeled an orange for her, placing the segments one by one into her mouth as if she were feeding a child. The sun came up, spreading a film of colour over the sand. On the crests of the dunes it turned to pale sparkling gold, and on the cheeks and flanks it was beige and terracotta and khaki. The air had already lost its chilling bite. Iris sat propped up against the shaded side of the car with her mottled bare legs stretched out in front of her. Ruby took one last gulp of water, then half buried the bottle in the sand beside Iris and put the basket containing the rest of the fruit and the dried apricots within reach. She made sure that her grandmother had her hat and her scarf, then she squatted down directly in front of her, looking into her eyes to see if she took in what she was telling her.

'I'm going for help. I'll be as quick as I can. Stay here in

345

the shade, don't move away from the car. Drink a sip of water once in a while, and – look – here are two oranges and two pomegranates. Iris?'

'I am not deaf. You will promise to look where you're going, Lesley, won't you?'

Where was she, in her unreadable confusion? 'Yes.'

Ruby leaned forward and quickly kissed her. Her feet and head felt heavy, but her heart was racing with adrenalin. The sooner she went, she reasoned, the quicker she would be back again.

She began walking, towards the flaming ball of the sun. From the crest of the first dune she looked back. All she could see were Iris's feet sticking out beyond the car and her own footprints leading away, already fading, like a betrayal.

She scrambled up a dune, down into the hollow beyond and up again, always heading into the sun. It was hard work and she was soon out of breath. The next dune was higher and she had it in her mind that once she was on the summit of this one the road would be there in the distance, with trucks and tourist buses catching the sunlight and winking rescue at her.

As she laboriously climbed, the sand carried her backwards. Sweat ran into her eyes, and she flopped onto her hands and knees to crawl the last few metres.

She poked her head over the ridge. There was no road in sight. Only more dunes, in every direction, identical.

On her knees Ruby shuffled in a circle. A breeze fanned her face but it also stirred the sand. The tracks leading backwards and linking her to Iris were blurred hollows trapping a fingernail of shadow, becoming less distinct with every puff of wind. As soon as they were rubbed out Iris would be lost to her.

It was unbearable, unthinkable to leave her lying there alone.

Ruby staggered to her feet and began running back the way she had come. Already it was hard to distinguish the footprints from the natural dimples worn by the wind.

Oh please, let me find her. Please, please let me.

Faria's wedding was exquisite. Every opulent detail proclaimed the wealth of both families and their satisfaction at this dynastic amalgamation.

The medieval Coptic church was lit entirely by candles. Along with the whole of fashionable Cairo, Sarah and I sat under the branched golden candelabra and watched Ali waiting to receive his bride. He stood with his father and brother beside him, all three of them in pearl-grey cutaway coats, expressionless, dark-faced, massively convinced of their collective power.

Faria was almost half an hour late. I remember thinking that this was her very last gesture of independence. From now on, Ali would require her to behave like a good and pliant Egyptian wife. She came down the aisle at a slow pace with the huge pearl-embroidered train of her dress swishing over the floor. Her waist looked tiny. The diet and some punishing French corsetry had done the trick.

When Ali stepped to her side she allowed him to take her arm but her face was turned aside, as if he were merely an usher or a major-domo who had hurried forward to help her out of her limousine. I glanced at Sarah, to see if she was also wondering how this marriage could work, but her head was bowed and she was picking at the hem of her kid glove.

Faria would find a way to arrange her life to her own satisfaction, I decided.

In five days' time I would be Xan's wife. The dozens of candle flames shivered in the incense-heavy air of the packed church as I listened to the Coptic liturgy.

*   *   *

347

The wedding feast was held at Faria's parents' mansion. The bride and groom led the way from the church on foot, accompanied by the *zaffa* – a long parade of drummers and belly-dancers who played and sang and danced around them. The enormous reception hall of the house was decorated with tall sheaves of green wheat, representing fertility, tied with ribbons of gold representing – I supposed – money. Ali and Faria, king and queen of the day, sat between the wheat-sheaves under a golden canopy to receive their guests. The real King and Queen of Egypt were among them.

There were no field officers from any of the Allied armies. Rommel's long-awaited attack had begun two days earlier.

Out in the desert, after an Italian feint towards the north of the Gazala Line, the Panzer Army had hooked south around Bir Hacheim and were now fighting their way up through General Ritchie's armoured brigades towards Tobruk. The armoured cars and infantry of the German Ninetieth Light, meanwhile, ploughed into the exposed communication lines of the Allied rearguard.

I wandered through the glittering rooms. There were lilies everywhere, overpoweringly scented, and drifts of rose petals, and white-gloved servants, and more jewels than I had ever seen in one place. A little group of people I knew from the embassy appeared and I went with them into the supper room. The tables heaped with food stretched into the distance; much more food than the hundreds of guests could ever eat or even make much of an impression upon. There was enough to feed an army. The waistband of my best silk dress was much too tight. I turned aside from a swan sculpted in ice that lifted a crystal trough of Beluga caviar between its wings, and saw Roddy Boy coming towards me.

He took my arm, standing too close so that I made an awkward step to one side. My hip bumped against the edge of the table and the swan's beak seemed to peck at the scented air.

'Iris, come with me.'

'Where?'

My companions had fallen back and Roddy and I were standing in an empty space.

'I have something to tell you.'

I knew. I already knew.

There was a niche at the far side of the supper room. I sat down on a gilt empire sofa and Roddy Boy put his hand on my arm.

'Please tell me at once,' I said.

'I have some very bad news. I am afraid that Captain Molyneux was killed in action two days ago, in the Qattara.'

I must have asked for more information.

A few feet away from us, Ali's and Faria's guests were scooping lobster and caviar on to white-and-gold porcelain plates. There was singing and dancing and loud applause in a neighbouring room. The wedding banquet was in full swing.

I listened to Roddy Boy's words as if I had already heard them.

He told me that Xan and his Arab scout had been leading a small exploratory detachment over the route that their patrol had devised as a means of bringing Allied armour in on the southern flank of the Eighth Army. It was a highly secret operation, known to very few people outside Special Operations Executive. But as the little column wound its way through the wind-sculpted buttes and mesas of the Qattara, a formation of six Italian Macchi aircraft had appeared and homed in on them with a level of accuracy that ruled out coincidence. Most of the men had been mortally wounded by machine-gun and cannon fire, and several of the vehicles had burst into flames.

The heavy armoured trucks and cars had been drawn from the Eleventh Hussars, the Cherry Pickers, and their second-in-command was Captain James. Captain James had been very seriously injured but he had been brought in from the desert and was now in the Queen Mary Hospital. It was Jessie James who had given an account of the skirmish, and of Xan's death, to a staff officer from GHQ.

'I am so sorry,' Roddy said. 'As soon as I heard I came straight here.'

Somehow I spoke. The words sounded as though they came from someone else. 'Thank you. Colonel Boyce, how could the enemy have known that Xan's patrol was in the Qattara?'

I must have been unbalanced with shock. Part of my brain seemed crystal clear, with a sequence of sharp, angry throughts running through it. The other part was black, closed, disbelieving.

'I am afraid I can't answer that, Iris. I wish I could.'

Can't or won't, I thought. There was a security leak, exactly as Xan had suggested. Roddy's eyes flicked towards the door of the supper room. He was under unusual pressure and there were heavy demands on his time; he had broken the news and he wanted to be gone.

'I'll go to the hospital,' I said.

'Are you sure you want to do that?'

I was already on my feet, walking unseeingly through the crowds of guests and past the sheaves of green wheat for fertility.

'I've got a GHQ car,' Roddy mumbled as he tried to keep up. 'You could take it, I'll walk.'

'Thank you,' I said again, not even looking back.

In the car, on the familiar route, I stared at the people in the streets who were walking and talking as if nothing had happened. I was still alive myself, I was breathing and sitting back against creased leather with my hands like wax in my lap. I stared down at them. It was impossible that Xan was dead. Xan, who had been more alive than any of them. My mouth moved and I found I was saying his name.

At the hospital, crowded with MTC drivers and medical staff and injured men, people stared and then fell back to let me pass. I was in wedding clothes and my face must have been a mask of shock. I went to the clerks' office and with Christina Tsatsas's gentle help I found out where Jessie had been taken.

He was lying behind screens in a ward full of men who had just been brought in from the battle. His face was paler than the dressings that covered his upper torso and his light hair was dark with dirt and blood. At first I thought he was unconscious but when I took his bloodstained hand and held it his eyes opened.

'Iris.'

'Yes.'

His lips moved but his voice was barely audible. 'Xan. I'm sorry.'

'Shh.'

There was a silence while he summoned up a reserve of strength.

'Air attack. Out of nowhere.'

'Roddy Boy told me.'

'I saw . . . came straight at us.'

'Jessie. I have to ask you this. Are you certain he is dead?'

Maybe there was the possibility of a mistake, maybe the smallest chink of doubt that would allow me to hope. At the same time I prayed that there could be no doubt at all, no chance that he might be lying alone and mortally wounded in the sand.

There was a carafe of water and a sponge on the table

351

beside the screen and I moistened the sponge and dabbed it to Jessie's mouth.

'He was in the lead truck. The rest of us were spread out on a broad front behind. Xan's vehicle took the brunt of the fire.'

This much seemed to cost him all the strength he had.

'Shh,' I said again. I held his hand and a nurse looked in through the screens, glanced at me and went away again.

Jessie collected himself once more. 'The truck burst into flames. A ball of fire. None of them got out. I tried to run across to see but the planes came back to finish the job and . . .'

Jessie's eyes closed. A breath sighed out of him. He didn't say anything more and I sat there with my hand linked in his as the life seemed to recede, from his fingertips, from his arms and legs, until it was just concentrated in a flutter round his heart. I felt hard and heavy, like a piece of wood.

I thought it was the nurse again when the screens parted but someone put a hand on my shoulder and I looked up to see Daphne. She was wearing an apron and her horizontal hair was flattened under a white stocking cap. There were purple circles of exhaustion under her eyes. I watched her as she moved round to the other side of the bed and put her fingers on Jessie's neck, then shone a small torch into each of his eyes. Her expression didn't change.

'Well?' I demanded.

She shook her head.

'Xan is dead,' I said.

She came back to my side of the bed, unlaced my fingers from Jessie's cold ones and put her hands on my shoulders. Then she pulled my head against her. She smelled of carbolic and disinfectant and also, I thought, of carnage.

'Xan is dead,' I repeated. I knew I hadn't begun to register what the words meant.

352

'Iris. Listen to me. Come with me to the mess. I'll get you some tea.'

'No. I'm staying here.'

She nodded wearily. 'All right then. I've got to go now, but I'll come back when I can.'

I turned back to Jessie and held his hand again. I put my mouth close to his ear and reminded him of the night we met at Lady Gibson Pasha's, and the mule at Mrs Kimmig-Gertsch's New Year's party. I said that I would go and see his family back at home, and I told him that I loved Xan and I would always love him. What I really felt was angry, but I told him that I was proud of them both.

Jessie never regained consciousness and he died in the early hours of the morning.

Afterwards Daphne led me out of the ward.

'You have to go home and rest now,' she ordered. 'Remember the baby.'

Since the moment when I saw Roddy Boy heading towards me, I had not given it a thought. I had forgotten that I was pregnant.

Another slope of dune and her gasps for breath keeping a rhythm with the words *please, let me find her*. Her outward tracks were barely discernible.

Ruby crested the dune and the Beetle lay in the hollow below. Her legs wobbled and she sat heavily down in the sand, slip-slithering to the bottom. Iris seemed not to have moved at all, but there were tears running down her face and glimmering in the sun.

Ruby knelt in front of her and gathered her up into her arms. She mumbled a rush of words. 'It's all right, here I am, you're safe, we're going to be all right, look, I won't leave you again, Ash will find us, Ash and Mamdooh and Auntie, I promise, they have to find us, don't they?' She attempted the reassurance out of a complete absence of conviction, and she thought how frail and improbable the words sounded. But in any case Iris was staring at her, through her tears, as if she had never set eyes on her before. She wasn't crying over their plight, or out of fear at being left alone. She was crying for something inside her own head and Ruby couldn't reach that.

She let go of her and Iris sank back against the half-buried car.

It was for the best, probably, Ruby thought. Let her be, with her memories. Better that than be aware of this reality.

She unscrewed the bottle of water and gave it to Iris; then she took some herself. It was the hardest thing she had ever done, not gulping the last mouthfuls straight down. They had less than half a litre left now.

The day slid onwards. At noon, sitting shoulder to shoulder in the little ellipse of shade beside the car, they shared a pomegranate and each bead of sweetness burst a tantalising droplet of moisture on their parched tongues. Iris was silent, lost in a reverie, and Ruby's thoughts went round and round in tighter and increasingly desperate circles.

The planes continued to glide overhead. Maybe if she could light a fire, they would see the smoke? The car tyres would burn with thick black smoke, but how could she set fire to them with no matches?

She rummaged in her memory for the vestiges of television survival programmes, the kind of thing her stepfather liked to watch. Focus the sun's rays through a lens, or use a camera battery? They had neither.

The sun crept across the sky.

Lesley had been in the garden for most of the afternoon, sweeping fallen leaves off the herringbone brick paths, but now it was getting too dark to work. Through the drawing room french windows, she could see Andrew sitting in his armchair reading. At least he wasn't clicking at his laptop, or checking messages on his BlackBerry. She would take him a cup of tea and draw the curtains. She put her broom away in the garden shed, carefully padlocking the door behind her because the Macys' shed had been broken into last week and their lawnmower and gas barbecue had been stolen. Colin Macy was burning leaves this afternoon; the damp air was thick with the smell of bonfire smoke.

In the kitchen she washed her hands and filled the kettle. She could hear Andrew talking on the phone. It must be Ed, calling to say what time he wanted to be collected from Saturday rugby practice.

Then Andrew appeared in the kitchen doorway.

'There's some French doctor on the phone from Cairo. It's about Ruby.'

Lesley's hand reached up to her mouth. 'Is she hurt?'

'He says your mother and she went out yesterday morning and they haven't come back.'

Lesley took two steps to the kitchen phone. French, her mind obstinately retained that. She cleared her throat.

'*Bonsoir? Je suis la mère de Mademoiselle Ruby Sawyer* . . .'

'Good evening, Madame. I am afraid there is some anxiety concerning your daughter and your mother,' the doctor began in accented but perfect English.

When Lesley replaced the phone her hands were shaking. Andrew was still standing in the doorway.

She said, 'We'll have to fly out. Tomorrow, as soon as we can.'

He didn't try to contradict her, or tell her that she was overreacting and ought to calm down. He just nodded. 'I'll see what flights there are.'

*   *   *

355

Ruby stood up and walked a little way from the car to where the sand sloped upwards. Her body was twitching, small jerks of electricity ran through her limbs and made it difficult to keep still. The sky was unbroken blue, and along the line where the crest of the dune met the sky there was a multicoloured zigzag of dancing light, as if the sand were narrowly on fire. The sight made her thirst burn more fiercely and she turned her back and slumped down on her haunches. The sand around her feet was criss-crossed with tiny braided patterns, and after a while she worked out that these were the tracks of toktok beetles. Her fingers burrowed aimlessly in the sand and encountered some coarse strands, and when she disinterred them she saw that it was a few blades of rough, bleached grass that had been buried by the storm.

Grass, beetles, they could survive.

Can we?

Iris was lying on her side next to the car, her head shaded by her white scarf. Her quietness, her seeming acquiescence, frightened Ruby. But Ruby was frightened of everything now. Their water was gone, all they had left was a pomegranate. In an hour or so it would be dark again.

Ruby was thinking so this is how you die, is it?

Tears of pity for herself burned behind her eyes, but her whole body seemed too dry for the relief of falling tears. A voice quite unlike her own broke out of her instead.

'I don't want to die. I don't *want* to fucking *die*.'

CHAPTER FOURTEEN

Under a sky blown clear of cloud, the temperature dropped as soon as darkness came. Ruby helped Iris into the back seat of the car and held her with her head cradled in her lap. Iris folded her arms across her chest and drew up her knees to fit in the cramped space, and Ruby took off her own T-shirt and tucked it over her hips as if it were a blanket. They were both shivering but the cold was only a partial distraction from their thirst.

Ruby decided that they would share the remaining half of a pomegranate when the sun rose again, then she would plan what to do.

But *what to do* suggested a breadth of choice belonging to the precious world that had just slipped out of her reach.

Go out, stay in. Smoke a cigarette, or not. Tea or coffee, pizza or curry, cinema or telly – mundane choices that she had never bothered to savour, let alone acknowledging that it might also be luxurious to weigh company against solitude, the possibility of action against lingering inertia, the greasiness of indulgence as opposed to glowing self-denial.

Her mind racked up the pairs of alternatives, her imagination lending them a luminosity that reality had never bestowed.

She thought if I ever get out of here, if we get out, I'll *never* not value every ordinary minute of every day, however drab or annoying the moments seem.

Life is exquisite. Why had she never known this before?

It is precious. Colours. Voices. Streets. Love, music, laughingsingingtouchingdancing. I wish I could even find the words for it. I wish I'd done something I was proud of.

I wish . . .

Thirst racked her throat and made her tongue raw and puffy. The recesses of her teeth and gums tasted foul, and she couldn't draw down enough saliva to swallow properly.

I wish I could see Lesley and Ed, and my dad and Andrew.

She realised that her lips were moving, forming the words even though her throat was too sore to voice them. She stroked Iris's hair, feeling the gritty sand coating her scalp. It was cold, and the rear window framed a patch of sky packed with aloof stars. A cold quarter of moon hung in a faint veil of silver. To see the jets drifting overhead towards the glamour of the airport made the desert even lonelier.

'Iris?' she croaked.

There was no answer; they had hardly spoken since they had taken their last mouthful of water. Ruby hoped that she was asleep, and at the same time she was afraid to realise how silent and still she had become. Iris was frail and every hour left her weaker.

Ruby lifted her head, wincing as a cramp tighened in her leg.

Choice. She had been considering the stark options that would be open to her when the sun rose again.

They could sit here and hope to be found. In the end, a search would be mounted and they would be discovered, sitting in their car that was slowly turning into a piece of the desert. But this was Egypt. Realistically, how long would it take for Mamdooh and Auntie to summon the rescuers?

Most probably Iris would be dead before anyone came.

Or she could set out again, as she had done this morning, and this time instead of losing her nerve and turning back she would have to keep on and on walking until she found help or until she dropped.

Either or. The richness of the whole world reduced to a choice that was not a choice at all, but a sentence.

All right. Wait till the morning. Think.

Ruby now couldn't think of anything but the few drops of moisture held in the pomegranate seeds. She had to clench her fists to stop herself reaching for the fruit and cramming it into her mouth. Then she relaxed her hands again and continued to stroke Iris's hair, concentrating on the slow rhythm, trying to subdue all her love and longing for the world into the caress.

Mamdooh walked through Qarafa with the folds of his *galabiyeh* drawn up round his ankles, following the ragged boy who dashed ahead of him, and at the same time trying to avoid the heaps of rubbish and scattered animal dung. It was the point of the day at which the light faded and the sky turned indigo. In the City of the Dead the flat brown tombs and the colourless dust darkened, and their sharp edges were picked out with the silver-bright tracery of rising moon-light, so that the arid daytime scenery was transformed by exotic twilight.

Mamdooh did not linger even for a glance at the Mamluk tombs in the moonlight. He kept his eye on his skinny little guide instead, who was ducking between the low tomb houses of the ordinary dead. The alleys were apparently deserted but they contained a sense of watchfulness. A few more turns brought them to a closed door and the child wordlessly pointed to it. He held out a hand and pulled at Mamdooh's sleeve until Mamdooh tipped a couple of coins into his palm.

Then the child skipped over a broken pillar and vanished into the dusk.

Mamdooh banged hard on the door. It opened by a crack and Nafouz's face was revealed. Mamdooh reached in and grasped him by the collar of his leather jacket. With unsuspected strength he hauled him out into the open and in the crack in the doorway the faces of Nafouz's mother and his grandmother immediately appeared instead.

Mamdooh shook Nafouz and poured out a stream of questions, and Nafouz twisted his shoulders and tried to break out of his grasp.

He shrilly insisted that Ashraf was at his work at the Bab al-Futuh hospital, and had been at work the night before too, as usual, and he had not seen Ruby for two whole days.

The two women emerged from the protection of the tomb house and now they all stood in a little circle in the indigo dusk. Mamdooh turned on them and demanded to know if this was the truth.

It was, Ash's mother protested. Several times Ashraf had brought the young girl to this place, but not in the last two days. And yesterday afternoon he had said that he would go to meet her but he had come back and told his family that the girl was not in the usual place at the agreed time. Today, the same thing.

What was Ashraf to do about that, she demanded? Was her son to blame if an English girl was not reliable?

Mamdooh retorted that what her son should now do was tell the truth to the police.

The two women pressed closer to Nafouz and murmured anxiously to each other, and Nafouz stepped in front of them and loudly insisted that his brother and the police had no business together.

'That we shall see,' Mamdooh warned.

He told them that the police were now looking for Miss

and for Doctor Black, her grandmother, who was missing also. The young girl's mother and father were coming from England to take charge of the search. They would all want to speak to Ashraf, and to the rest of his family too, and it would be advisable if they remembered every smallest thing and spoke nothing but the purest truth.

Ash's grandmother covered her face with her headscarf and began to wail.

Mamdooh walked away, back in the direction he had come.

Ruth is stroking my hair.

After Xan died I went through the motions of living, although I felt hardly alive myself. On what would have been our wedding day and for two weeks afterwards I did my job for Roddy Boy, went to the hospital for my voluntary shift and came home again to Garden City. It was a meaningless triangle and at each point of it I longed to be at either of the others because surely the pain there would be more bearable than at the present one. But it never was and so there was nothing to do but continue.

I told Roddy Boy and Sarah and Daphne and Ruth that I was all right.

By the middle of June Rommel was once more within reach of Tobruk, and after days of fierce fighting and huge losses on both sides the city fell to the Germans. The Panzer Army moved on towards el Alamein and the Egyptian frontier, driving the tattered remains of the Eighth Army ahead of it. The threat to Alexandria was imminent and Cairo was in uproar. It seemed inevitable that Axis forces would reach the delta within days.

Ruth and Daphne did their best to look after me. Daphne drove me out to the flat on the Heliopolis road one evening, and I sat in the same chair as on my first visit and accepted the last of the malt whisky that I had brought them as a present. I tried to think back to the happiness that had suffused everything then, but I couldn't grasp it. All that remained was darkness.

'Come on,' Daphne insisted. 'Try to eat some of this.'

I took the plate of their good food and lifted a forkful to my mouth.

When I set out for the evening I had not bothered to distinguish one pain from another, but now I realised that I was ill.

I reached across and caught Daphne's arm. 'I'm sorry,' I said.

My friends looked at me, then at each other. A belt of pain tightened round my middle.

'I'm so sorry,' I heard myself mumble as I put my head down and tried to assimilate the pain.

Ruth and Daphne were talking in low voices. Daphne put one hand to my forehead and held my wrist in the other. When I could stand up, I went into the bathroom and found blood. There was a thin seam of blood running down the inside of my leg and dark droplets on the tile floor.

My friends made me lie down on their bed. I was very thirsty, burning up with thirst.

Ruth sits beside me and strokes my hair again, but there is nothing to drink and I am too parched to ask for water. The stroking soothes me, but I am cold, shivering. It's dark and my arms and legs are bent and hooked in a narrow space.

Ruby did not sleep. Between wishing for and dreading the dawn it was the longest night she had ever known. The moon set and in the darkest hours there were not even any planes to offer a link with the friendly world.

At last the stars began to fade and a pearl-grey line touched the horizon. As the light came again Iris stirred and moaned.

362

Ruby helped her to sit up, then held her face between her two hands.

'Iris, listen. Look at me. I've got to go for help, otherwise we are going to die.'

Iris's cracked lips twitched as she tried to speak. No sound came out, but her eyes held Ruby's and she seemed to understand what she was saying.

'I don't want to leave you, but I don't know what else to do.'

Then Iris nodded, very slowly but definitely.

'I'm going to set out as soon as it's properly light.'

Again the nod.

'Let's share this,' Ruby said. The hoarded pomegranate half was dull with dust. She tore the peel, careful in case of spilling even a drop of juice, but the fruit was almost dry. She gave two-thirds to Iris and dug her teeth into the remaining third. There was an ecstatic second as the seeds split on her tongue and yielded a few drops of liquid, but then it was gone and she chewed on the stiff pulp that was left. Iris did the same.

The sun was not yet up and the air was still cold, but it was light. Ruby climbed out of the car and sank up to her ankles in chilly sand.

'Let me make you comfortable before I go.'

She took Iris's hands and helped her from the car to sit in the sand beside it, putting one arm round her waist and lowering her gently. Iris was very weak now. Ruby knew that if she didn't go immediately, she would not be able to leave her. She leaned down and kissed her on the forehead. 'I love you,' she told her. 'I'll be back very soon. Just wait for me, all right?'

She was straightening up when Iris grasped her wrist. Ruby had to bend down again with her ear close to her grandmother's mouth to catch the words.

'Just go. Don't worry.'

She knew what Iris was telling her.

'I'll be back,' she repeated angrily. She pulled herself away and began to walk.

She didn't look back until she reached the crest of the nearest dune. The Beetle looked even more like a chunk of the desert than it had done yesterday.

Only *yesterday*.

She did her best to memorise the shape of the surrounding dunes, searching for a single feature anywhere in the landscape that would help her to fix this place and lead the rescuers back again. But the dun-coloured curves and hollows were all the same, implacable.

Ruby turned her back on the car and her grandmother, and trudged eastwards through the sliding sand, as fast as she could, while the sun still told her which way to go.

Daphne called a taxi, and she and Ruth took me to the Cairo Hospital for Women and Children, run by the nuns. In a shuttered white room there I miscarried my sixteen-week pregnancy, Xan's son.

The placid, smooth-faced nuns nursed me. For two days I wouldn't see anyone except Ruth, who came after she finished work and sat with me for a few silent minutes. I lay and stared at the white walls and waited to die.

Xan was dead and now I had lost the precious link to him. I remembered his delight when I told him that I was pregnant and I grieved twice over, for myself and for Xan too because it was his child as well as mine that was lost. It seemed beyond bearing that I could not share my desolation with him. It was incomprehensible that I would never share anything else with him, and I lay and wept until no more tears would come. Death would have been a welcome solution but my body refused to oblige; rather than letting me sink into oblivion it began obstinately to recover.

On the third day one of the sisters made me sit up and wash my face and comb my hair.

'There's a different visitor to see you,' she said.

'I don't want a visitor.'

'Yes, you do,' she told me. The door opened and Sarah came in. She had a bunch of marigolds and cosmos in her hand, flowers that made me think of my mother's garden.

'Oh, darling,' she cried. 'I'm so sorry.'

She put the flowers in a toothmug, then sat down in the chair beside my bed and took my hand.

I stared at her as if she had walked in from another world. A minute passed in silence, but then I squeezed her hand in mine.

To see Sarah made me feel, for the first time since I had lost the baby, that there was a chink of light in the world. As well as the flowers, her pale complexion and pale eyebrows and even the neat collar of her starched blouse all seemed to stand for Englishness, and a distant, quiet normality separate from this present agony. The continuity that she represented gave me an inkling that I might be able to go on living.

'I'm glad you're here,' I whispered finally. Her fingers tightened on mine.

Sarah let me weep again, and in the end I shouted and sobbed at her, 'If I can't have him, why couldn't I at least have had his son?'

Sarah bent her head. 'It's cruel,' she agreed.

I thought she couldn't possibly know how cruel it felt. Sobs of self-pity racked me, until she raised her head and looked me in the eye.

'Listen to me, Iris. It's hard, but you do know that Xan loved you. You have that memory and the certainty will always stay with you.'

'Yes,' I agreed.

'The tragedy is that he was killed. The double tragedy is that you lost the baby too. That's terrible, almost unbearable, but in some ways you are lucky.'

I stared at her, wondering where this was leading.

'In what ways?'

'You were loved. Loved passionately and with all his being, by a man you deeply loved and admired in return. You may only have had a few months, but you did have that much. You conceived a child together, out of love and hope, and now it's ended you can at least mourn them both without feeling ashamed.'

The grief that had blinded me shifted a little and I was able to take a glance beyond it.

It was suddenly plain to me that she had suffered a loss too, although I had never seen as much before now. 'What happened?'

'I wasn't loved,' she said simply.

'Who didn't?'

'Jeremy.'

Jeremy the poet, shabby and blinking, Faria's helpless and hopeless admirer.

'But he was in love with Faria . . .'

'I know that. It didn't make any difference. When she was too busy for him, didn't require him as an escort – well, then there I was. It was much better than nothing, for me. Iris, can you understand that?'

I hesitated. 'In a way.'

'Faria wouldn't sleep with him, of course. But I did. That was better than nothing for *him*, do you see?'

Her sadness cut my heart. 'You love him.'

'Yes. Terribly. And then, I was pregnant.'

The white coif of one of the nuns nodded at the little observation window in the door of my room, then passed on down the corridor. The marigolds in the glass mug bled their colour into the dim room. The louvred shutters were closed but I knew that outside the afternoon heat would be at its white, blinding height. Cairo was a cruel city.

'What did you do?' I asked, already knowing the answer.

'I told him, of course.'

Her hand that was not holding mine tapped out the words on the folded bedsheet.

'What was I hoping for? That he would say to me that this changed everything, ask me to marry him, announce the glad tidings to all our friends, as you and Xan did?'

Your friends would have greeted the news with frank disbelief, I thought and immediately felt ashamed of myself.

'He didn't, in any case. Of course. He just said that he was very sorry and he would do everything he could to help me. So I had an abortion. I went to Beirut, do you remember? Jeremy gave me some money towards it. Not much, because he doesn't have much. I had some savings, luckily.'

In my self-absorbed happiness I had been quite ready to accept the story that Sarah had had Gyppy tummy and had gone to Lebanon for a holiday in order to recover.

'I'm so sorry,' I said.

She looked at me. 'Are you shocked? Disgusted?'

'No. Surprised, that's all, although I really shouldn't be. I could have worked the whole thing out for myself, if I had bothered. I wish you'd felt that you could tell me. And I wish that I had been a better friend, when you needed one.'

'I couldn't tell a soul,' Sarah whispered. 'I am only saying this now because I can't bear to see you so stricken and I'd admit to worse if I thought it might help. The truth is that I wasn't loved and I didn't even have the courage to keep my child. Now that it's too late, I wish I had kept it. I dream that I'm cradling it, then I wake up and my arms are empty. That is what I did.

'So I'd trade my place for yours, you know. You have no reason in the world to feel ashamed, at least.'

'No,' I said.

Sarah was right.

We held each other and cried, and I hoped that I was not only crying for myself. Then she sat upright in the chair and wiped her eyes.

'That's enough,' she said. Her Anglo-Saxon stoicism made me think of my mother again. My mother, who didn't yet know that she had lost a son-in-law and a grandchild before they had even existed.

'What are you going to do?' Sarah asked, taking a powder compact and a lipstick out of her handbag. She snapped open the compact and began to repair her face.

I might have replied that I didn't know, or care, but I stopped myself. 'I'm going to come home to the flat as soon as I can. Could you bring me some clean clothes, perhaps?'

'Of course.' Sarah liked to be given a defined job. 'There's a bit of a flap on, even more than usual, actually. Have you heard the BBC?'

Since my miscarriage I had almost forgotten about the war. I hadn't heard the wireless news, but one of the sisters who spoke some English had told me that Alexandria was likely to fall to the enemy in a matter of hours. The threat of air raids on the harbour was so strong that British Navy ships moored there had been suddenly withdrawn to Haifa and Beirut, leaving the busy harbour deserted and causing panic in the city. Alexandrians were packing up their belongings and flooding out into the delta to avoid the coming enemy invasion.

'Battle for Egypt, BBC is saying,' the nun told me. Her long, pale face was calm and resigned under the folds of the coif.

'Women and children are being evacuated. The embassy's

in charge of allocating places on the Palestine train. People are pulling strings all over the shop, just to get a seat,' Sarah went on. 'It's chaotic. What do you think you'll do?'

I had no idea. I had no sense of purpose and I couldn't think where I would go if I were to leave Cairo. Heavily I said, 'Go back to work again, if Roddy Boy wants me, I suppose. What about you?'

'I'd like to get out to Palestine. Why sit here and wait to be invaded? Mamdooh says half the shopkeepers in town have got German swastikas and bunting all ready, to welcome the troops when they arrive.'

'They would do.' I smiled, against the odds.

Sarah promised that she would bring in my clothes the next day. We clung briefly to each other before she left.

'Thank you for coming.'

She patted my shoulder. 'Got to stick together, eh?'

I suddenly wanted very much to be back at the Garden City flat, the nearest approximation I had to home, but if Sarah was leaving Cairo and Faria's parents wanted us to move out in any case, I would have to look for somewhere else to live. The effort involved seemed insurmountable.

That evening, when Ruth visited me, she told me that I was looking much better.

'I want to get out of here. Tomorrow, if I can.'

'That can only be a good thing.' The Hospital for Women and Children was a sepulchral place, scented with iodine and boiled vegetables.

We walked slowly down the corridor to the patients' sitting room to listen to the BBC news together. Alexandria had been heavily bombed the night before and Cairo itself was reported to be braced for an aerial invasion. It was 30 June.

At the end of the bulletin Ruth switched off the wireless and we stood out on the veranda at the far end of the room.

The hot night was unnaturally quiet. A curfew had been imposed on all the troops, making the city out of bounds during the hours of darkness, and the streets were deserted. The cafés and nightclubs must all have been empty too. A horse-drawn gharry clopped beneath us, the driver's whip trailing at an angle.

'He's probably thinking about how he'll be taking some German staff officer to Shepheard's in a couple of days' time,' I said.

Ruth laughed. 'The service at Shepheard's will slow Rommel down, if nothing else does.'

Ruth told me that Daphne intended to stay and work in Cairo for as long as she could be useful. 'And where Daphne is, that's where I want to be.'

I nodded. Ruth was devoted to Daphne, and Daphne was devoted to her work. Neither of them lacked a sense of purpose. I thought again about returning to London, after the war, to study medicine. I would not be Xan's wife, but I could make myself useful somewhere.

After Ruth had gone I lay on my hospital cot, half expecting to hear air raid sirens, but no German bombers reached Cairo that night.

Sarah brought in my clothes, and offered to wait with me and see me back to the flat, but I told her to go off to work. I didn't know how long it would be before the French doctor came to discharge me.

In the end, I was free to leave hospital by the middle of the morning. The doctor examined me once more and told me that I should rest, but that I was a strong young woman and he did not think there was any reason why I should not have a healthy baby in due course. I knew the reassurance was kindly intended, but I ignored it. I didn't want another baby, or another lover to give me one. Only the ones I had lost.

As soon as I walked out through the hospital gates I understood that there was a flap on unlike any that had gone before. I had told Sarah that I would take a taxi back to Garden City, but Sharia Port Said was a solid, hooting mass of motionless traffic. The few taxis I could see were all taken, and in any case were going nowhere. Wedged into the jam I could see at least two dozen dust-caked lorries packed with troops. Their weary faces and dejected postures told the story of what had been happening in the desert. The nearest lorry was only a few feet away from where I stood. Several of the men were asleep, their heads lolling against the camouflage canvas. Others were wounded, and their field dressings were caked with blood and dust. All of them looked too exhausted and too dejected to move.

An Egyptian street vendor came along the pavement under the banyan trees, pushing a cart packed with ice and bottles of lemonade. As he drew level with the lorry he suddenly stopped, looking up at the rows of soldiers. Then he twisted the stopper out of a bottle and handed it up to the nearest man, who nudged the wounded soldier slumped next to him. The other man's hands were bandaged, so his friend tilted the frosted bottle to his mouth for him.

The vendor went on unstoppering his bottles and the big, dirty hands reached down and gratefully took them, until the vendor's cart was empty and the dust at his feet was spattered with melted ice.

'Ta, mate,' one of the men called. 'Rommel ain't getting anywhere near Cairo, don't yer worry.'

Revived by the lemonade, the soldiers at the back of the lorry caught sight of me and waved.

'Hello, Miss. Want a ride?'

'Come on, hop up here with us.'

I waved back at them and smiled.

The column briefly shuddered and the lorry edged forward

371

in a cloud of exhaust fumes. I took some folded notes out of my purse and gave them to the street vendor, the money disappeared into the folds of his *galabiyeh* and I crossed the road through the stalled traffic. I decided that I would head for GHQ because it was nearer than the flat.

Apart from army lorries pouring in from the desert and staff cars with preoccupied brass fuming behind their drivers, most of the cars belonged to ordinary Egyptians. They were packed with people, families and grandmothers and tiny children, and laden with possessions of all kinds. Suitcases and furniture and baskets of provisions were strapped onto the roofs, and many of the people had tied mattresses on top of all that, to offer some protection against flying debris. It seemed that the whole of Cairo was flooding out into the delta before the war could reach it.

In the street before Qasr el Aini a thick line of people wound from the steps of the Bank of Egypt all the way back down to the next corner. The people who still remained in town wanted to withdraw their money while they could. I passed the queue and walked on to the entrance to GHQ, as automatically as if it were an ordinary day.

I didn't have my entry pass, but the guard sergeant at the perimeter hut recognised me.

'Morning, Miss. Business as usual for some of us, isn't it?'

The dingy, rabbit-warren corridors smelled of burning. Staff officers were dashing up and down the stairs and telephones rang behind closed doors. I found Roddy sitting at his desk behind a pile of 'Most Secret' folders that were normally kept under lock and key in our filing cabinets. He got up as soon as he saw me, concern fighting embarrassment in his face.

'Miss Black, what's this? Are you well enough to be here?'

Very few people had known that I was pregnant. As far as Roddy was concerned I had just had a stomach upset.

I was at a loss myself and I didn't know where else to be.

'I'm well enough. Can't I do something for an hour or two?' I begged.

I liked Roddy more than I had done. He had said nothing after Xan died except that he was sorry, but he had given me work to do and he hadn't treated me as though bereavement made an outcast of me.

He rubbed his jaw now. He was pink and well-shaven, and his service dress was as impeccable as always. 'Ah. Yes, yes, all right then, plenty to do. Today of all days.'

I made him his mid-morning cup of tea and put the two custard creams in his saucer.

'What's going to happen here?' I asked.

'If our lines hold at el Alamein, nothing. If not' – he snapped a biscuit in two – 'we had all better be ready to evacuate. Half of the GHQ sections and Special Operations are already moving to Jerusalem for safety. And General Corbett has ordered the most sensitive documents to be burned, in case they fall into enemy hands. If you are sure you are able, you could take this lot down for me now. Out to the back of the building, you'll see when you get there.'

I took the pile of folders off his desk and went downstairs. Several of the offices I passed were empty of their colonels and brigadiers, dusty shelves swept bare, metal filing cabinets gaping open. The smell of burning had grown much stronger.

Out on a bare patch of ground stood a line of blazing forty-gallon oil drums. Sweating men, their faces blackened with smoke, were dashing up to them and tossing huge sheaves of classified documents into the flames. Captain Frobisher was supervising the operation.

'Hullo, Martin.'

He greeted me respectfully. Since Xan's death I had become

373

an awkward figure, no longer someone to be joked or flirted with.

'This is a bit of a show, isn't it?' He took the folders out of my arms and consigned them to the waiting heap.

I stood beside him for a few minutes, watching the columns of black smoke rising over the rooftops of GHQ. The updraught carried flakes of singed paper with it and they swirled down again like gingery snow.

I went home to the flat that evening with my clothes reeking of smoke. Roddy and I had cleared our files of anything remotely sensitive and the oil drum fires were still burning brightly.

Mamdooh was full of the news. He told Sarah and me that shopkeepers had started putting up pictures of Mussolini in their windows. Indignantly he muttered, 'British not so very bad in Egypt, whatever these ignorant people think, and Germans and Italians much worse, hear my words.' His little boy sat on a stool, watching and listening.

Sarah's job was in the embassy, and her contribution was that the ambassador had made a great show of normality all day and had now taken his lady out to dinner. But Sandy Allardyce, the embassy's best German speaker, had been told that he would have to stay behind to liaise with the Germans once the ambassador and the rest of the staff had travelled to safety. Remembering the rumours about Sandy being a spy, we looked at each other and laughed.

It was bedtime, but I couldn't sleep. The drama of the day had kept my mind busy but now that I was alone I felt empty and despairing. I stood at my window for a long time, staring at the outlines of my jacaranda tree. If the Germans came or if they did not, it seemed hardly to matter. At last I sat down at my table and wrote a letter to my mother and father, telling them the news about Xan and the baby.

* * *

374

As soon as they stepped out of the air-conditioned order of the airport, Lesley and Andrew were assaulted by Cairo. Taxi drivers and touts mobbed them and tried to yank the suitcases out of their hands. Andrew pulled away from the insistent grasp of one man, only to be seized from another direction and when Lesley shrank behind him for protection he trampled over her feet when he staggered backwards. They both almost fell over.

'Sir! Lady! Coming with me, please!'

'This way, with me, very good ride.'

When they finally reached the taxi park it turned out that they had somehow promised their custom to two different drivers and the two men were bitter enemies. A storm of threats and yelling broke out, with each driver seizing one suitcase and locking it into the boot of his taxi. In the end Andrew had to bribe one driver to leave them in the clutches of the other, and the loser drove away with a torrent of abuse and a volley of hooting. Sweating, they sank into the winner's cab and he celebrated by accelerating at reckless speed across a swathe of oncoming traffic. Lesley gave a little yelp and covered her eyes.

'It's Cairo, isn't it? This is what it's going to be like,' Andrew said through clenched teeth.

By some miracle they avoided a collision with an oncoming bus. The cab swept past huge concrete apartment blocks and up on to an elevated section of motorway that gave them a glimpse of the city's dust-shawled grey extent. Lesley sat forward and stared at it.

'It's so big. How will we find them? Where will we even begin?'

Andrew's forehead and his broad nose were pearled with sweat. He hated the unpredictable and he hated being caught off balance, and Egypt threatened to deliver the worst possible circumstances.

'That's a job for the police,' he snapped, masking his uncertainty with brusqueness.

Lesley turned her head away from him and looked at the black windows in the concrete faces of buildings stretching away in a dust haze as far as the eye could see. Ruby could be behind any one of those windows. She could be ill, kidnapped, assaulted. Lesley's heart was pounding with adrenalin. She wanted to jump out of the cab and run or climb or tear down walls, anything that might bring her closer to her child, but all she could do was sit on the sticky brown plastic seat of the cab and clench her sweating hands into tight fists.

The cab driver looked back over his shoulder. 'Holiday in Cairo? Nice tour for you, maybe, good price?'

After a long time in dense traffic, they arrived in a cobbled alley that became too narrow for the car to pass. Three minarets rose behind a high wall. The affronted driver pointed ahead to a shabby unmarked door.

After he had reversed away Andrew and Lesley stood in the street with their bags at their feet. The high walls trapped the polluted air and there was rubbish silted in the the corners. Ruby had come all this way alone, Lesley thought, and she must have stood here in this same decaying cul-de-sac wondering if she had come to the right place, and yet she had made nothing of it. What kind of a child was she, to do such things? Where was she now?

Andrew said, 'Come on. Let's get on with it, if this really is the place.'

She followed him to the door, and they stood on the hollowed step and waited for someone to answer their knocking.

Ruby was lost by the time she had climbed up and skidded down the first two or three dune ridges. From down in the shadowed hollows the swelling mountains of sand were fore-shortened, and it always took her much longer than she anticipated to climb to the summit. It was too disheartening to look upwards to the sizzling light line where sand met sky because it never seemed to come any closer, so she trudged upwards with her head hanging, listening to the wheeze of her own breathing. Jagged pain shot through her cranium and down into her spine. Her mouth and throat cracked with drought and her lungs burned, but she kept on putting one foot in front of the other.

When she did crawl up to the summit, there was only ever another dune rising beyond it.

After she had been going for two hours she stopped and tried to take her bearings, although it was pointless trying to memorise the features of the landscape because there were none. Only her tracks stretched backwards, looking like irrelevant wrinkles in the wind-fluted landscape. But they were at least still visible. There was only a light breeze blowing, puffing a little veil of sepia dust off the exposed slopes.

Steering by the sun was much harder than she had antici-pated. It had risen fast and she couldn't gauge whether it was now more in the south than the east. It would be a bad mistake to head too far south, she reckoned, because that would simply lead to more desert, although she had only the sketchiest idea of the geography beyond the delta. There was no point now in being angry with herself about that. The only thing to do was keep walking.

Keep walking. Leave the sun more or less on her right cheek now.

She plodded on. Help, help, hurt, hurt, home, home. The words drummed meaninglessly in her burning head. It was too much effort even to think. It was better to be somewhere else, outside her own body. She could be separate from the little beetle figure that was Ruby Sawyer as she toiled up and down the sand slopes.

I am tired. I would like to surrender and sleep, but I know that I can't because there is more to be done. The child was right when we talked about an empty place at the centre.

I try to swallow on a throat full of sand and the parade of memories starts up again.

The line held at el Alamein.

After twenty-eight days of almost continuous fighting the battle ended in a stalemate, but the Panzer Divisions had been halted and the enemy forces never reached Alexandria or Cairo.

The curfew was lifted and the city streets filled up with soldiers once more. People slowly filtered back from their refuges in the delta, and the pictures of Mussolini and the bunting disappeared from the shop windows as quickly as they had appeared. At GHQ Roddy Boy and the remaining top brass bewailed the loss of all their classified files.

I remember the exhausted sense of anticlimax that descended after the days of the flap, and the terrible July heat that weighted every movement. My second summer in Cairo was long and painful.

Sarah's French diplomat boyfriend was posted to Baghdad and she decided that she would follow him.

'Why not?' She shrugged. 'What else should I do?'

Jeremy had left Cairo for Palestine at the height of the crisis, without taking the time to say goodbye to her.

Faria came back from her honeymoon and settled into Ali's opulent house. She spent much of her time shopping for linen and upholstery fabrics. I went once or twice to dinner with the newlyweds, but the other guests were mostly business associates of Ali's and Faria herself was uncommunicative.

'That is very sad,' she sighed, when I told her about the

baby. 'But maybe in the end, you know, it is for the best?'

I began to look for somewhere else to live, without having any heart for it. And then one day at work, Roddy Boy put his head out of his office and announced through tight lips that my father was on the telephone and wished to speak urgently to me. I took the receiver and in the familiar dingy office environment of spilling folders and metal cupboards I heard my father saying that my mother was ill and maybe I should consider returning to England as soon as possible. I knew he wouldn't suggest such a thing unless it was serious.

'I'll be sorry to lose you, Miss Black. But your family must take precedence,' Roddy told me. And apart from Ruth, Daphne and my inessential voluntary work there was nothing else to keep me in Egypt.

I booked my passage home on a ship sailing via the Cape and then, when my belongings were packed and I was waiting out the last few hours in the empty Garden City apartment, Mamdooh came to tell me that I had a visitor.

'Who is it?'

In the dim hallway with its over-elaborate furniture, a tall dark-faced man was standing.

It was Hassan, who I believed had been killed beside Xan in the Qattara Depression.

For a moment I didn't know whether I should turn and run away from this apparition. Shock rooted me to the ground and my voice dried in my throat, but Hassan slowly extended his hand to me and I reached out and grasped it. I hung on to him as if he were a connection direct to Xan, and Hassan bent his head and touched his fingers to his forehead in greeting.

'You are alive,' I croaked. 'How? Wait, don't stand here. Come in, sit, let me give you some tea. Mamdooh, will you bring some?'

If it seemed foolish to welcome a man back from the dead

with a glass of mint tea, but I didn't know how else it should be done. I took Hassan into the drawing room where the furniture was already partially shrouded in dust sheets and we faced each other across an inlaid table. Hassan sat upright, his hands folded, as if he could not make himself comfortable in this Westernised setting.

'I come to pay respect, Madam,' Hassan said. 'The Captain my friend. From a boy, Bedouin and British man, friend.'

'I know. You must have known Xan better than anyone else. Will you tell me what happened?'

Hassan described how the planes had come from nowhere, out of an empty sky, straight at them. Xan's driver had jinked and swerved, trying to avoid the fire, and they had fired back at the aircraft, but they had stood no chance. The truck hit a patch of soft sand and sank down to the wheel arches, and Hassan dived out and began to run. When he looked again he saw that Xan was trying to pull the driver, who had been shot in the back, out of the burning truck. He shouted at him to run, but Xan wouldn't leave the wounded man. Then the ammunition and the fuel stored in jerrycans in the back of the truck had exploded in a huge fireball.

Hassan had turned from the scene of his friend's death and melted into the moonscape. It had taken him many days to make his way back, walking at night and hiding during the day in case the planes came again.

'I should have stayed by his side.'

'No. What good would that have done?'

'I did not know if to come here,' he explained at the end.

'I am so glad you did. I'm happy to see that you are alive. Thank you.'

He stood up then and bowed his head once more. 'You go back to England?'

'Yes, my mother is ill.'

'I am sorry for that.'

'What will you do now, Hassan?'

His eyes met mine. I remembered the desert oasis and the men gathered round a fire, just as they must have done for hundreds of years. He said quietly, 'Like you, I believe I will continue my path, but I will keep a memory always.'

He stood up then and bowed his head once more.

Hassan had brought me a connection to Xan that I longed for and now I knew how bravely he had died. When we reached the door I caught his arm once more.

'Hassan, I would like you to keep this. Xan gave it to me when he asked me to marry him, and I would be happy to think that it will stay here in Egypt with you.'

I took the amethyst off my engagement finger and put it into his hand. He held it in the cup of his palm and we both looked at it. I felt an unfamiliar movement in me like a bird's wings and realised that it was a beat of happiness.

'Madam?'

'Please take it. It will be a link between us, you and me and him.'

Hassan touched his lips to the ring. Slowly, he took a worn leather pouch out of a fold of his clothing and put the ring into it. Then he pulled the strings to close the pouch and tucked it away next to his ribcage.

'Goodbye, Madam,' he said. 'May God be with you.'

'And with you,' I answered.

The next day, my goodbyes already said, I left Cairo by train for Suez. It was Major Gordon Foxbridge, the photographer, who drove me and my luggage to the station. It happened that he had the morning free, he told me, and he had a staff car at his disposal. As we parted he asked if he might have my address and, grateful for his assistance, I gave him my parents' address in Hampshire because I had no other.

It was thirty-five years before I saw Cairo again.

My mother recovered from her illness and I spent a few months nursing her. But she died suddenly a year later, in September 1943, from bronchial pneumonia.

Under the terms of her will I inherited a share of her family trust and with this money to live on, I began the long battle to get into medical school. Daphne Erdall, who was by then living in Athens with Ruth, sent me to see a one-time colleague of hers at the medical school of St Bart's. In the end, probably because it was easier to offer me a place than to continue to refuse me, I was accepted.

I kept in touch with Daphne and Ruth, and from time to time I also heard from Sandy Allardyce. He married Gerti Kimmig-Gertsch and they moved between Cairo, Italy and Zurich.

My father died in 1946, and not long afterwards I agreed to marry Gordon Foxbridge. I didn't love him but I liked and respected him, and I didn't expect ever to fall in love again. I had had my great passion and that was more than many people would ever know. I had my memories and I continually returned to them. For sixty years I reached up to the shelf and took the familiar cup down, wrapping my fingers round it and letting the warmth nourish me.

My second pregnancy was unplanned. Gordon was overjoyed and we bought a house outside London in a hurry.

Lesley was born in 1950.

I shift my legs in the sand and my head rolls against the metal flank of the car. I want to sleep, to slide under the surface of consciousness, but a hand holds me back. The clutch torments me even more than thirst and the white eye of the sun.

My daughter clings on to me. I try to creep backwards, like a hermit crab pulling into its shell, but it is Lesley who follows me into my refuge. She stands there with her hands on her hips, in the middle of the space in my life, staring at me as if she is waiting for something.

There is still more to be done.

Andrew went out to see the police.

'I'll come with you,' Lesley said, but he insisted that she should stay in the house in case there was any news.

'I'm going to meet a senior officer. It's nearly three days since Ruby and your mother disappeared, and they are taking it seriously. After that I am going to the British embassy.'

Even though it was quite cool inside the house, sweat broke out on his forehead whenever he moved and strands of his sandy hair were pasted to his skull.

'When will you be back?'

'How can I tell? I have no idea what it will be like dealing with these people.'

There was nothing for Lesley to do but sit and wait.

The gaunt, dusty house was quite unlike the Moroccan fantasy she had dreamed up. It was impressive in its way but uncompromisingly austere; Lesley tried and failed to imagine the solitary existence that her mother must lead here. It was as if she were speculating about a stranger, not the woman who had given birth to her, yet Ruby had made a connection with her at once.

The manservant's presence was disconcerting. He moved through the rooms like an airship, stately and silent, squeezing his bulk through the doorways and round tight corners. Whenever his helper, the little old woman with a face like a walnut, saw Lesley she started to cry, mopping her eyes with a corner of her white headdress. Lesley had learned from Mamdooh that Auntie – she didn't know whose aunt – had been the last person to see Ruby, two mornings ago, but Ruby hadn't told her anything about where she and Iris were going. Auntie seemed to think that Lesley might still blame her in some way for what had happened and Lesley's attempts at reassurance only made her more upset. The minutes of waiting dragged by.

Whenever the telephone rang Mamdooh answered it. He spoke Arabic, and after the call was finished he pursed his lips and shook his head.

'I am afraid no news, Madam.'

Lesley was in Iris's sitting room when someone came to the door. She heard Mamdooh bringing him up one of the house's several confusing sets of stairs and jumped up to see who it was.

'Good evening,' a suave little man said. 'I am Nicolas Grosseteste.'

'I'm so pleased you have come. My husband's gone to the police and the embassy. I'm so worried and sitting here is making it worse.'

The doctor shook her hand. 'I understand that you will be worried. It is a matter for concern. But they may be found safe and well, we must not lose sight of that. The police will do everything they can, I assure you.'

Lesley pinched the bridge of her nose and tried to think coherently.

'Have they been kidnapped?'

'I think that must be considered as one possibility. But myself, I believe it is more likely that they have got lost, or stranded in some local difficulty. That seems to me to fit more with the two people I know.'

'What do you mean by that?'

Doctor Grosseteste considered for a moment. He was the kind of person who would not say anything without weighing it up first.

'Your mother has been ill.' He left a delicate, interrogative pause that Lesley did not try to break. 'But since your daughter arrived in Cairo I have noted a great improvement

384

in her health and her state of mind. She has rediscovered some of the enthusiasm for the world that marked her out when it was my privilege first to meet her. The two of them appeared to share a remarkable rapport and it is my guess – my hope – that they have embarked on some excursion together. This may have gone wrong, but your daughter is a young lady of considerable energy and resource. I would place trust in her.'

'I see,' Lesley said.

She was on the point of asking the doctor whether he would like a drink, but Mamdooh was already at the door with a silver tray and a small glass of wine. Obviously Nicolas Grosseteste was a regular visitor. The two men murmured in Arabic while Lesley looked on. A pulse beat in her neck. It was her role always to be excluded, she thought. Andrew was the master at it; now her daughter and her mother had established a *remarkable rapport*.

It didn't matter. She would volunteer at this moment for an entire lifetime of physical and emotional isolation, so long as Ruby could be found safe.

Mamdooh left them together again and Nicolas sat down with his glass of wine in a chair that was obviously the one he always took. There was nothing to do except wait and the silence pressed in on them. But then a moment later Mamdooh was back and this time he was showing a young man into the room. He was thin, with slicked-back black hair and smooth skin. He looked from one to the other and burst into a torrent of words.

'This man Mamdooh tell me the police look for me. I don't hide. Ruby is my friend,' Ash said hotly.

'I am Ruby's mother. Who are you?'

'*Umm* Ruby,' the young man said. He bowed to her and Lesley understood that this was a polite greeting. 'My name is Ashraf. Ruby is my friend and I show her Cairo and we

385

speak English together. I would not do to her any thing that would harm one hair of her head. I take her to meet my own mother.'

Lesley saw that the boy was on the verge of tears.

'It's all right. We are friends here. You had better sit down, Ashraf, and tell us whatever you know.'

They were an incongruous group, sitting in Iris's under-furnished room.

Andrew found them there when he came back to the house. He told them that the police had talked to a café owner on the road to Giza, who said that Iris and Ruby had stopped there for breakfast two days ago at dawn. Another roadside vendor reported that he had seen the old Beetle a little later, beyond Giza, heading out on the desert road.

It would soon be dark again.

In the morning, a police search would start. But the officer had warned him that the desert was very big.

Ruby no longer had any idea what she was doing.

She moved slowly, dragging up the ridges and sometimes falling down the other side. After the falls she took longer each time to stand up, but she always did get to her feet again and stumble on. The words had stopped beating in her head and she was too exhausted to think about the world that had slipped away from her. All she was left with was a dull awareness that she must keep going or Iris would die. As the day drew on, drying and shrinking her until she felt no bigger than a toktok beetle, even that certainty began to fade. She couldn't go much further. Her body was shrinking but her tongue had swollen. Soon it would fill her mouth and throat and choke her.

Soon it would be dark again.

She reached the top of another dune, slid down the other side. From this hollow she could see off to the right, where the shoulders of the dunes overlapped in a series of leaves like a deep stage set. The way between them looked almost like a track and she began to hurry along it with hope clicking on like a bright light. But only a few steps showed her that there was no track, only the illusion of one.

The despair that followed was complete. Ruby stopped walking. She sat down in the sand and her head dropped to her knees.

A rest. She would just rest for a while, staring at the infinity of sand between her feet.

When she did look up again she saw a camel.

It paced between the dunes ahead, close enough for her to hear the small jingle of its harness bells. There was a man in a *kuffiyeh* on its back. Behind the first camel came another, its haughty head up, rolling with its steady camel gait through the solid waves.

Ruby staggered to her feet.

Now she saw that there was a string of camels, some with riders and others carrying baggage, passing between the dunes a hundred feet ahead of her.

She shouted, but no sound came out of her scorched throat.

She began to run, waving her arms, zigzagging through the sand with the breath like a razor-blade in her lungs.

The camels and their riders were real. The animals at the rear of the train slowed and turned their heads to inspect her. She could hear voices.

'Stop. Someone's coming.'

'Lindy, wait . . .'

'What's happening?'

They had seen her. It was all right.

Ruby stopped running and her arms dropped to her sides. Her head was pounding as if it would explode, but there was also a *whoosh* inside her as colour and possibility and the future flooded back to her.

'Help,' she managed to say. 'Help my grandmother.'

She dropped to her knees in the sand.

The camel train came to a halt. It seemed neither likely nor particularly improbable that the riders were speaking English, or even that they sounded like her mother. There were five women and they were all dressed like Lesley, talked like Lesley. The nearest one slid down from her saddle and came towards her.

'What's wrong? Are you in trouble?'

She was wearing a water bottle in a kind of woven holster on a shoulder strap. Wordlessly, Ruby held out her hand for it.

The water dripped on her tongue and then flowed. She huddled in the sand and drank and drank until the bottle was empty.

The Lesley-voices were babbling. 'Hammid, I think she's lost.'

The Arab man in the *kuffiyeh* knelt down in front of Ruby, blocking out the sinking sun. 'Where have you been?' he demanded. 'Where are you going?'

CHAPTER FIFTEEN

They formed a circle round her. One of the women told the others to give her some space and air, another said here, she had some more water in her bottle.

Ruby grasped the man's arm. 'My grandmother. Help us. You have to find her.'

The camels and camel boys made a subsidiary circle. Ruby felt crowded by so many faces hanging over her and she rolled her head against a wave of panic. Everyone except the man in the *kuffiyeh* fell back a step.

'Where is your grandmother?'

She pointed to her tracks emerging between the dunes.

'Where? How long have you been walking?'

With a struggle, she put the words together. 'All day. I left her in our car early this morning. We have been lost for three days. She's got no water.'

'All right.'

The man pushed back his head covering, reached inside his blue robes and pulled out a mobile phone.

The women closed in on her again.

It hadn't been a hallucination: they were speaking English, and they did look and sound like her mother. As she listened

389

to the guide's rapid Arabic, Ruby took in the women's linens and khakis, their broad-brimmed hats and sunglasses and pearl ear studs, and on the camels' backs saw their baggage with the words Ideal Desert Safaris in white stencil lettering, decorated with a palm tree.

There followed a perfectly still, crystalline moment when Ruby knew that she understood everything.

The stitching on the pockets of the nearest woman's combat trousers, the jingle of bells when one of the camels shifted its feet, the oblique shadows cast by the setting sun, these were vivid and as significant as if they had just been created. The world was still beautiful and after all it behaved as it was supposed to do. She was safe again, she was going to live.

She saw the man fold his little silver mobile and tuck it back inside his robes, and she registered the incongruity of it. The guide was dressed up as a Bedouin tribesman and the tourists were dressed up for the dune safari, and they all had mobile phones and expensive watches. A gust of laughter surprised Ruby and she almost choked, then sanity caught up with her again and she remembered that Iris was still lost and maybe dead.

Her face changed and a sob broke out. She jammed her knuckles against her teeth, her face contorting as the sobs came faster.

'Help is coming,' the guide said. His phone rang, a tinny jingle, and he busily took it out.

The women clustered round her, stroking her hair and trying to hold her hands and murmuring reassurance and pressing their bottles of water on her. They were a collective force of motherliness. Ruby drank some more water and rubbed the silky remainder all over her face. Dust scraped under her hands, and she realised that her skin was burning and her lips were swollen and cracked.

'Hammid is a wonderful guide. He'll find her,' said the woman who was holding Ruby's hands. She wore perfume, as Lesley did, a heavy cloud of it wafting around her and catching in Ruby's throat.

If only her mother were here. Ruby wanted her mother all the more because of the resemblance in these camel trekkers. She blinked through her tears.

'How far is it? How far are we from the road?' Ruby mumbled.

Hammid looked up. 'From here? Maybe three kilometres.'

'That's quite close.'

'But you were walking away from it.'

The tourists wanted to stay to see the rest of the drama, but Hammid told them there was nothing to wait for and they were to go on with the camels and the boys to the oasis hotel where dinner would be laid out for them as planned. They were to take Ruby and look after her, and he would stay here to meet the rescue party, which would then move out into the dunes to search for the lady. He clicked his fingers and beckoned, and the camels came jingling forward. They went down on their knees in a chorus line, ready to be mounted.

'No,' Ruby said loudly.

They all looked at her.

'I'm not going to any bloody oasis. I am going to find my grandmother.'

The perfumed woman squeezed her hand. There was a short argument but Ruby won it because she shouted at them all, surprising even herself with the violence of her determination.

'Very well.' Hammid frowned. 'But I assure you that you will be in the way and you will make matters difficult for us.'

391

'I won't, she said wearily.

The safari women hugged her, and put a warm shawl round her shoulders and gave her more bottles of water. Then the camel boys helped them to climb onto the kneeling beasts, the boys gave low whistles of encouragement to the camels, who rose to their feet and swayed in a line to the ridge of the first dune, heading in a direction that left Ruby disorientated again. The sun was now a lemon-yellow ball tumbling towards the western horizon.

Hammid was talking into his phone again. Exhausted, Ruby lay down on the sand and pulled the shawl round her.

Lesley stands there with her hands on her hips. Her feet are planted in the sand and her face is screwed up with childish accusation.

I shake my head to clear the image, but she is still there when I look again.

I try to close my eyes. I want to sleep and not to feel the various forms of pain as my body slowly shuts down, but I can't do it with Lesley's glare burning into me.

'What do you want?'

I must have mumbled the words. Small stabs of pain radiate from my cracked lips, a flash of agony explodes beneath my cranium and subsides in a series of throbbing waves. At the periphery of my mind I know that I am experiencing the effects of extreme dehydration. Quite soon, if I am lucky, delirium will be succeeded by unconsciousness.

I am lying in the sand. It is in my mouth, in my throat, scraping in my lungs.

I am apart and looking down at myself, an old woman lying in the sand, bits of clothing pulled round gaunt legs, thin hair spread like the wing feathers of a dead bird.

Lesley is still there, sturdy legs and sandalled feet, a gingham summer dress too tight for her. She's growing, every holiday when I see her she seems an inch taller.

She doesn't answer me.

Lesley and Andrew and Doctor Grosseteste were still waiting.

Ash had explained that he must go to his switchboard night shift at the hospital and when Andrew demanded to know where he was to be found if they or the police needed to ask him more questions he answered politely that he would come straight back to the house in the morning, as soon as he had finished work.

If they would allow him, he added.

'All right,' Andrew said.

'Thank you for coming.' Lesley tried to smile. Mamdooh appeared and escorted Ash down to the front door.

Andrew turned to Nicolas. 'How on earth do you deal with this place on a daily basis?' he asked.

'Cairo?' The doctor looked at him, then gave a delicate shrug. 'One learns the technique.'

'I'm glad I don't have to.' It was Andrew's way to respond to pressure by becoming more critical. They lapsed into silence again.

'I had better talk to her father,' Lesley said at length.

Sebastian was about to leave his office.

'Lesley, Lesley,' he sighed. 'Don't panic yet. It's not the first time Ruby's gone missing, is it?'

'Not like this. This is different.' The heavy receiver of Iris's old-fashioned telephone was slippery in her sweaty hand.

'Well, let's just hope it will turn out to be the same. Keep in touch, all right? Let me know as soon as there's any news. Try not to worry.'

Lesley replaced the receiver. Ruby was his *child*, she thought. How had Sebastian developed such a degree of detachment? With an effort, she steered her thoughts away from making the same old speculation about Iris.

She had resumed her seat when Andrew's mobile rang. Lesley and Nicolas stared at each other in equal hope and dread as Andrew took the call.

'Yes. Yes. I see. That's good. Thank you.'

Lesley shouted at him, 'What is it? What did they say?'

The police reported that Ruby had been found by a group of camel trekkers, wandering in the desert not more than a mile or so away from a little-used track leading back to the Fayoum oasis road. A search party was about to set out to look for Iris and the car.

'Oh, thank heaven.'

Lesley leapt out of her chair and blindly ran to her husband. He held her while she fired questions at him. 'Where is she now? Is she hurt? Can I talk to her?'

Andrew kept one arm round her shoulders and rubbed the free hand over his sagging face.

'Ruby insisted on going with the searchers.'

Nicolas Grosseteste looked down at his folded hands.

Ruby crouched in the back of the four-wheel drive. Her head bounced against the canvas roof as the vehicle swayed to the crest of a dune and tipped over the other side. It was fully dark now, and the headlamps raked over an unending slice of rippled sand that just showed the faintest impression of her footsteps. The police driver and Hammid next to him were hunched in silence, intent on their task. To the left and right of them were two other trucks, covering as broad a sweep of the desert as possible. They moved forward slowly but steadily. Ruby was shivering, and her eyes stung from staring into the darkness and willing the darker hump of the Beetle to emerge in the next black hollow.

The men were muttering to each other. Then Hammid's profile was briefly outlined as he half turned to her.

'You see? You walk almost in a circle.'

'Are we going to find her?'

'In time. But you should not have left the car.' The guide was angry.

Ruby wasn't surprised, but her own anger flared to match his. 'So I was supposed to sit there? Just watch my grandmother die of thirst and do nothing?'

The truck was slowing and the driver craned over the wheel, his head turning from side to side as he scrutinised the ground.

'It is hard enough to find a car, out here. What chance to find one person, just walking alone? I think you do not know how lucky you were, to discover my group in this way. It is much more likely to walk until you drop.'

Ruby's mind closed that off. There was no available space to consider it. She didn't think about being hungry or cold or tired either. Every point of her concentration was fixed on catching sight of the Beetle and finding Iris alive.

The driver said something and the truck came to a halt. Hammid jumped down and Ruby watched as he walked round the front of the bonnet. He crouched down in the beam of the headlamps and studied the rampart of sand as the other trucks stopped too. Ruby scrambled from her seat and ran to shake his shoulder.

'Why have we stopped?'

But she could see why. As they followed the tracks they had become progressively fainter, to the point where there was now nothing to see at all.

Hammid swung a torch in a circle, and only the smooth silent expanse of the desert was revealed. He shook his head. 'We will go back now and wait for daylight.'

Ruby took a breath, mustering her last reserves. She looked up and overhead were the winking lights of a plane dipping towards the airport. She gripped Hammid's arm and her fingers dug into his skin as she begged, 'Please. I know it's near here. I *know* it is. If we give up now she might die before the morning.'

Ruby felt as if she were standing outside herself somewhere, watching and listening to this scene being played out by the light of torches and truck headlamps, but at the same time she knew exactly what she must do. This was the most crucial and urgent plea she would ever make. 'We have got to go on. It's only a few hours out of your lives but it could make the difference between life and death to my grandmother.'

'You don't know the desert. We could search all night and miss by a few metres. It is much better with daylight and more people. A helicopter can come.'

Ruby clenched her fists, raised herself on the balls of her feet, ready to punch the man or claw his face, or fall on her knees in the sand in front of him if that was what it would take. She raised her voice until she was shouting, her own urgency almost deafening her. 'If you won't go on, I'm not going back with you. Give me as much water as I can carry and I'll search until I find her. Understand me?'

Hammid considered. A small breeze fanned across the sand. At last he said, 'Very well. We go one more hour.'

Ruby ran back to her seat before he could change his mind. She was shivering convulsively now and she bit the insides of her cheeks in an attempt to suppress the shudders.

The trucks started to roll again.

They drove on, up the curved dune faces, down the other side. The grind of the engine in low gear vibrated all the way through Ruby's bones. They teetered at the crest of yet another summit, hanging in a vacuum before plunging into the descent.

Then Hammid's head jerked forward and he called out. Ruby pitched forward to look down, over his shoulder, into the depth of darkness below.

There was the car, almost submerged in sand on its windward side.

The driver flashed the lights and hooted, and the other trucks swung inwards from their parallel routes and slowly converged.

Ruby kept her eyes fixed on the hump of the Beetle, fearing that even now it might disappear if she blinked.

Iris was lying on her side in the shelter of the car. She didn't move as the headlamps swept across her. Ruby flung herself out of the truck before it had stopped moving and ran, sinking up to her ankles as the sand tried to the very end to hold her back. She threw herself down and pressed her head to Iris's ribcage, praying to hear a heartbeat or feel the faint exhalation of a breath.

There was nothing, but Iris's skin under her clothes was still warm.

Ruby rocked back on her heels.

After all this, she didn't know what to do to save her. The men moved her aside and bent over Iris's motionless body.

Their heads turned this way and that as they exchanged terse words. Hands felt her wrists and touched her throat, then suddenly two of them lifted her from the hollow of sand that looked like a shallow grave. Iris was so light that they ran with her body between them as if she were a feather pillow.

'She is alive,' Hammid said. 'We must get her to the hospital.'

One of the trucks had a stretcher mounted down one side and they strapped Iris on to this. Ruby resisted the hands that tried to restrain her and forced her way in next to the stretcher. The rear doors were slammed shut and at once the vehicle swayed and bounced over the dunes, much faster than they had come. She kept her eyes on Iris, not daring even to reach out and touch her. A man in a blue police uniform held his hand on her chest instead, monitoring the rise and fall of breathing.

Hammid was up in front with the driver. He called back over his shoulder to Ruby, 'Your mother and father are at the hospital, waiting.'

'My mother and father, in Cairo?'

'They came here this afternoon.'

Lesley's and Sebastian's faces flashed in front of her. She couldn't work out how they could be here; reality seemed to be receding under the pressure of her anxiety. If Iris died they would blame her. They would be right to blame her.

'Will she live?' she breathed to the policeman. Her eyes were wide in her skull.

'*Inshallah.*'

It took only ten minutes to reach the track that she had left so unthinkingly in the Beetle.

A long white car, a private ambulance, was waiting. Iris's stretcher was rushed into it and Hammid held open the door for Ruby to climb in alongside.

'You will go to the hospital. I must go back to my group.'

Ruby lifted her smudged face to meet his eyes. 'Thank you,' she said. 'Thank you.'

They were already moving. Hammid and the desert dropped away.

Lesley and Andrew were in the ante-room where Nicolas Grosseteste had advised them to wait.

Lesley thought distractedly about how all hospitals were the same, even though in this one she couldn't read half the signs or decipher the handwritten notices under peeling laminated shields. There was always the unwieldy pounding of human needs against the fragile struts of medical provision, surf against a rickety pier. A very old woman sat opposite them, soundlessly weeping and holding a folded coat. She

398

kept stroking the folds and turning the coat in her hands as if to settle it more comfortably, and her tears glimmered under the overhead lights. Andrew held his mobile phone and checked the display, over and over again.

Ruby and Iris were both alive, they would be here soon. Lesley would have liked to hold her husband's hand for the warmth of it, but he was checking his mobile phone. She sat and studied the hem of her skirt instead, smoothing it over her knees and listening to the passing footsteps.

A pair of feet eventually stopped in front of them and an orderly in a grey overall led them down cracked corridors to a cream-painted cubicle with a bed in it. They saw her before she saw them: Ruby was sitting on the bed with her head hanging and her upturned hands resting on the sheet beside her, the fingers loosely curled. She looked utterly exhausted.

'Ruby.'

Her head came up when she heard her mother's voice.

She slid off the bed, dragging a corner of the sheet with her and almost tripping over it.

'Oh, Mum.' The words came out of her as a choked whisper. Lesley folded her arms round her and cupped her head against her shoulder. 'I'm so glad you're here.'

'It's all right, it's all right now.'

Ruby was crying. Her tears were hot against her mother's neck. This was a much younger Ruby, without the metal studs piercing her skin and with her eyes unpainted, and her hair flattened and gritty like a child's in a sandpit. She was younger even than a child; she was no more than a baby.

Lesley held her, and as Ruby clung to her she felt a surge of happiness so sharp and complete that it came close to ecstasy.

Nothing else mattered. Not Andrew, not loneliness, not even Edward nor that her own mother might be on the point of death. Ruby was here, the smell and the solid shape of her, and she was safe. The fuse that lit the bright delight for Lesley was Ruby, it always was. And the flare of delight itself now, so white-hot that it blinded her, was that Ruby was vulnerable and knew that she needed her mother and hadn't concealed it.

'You're safe, I'm here,' she said. She rocked her, smiling with her mouth against Ruby's matted hair.

A chair squeaked as Andrew heavily sat down.

The moment extended itself, opening as silently as a flower.

'I was so stupid. I didn't mean it,' Ruby sobbed.

Lesley could have flown, out of the door and over the orange glitter of Cairo. All would be well. All would be miraculously well. 'No, darling. You weren't stupid. It isn't stupid to be young,' she murmured to console her.

Ruby's shoulders had been boneless, soft as an infant's, but now a rigid spot developed and she lifted her head an inch. She wiped mucus from her nose with the back of her hand. 'I drove the car off the road, didn't I?'

Lesley understood instantly that she was meaning the desert misjudgement had been stupid. It wasn't a bigger acknowledgement than that; in her own eager haste she had misinterpreted it. It wasn't that Ruby had looked back over the years of rebellion and defiance, and finally seen them for what they were.

'Oh. Well, yes.'

Hot dismay flashed through her at the thought that Ruby might register the scale of her misunderstanding. The white light faded to grey and she was heavy again, feet locked to the floor.

'You didn't know,' Lesley said quietly. She let her arms fall, then took Ruby's hands in hers. 'What happened?'

Ruby twisted in her grasp. It was still too close to be talked about. 'I got us *lost*. We could easily have died.'

'Shh. You didn't die.'

Ruby was looking at her now, the old Ruby expression forming somewhere behind the baby-soft, tear-stained mask.

Lesley let go her hand and searched in her pocket for a tissue. 'Here, blow your nose,' she said. When she looked round she noticed suddenly that her husband's face reflected equal parts of relief and exhaustion. She made a small gesture and he stood up at once. The three of them stood linked in an awkward embrace. Even Ruby stood still for a few seconds.

A doctor told them that Iris's condition was serious. They were briefly allowed into a room where she lay hooked up to bags of fluid, the tubes taped to her thin grey forearms. Her eyes were closed and her mouth hung open, and there was a tube in her nose as well. Andrew and Lesley stood one on each side, and Ruby briefly hovered at the bed end. But these positions made her think of a funeral and she swung away to the corner of the room, crossing her arms and rubbing angrily at the skin of her elbows. Each time Iris took a breath it was like a snore; then it subsided and it seemed that she was never going to take another. Go on. *Breathe*, Ruby furiously and silently commanded.

There was nothing further they could do, the doctor said. The next twenty-four hours would tell. Nicolas had gone home, but he had left them a message to say that he would see them in the morning.

'We all need some sleep,' Andrew said.

Ruby squashed into the back of a taxi beween her mother and stepfather. The enclosed space filled up with Lesley's perfume. She wondered briefly about Ash and what he would have made of her disappearance. Then she asked herself why she had leapt to the conclusion that it would be Sebastian who had come all the way out to Cairo with Lesley. Because that was what she wanted, Mummy and Daddy together, just as if she were a kid?

But it was Andrew who really had come and was sitting solidly beside her in his seersucker summer jacket that she remembered from dull holidays.

She put her hand awkwardly on his sleeve, realising that at the hospital she had hardly acknowledged his presence. 'Thank you,' she said humbly. 'I'm really sorry.' She had parroted that often enough. But this time she meant it. Lesley stirred on her other side, making Ruby aware that she was grateful for this offering. It was such a very small offering, too, Ruby realised.

'You're in one piece. That's what matters.' Then he leaned forward. 'Do you think this driver is taking us all round the houses?'

'No. This is the right way. Where's Ed?' she asked Lesley.

'Staying with his friend Ollie. It was the best we could do at short notice.'

'Are we ever going to get there? Where on earth are we?' Andrew muttered.

'It's just down here.' The sight of the three minarets touching the sky made Ruby's stomach turn over with renewed anxiety for Iris. 'You don't think she's going to die, do you?'

'No, I don't,' Andrew said.

In that moment she loved him for always having to know best and for always having an opinion to express, right or wrong. It was weird, that, because it was one of the things about him that had always annoyed her most. Lesley didn't say anything. She had been very quiet since they had left the hospital.

Mamdooh opened the door almost as soon as Ruby knocked. His moon-face was heavy with gloom. 'Miss, you are safe. And Mum-reese?'

'They're looking after her,' Ruby said.

Auntie appeared and swept Ruby into a flutter of hugging

and patting. She was rapidly murmuring in Arabic and Ruby couldn't understand her any better than she ever had done but she whispered back just the same, telling her that she was sorry and it was all her mistake and Mum'reese was in the hospital and being cared for and they would all have to hope and pray that tomorrow she would begin to get better.

'*Hasal kheir*,' Auntie said. Ruby did understand that, it was one of the phrases Ash had taught her. It meant something like, it could have been worse and we should be thankful that it was not.

'*Inshallah*,' Ruby added. That it might not yet turn out to be worse.

Turning back to Andrew and Lesley she noticed how lost and incongruous they appeared in the dim, bare, stone heart of Iris's house, flanked by Mamdooh in his *galabiyeh* and Auntie with her white-shawled head. Andrew was wearing his summer blue chinos with the seersucker jacket, and Lesley had low-heeled sandals and fine tights and a good handbag. They must have hurried to find lightweight clothes that would have been stored away for the winter. Knowing how long and how careful the preparations were for an ordinary holiday, Ruby could only begin to imagine what it must have been like for them to pack for Cairo at a few hours' notice. Yet here they were. She felt a weight dropping off her as she looked at them. They were only people, as kind and as blinkered and as likely to be correct or mistaken as any others. Maybe the weight was resentment.

'It's late. You should go to bed now,' Ruby said, as if they were the children.

Lesley nodded her head obediently, and then collected herself. 'But you need some food, darling, and you remember what they said about fluid intake.'

At the hospital, Ruby had been examined. She was dehydrated and hungry and sunburned, that was all. She had

403

felt quite proud of her resilience, and then bitterly ashamed of her thoughtlessness in taking Iris with her, who was neither young nor strong.

Ruby was still wearing the wrap that one of the trekking party had given to her and now Auntie was insistently tugging at the folds of it. She was murmuring about food.

'Auntie will fix me something in the kitchen. Have you got a bedroom?'

'If we can find it, in this place.' Andrew peered up into the shadows of the gallery.

'Good night, then.' Ruby hugged them both and thanked them, as best she could. The words were just words but she meant them. Lesley held on to her for a second and then turned away in Andrew's wake.

'It's this way,' he told her, heading for the wrong stair-case.

In the kitchen it was warm and quiet. Mamdooh sat in his chair next to the stove with his hands laced together over his belly, as he always did, and Auntie laid out an earthen-ware bowl and a dish of flat bread. Ruby tore off papery chunks and soaked them in bean soup, and crammed the rich hot mush into her mouth so the overflow dribbled down her chin and she rubbed it away with the heel of her hand. With her head on one side, Auntie watched her and nodded encouragement.

There was no need for any of them to speak. Their thoughts were with Iris and the collective wish for her pooled between them in the silence.

When she could eat no more – and she was surprised by how little she had managed, believing that she was ravenous – Ruby washed up her own plate and spoon even though Auntie tried to stop her. She touched each of the old people on the shoulder, reaching up to Mamdooh and down to Auntie, and told them that they should try to sleep. Then she went upstairs, passing along the gallery where the faint light from below shone through the crescents and stars in the pierced screen. She was dirty, her skin and hair were caked with dust, but she was too tired to do more than strip off the borrowed shawl and her stiff clothes, and drop them in a heap on the floor. She crawled under the covers and closed her eyes.

The desert rose up, with Iris lying in what looked too much like a shallow grave scraped beside the car.

'It's not time for you to die,' Ruby told her. She listened in the dark room, but she couldn't hear Iris's response.

The metal clash and footstep squeaks of hospital. Familiar from layers of memory and experience, but I can't place myself in any of them.

Pain at the periphery, or rather within a separate place that I don't want to re-enter. So I am the patient, not the doctor.

Either way I would prefer oblivion and I am trying to retreat into it, but awareness scratches and then batters at me. There are voices, talking across me, and as soon as I can decipher the words pain sweeps in. It is no longer on the margins but everywhere, behind my eyeballs and within my ribcage and in my mouth like a hot stone that I can't spit out.

I open my eyes and pain shoots through my frontal lobes.

In my immediate field of vision there is a doctor's face; he has thick eyebrows and nasal hair and a deep cleft in his chin in which a line of bristles is embedded. Beyond him, standing against a window so that it is haloed in light, is another figure. A woman in a flowered dress, not a nurse. The woman steps forward, away from the sunlight, and the troubling familiarity surrounding it like another light halo suddenly crystallises.

405

It is Lesley.

'She's awake,' the doctor says, in English.

There are painful – agonising – prods and shifts of examination. My wrist is lifted and turned, then my head. I close my eyes against the intrusion.

When I look again, Lesley is close at hand. Her face leans down over me, her forearms are resting on the bedsheet. The doctor has gone. Lesley lifts a hand and touches her fingers to my forehead. She is smiling, rather tremulously, her characteristic smile that might at any moment melt into tears.

'It's all right,' she whispers. 'You're going to be all right.'

I look past her, to where an IV pack hangs on its stand. The tube is taped to my arm. They're putting in fluids, that's all. We were in the desert, I remember, without water. The pain is mostly in my head, I realise; the after-effects of severe dehydration. Lesley is correct, then. I am not going to die today, or even tomorrow.

A shadow falls for a moment, a compound of weariness and exasperation.

But then I look back at my daughter's face. I don't know why she is here and the effort of working it out is too much. But I have the sense that Lesley has been in my mind. It was her absence that was like a butcher's hook, holding me up and stopping me from slipping down and away. Now the negative is reversed to positive, absence has become presence, and I realise that I am profoundly glad.

I make an effort of concentration and lift the fingers of my left hand. The plastic IV tubing faintly chafes my skin and Lesley sees the movement. She takes my hand and laces her fingers with mine.

I say her name. The smile flowers all over her face.

'Yes. I'm here, Mummy. Everything is going to be all right. I love you.'

Love. The wide sea that one word conjures up, all the

currents and tides and storms and oily swells of it. But I manage to nod my head.

As soon as she woke up Ruby knew that she had been asleep for a long time. The light was bright behind her half-closed shutters and Auntie was at the door of her bedroom. She was bringing morning tea; at least, a glass of hot water with a Lipton's tea bag laid in its yellow envelope in the saucer. A cup of tea English-style, a special treat.

Mamdooh eased into the doorway and decently hovered there. Ruby instantly hoisted herself upright, keeping the sheet pulled up to her chin.

'Mum-reese?'

'Today better. She is weak, but now awake. Your mother with her.'

The cup and saucer rattled. 'God. Oh, what a relief. That's so good. She's going to be all right, isn't she?'

'God is merciful,' Mamdooh agreed. 'Your friend has called to the house. He waits for you outside.'

'Ash?' Ruby wanted to see him, very much. She began to get out of bed and Mamdooh hastily withdrew. Auntie dipped the tea bag into the hot water and pressed the glass of cloudy brownish fluid into Ruby's hand. She was very thirsty, sticky-mouthed with the taste of sand and the residue of bean soup, so she drank it in a single draught. She shook her head like a horse and Auntie tittered.

Ruby pulled on the nearest clothes that were not actually in the reeking desert heap, raked her fingers through her hair and leaned to open the shutters. Ash was standing against the opposite wall, one knee bent and the foot propped under him. He was wearing his leather jacket and a red Coca-Cola T-shirt. She rapped on the window to attract his attention but he was smoking, frowning and looking away down the alley.

She ran down the stairs and out of the front door.

Ash straightened up and threw his cigarette aside. 'You look very terrible,' he said.

She stopped short. 'Well, thanks very much.'

He caught her by the wrist. 'It is not being rude, it is the truth.'

Her hair was flat to the back of her head and stood up in matted spikes from the crown. Her lips were swollen and cracked, and her cheeks and eyelids were reddened and puffy from sun and windburn.

'I am sorry,' he added.

Ruby pulled angrily back but then she realised he was only shocked at the sight of her. She hadn't bothered to consult a mirror and wondered briefly just how bad things were.

'I've been in the desert. Three days. It was . . . it was . . .' She stopped there and shrugged. She supposed that in time she would develop a routine for describing the experience, it would become her desert story, but she was nowhere near that yet. How it had been was too unwieldy to put into words. 'Can we go somewhere? Not in the house.'

'I will never put foot in there again,' Ash almost spat.

'Why? Why not? What happened?'

'Let us go somewhere, yes.'

'I want something to eat.'

'Come, then.'

He took her hand. They went down the alley and into the street that led to the busy road. Ruby looked all around her, at the crowds of people in which each person had his own precious history, and at the garish colours of the overbearing advertisement hoardings, and the peeling walls and telephone wires and glinting traffic and exuberant density of ordinary Cairo, and she was almost overcome with gratitude for it. Her legs felt unsteady and even though she was hungry her

408

stomach contracted and rose as if she was about to be sick.

'Are you all right?' Ash wanted to know.

'Yes.' She was shocked, Ruby thought, with another faint frisson of surprise that she should be knowledgeable enough, somehow old enough, to recognise this so precisely. But that was what it was. She swallowed the sharp taste of delayed terror and followed Ash's leather jacket as he shouldered through the crowds. At a café on the edge of Khan al-Khalili Ash pulled out a chair for her and Ruby quickly sat down. Immediately the usual crowd of newspaper vendors and shoeshine boys and children trying to sell lighters and bottles of water swarmed around them. Ash waved them away, and from the waiter in a stained white jacket he ordered yoghurt and coffee and fried eggs with flat bread for Ruby, the same as he had ordered for her first breakfast in the bazaar.

Ruby helped herself to one of his Marlboros. Inhaling the smoke brought a wave of giddiness.

'The *suffragi*, and your mother and father, they think *I* have taken you and Madam Iris and done harm to you,' Ash blurted out.

'Did they? Why?'

'How should I know this? The *suffragi* came to Nafouz and my mother, and talks about the police. And then of course, to help in any way I come to the house as soon as I can and your mother and father . . .'

'My stepfather,' Ruby interrupted, but Ash only stared at her.

Angrily he said, '. . . They look at me as if I am guilty for something. Why do they think that when I am your friend and you are mine? I tell you why. It is because I am Egyptian boy and you are English girl.'

They were looking at each other across a gulf that had not been there before.

'I'm sorry for whatever it was they said, or did. It was

409

probably worrying about me that caused it, and my step-father's like that with pretty much everyone, not just you. My mother always tries to do the right thing. And weren't you concerned about what had happened to us, or were you only thinking about yourself?' she snapped back at him.

'Ruby, Ruby. What do you think, since you know me?' Ash reached out and took her hand. He was very good-looking, especially when he was angry and serious. She felt raw and needy, and the need translated itself into wanting him. She held on to his hand, turning it over and studying the flat purplish ovals of his fingernails. 'And besides this, did I not tell you not to go past Giza, in the car with your grandmother?'

Anger flashed in her too. She banged the tin table with her free hand and the holder of paper napkins and the plastic menu card in its claw holder rattled and bounced. 'I am not your possession, to be told what to do and not do.' She was shouting, and the tourist couple at the next table glanced curiously at them.

'There are good people in Cairo, and some bad. I was afraid that you were dead,' he muttered.

'I was afraid that I was dead.'

She said it in such a way that he caught her hand more tightly and hauled the rest of her closer to him so that their mouths awkwardly met across the table. He kissed her very hard and it was the more startling because Ash never made demonstrations in public.

Ruby caught her breath with difficulty and sank slowly back in her seat. The cracks in her mouth stung and she touched her fingers to them.

'You see?' Ash whispered.

She was the first to look away. Her face was burning twice over.

The waiter came and banged down the plate of fried eggs.

Ruby looked at the clouded yellow eyes and the brown lace-work at the edge of the glistening white and her mouth watered. 'I'm so hungry.'

Ash smiled at her, a sunny smile from which the anger had melted away. 'Eat, then,' he said.

Lesley sat beside Iris's bed, letting the time pass.

Andrew told her that he had work calls to make and needed to check and respond to his e-mails.

'Couldn't have happened in a worse week, all this,' he sighed. 'If you're going to sit here with your mother, I'll come back later. Will you be all right?'

Lesley smiled at him. 'Yes,' she said. 'We will all be all right.'

Iris woke up and Lesley told her that she loved her. During the night, lying awake in the dusty bedroom while Andrew snored beside her, she had resolved that she would tell her mother this much before anything else. She had said it as soon as Iris seemed briefly aware of her surroundings, and she thought that Iris had heard her and even nodded her head. It was a comfort to Lesley that they had made this connection, at least.

Ruby had been deeply asleep when they left the house, and she was glad of this too. It was a different world from this time yesterday. She had Iris's life to be grateful for, and Ruby's youthful resilience. The edge of loneliness, the sense of never being quite what any of the people she loved wanted or expected her to be, was nothing compared with this.

'Hello?' an English voice said.

Lesley looked up and saw a woman in a khaki T-shirt with the LandRover logo on the front, only it had been changed to read SandLover instead.

'Hello,' Lesley answered uncertainly.

'How is she?'

411

'A bit better. She woke up about an hour ago.'

'That's good news. And your daughter?'

'She was asleep when I left the house. Um, do we know each other?'

The woman laughed, then hurriedly looked around in case she had disturbed any of the other patients.

'I'm sorry, my fault. I was in the group who found your daughter last night, or perhaps she found us, I'm not sure which. She was marvellous, you know. We just wanted to make sure everything had turned out all right. I'm Ros Carpenter, by the way.'

Lesley came round the foot of Iris's bed and shook the woman's hand, and the woman gave her a friendly hug and said that she was sure Iris would soon be on the mend and this seemed quite a good hospital, better than you would expect, really, at least it looked clean, and what kind of treatment would you hope to get at home these days? The other members of the group were having coffee at a place round the corner, actually, and would she like to take a break for a few minutes and come and meet them?

'Well . . .' Lesley hesitated, looking back at Iris. Then she decided quickly, why not? Ruby was marvellous, this woman had said. She smiled at her. 'Just for half an hour. I want to say thank you to all of you. My name's Lesley Ellis.'

The other four women were gathered round a table, and they waved them over and shuffled up their chairs to make room.

'This is Lesley,' Ros announced proprietorially. 'Her mum is recovering and our desert wanderer is at home fast asleep.'

There were exclamations of relief and satisfaction, and the largest of the women cheered. Lesley looked around the table, touched by their warmth.

The blonde one said, 'Your daughter was very brave. She was exhausted, terribly thirsty, sunburned – she had walked

412

all that way, but she didn't think about herself at all. The one thing she had in her mind was to get help to her grandmother. Our guide tried to send her to the hotel with us but she just stood there and shouted at him until he said she could join the search.'

Lesley smiled. 'Yes, that's Ruby.' It was, too. It came to her that her beloved child was a different person from the one all her misgivings and anxieties had rested upon. 'That's Ruby,' she repeated, almost to herself.

A woman with sunglasses pushed up on her head took Lesley's hand and patted it. 'This must have been a horrible few days for you.'

They gave her coffee and a croissant, introduced themselves, told the story again of how Ruby had stumbled from between the sand dunes and almost collapsed at their feet.

'Our guide, Hammid . . .'

'Lindy's in love with Hammid.' The one called Clare laughed. 'Can't stop saying his name.'

'No, I'm not. I'm just saying that *he* said you should always stay put if you lose yourself in the desert, but if Ruby had done that it might have been days before anyone found them and by then it might have been too late.'

'She did the right thing in this instance,' Jane agreed.

'I'd never have been able to do what she did,' Louise added. 'How did it happen, by the way? How did they get lost?'

'We don't really know yet. I expect we'll get the full story when Ruby has recovered.'

Or maybe not, knowing Ruby.

Even though they were praising Ruby, Lesley wanted to shut out the rest of it; to think of how lucky she had been and what would have happened if she hadn't met the safari party was too much for now. She made the right faces and responses to the talk, but to distract herself she studied the women. They were about the same age as she was, and Lesley recognised their clothes and their discreetly highlighted hair, but there were other aspects that were less familiar.

Their friendship, for one thing. They seemed very comfortable together. Lesley had friends of her own, from business and from the village, but she couldn't imagine setting off to ride a camel across the dunes with any four of them. And the other unusual factor was the absence of men; husbands, specifically. For Lesley, holidays meant Andrew and the boat. Or, rarely, Andrew and not the boat.

They were ordering more coffees now, and debating whether it was too early to think about lunch and maybe a glass of wine.

'We *have* just spent five days sitting on a camel's back.'

'And it is our last day but one.'

'I don't want it to be over,' Ros sighed.

'Do you always take your holidays together?' Lesley asked them.

They all laughed. 'Last year it was Sri Lanka. Next year we're thinking Machu Picchu,' Clare said.

'Well, you might be,' Lindy protested.

'But yes, we do. Three of us are divorced, two still married . . .'

'Just about.'

'. . . and we don't all like the same things. Some of us will spend this afternoon at the Egyptian Museum, for example, others . . . well, they won't. But we all like each other. And it works.'

Lesley smiled, envying them their apparent freedom. Then she looked at her watch. 'I'd better go. Wait, did any of you lend Ruby a shawl yesterday?'

'That was me,' Ros said.

'How can I get it back to you? Where's your hotel?'

'Tell you what,' Clare suggested. 'Why don't you meet us for dinner tomorrow? Our last night?'

414

To her surprise, Lesley agreed without even thinking about it. Nor did she say that she would have to bring Andrew with her.

'See you tomorrow, then,' she said. 'Enjoy the museum.'

'Or a nice sleep by the pool,' Lindy murmured.

When she reached Iris's side ward again, Ruby was sitting in the visitor's chair. She looked clean and almost her normal self, apart from her cracked and swollen lips.

'Darling, you're here. Did you sleep? Have you had something to eat? How do you feel?'

'Mum. Where did you get to?'

'I went for a cup of coffee with the camel trekkers, they came to see how you both are. How did you get here?'

'Really? That was nice of them. I'm fine, I woke up and had breakfast with Ash. Then I had a shower and he gave me a lift on his scooter. Iris was awake a minute ago. She looked around and asked for you.'

'She asked for me?'

'Yes. She said to me, "Lesley, you'll have to speak up." Then she sort of blinked, and said, "Where's Lesley?" I told her you'd be back soon.'

Lesley sat down quickly on the other side of the bed. She took her mother's hand, so thin and small that there was no weight in it, and held it tight. Ruby was quiet, sitting with her head propped against the back of the chair, and Lesley sat watching her and letting the wordless phrases of gratitude rise slowly through her mind, like bubbles in the sea.

CHAPTER SIXTEEN

Ruby talked to Sebastian, who was in his office in London.

'You gave us all a fright,' he said.

'Sorry. I gave myself a fright as well.'

'Are you sure you are all right?'

Ruby was using Andrew's mobile. Andrew was trying to work, with his papers spread out on the divan in Iris's sitting room. He complained that the overhead light was too dim to read by, and if he opened the shutters the muezzin and the noise from the street below was too disturbing. Ruby saw no point in trying to pitch a conversation somewhere between two fathers.

'I'm OK. Iris's getting better as well.'

'That's good news. All right, darling. I've got to go to meet an author. Give me a call later in the week, eh? And we'll have to make a proper plan for that New York trip, once you're back in England.'

'Yeah. OK, Dad.'

'Love you, darling. 'Bye.'

Ruby put the phone down beside Andrew's papers, but he didn't look up. She wandered out and glanced down from the gallery into the hall. With a scarf tied over her hair, Lesley was balancing on a stepladder. She was taking the red glass lights out of the huge lantern that hung on chains from the carved roof and dusting them one by one. Mamdooh hovered at the foot, his hands raised and upturned as if he hoped to catch her when she fell. Ruby went slowly down the stairs. Between them, Lesley and Andrew were re-creating Kent in Cairo.

'I'm going for a walk with Ash,' Ruby called.

'What? Oh, wait. Where will you be going? Take my phone. You'll be back to have supper with Andrew, won't you? I'm going out, remember.'

'Dunno,' Ruby breathed. 'Don't fall off.'

She skipped out of the door, closing it tight and automatically squinting as the low sunlight hit her face.

Ash detached himself from the wall and sloped towards her. 'You are late. But you are looking like yourself again, I am glad to see.'

'I was talking on the phone to my dad in London. And thanks.' She sketched a mocking kiss at him.

'On the phone, why? I thought he was here also.'

'This one here is my stepfather. The other one in London is my real father.'

Ash sighed. 'This is very complicated for you.'

'It's pretty simple, actually. I don't worry about it.'

He took her hand and they began to walk, slowly and with no particular objective, the way Ruby enjoyed.

Mamdooh puffed out his cheeks with relief as Lesley replaced the last of the red glass globes and clambered down the ladder. She stood with the duster in her hand, looking up at the result of her work. She now saw that it wasn't an improvement. When it had been furred with dust the lantern had at least looked old and important. Now, with the clumsy joints in the metalwork and the machine-made glass fully revealed, it was obvious that it was a piece of modern junk

417

that anyone could have picked up in the bazaar. Which was probably exactly what Iris had done. Most of the rest of her furnishings looked the same. Iris didn't care about clothes or possessions or aesthetics, perhaps never had. Lesley had inherited all her enthusiasm for such things from her father. When he died, he had left her his good furniture and his library of first editions on photography, nearly all of which she had sold, although that wasn't particularly relevant.

It was the ability to appreciate in the first place that mattered, Lesley thought.

She went through to the kitchen to rinse out her duster, surprising Auntie into a nervous flutter in her wake, then retreated upstairs to have a shower in the bathroom in which the pipes ominously clanked and the water swirled away into a scaly hole in the tiling.

'What am I supposed to do for the evening?' Andrew demanded when Lesley reappeared changed and ready to meet the women at their hotel.

'Have some dinner here, with Ruby if she's back. Auntie is cooking something.'

'Bean soup.'

'Very good for you. I won't be late.'

'This is getting more and more awkward, Lesley, you know. How long are you going to need to stay? I'm right in the middle of the Elligott deal, and I can't handle the whole business from here.'

She crossed the room to him, making a show of folding down and settling the collar of his shirt just because she wanted to touch him, to make the smallest connection, and wishing at the same time that they could laugh together or tease each other. Two creases familiarly showed between Andrew's eyebrows.

'Thank you for coming out here with me and taking charge of everything,' she said.

418

It was Andrew who had tracked down the office of Ideal Desert Safaris and made sure that the camel guide received 'an appropriate gesture', as he put it, and he had dealt with the police and the embassy officials too. I couldn't have done it on my own, Lesley thought automatically.

But now, suddenly, she reflected that there was no real reason why she should not have done. She ran her own business, even if it was only to do with lampshades and storage solutions, not corporate takeovers. It was Andrew's way to make little of what she did and, by extension, to make little of her. And she accepted this because she also understood that he needed to emphasise his own adequacy by doing so.

He looked surprised, but pleased. 'I couldn't just stay at home, could I? And I was as worried about Ruby as you were.'

Maybe, Lesley thought. Her husband felt what he ought to feel, as if love or anxiety or responsibility had been placed on an agenda for him to consider. None of these emotions came spilling out of him, unstoppable. Passion was nowhere on the list. Except maybe where his boat was concerned. Lesley found herself smiling.

It wasn't that he was a bad man.

But she didn't know any more if he was what she wanted.

And then Lesley realised that even to consider what she wanted was such an unfamiliar course that she was startled by the exposure of it.

She said quickly, 'So what do you want to do? I'm not going to leave Cairo while my mother is seriously ill in hospital.'

Andrew closed the lid of his laptop and gathered up some of his papers into a sheaf. 'I might have to go back before you, then.'

'That's all right. Ruby and I can take care of ourselves.

You'll have to look after Ed for a few days; we can't leave him at Ollie's for ever.'

'Well. I suppose so.'

'I'd better go.' Lesley stooped and kissed the top of his head, where the hair had retreated. He caught her wrist and held it, and it was Lesley who straightened up in the end and said that she really must go.

Dressed up in bright tops, sparkly earrings and strappy sandals, the trekkers were drinking cocktails in the bar of the hotel.

'Here she is! Come on, Lesley, you're a cocktail behind.'

'I'll have a margarita,' Lesley said.

The first was quickly followed by a second.

Later they went out in two taxis to a Lebanese restaurant where they sat on cushioned divans and ate a long succession of little dishes accompanied by bottles of heavy red wine. The conversation was a choppy stream of anecdote cut with intimate confessions that were received and then neutralised by a lot of laughing, and Lesley felt buoyed up by the giggly camaraderie of it all. The waiters played up to them and brought them free silver dishes of sugary pastries at the end of the meal, and everyone swore that they never touched such things before gobbling up every one as they drank thick coffee from tiny gold cups. After they had divided up the bill Lesley said that she ought to go home, but the others insisted that this was Cairo, they were going to a belly-dancing show and she must come with them.

To begin with, the dancer wore diaphanous turquoise voile harem pants and a matching veil, and a bodice and wrist bands glimmering with sequins and pearls. Bells jingled at her wrists and ankles, and her bare feet padded on the dusty floor. She had long, eloquent fingers and her sad eyes were heavily outlined with kohl.

420

'I wish I could dance. I want to be a belly-dancer,' Lindy wistfully sighed. Her eyes were shiny with admiration.

'Right then. We'll leave you here and come back next year to catch your show,' Ros said.

Towards the end of her act the dancer shed most of her voile. Her thighs and the flesh of her belly shimmied extravagantly as she shook her hips and the jewel in her belly button flashed in the lights. The tourists all clapped.

'I feel better about myself,' Clare murmured.

'Me too,' Louise said. 'I'm not going to suck in my stomach any more. I'm going to let it all hang out in a sequinned bikini.'

Lesley felt sorry for the dancer, who looked tired under her thick make-up, and then a more general sadness. The musicians were old men with greasy marks on their red waistcoats and their tarbooshes tipped to one side. Everyone was sad, and herself most of all.

Too much to drink, she told herself.

It was the end of the evening. Jane's eyes were shut, her head resting on Lindy's plump shoulder, and the dancer was taking her last bow.

Outside in the street there was the ubiquitous line of waiting black-and-white taxis. It wasn't hard to travel around Cairo, Lesley had discovered, if you had a few Egyptian pounds for the fare.

The women all hugged her, and Ros made sure she had her shawl, and Lesley thanked them all again.

'We didn't do a thing.'

They had her address, she had theirs. They would meet up again. Lesley had been invited to join them next year.

'Machu Picchu.'

'*Not* bloody Macho whatsit. I fancy Parrot Cay, myself.'

They climbed unsteadily into two taxis. Lesley waved them off and then got into a third. She gave the driver Iris's address

421

and looked ahead into the thick of the traffic. She was wondering what would happen next and at the same time realising that there were possibilities, definite possibilities. The answer might be as simple as taking a holiday on her own once in a while, or as complicated as admitting that her marriage needed work. It was like a door opening. She couldn't quite see into the room beyond, but neither did she feel locked into the same old space.

Ruby was in bed, reading a book.

'You're still awake.'

'Andrew went to bed hours ago, so he won't be. I wanted to make sure you got in safely.'

They looked at each other, acknowledging the perfection of this reversal, and started to laugh.

Lesley sat down on the edge of the bed, as she used to do when Ruby was a child. 'What are you reading?'

Ruby held the book up so she could see the cover. It was a history of pharaonic Egypt.

'Is it interesting?'

'Yes. We could go to the Egyptian Museum, if you like. I'll show you some of the exhibits, there are some amazing things.'

'Let's do that. Andrew might have to go home in a day or so, but I'm going to stay.'

With her eyes on a photograph of excavations to unearth the tomb of Ramses II, Ruby said, 'We'll be fine on our own here.'

For its steady inclusiveness it seemed to Lesley that this was one of the most musical sentences she had ever heard Ruby speak, at least since she had been old enough to give voice to the opposite kind.

She smiled at her. 'Are you coming to the hospital with me in the morning?'

'Yeah, 'course I am.'

Lesley kissed her and Ruby didn't duck or wince. 'Good night, then. Sleep well.'

In their bedroom she eased herself into bed without turning on the light, careful not to disturb Andrew. She lay on her back, looking up at the domed ceiling.

I am recovering. The figures coming and going at the edges of my awareness gain definition as the pain recedes. I recognise the nurses, who do what they must with reasonable efficiency, and the doctor, who when he leans over me smells of coffee and tobacco overlaid with cologne. And I have four visitors. Nicolas is the easiest. He sits in the chair beside my bed and reads to me, paragraphs from the *Egyptian Gazette* or one of the Cairo newspapers, or sometimes a short story by Somerset Maugham, a writer we both admire. Nicolas always kisses my cheek before he leaves, and tells me that I am doing well and will soon be home again. When Mamdooh comes he brings a small covered basket of food, cooked by Auntie, which I cannot eat. He sits for a few minutes, uncomfortable, too large for the spindly chair, and anxiety radiates out of him.

And then, my daughter and her daughter.

Earlier, because they have the same eyes and their mouths move in the same way, their faces slipped together and I had trouble distinguishing them. But now they are distinct. Lesley's skin falls into vertical creases to her jawline and her expression is hesitant and at the same time expectant. Ruby looks as if there is a light behind her eyes. The future offers her everything, by right. She has only to reach out and take whatever she wants.

I am too tired to say more than the occasional word, but I like it when they are here, separately or together.

Now they have put more pillows behind my back and

slipped their arms round me for further support. Ruby is holding a cup and Lesley dips a spoon into it and pushes the tip against my lips. I open my mouth and taste, like an infant feeding, and then I swallow. It is warm, sweetened porridge. The first solid food I have eaten in – how long? I have lost track.

I am in the house that Gordon and I bought, in haste, before Lesley was born. There is a ceanothus bush in the garden and a high-sided pram placed in the shade of it, with netting stretched from the hood to the handle to keep off the cats. I unhook the net and peel back the white coverlet, but what I find beneath is not a baby but a fat tabby cat.

I force my eyes open. My tongue is parched and swollen, my lips gummed at the corners. Someone holds a cup to my mouth and I gratefully swallow. I see that it is Lesley, with her expectant look.

'How long have I been in this place?' I demand.

'A week.'

I am assimilating this information when she says, 'Mummy, it's me. It's Lesley.'

'I know who you are.'

'You do? Well . . . good. That's very good.'

'I want to go home, Lesley. I want to be in my own home,' I say. At home I will be able to concentrate on what I have to do.

'Do you like them?'

Ruby and Lesley were at the museum. They had queued to enter the Mummy Room, where Lesley recoiled slightly from the shrivelled faces with leathery dark skin drawn back from the bleached bone in what looked like a snarl. Ruby wandered between the cases, pausing beside each king and queen with what seemed to Lesley to be close to tenderness.

They had stood in front of the mask of Tutankhamun, and as with the *Mona Lisa* and *The Birth of Venus* Lesley experienced the same small shock at the familiarity of the real thing, the parallel absence of astonishment. You expected more from it, but all the images and reproductions that you had pre-absorbed meant that there was no more; how could there be?

She remembered that as a teenager her father had taken her to the British Museum when the boy king was on temporary display there, but the queue for admission had stretched a long way beyond the gates and they had both decided that however magnificent it turned out to be, the exhibit would hardly repay such a wait. They went to the pictures in Tottenham Court Road instead, the faintly illicit afternoon fug of the cinema acquiring an extra charm following their mutual rejection of planned culture. In their enclosed, affectionate relationship Lesley and Gordon often did things like that together.

Now Ruby led her down the stairs again and they passed between the dingy glass cases that cluttered the ground floor. There were incoherent heaps of antiquity everywhere, looking like nothing more than bric-a-brac, crying out to be labelled and separated and properly lit, yet Ruby was obviously entranced by it all. They came into another tall room and Ruby took her arm in front of a series of statues with enigmatic sloping faces and massive bellies and thighs.

'Do you like them?' she repeated. 'They're my favourites.'

'They are certainly impressive. Who are they?'

'Pharaoh Akhenaten. About 1300 BC. And look, here's his wife, Nefertiti.'

'Really? That's Nefertiti? You are very knowledgeable, I must say.'

'I am interested,' Ruby said, faintly reproving.

She pointed out a carved panel, calling it a stele, that showed the pharaoh cradling a child and his wife nursing two smaller infants. The domestic intimacy of the scene was in sharp contrast with all the funerary pomp and symbolism elsewhere, and Lesley lingered in front of it. Even these ancient stone-carved kings and queens had babies, and held them in their arms. She wondered if any of these children had grown and died, and then been interred in their pyramids, only to be dug up again centuries later and laid out under the lights upstairs for inspection by daily parades of German tourists. It was a harsh fate, she thought. Death ought to be a private matter, whoever you were.

She became aware that Ruby was shifting at her side, preparing to say something.

'I'd like to stay here, you know.'

'To do what, darling?'

'Look, Mum. You've got to go back home soon, haven't you? Ed needs you, and so does Andrew.'

Andrew had returned to England four days earlier. Ed had insisted that he was fine, he came home from school and made himself some cereal and did his homework, and then Andrew came in and they had supper together. Takeaway, sometimes, he had added with satisfaction.

But she would have to go back soon, whatever Ed might say. Christmas was coming. She had a lot to do.

Ruby continued in a voice of calm reason, 'On the other hand we can't leave Iris here on her own. She'll be out of hospital in a day or so, and I can't really see her packing up and coming back to Kent with us. Can you?'

'No,' Lesley conceded, although that was more or less what she had been anticipating.

'So I thought, like, the best thing would be for me to stay on. Seeing as it's what I want to do anyway. I could maybe study Egyptology? Or something like that,' she added.

Carefully, Lesley said, 'You want to stay here, look after Iris, and be a student?'

Ruby met her eye. 'Yeah. That's it, pretty well.'

'I know you want to be with Iris. That's good. But she could live for a long time yet, you know.'

'She will do,' Ruby insisted.

'Then tell me something else,' Lesley continued.

A big tourist group led by a man holding up a striped wand passed through the crowd, the tourists flowing intently behind the wand as if it were a religious icon. They were mostly grey-haired women with broad hips and flat shoes, and a few men in short-sleeved shirts with little knapsacks on their backs. Dutch, perhaps, Lesley thought.

'How much is this to do with Ash?'

'Not all that much.'

Lesley's back and feet ached.

'Let's sit down.' She pointed to a bench against a wall, out of the stream of visitors. Ruby followed her and they sat, identically puffing with relief, Ruby shuffling herself sideways a little so that she could go on looking beyond a pillar at the Akhenaten statue.

They had spent four days almost alone together. They had established a routine of breakfast in the inner garden, visits to Iris, small excursions and suppers eaten together after Ruby came back from her afternoon walks with Ash. They had mild conversations about Iris's progress and Ash's family and the geography of Cairo. Ruby had been almost meek; Lesley understood now that she had been working out this idea.

She's my daughter, the refrain started up. I love her and I don't want to lose her to Cairo and Iris and pharaohs. What will she get up to if I am not there to restrain her? The thought of the desert and what had nearly happened blew a hot blast of fear straight into her head.

427

'It's certainly worth thinking about,' she temporised.

Rather to her surprise, Ruby nodded instead of launching into a further attack.

Ros Carpenter and the others had given Lesley a picture of a different Ruby, one who had been notably brave and who had only thought about rescuing Iris. What if it was this *other* Ruby who had been the real one all along, Lesley speculated, while as her mother she had kept a deficient version of her in her heart for her own purposes?

To fortify herself, by seeming strong in comparison?

To convince herself that she was needed?

And if this was possible maybe something similar, some other faulty construct, might also be at the heart of her relationship with Iris?

'Do you think I have been a good mother?' Lesley asked abruptly.

The question was out before she could stop it or even edit it and she disliked the imploring note it sounded.

She had never asked such a thing before. Lesley tried always to do what was right without expecting outside validation, however much she hoped for it. That was, she supposed now, a pattern that she had learned from her own mother.

Ruby stretched her thin arms and sat on her hands, revealing her discomfort.

'*Do* you?'

'Mum, I don't know. You gave me plenty to kick against. Well, yes, of course you've been a good mother, like you came out here to rescue me. You've always been there, doing the right thing.'

Ruby made the same judgement as she did herself.

Doing the right thing: how dull it made her seem.

Ruby added seriously, 'There are all the good people in the world, and you are one of them. Then there are all the

428

other people, and they're Iris and me. D'you think that's true?'

Iris and Ruby on one bank, herself on the other, and the river of opportunity and experience flowing between them. She was stricken with a sense of absolute isolation.

'Maybe,' she whispered.

Ruby turned from Akhenaten and saw her mother's face. 'Oh, Mum,' she whispered. 'What's wrong?'

Lesley shook her head. Not here, she pleaded with herself. Don't cry in front of a hundred Dutch tourists and a haughty statue of Nefertiti.

Ruby slid back along the bench and put her arm round her shoulders. 'What is it? Is it about Iris?'

Lesley pressed her lips together, then retrieved a tissue from her bag and blew her nose. 'In a way it is.'

'What way is that?'

'I haven't ever understood why she was never there.'

Ruby chewed the corner of her lip; the cracks and fissures had healed, and the swelling had gone down days ago. Her face was smooth and her mouth was her own again. Lesley saw her making the connections as clearly as if the chain of thoughts were projected on a screen.

'You wanted to do it differently for Ed and me. You wanted to be there every hour of the day.'

'Yes.'

She nodded. 'I understand. Haven't you ever asked her why?'

'No.'

'Then you must. Before she forgets everything. Will you?'

'I will try,' Lesley said. The tiny, leaf-light figure in the hospital bed was awkwardly, painfully dear, and even though she had tried to tell her so she remained as remote as ever.

'Good. Come on. Let's go.'

They walked out of the museum into the winter twilight.

Lesley was glad to get out of the gloomy halls, even though the low clouds spat rain on them. Ruby marched past the line of taxis and led them through the churning traffic of Midan Tahrir to a local bus. She grasped Lesley by the wrist and expertly dragged her through the press of people trying to climb on board.

It is as if she already lives here, Lesley thought.

Iris came home. They went to the hospital together and brought her back in a private ambulance. Iris tried to insist that there was no need for such a thing, but she was shaky on her feet and she walked very slowly with the aid of a stick. Her wrists and ankles looked like twigs.

Mamdooh and Auntie were waiting for her in the hallway, under the traffic-light red glass of the big lantern. They swooped on her and tried to take her arms as if she was going to be lifted up between the four of them and carried up the *haramlek* stairs.

But Iris held up her hand. 'Wait.'

She stood still instead, propped on her stick. Her head rotated, then her chin lifted as she gazed upwards into the painted rafters.

She's going to notice the lantern, Lesley thought.

But she did not.

She has gone much further away, Ruby thought. She's looking at Mum and me as if we're other people.

They all hovered, watching, ready to dash forward if she fell.

'I love this house,' Iris said.

Then she consented to be helped upstairs and put to bed.

The house was quiet. It was as if they were waiting, the three of them, for one of the others to choose a direction. The shuffle of Mamdooh's slippers was amplified in the stillness.

Lesley tried nervously to make plans.

'Christmas?' Iris said in response. 'I don't celebrate Christmas. Neither does Mamdooh, or Auntie. They are Muslim, you see. Doctor Nicolas sometimes calls. He brought his young friend with him once and we played canasta and got rather drunk.'

It was a winter's day. The parallelogram of sky overhead was pewter grey, but the garden offered shelter from the cold as well as the heat of summer. Iris sat wrapped in blankets, her stick laid beside her chair.

Lesley bowed her head. 'I understand. But you see, Mummy, I have to go home to Andrew and Ed because we do have Christmas; Ed's still a little boy, really. But I am torn because I don't want to go and leave you when you are not strong, and I don't want you to be lonely.'

Ruby looked quickly away, up at the needle points of the minarets that now seemed almost to pierce the heavy clouds.

'Lonely,' Iris repeated, in a voice that sounded as cold as frost.

Lesley persisted, unwisely. 'Yes.'

Iris's fingers tapped on the wooden arm of her chair. 'It takes some initial determination to be alone. After that it is easy.'

'But . . .'

'Perhaps you are the one who is lonely.'

Ruby drew in a sharp breath and stole a look at her mother. Lesley sat very still. There were tight lines drawn from her nose to the corners of her mouth. 'Perhaps,' she agreed.

No one said anything else and raindrops suddenly scattered on the tiles.

'Let's see you indoors,' Lesley murmured and went to help Iris to her feet.

*   *   *

431

'It's weird and uncomfortable,' Ruby complained to Ash.

They were in what had come to be their place. It was a single-storey concrete building at the side of the yard where Nafouz kept and serviced his taxi, a lock-up space containing bald tyres and empty oil drums and a few tools. There was also a brown plastic bench seat taken from a car, on which they sat with their legs splayed to smoke and drink Coca-Cola. Ash had a cassette player, and a selection of Michael Jackson and Madonna tapes. They belonged to Nafouz, really, he had protested. Ruby promised to get him some good music.

'There we are in that house, the three of us, mother, daughter, mother, daughter. There's a lot to talk about but no one says anything. Iris is so old and so locked up in herself and her memories. When there was just the two of us it didn't matter, she talked or she didn't, it made sense or it didn't. I didn't expect anything, why would I? I hardly knew Iris before. But with my mother, she's all tucked-in, she smiles all the time and you know she's really close to crying. She still wants Iris to be her mother. Even though she's fifty-whatever herself, she still wants a mum.

'That's what's really surprised me, you know? That you don't get to some point in your life where, right, you've joined the mother crew and fully left the daughter one and it's all fine because you're grown up.

'And I've never really noticed before that it's made my mum unhappy. Never noticed it. That's really bad, isn't it?'

Ash sighed. 'I do not understand. You are rich people, you have a fine house and money for everything you need.'

'I know. And your gran and your mum and your little sisters don't, and they get on fine.'

'It is family.' He shrugged.

As if that contained everything, instead of next to nothing, Ruby thought.

Ash slid closer and hooked one leg over hers. 'Let us talk about something else. I would like you to know that I love you. You have ideas that I do not understand but I love you anyway. I do not say this lightly.'

Ruby slid closer. She pressed her nose to his, flattening the tips, then found his mouth.

'I know,' she murmured.

Two weeks before Christmas, Lesley remarked that she had booked flights home for herself and for Ruby.

'I am not coming,' Ruby said immediately.

It was a chilly, grey afternoon but the three of them were in the garden. Iris had grown stronger since coming home and she liked to sit out there until the winter twilight fell, when Mamdooh would help her back up the stairs to her sitting room. Sometimes she seemed to be dozing, but a second later she would be wide awake. Her head had fallen back against the chair cushions now and her mouth sagged open. Ruby was reading her book and Lesley had been writing notes and making lists.

'It's Christmas,' Lesley repeated.

'You and Ed and Andrew can have Christmas. You don't need me.'

'Yes, we do. I do.'

'I don't want to leave Iris. Iris doesn't want to leave Cairo.'

In the following silence the fountain insistently splashed.

Iris opened her eyes. 'You will do as your mother tells you,' she said precisely.

'But . . .'

'You heard what I said. Remember, you stay in this house only at my invitation.'

'Well, yes, I know, but . . .'

'That is enough. You will go back to England for Christmas, because that is what Lesley wants you to do.

433

Will you call Mamdooh, please? I would like to go inside.'

Later, Ruby slipped into Iris's bedroom. Auntie had put Iris to bed and she was lying back against pillows with the sheet folded across her chest. The picture of her and Xan Molyneux stood on the bedside table, as always, with the little wooden ship with the numeral 1 painted on it placed alongside.

'Can I talk to you?' Ruby asked.

'Yes.'

'We were quite happy before I got us lost in the desert, weren't we?'

'You did not lose us. If anyone was responsible it was me because I know the country and the desert and you do not, and I should have taken proper precautions instead of letting you joyride into nowhere. I can't even remember how it happened.' Iris gave an exasperated sigh. 'In any case, no harm was done. We are both here now.'

'No harm? No *harm*? We could both be dead. You were in hospital for days. You could easily be dead instead of lying here.' Ruby's face turned crimson and she twisted in her chair, unable to sit still while thinking about what had almost happened.

'The shame is rather that I am not. Death is not an unthinkable prospect for me, remember.'

Ruby shouted, 'How can you say that? What about Lesley? What about *me*? I've only just found you. I've only just begun to know what you are like and I've hardly found out anything about your life, and yet you say that it's a shame that you aren't dead?' She clenched her fists and angrily pounded her own thighs.

Iris stared at her. 'I am sorry,' she said in the end, through pale lips.

'Don't say it ever again.'

'But I am old. Death will come as a relief.'

'Not to us left behind.'

'Don't shout. It is my life and the end of it is mine also. I am selfish, but you are the same.'

Ruby considered this. 'Am I? Actually yes, I suppose so.' There were the good people, like Lesley, and then there were the others. 'It's quite funny, isn't it?'

They looked at each other and suddenly it was funny. They laughed, Iris wheezing and runny-eyed and Ruby uninhibitedly, showing her white teeth and with her hair springing back from her face.

'It's weird that we're alike, since we hardly met until a few weeks ago.'

'Not so very strange, really. There is the matter of genetic connection.'

'But Mum's so different.'

'That's true.'

Their amusement subsided.

'Have I got to go home for Christmas? Won't you let me stay here with you?'

'No, I won't let you. I prefer to spend Christmas as I always have done in this house. Maybe I will play some canasta with Doctor Nicolas. And I have a lot to remember.'

'The cup on the shelf?'

'Yes, something like that.'

Iris spoke very softly. Ruby worked out the truth, that she probably would have liked her company, might even have liked it very much, but her insistence on her going home was for Lesley's sake. Her grandmother was not so very selfish after all.

'Won't you come to Kent? There's underfloor heating and power showers.'

'I have no idea what either of those might be. No, I will not.'

'All right. I'll go. Can I come back in the new year?'

'That's for you and Lesley to settle between you.'

'But if Mum does agree?'

The skin round Iris's eyes and mouth was now so papery that Ruby could see the tiny muscles move beneath. There was a hesitation, a twitch of conflict between habit and desire, all plain in the widening of her grandmother's watery eyes and the pursing of her lips.

Then Iris said, 'You may. I would like that, if you are sure.'

'I'm certain,' Ruby said firmly. She grasped Iris's hand and held it. 'There's something else, as well.'

'Oh dear,' Iris sighed.

'It's Mum herself.'

The muscles tensed once more. 'Yes?'

'She wants something, I don't even really know what it is but it's to do with you and her and the past.'

'I know.'

'Well?'

'Well what?'

'Can you give it to her?'

There was a silence compounded of reluctance and denial and apprehension. Deliberately, Ruby let it stretch.

'When is it you are supposed to go back to England?'

Iris never referred to England as home. Obviously she would not, Ruby thought.

'In two days' time.'

'That's sooner than I expected. I might give you and Lesley a farewell party. A dinner,' Iris said grandly. 'I could ask Doctor Nicolas and his friend. And your two young men. I like them.'

Ruby gently stroked her hand, feeling the rigid tendons beneath the skin.

'A dinner's a very good idea. I think, though, it should be for just two guests. Me and Mum.'

'You do? That doesn't sound very festive, does it?'

'I think we can make it festive, if that's what we want.'

Ruby and Lesley confirmed their flights, and Ruby collected a few belongings and stuffed them into a rucksack. Most of her possessions she left as they were, tidied away in her spartan bedroom. The more she left behind, she reasoned, the more certain her return would be.

Iris conferred briefly with Mamdooh and Auntie. Mamdooh nodded heavily, put on his tarboosh and went out to the market.

'Do you think it will be too much for her, this dinner?' Lesley worried to Ruby.

'No. It's giving her something to think about. She's been much livelier since she had the idea. And she wants to do it for you.'

Lesley didn't say anything, but Ruby could see how this notion pleased her.

The day before their departure was dark and windy. Rain swept in from the north in unpredictable gusts and the garden became an unwelcoming space of dripping water and slippery glazed tiles. Auntie dusted the table in the domed room that led off the hallway and put fresh candles in the branched candlesticks, Mamdooh took deliveries from local shopkeepers, and the two old people retreated into the kitchen. Auntie shooed both Ruby and Lesley away when they tried to insinuate themselves.

At breakfast time, Iris told them that they were to join her for drinks at 6 p.m. She spent the rest of the day in her room.

At six o'clock precisely, Ruby and Lesley were both waiting under the lantern in the hall. Mamdooh had climbed the stepladder and placed tea lights in the crimson glass lights, and a smoky reddish glow now suffused the bare space. Ruby put on a plain black T-shirt, pulled well down to cover her midriff, and made up her face with not too much black eyeliner. Lesley thought how pretty she looked, the daughter that the trekkers had pointed out to her. Lesley herself wore heels with a blue embroidered skirt, and elaborate turquoise and silver drop earrings bought on an expedition to the jewellers' quarter of the bazaar.

Iris came slowly along the gallery. They caught a glimpse of her as she passed an open screen. A moment later she turned the corner of the stairs, descending one step at a time, leaning on her stick. Ruby moved forward instinctively, but she held up her hand.

'Thank you,' Iris said. 'I can manage.'

She had put on a white lace blouse dotted with rust spots, and a full skirt made of some rustling greenish black material. It was too big for her now and she had bunched up the folds and knotted a silk scarf round her middle to hold it up. She had powdered her face and her sparse hair was brushed upwards and held with ivory combs on either side of her head. She came to stand between them, upright even with the stick, but her gaze slid past them to the other end of the room. There was a long pause.

Iris was looking at the spot where a mule wearing a sable wrap and an orchid corsage had defecated on Mrs Kimmig-Gertsch's rug in the first minutes of 1942.

'Mummy?' Lesley said softly.

Iris turned her head, very slowly. Her eyes finally settled on Lesley's face. She looked startled.

'I was thinking of something else. Something reminded me . . .' It was the candlelight. With an effort she came back to the present. 'We are going to drink a toast,' she announced.

Wearing his tarboosh and a red cummerbund stretched round his waist, Mamdooh brought in a tray and three glasses and a bottle of French champagne. He extracted the cork with a little difficulty.

Iris raised her glass. There was another long pause while she searched her mind. Ruby looked away, concentrating hard on the Ottoman harmony of arches and domes.

'To the future,' Iris managed, commendably. They echoed the word, and drank with eager smiles and murmurs and little shrugs of relief.

There was nowhere comfortable to sit and the occasion seemed too formal to allow them to go upstairs to Iris's sitting room. Iris soon tired of standing and so they led her through to the dining space where the candles flickered in the faint draught. She clapped her hands at the sight of the napkins and glasses and polished cutlery.

'How pretty. Isn't it pretty? Now, you here, Lesley.' Iris took the head of the table and Lesley the foot, with Ruby in the centre of the long space between them. Lesley quickly finished her champagne and drank a second glass, the rim clinking faintly against her teeth and betraying that her hand was shaking.

Mamdooh brought in an earthenware dish and served with great formality. Auntie had made chicken stew. He uncorked a bottle of red wine and poured that for them too, then he withdrew.

Ruby thought, God, what are we going to talk about?

'I'm sorry I have to go back,' Lesley began. She lifted her glass of red wine.

Iris answered, 'I'm grateful that you came.'

Fuck, this isn't going to work at all. I should have encouraged her to ask Nicolas and his boyfriend. Even Ash and Nafouz.

'Well, here we are,' Lesley added brightly, looking around as if to admire the setting for the first time.

Iris picked very neatly at her chicken, then touched her napkin to her lips. The candle flames shivered and sent up thin trails of smoke.

Lesley made a bold effort. 'Do you know, Mummy, I was thinking about this while you were in the hospital. You've never told me how you and Daddy first met. Was it during the war?'

Iris's cutlery clinked as she laid it down. Don't say anything mean to her, Ruby silently begged. But to her surprise Iris suddenly smiled.

'He was a major, working in Intelligence here at GHQ Cairo. We knew him a little in those days. Then, after the war, I met him again in England.'

Lesley smiled back over her glass. 'Go on.'

I can remember the day, almost the exact date.

It was in Hampshire, to be precise, at the end of June 1946. My father had died a few weeks earlier and was buried next to my mother in the village churchyard.

I was at medical school, living in a rented flat in Southwark with a fellow student and his sister. I worked very hard, spending long hours in lecture halls and dissecting rooms, then coming home on the bus to sit with my textbooks until bedtime. I didn't find the course easy but I was keeping up, and my marks in that year's exams were adequate. One weekend, telling myself I must make the time sooner or later, I took the train down to Hampshire, intending to begin the job of clearing my parents' house. Among the post that had accumulated there I found a letter addressed to me. It was from Major Foxbridge.

'He had your address, then?'

'I gave it to him as I was leaving Cairo. Your grandmother was very ill and I was rushing home to be with her. The world was upside down; it was the middle of the war. We didn't automatically expect to see people again.'

'You don't have to make excuses for giving your address to a handsome major,' Lesley teases.

440

I look at my daughter through the candle glow. She has her tremulous look, accentuated by smudgy colour rubbed onto her eyelids. The child watches us both.

'I don't know about excusing myself. It was a hot afternoon and there were roses, Albertine, growing over a wall in the garden. I saw that Gordon's address was not very far away from your grandparents', so I poured myself a glass of lemonade and sat down at my father's desk to telephone him. It was a Saturday and he was at home. The result was that he drove over, perhaps twenty miles, and we had a drink in the garden and then he took me out to dinner.'

'The rest is history,' Lesley says.

I am surprised to find myself talking so much.

'History?'

'Tell us some more,' Ruby says quickly.

I am a little dizzy with champagne, but suddenly I can find the words.

'The Qattara Depression.'

'What's that?' Lesley asks.

'Mum, just let her tell it in her own way.'

My poor daughter. Gordon's daughter. I look straight at her as I recall.

'When I lived here during the war, Lesley, I met a soldier and I fell deeply in love with him. We were going to be married. His name was Xan Molyneux and he was killed in 1942 in the desert, a few days before our wedding, in a place called the Qattara Depression. He was on a special operation with his commando group and five Italian aircraft came out of the sky and shot them to pieces. Only two members of the group survived. One died three days later in hospital, the other was an Arab scout who escaped by walking across the desert.

'Before he went out there Xan told me that the enemy forces had developed an uncanny ability to pinpoint Allied movements in the desert. He suspected that there must have been some large-scale signals Intelligence leak.'

Gordon was by that time out of the army and working in the City.

I remember that he took me to the restaurant of a local hotel, where we sat at a table next to some open french windows overlooking the garden. Moths swept towards the lights, and the heat and the scent of stocks and jasmine made the night seem exotic, more Egypt than Hampshire. It didn't matter that the food was terrible and there was no wine. We drank beer, and talked and talked about the war and Cairo and people we knew. It was a joy to be with someone who shared those memories. And we talked about Xan, of course.

During that talk, Gordon told me what I could not have learned as an ordinary civilian, that the US military attaché in Cairo had been responsible for allowing a stream of top-secret information to fall into Italian and then German hands.

Xan's suspicion had been correct.

Every night, between September 1941 and the middle of 1942, Colonel Bonner Fellers used a code called the Black Code to relay information about the Allied movements in North Africa to Military Intelligence in Washington. It was the Colonel's bad luck that the Italians had broken into the US embassy in Rome, stolen the black notebook in which the code was written, copied and returned it before anyone noticed it was missing. The Italians wouldn't share their prize with the Germans, but they did pass over decoded transcripts of early messages and Fellers's encryptions, always starting off and ending in the same way, meant that the German cryptographers soon cracked the code for themselves.

Rommel referred to these priceless bulletins as 'my little Fellers'.

After Pearl Harbor and the American entry into the war,

Fellers had access to even more sensitive material from GHQ. Among countless other pieces of information the intercepts would have revealed the covert movements of Tellforce, plotting their surprise route by which heavy armour might strike northwards towards el Alamein. And so the Italians had been able to direct their air attack straight at them.

Gordon's light hazel eyes met mine across the dinner plates. He had a tidy moustache, slightly receding dark hair, well brushed. In a nearby room I could hear someone playing dance music on a gramophone. The dining room had emptied out and we were alone.

Slowly but very deliberately he reached for my hand. 'Has it upset you, to know more about why Xan died?'

I thought about it for a moment. 'No. Anything that makes it easier to understand makes it a little easier to bear.'

He went on holding my hand, looking into my eyes. 'Do you have a lover, Iris?'

'No,' I said. 'I don't.'

It was true. I had medical studies, my father's brother and his wife Evie and their children, a handful of friends. When Gordon asked if he might see me again I agreed, almost eagerly. I longed to talk again about Cairo and remember the places and people we had both known.

Lesley and Ruby are both gazing at me. Lesley looks rapturous. She fills her glass again, sketches a toast to me, and drinks. 'That's so romantic,' she breathes.

From that night onwards, Gordon Foxbridge pursued me with single-minded determination. He told me he had loved me even when he took Xan's and my photograph on that breathless afternoon at the Gezira Club, and after Xan died he resolved that if he couldn't have me he didn't want anyone.

'Why?' I was amused and rather impressed.

443

'Why do we love one person rather than another? There is no recipe, only certainty that has its own logic.'

True, I thought.

At length, after more than two years during which I readily became his lover but always refused his proposals, Gordon's kindness and considerateness wore me down. Exhausted with the end of my training that meant long hospital hours, and vulnerable to the stability and security he offered, I finally agreed to marry him.

Lesley claps her hands and the candle flames waver in the moving air.

'Bravo,' she cries. 'Love triumphs.'

Here is the point, now.

I remember the baby, an inconsolably wailing bundle, and the small child she became, plump in a gingham dress. Did I dream about her in my desert delirium? Waiting, accusing me, refusing to release her rightful hold and let me go.

I gather my breath again. I have talked so much, more than I have done for years. My food lies cold in front of me, almost untouched.

She deserves the truth. It is all I can offer her.

'I shouldn't have done it. Shouldn't have married him.'

'Why ever not?'

'I didn't love him. I loved Xan Molyneux.'

'But he was dead.'

'And so was the child I was expecting. I was going to have his baby but I had a miscarriage. I lost them both in the space of two weeks, you might say that I lost everything. But it was wartime, and I wasn't alone in that.'

Lesley's gaze wavers and drops from mine. I can see her mind working. Ruby has cupped her chin in her hands. She looks concerned but not very surprised.

444

Then Lesley lifts her head again. There are spots of high colour on her cheekbones and she is more than half drunk. She is angry, not sympathetic in the least. Not that I am looking for sympathy.

'So all the time, all those years, when you left Daddy and me behind and went off to look after other women and their children in bloody Africa, you were wanting the family you lost instead of the one you actually had? You discarded us because we made the mistake of being still alive, not a heroic memory?'

She pours herself another glass of wine and drinks deeply. Ruby begins a move to restrain her, but I shake my head. If it takes alcohol to get Lesley to unbutton and say what she feels, instead of smiling with the corners of her mouth and hiding it all, then the headache and the nausea will be worth it.

There is still more that I have to say. My garrulity is startling.

'No. I have had long enough to think about it and I believe that it isn't quite as you see it.'

I need a drink myself. I take a mouthful, choking a little as the fumes go to my head.

'Perhaps if Xan and our son had lived, it wouldn't have been so very different.'

'Wha' d'you mean?'

'Death preserves an ideal. Ideal love, lover, infant. Can you follow that? *Can* you? No romantic story. No *bravo*, nothing. Just plain, stony reality. Because in the end, Xan, Gordon, your brother or you, I might not have been so different. I might have betrayed them, neglected them too. I did what I did and I am the person I became. Bad, good, flawed. Indifferent. Better alone, preferring to be. I knew that, living in a hut up country, a hospital annexe, Tanganyika, Nyasaland, Namibia. Here, finally, in this house.

445

I knew that where I was and the way I lived was the best I could do.

'An ordinary life didn't mean enough, it wasn't precious enough, after Xan died. I found the rigour I needed in practising medicine. I was passionate about my work and the detachment in me became an asset, not a shortcoming. You need to be able to stand back a little, when you do work like that. I don't think, Lesley, I would have lasted in the role of good mother or proper *wife* to anyone. Maybe . . .' My voice is beginning to fail me. '. . . Maybe not even Xan Molyneux.'

I raise my hand and let it fall again. I am utterly exhausted by this confession, because that is what it is.

'Gordon deserved better than I gave him. And so did you, my dear.'

Lesley stares. Then she stands up, the high heel of her shoe catches in the hem of her pretty skirt, and she snatches at the back of her chair to stop herself falling. The chair and she rock dangerously for a second before coming to rights. Ruby sighs heavily, preening her maturity in the face of our messy revelations.

I get to my feet too.

'I'm sorry,' I say.

Lesley's face swims, then tears begin to slide down her face. She reaches out to me, and we shuffle into an awkward and unpractised embrace.

I don't know how long we stand there. I am aware of Ruby still sitting at the table, picking the wax runnels from the candles and frowning as she moulds them in her fingers.

'Iss all right,' Lesley says in the end. There are black marks under her streaming eyes and she is tending towards maudlin. 'Got to go on, haven't we? Life goes on.'

'Yes.' But I disagree.

Now Ruby stands. 'You ought to go to bed,' she says, into the space between us.

Lesley and I take each other's arm and we move slowly, unsteadily, towards the *haramlek* stairs.

Ruby started after them, but then she looked back at the candles and the panelling. She leaned across the table, pinching the wicks in turn between her fingers to feel the split-second smoulder as each flame was extinguished.

'Fucking *families*,' she said into the smoky dark.

CHAPTER SEVENTEEN

Christmas in England. Christmas with all the re-enactments of family tradition, performed in the same way for as long as Ruby could remember. The difference was that this year she noticed how hard her mother worked to make it look effortless.

Lesley lifted her antique glass tree ornaments out of their cottonwool nests and hung them on the guaranteed-not-to-drop tree. Presents were bought and wrapped and handed over. Will and Fiona and their children came to stay. There was even the diversion of a party given by one of Ruby's friends, at which Ruby was told that she was looking cool these days.

She participated in all this and even, to her surprise, enjoyed approximately half of it. At the same time she thought constantly about Iris and about Cairo like a parallel world that was waiting for her to slip back into it. The knowledge that she had a separate resort, another place to which to retreat even if it was only in her mind, made it easier to forgive the shortcomings of the present one.

On Boxing Day when Fiona and Lesley took the wound-up children out for a walk and Andrew immediately fell asleep, Will followed her into the kitchen and casually dropped his arm round her shoulders. He tilted her chin in order to gaze into her eyes.

'How is my special girl?'

Ruby considered, giving herself plenty of time to do so, while Will's finger traced a line down her neck to her collarbone.

I don't need to have any kind of weird contract with you, not any more. I'm never going to live in your house again. You can't confuse me any longer with your creepy blend of authority and sleazy secret advances, was what she was thinking.

'I am not yours,' was what she said. She was pleased with the splinters of ice in her voice.

She detached his hand from her shoulder and let it fall, then she added, 'I don't want you to touch me ever again. And if you do, I will tell my mother and your wife about it.'

As an afterthought she picked up the tea cloth and pointed to the washing-up.

'Here.' She smiled at him, putting the cloth into his empty hand. Will had not cleared up a plate or a glass throughout the whole of Christmas. That was women's work.

When she came back from the walk Lesley said, 'Ruby, darling, you've done the saucepans. Thank you.'

'Not me. It was Will,' Ruby told her.

She couldn't be sure, but Lesley seemed also have adopted a different attitude to Andrew. She told him once that he and his papers were in the way, and if he really had to work all through Christmas could he perhaps go and do it in the study?

Andrew gave her a look, but he gathered himself up and went.

She didn't shrink, either, when he told her that those brown

449

trousers didn't suit her. 'Don't you think so? I am quite pleased with them,' she said, smoothing the front pleats across her stomach. 'And they're taupe, actually.'

Instead of changing into a different pair she wore them all day, and the next day as well.

It wasn't much, Ruby acknowledged, but it was something.

Lesley seemed to occupy more space. As if she had decided that she deserved as much light and air as everyone else.

'Thanks for doing all the cooking and shopping and everything,' Ruby said to her, when Will and his family had at last gone home. Andrew and Ed were watching the football. 'Everyone enjoyed themselves.'

'Did they?' Lesley said eagerly. 'Did you?'

'Of course I did. I never thought about it before but Christmas works like glue, it keeps us all sticking together, eating the turkey and playing the games and going for the walk. Now we've done it and that's it for another year. But I understand why you wanted me to come home for it and I'm glad I did.'

They looked at each other and a slow smile curved Lesley's face. She seemed suddenly younger and almost relaxed.

Ruby said, 'You never got an answer, did you?'

Lesley knew instantly what she was talking about.

'In a way I did. It wasn't exactly a revelation that Iris wasn't a good mother. But it helped, rather, to hear her admit that she probably wouldn't have been to anyone else either. That it wasn't just me who had somehow failed to capture her interest, which was what I always felt.'

'You didn't know about her great love affair, and the lost baby?'

'No. Nothing at all. When I was young Iris was either away, or I was visiting her in difficult places where she was

450

always needed more urgently than I seemed to need her. I was rather afraid of her.'

'I'm pleased she told us. She must have wanted to, the way it all came out in a great rush.'

'Did you talk a lot, when you were there together?'

'She told me a few stories, but they never connected up, not the way they did when she told us about Grandad and the Black Code and the Qattara Depression. Now I come to think about it, most of the time I talked and she listened. I probably moaned about how unfair life was.'

'Was?'

Ruby grinned. 'I'm saying nothing more at this stage.'

'Of course not.'

'You know? I think Iris had forgotten *how* to talk. She's been on her own for so long, it's just not what she does.'

'I think you are right.'

Abruptly, Ruby asked, 'When can I go back there?'

It was the last day of the year, a pale glimmering afternoon with raindrops on black twigs and a low English sky folded on the tops of the hills. The world seemed to leak water and to be so exhausted with bearing the weight of it that it heaved itself out of darkness only to sink back into twilight again.

Lesley said, 'Can you tell me why you want to, so much?'

Ruby considered window-dressing her proposition with more assurances about language courses and pharaonic studies. She was eager to do those things, if she could find a way that wouldn't make her feel stupid all over again, but she was afraid that concealing the real reason for going back to Cairo would be to deny Iris herself.

'To be with her. She's old.'

'I know that.'

Lesley had been staring out at the smeary lead-grey and russet enclosure of the garden but now she turned to face

451

Ruby. She had watched her since they had come home, expecting that there would be a bad reaction after her ordeal, but all that had happened was that her daughter had acquired a new stature. Since her days in the desert she had become more measured, she spoke more slowly and gave more thought to what she did say. Even her voice sounded less strident.

But was she old enough for what would come next, Lesley wondered? Did Ruby even understand what was involved?

On the morning they left Cairo, Lesley had a serious headache. Iris was tired and peevish too, and she had waved them off with visible relief. But Lesley noticed that her eyes followed Ruby all the way out of the room.

If Ruby went to Cairo she would be doing what Lesley would have been glad to do herself – but Iris wouldn't want that. She wouldn't look for Lesley's company now, any more than she had done before. But at least Ruby could be there. Ruby would be the thread. And if Iris's condition worsened – past the point, Lesley secretly calculated, when she would be able to exert her iron will – then it wasn't so far for Lesley to travel to be there herself.

Lesley beckoned and Ruby took a sideways step, to come under the shelter of her arm. They stood close together, their cheeks touching.

Lesley didn't say that they should discuss the matter with Ruby's father, or even with Andrew. This was between the two of them.

'I think you should go,' she said at last.

Ruby's head lifted at once. 'Thanks, Mum,' she said.

This time, she knew exactly how much to pay the taxi driver for the ride in from the airport. The smell of diesel fumes and frying offal, underpinned with the amalgamated spicy, rotting, fermented odours of Cairo itself, was perfectly familiar. As they sat in the dense pack of freeway traffic Ruby watched the navy-blue skyline jagged with domes and high-rise blocks and sharp minarets, and saw the first faint stars appear above them. The old city drew in around her.

The door in the high wall opened and Mamdooh's shape was outlined against the dim light within. 'Miss, you are here again,' he said. It was impossible to tell whether his gloomy tone was lightened by a briefly welcoming note.

Ruby stepped inside and he took her bag. The quietness of the house struck her again. It was all shadows and arches, shadows within the arched recesses and in the angles of the old walls, muffled with dust, populated by ghosts. Auntie hurried out of the kitchen and grabbed her hands, looking up into her face and talking volubly.

'How is Mum-reese?' she asked them.

'Doctor Nicolas has visited her. She is a little tired, but she waits to see you.'

The door to Iris's sitting room stood open, letting a slice of light out into the dim breadth of the gallery. Ruby stepped inside.

'You are here at last,' Iris greeted her.

The child.

She gives off energy like heat from a fire.

She sits down in her usual place, takes my hand. I think she is talking about England and Christmas and Lesley, but it is too tiring to catch and catalogue the sense of what she is saying. Instead, I watch the way her mouth moves, the lower lip pushing forward to form her words. Her lips are shiny, pinky-red, and her tongue taps her white teeth with a rhythm like music.

After a while she stops talking and looks at me, with a question that I haven't heard left hanging in the air. I have no idea how to answer it.

'I don't know,' I sigh. My eyes are closing.

Tonight, it is Ruby who helps me to bed. The determination that has gripped me ever since they left eases, suddenly mutating into drowsiness.

Sleep.

In her own room, Ruby sat on her bed and stared into the darkness outside her window. Just in the space of a month Iris had become much smaller, frailer, except for her eyes which appeared huge in her shrunken face. Ruby didn't even know if she had been able to conceal her shock at the sight of her.

She would have to talk to Doctor Nicolas, find out from him what treatment or medicine Iris could have that would make her better. And even as she resolved to do this, the recognition of its futility crawled up her spine to grasp the nape of her neck.

Iris wasn't going to get better and there was no medicine she could take. She was dying.

No . . .

I won't *let* her die, was Ruby's first reaction. It isn't fair. I didn't let it happen in the desert and I won't now.

Then she bowed her head. The splintered old floorboards were dull with dust, her feet were placed on the familiar garnet-and-maroon pattern of a frayed piece of Persian carpet. She traced the lozenges and interlockings with her eyes, until tears blurred the geometry.

'You like pomegranate,' Iris announced as triumphantly as a child.

'Yes, I do.' Ruby gnawed the seeds from their caul of pith and burst them between her teeth.

The light in Cairo even in January was bright after the English murk, and the sun was gentle on the tops of their

454

heads. Iris blinked in the warmth, her eyes watering, and Ruby picked up her hat from where it lay and placed it on Iris's head.

'Is that better?'

'Thank you.' She smiled vaguely.

'Have you finished your coffee? Would you like some yoghurt, look, with some of this honey? You haven't eaten anything, hardly,' Ruby insisted.

'I'm quite happy.' Iris smiled again.

It was true, she did seem happy. They sat in the garden together as they had done before, and if Iris wasn't too tired they talked.

'Tell me more about Xan Molyneux?'

Sixty years ago there were soldiers in these streets. Officers and men in their dusty khaki, Xan among them. The war was just another layer of history in the making.

'Ah, Ruby. If you had only known him. He was an extraordinary man.'

'How did you meet him?'

That was the question that Lesley had asked about her father when they were having dinner on the last night. Ruby remembered that she had cringed a little, thinking that her mother was too direct, but Iris had come straight out with the story.

In Lady Gibson Pasha's garden. Dancing with Xan and then falling and spraining my ankle. I had been drunk on whisky and champagne, and then drunk on Xan himself.

The child's eyes as I talk, rounded in surprise.

She thinks as all the young do – as I thought myself, when I was her age – that passion is their own invention.

I find that I am laughing because I remember the night and the joy of it, when it was the loss of memory I feared more than anything else.

And I talk and talk. The words come easily now, bringing relief. Ruby sits and listens, her hand linked in mine, her eyes on my face.

'How is your grandmother today?'

Ash and Ruby were sitting on the old car seat. The door of the garage stood open and a bar of white light lay across the oily floor, slicing across their ankles.

'She's weak. She doesn't eat anything, so that's not so surprising. But she's full of memories. I've heard about how she met her great love, when they lived here during the war. You'd think it was all tennis parties and chaperones, but it wasn't like that a bit. They were quite wild. They slept together. Iris said it was because they didn't know if the men would be alive the next week, or even the next day, sometimes. You had to live for the minute, so what point was there in being good?'

Ash looked startled. 'You are discussing such things with your grandmother?'

Ruby laughed. 'Yes. We sit there with our coffee cups and she tells me about it; and while I'm listening it's as if we're the same age. She's talking all the time, as if she's suddenly discovered that she *can*.'

'It must have been quite near where we got lost.'

The child's face turns anxious. 'I don't like thinking about it.'

'Why not?'

'Well, obviously, because of what might have happened.'

'Not because of what did happen?'

She thinks about this. 'It was horrible. I was afraid and I was drowning in sand and burning up with heat and thirst. I kept thinking about how I didn't want to die and how precious everything is.'

'You are right,' I tell her. 'Life is precious. That's what to think about.'

'All right.' She shifts in her seat, looking at me. 'Go on, about Xan driving you into the desert.'

Hassan at the wheel and Xan in the back beside me. Holding my hand in the creased coral pink silk folds of my dress.

The Bedouin tent pitched in the shelter of the dunes, the view of the Pyramids and champagne frothing into tin mugs. The first time I understood the split in Xan, and Jessie James and all the others like them, who had to confront the unthinkable every day in the desert and who only wanted to laugh and get drunk and make love when they left it behind.

'Was that the first time you and Xan made love?'

'No, not that night. That came a little later.'

And I can remember it as if I have just stepped out of his arms. The joy of it.

Ruby is still looking at me, with a strange expression now. 'The cup on the shelf,' she says again.

'That's right,' I tell her. I have the sudden certainty that when I can no longer hold it, when it has slipped out of my hands, it will not be smashed into a thousand pieces.

Ruby will be holding it for me.

The car seat creaked as Ash moved closer. He put his mouth against Ruby's neck and she shivered, arching her back with pleasure at the heat of his breath.

'My grandmother had a good life. She knew what it was like to love and to be loved. It was tragic that he was killed, her lover, but that doesn't take away from the meaning of it, does it?'

'It does not.'

His hand slid between the tired plastic of the seat and Ruby's smooth back.

*   *   *

457

I was thinking of the oasis that I never found again, in all the years. It might have been a mirage that only existed for Xan and me. And then the other faces of the desert: Private Ridley, Jessie James, Gus Wainwright. The Italian planes coming out of the sky in their tight formation and fire springing from them. I was thinking of them, searching for all those lost places, in my old car with the child at the wheel. Of course I couldn't find them. The desert is full of bones.

I tell Ruby, 'It's all gone. Blown away.'

Her face puckers with determination. 'No it hasn't. It's here. Go on, tell me some more.'

Gordon with his camera. Elvira Mursi, dancing in her sequins. Ash Wednesday, when we burned all the GHQ files. Faria's wedding, Roddy Boy coming across the marble floor to tell me that Xan was dead. Ruth and Daphne and how I wanted to be like them, instead of a girl on the cocktail circuit.

Ruby sits beside me and holds my hand, her eyes on my face.

Ruby *is* the cup.

The thought makes me feel so happy that I am light, ready to float. The first warmth of the year is in my bones. Soon the heat will flood back, like the Nile itself.

Nicolas has come, he is leaning over to examine me, but his investigations are painful and I don't want to be interrupted. I turn back, searching for Ruby again, and she is here.

'Good,' I say. 'That's good. I like you to sit where I can see you. Can you hear me?'

'Yes. I can hear every word.'

'How is she?' Ruby demanded of Doctor Nicolas as he put on his coat.

'In good spirits.'

'I don't mean that.'

'I know.'

'Well?'

'You want me to tell you that she is going to live for another twenty years and I can't do that.'

'No, but . . .'

'She is not ill, Ruby. Old age is not a viral infection, or some acute condition that I can treat with medicine.'

'Of course not,' she said fiercely.

Mamdooh appeared. 'Excuse me, Sir. Madam Iris would like to speak with you again for a short moment in private.'

Nicolas followed him, and came back again ten minutes later to where Ruby was still sitting under the lantern in the hallway. He patted her on the shoulder. 'She could be with us for a long time yet.' He smiled.

When Iris was resting in bed, Ash and Ruby resumed their long walks.

They explored the city in trajectories that looped outwards from the clogged arteries of downtown. They passed cavernous art deco apartment buildings where the doorman sat sunning himself on the steps. In the medieval lanes of the Islamic quarters Ruby wrapped a scarf over her hair and stepped meekly at Ash's side through the donkey shit and rotting vegetables and running water from burst pipes. Beggars hunched in the shade of latticed balconies pulled at her skirt as she passed and muttered their imploring 'Ya Mohannin, ya Rabb'. Or they went southwards to the Coptic quarter and slipped between the ancient, dark, inward-looking Christian churches and the ruined stones of the Roman walls. Once, close to the river, Ash pointed out the great stone-built aqueduct that for a thousand years had carried water from the river to the Citadel and they peered into the slots that had held water wheels turned by teams of oxen.

They went further, to the ordinary suburbs of Helwan and Ma'adi, and walked sunny residential streets that Ash had never seen before, peering up at shuttered windows and into gardens where lawn sprinklers pattered on thick leaves. But the areas that Ruby liked best were ordinary inner suburbs, where Cairo crowded into the polluted isthmuses between tall concrete apartment blocks and modern mosques and clattering railway lines. There were no tourists or grand sights here, only shoe shops and cafés and electrical stores and the blare and tumult of everyday life. It was the ordinariness itself, and the sheer momentum of it, that she found reassuring.

When she returned to the old house, the unbreathing silence seemed to unfurl within her head. She would almost run through to the garden or up the stairs, her chest tight with anxiety, looking for Iris.

'Here you are,' Iris would murmur. 'Sit down, don't loom over me.'

At other times she didn't even notice that Ruby had been away. She would pick up on an anecdote that she had lost her way in yesterday, or begin in an entirely new place, with a birdlike peck of her head towards Ruby to indicate *listen*.

Ruby did.

It was like making two different sets of excursions, she thought, the one imperfectly superimposed on the other. There were her explorations with Ash, and these were matched with the khaki-flooded streets of Iris's much more confined Cairo. Iris never went much beyond Garden City and Zamalek, but those dust-lined roads and party-scarred apartments, and the nightclubs and horse-drawn gharrys and all the sights of wartime Egypt in her grandmother's fading memory became almost as real to Ruby as the modern city outside the shuttered windows.

Iris backtracked, repeated herself, dropped into a doze in mid sentence, but the impetus of telling her story seemed enough to rouse her again. Sometimes the narrative drifted away to Swakopmund, or Blantyre or some other African town, but she always came back again to Cairo.

'You love this place,' Ruby said.

Iris opened her eyes. 'Do I? I don't know. Maybe I should have gone somewhere else, while I still could.'

'But where?'

'I have no idea.'

'Not England?'

'No, not England, thank you.'

'How is she?' Lesley asked. She telephoned every other day.

'Mum, she's OK. Doctor Nicolas says she could be around for a long time yet. She sleeps a lot, and wakes up and tells me about Captain Molyneux taking her to a nightclub and then going to bed with him. People seemed to have quite a lot of fun in those days, even though there was a war on.'

Lesley laughed. 'I've heard that.'

'They all got pregnant. Her friend Sarah went to Beirut for an abortion.'

'You sound shocked.'

'No. Well, you know. She is my grandmother.'

Lesley laughed again. 'Everyone was young once. When I was twenty . . .'

'Mum, please. I so don't want to hear what you got up to in the sixties.'

'All right. Ruby?'

'Yeah.'

'I'm glad you and Granny are talking. I'm glad you're listening.'

'Yeah. It's OK.'

A few days later Ash came for Ruby and instead of letting her go outside to join him Iris ordered her to bring him inside.

461

They had been sitting in the garden, and Ash came awkwardly through the summer rooms and stood in the slice of shade that sheltered Iris's chair. He was never very comfortable inside the house and Ruby blamed Mamdooh's attitude for that.

Iris tilted her head to look up at Ash. 'How are you today?'

'I am well, thank you, Madam. How are you?'

'Give me your arm,' she said.

'What? You are going somewhere?'

'Give me your *arm*, please.'

Between them, Ash and Ruby helped her to her feet. Fastened tight on their forearms, her hands looked like the claws of a rooster, but Iris still managed an imperious air. She indicated that they were to walk her round the little garden, and they made a slow circuit that allowed her to look closely at the fountain water trickling into its bowl and the crisp green folds of the new geranium leaves, and the cool submarine glimmer of the green and turquoise tiles.

Next they negotiated the worn stone step that led through an arch into the house. The summer rooms were bare; even the kelim cushions on the divans had been put away by Auntie for the winter, and there were velvety cobwebs draped in the high corners. Iris stopped in an inner door and looked back to see the garden framed by its arch. From this perspective it shone like a little green jewel in the heart of the old stone house.

When they slowly processed into the celebration hall she said, 'Wait. Stand still, please.'

Ash and Ruby glanced at each other. Silently, they surveyed the dark panelling and the intricate patterns of the *mashrabiya* screens. Overhead, hanging from the apex of the painted dome, the lantern was slowly acquiring a fresh mantle of dust.

Iris nodded, as if confirming something for herself. Her hands twitched, to indicate that they were to move on again, through the empty rooms that led off the hall. There were a few tattered books on the shelves of the gloomy wooden cabinets, pewter jugs or a cracked blue Chinese vase positioned between them. Looking at it, Ruby was struck all over again by how minimal an attempt Iris had made to impose her personality on the old house. Now she was withdrawing even further, leaving it to its shadows and history. In the alcove where she and Iris and Lesley had eaten their last dinner, the table was still pooled with grey wax.

They reached the *salamlek* stairs and began painfully to climb them. Even though Ash and Ruby were supporting most of her weight, Iris drew up one foot with a great effort, then placed the next beside it and paused to catch her breath before attempting the next step. They came to the sharp angle in the stairs where a screened window projected into a side alley beneath the looming walls of the mosque and Ash couldn't stop himself, while Iris was resting again, from darting to the window and pressing his face to the screen. From here, the house was almost part of the mosque itself and the shadow from the nearest minaret fell across it like a warning finger.

When he turned back, his eyes were shining. 'Your house. It is beautiful, it is like a house for a sultan of old Cairo.'

Iris's hand settled on his sleeve again. 'It is a beautiful house,' she agreed. 'I have been fortunate to occupy it.'

They climbed the remaining stairs, shuffled along the corridors with their wide floorboards and came to the gallery. They made one circuit and Ash broke away once or twice to gaze down through the screens into the hall, as if he could clearly see the men and the musicians and the jingling dancers below.

At the door of Iris's room she stood up a little straighter, looking Ash in the eye.

'Thank you,' he murmured, meaning for letting him see the inner rooms.

Iris nodded. 'Good. I will go to bed for a rest now, Ruby, if you will send Auntie up to me.'

The next day Iris stayed in her bed. Auntie took up a tray and brought it down again, untouched. Ruby sat beside the bed, opposite the photograph of Xan and its attendant wooden boat with the shaky numeral 1 painted on the side.

'Are you sleepy?'

'No.'

'Do you want to talk, then? Or are you too tired?'

Iris swallowed. Under the tissue-thin skin Ruby could see the muscles working in her throat.

'What about?'

'You never told me how you came by this house.'

'It was a legacy.'

'From whom?'

Poor Sandy Allardyce. Never had children, with Mrs Kimmig-Gertsch or anyone else. Lived here alone the last ten years of his life and died in his sixties. He inherited the house from Gerti Kimmig-Gertsch, then left it to me, of all people, in his will; a letter from his solicitor reached me months afterwards, me in my rented two rooms next to the clinic in Namibia. I hadn't seen Sandy since I left Cairo in 1942, but we exchanged letters once in a while.

So I came back here, to live alone for the last years of my life, just like Sandy. It has been a good house for me, there have always been the shadows of people and the echoes of their voices. Always, until recently.

Now there is only the silence.

'I wasn't lonely,' I say, just to break it, not because it is the truth.

Ruby smiles at me. She is so vital, with a bloom on her like a fresh peach.

'Good. *Who* was it who left you the house?'

'Sandy,' I say.

I can't tell the story. Too much effort. 'He was in love with me,' I offer.

'He was in love with me,' Iris said.

Ruby caught a sudden sideways glance, darting under her grandmother's colourless lashes, a look of coquetry, utterly knowing and triumphant.

Iris remembered how she had once been. Maybe, Ruby thought, she even felt today as she had once done. Capable of rousing men to passion. Eager, with the man she loved, to return it.

'What was it like, the first time with Xan?'

'Like . . . ?'

Iris gave a small sigh, her chest just perceptibly rising and falling under the covers.

'It was like going to heaven.'

The short-lived, dewy cool of pre-dawn. Xan's flat, a staging post shared with unnumbered officers who passed through Cairo. A gun on a shelf, boots with the shape of stranger's feet in them, discarded in the hallway.

I didn't know that you could laugh and cry at the same time.

I loved his body and I loved Xan. Then and now.

Iris had fallen asleep. Ruby stood up, very carefully, so as not to disturb her, and slipped out of the room.

Now I am alone. That's right. Silence rests on my head, reaches into the ear, swelling in the chambers and pressing against the delicate bones.

Malleus. Incus. Stapes.

Nicolas. Nicolas witnessed my scrap of a will.

I have nothing to leave, only this house with its serene Ottoman arches and the garden where it is cool even in the summer's heat, and I have taken my leave of it.

I do not want my Ruby, my precious gem of a Ruby, to retreat here, to be caught here, with second-hand memories for company.

The house will be sold.

And whatever money it realises, a great deal of money I think, because people have tried to persuade me to sell it, will be divided into three.

. . . Groppi's garden, shabby and tawdry and not the way I remembered it. Those two boys, the taxi driver with his quick way to make a pound and his brother, Ruby's beau, shy and intelligent. Ice cream. Yawning waiters. Ruby herself, pushing her lips out and tossing her head, caught between me and her friends, anxious and defiant at the same time and the three of them so *young*, which I had forgotten . . .

Three ways.

One-third for Mamdooh and Auntie.

One-third for Ruby, which will be something but not too much.

One-third for Ashraf, so that he can go and study.

Two-thirds for Egypt, one-third for England.

That's good, I think.

And Lesley, my poor Lesley . . .

She will not want my legacy. Let it pass on to Ruby, who has love from both of us. Who is more like me than Lesley ever was.

More like me. Miss Iris Black, Mrs Xan Molyneux as never was, Mrs Gordon Foxbridge, returned to Doctor Black again.

* * *

466

'Hi,' Ash said and Ruby pressed her mouth to his.

'Let's go to the garage,' she whispered urgently.

It was dark, and when Ash groped for and pressed the switch there was still no light. Nafouz had disconnected it, or it had fused, or there was a local power failure.

'We cannot play music,' he grumbled.

'We'll have to think of something else to do.'

Ruby slid closer to him, winding her arms round his neck.

'What is this?' he asked, as she ran the tip of her tongue from the corner of his mouth to the angle of his jaw, and buried her nose in the warm cleft behind his ear. She breathed in the scent of him. Spearmint gum, cigarettes and skin.

'I want to,' Ruby said simply. More than wanting to, it had become an imperative. She needed to be joined to him, just as she needed to breathe and eat. Like Iris with Captain Xan Molyneux. She slipped her hands inside the creaking leather of his jacket, running her fingers downwards over the span of his ribs.

'Ruby . . .'

'You said you love me.'

'Yes. It is true.'

Her fingers reached the buckle of his belt.

'Well, then . . .'

It was too dark to see anything but the faintest outline of his face.

'It is not a right thing to do.' He was struggling to maintain control.

'Ash. You have to trust me when I say that it *is* the right thing.' Her fingers worked and she punctuated her words with little darts of her tongue. 'It's right and natural if we both want to, and I do and I know you do too. Life's precious, Ash. We won't always be here. We'll end up just bones, like in the Cities of the Dead.'

He bent his head. 'Perhaps you are right,' he whispered at last.

He locked his arms round her and pulled her off her feet, and in the black, oil-reeking darkness Ruby laughed. They staggered backwards together, the old car seat catching them in the backs of the knees as they fell. They landed in a tangle of limbs on the sagging plastic. Ash caught her wrists and pinned them above her head.

'Now you are mine.'

'Now, yes,' she breathed back.

Iris exaggerated, she thought. It wasn't like going to heaven. But it was pretty good.

Ash had to be at his hospital switchboard by midnight. At twenty minutes to they left their car seat and stepped out into the blue night, Ash twitching at his shirt to straighten it and Ruby raking her hair with her fingers. They linked hands and ran to the moby, and Ruby circled his waist with her arms and rested her cheek against his back as they raced back to the house.

They kissed in the hidden angle of a wall. It was hard to pull apart again.

'Tomorrow?' Ash begged.

'Tomorrow. Same time, same place.' Ruby stretched luxuriously. Life was precious; it promised a chain of tomorrows. She stood back to let him go. He wheeled the moby in a tight circle and roared away.

On her way to bed, Ruby looked into Iris's room. She was asleep, lying on her side, facing towards the photograph.

In the morning she was gone.

Ruby woke very early with a cold premonition in her heart. She blinked in the dim light, trying to identify what was wrong. Then in one movement she sat up and pushed back the covers. She ran down the corridor, her warm feet leaving faint prints on the bare floor.

Iris was still lying on her side, facing the photograph.

Ruby hesitated in the doorway. When at the beginning of her time here Iris had fallen ill, she looked into the room to see Auntie sponging her waxy forehead and had feared for a moment that her grandmother had died in the night.

It was not like this.

Without taking a breath Ruby crossed to the side of the bed.

She touched her hand to Iris's arm and it was cold.

When she saw Jas's poor body she knew at once that he was dead; the person who had been was no longer there. She thought of him now, with her warm hand resting on Iris's cold skin. Her head was pounding until she remembered to take a breath that started as a gasp and ended as a sob.

Iris was gone, just as conclusively as Jas.

Ruby slipped down to her knees and put her arm round Iris's shoulders.

She had left in her sleep, alone. As if she had chosen to do it that way.

Gently, Ruby leaned forward and kissed her cold temple, where the blue veins showed under the skin. She knelt there for a few minutes, holding her, then she stood painfully upright again with all her body aching. The absence was complete.

In the kitchen, Mamdooh stood up from his chair by the oven as soon as he saw her face.

Ruby took both his hands. 'My grandmother died in her sleep,' she said.

Auntie was standing beside the sink. A rising wail of grief broke out of her, loud as the first call of the muezzin. Ruby

469

briefly hugged her, then she turned away. She would have to telephone Doctor Nicolas, Lesley; she would have to perform the tasks that those who were left behind always had to perform, in one way or another.

But not yet, first she wanted some time to be alone and to think about Iris.

Ruby left the house. She turned the opposite way from the front door and walked the few steps to the *ziyada* that led into the courtyard of the great mosque. She had only looked inside a handful of times, peeking at the sea of praying men who pressed their foreheads to the holy ground. But now the great space was deserted. She walked slowly, under a sky heavy with rain, the pebbles sharp under the thin soles of her slippers. The court was surrounded by arcades: the court was as vast as the desert and the smooth rhythm of the arches was like a rolling sea. Ruby tipped her head back and the first raindrops needled her face.

She wanted to hear Iris's voice, but she couldn't summon it up. Not yet. The image of the empty shell that she had left behind was too clear.

The three minarets topped with crescent moons soared towards the sky.

It was like going to heaven, Iris had said. Suddenly Ruby glimpsed the look that Iris had shot at her. The knowing, confident, amused look of a passionate woman. Maybe that's what it was like, Ruby thought.

She hoped so.

A sudden gust of wind swept across the open court, bringing rain from the north, down from the reeds and water of the delta.

The rain on the pebbles smelled strangely, yet familiarly, of England.

Sun at Midnight

Rosie Thomas

In a quiet corner of Oxford, Alice Peel's life unfolds smoothly and predictably in the shadow of her pioneering mother Margaret. But when Alice's relationship collapses and Margaret is taken seriously ill, her ordered world falls apart.

She accepts an invitation to enjoy a small team heading to Antartica. There, in her new home – a tiny, claustrophobic research station – she meets James Rooker, a man on the run from his past. In this harsh silver and ice-blue world, a spark ignites between them.

But as Alice experiences a momentous awakening that will change her life forever, the barren beauty around them threatens the group. And when they return to the everyday world, can the fragile bond between them survive?

'Gripping . . . the beauty of the setting gives this love story a unique feel.' *EVE*

'This is an epic love story set against breathtaking descriptions of the Antarctic waste.'
Women and Home

ISBN: 0 00 717352 0

WITHIN ONE EXOTIC LAND
LIE THE SECRETS OF A LIFETIME...

Newlywed Nerys Watkins leaves Wales for the first time to
accompany her husband on a missionary posting to India.
Deep in the exquisite heart of Kashmir lies the lakeside city
of Srinagar, where the British live on carved wooden
houseboats and dance, flirt and gossip as if there is no war.

But the battles draw closer, and life in Srinagar becomes
less frivolous when the men are sent away to fight. Nerys
is caught up in a dangerous friendship, and by the time she
is reunited with her husband, the innocent Welsh bride
has become a different woman.

Years later, when Mair Ellis clears
out her father's house, she finds
an exquisite antique shawl, a lock
of child's hair wrapped within its
folds. Tracing her grandparents'
roots back to Kashmir, Mair
embarks on a quest that will
change her life forever.

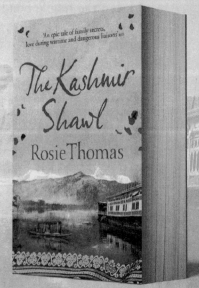

'An epic tale of family secrets,
love during wartime and dangerous liaisons'

The Kashmir Shawl

Rosie Thomas

'Spellbinding ... a delight
from start to finish'
Daily Express